To Boris, Kate, Sasha, and Anthony.

neš

Legacies

A Compilation of Short Stories by the
ACCESS Academy Class of 2013

A fundraiser for our school and gifted education around the United States.

Editor in Chief:

Michael Ioffe

Senior Editors:

Minhtam Tran

Liam Dubay

Cleo Forman

Chloe Jensen

Ari Bluffstone

Noah Gladen-Kolarsky

Editors:

Annika Steele

Ceara Adams

Duncan Gates

Ella Gleason

Justin Huang

Katherine Renner

Marissa Friedman

Nadia Siddiqui

Rebekah Goshorn

Sadira Urzaa

Tristen Wong

Dedicated to all the children of the world.

You are the future.

Table of Contents

Sunset on Mimosa Drive

Lian Prost-Hughart

"Why, hello!" said a voice above her head. Kaily looked up and her finger froze millimeters from the doorbell.

"Can I help you?" the frail old lady on the roof asked her. "If you're one of those salespeople, we're *not* interested! Really, you'd think that once you get this old you wouldn't have to deal with them anymore!"

"Um, no, actually my name is Kaily O'Conner and I'm looking for my grandmother Mirriam O'Conner. This *is* where she lives, right?"

"Huh? Oh. This blasted thing is off again!" the elderly woman reached up her hand and fiddled with something in her ear. "Okay, better. What did you say? And speak slowly this time."

"I'm looking for my grandmother Mirriam O'Conner," Kaily said, enunciating each word. "Is this where she lives?"

"Mirriam? Yes, this is her house. Who did you say you were?"

Kaily sighed, she was getting frustrated. "My name is Kaily, and I'm her granddaughter. I came for a visit."

"Kaily? Oh goodness, you should have said so to begin with! Just wait down there for a minute and I'll get off this blasted roof and show you where she is." The odd woman disappeared from her line of sight, and Kaily took a moment to look at the scrunched up paper from her pocket. In her mom's scrawl, her grandmother's address was written and the phone number to call her at while her mom was away on her cruise. Kaily took a deep breath. It wasn't that she wanted to go with her mom and her latest boyfriend on their little vacation, since at least she could have stayed with her best friend Sylvie. Now she was going to be stuck in South Florida in her grandmother's retirement community. On top of that, the first person she meets has to be a crazy, roof climbing lady with a salesmen phobia! A breeze rustled Kaily's waist-length hair, and a river of fiery red floated up in the wind. Then she heard a crash.

Kaily followed a moan around the corner of the generic white house and stopped dead in her tracks. The woman from the roof was lying face up on a crushed peony bush, a ladder standing a few feet away, balanced against the house and perfectly erect.

"Shoot! Well, are you just going to stand there?! Help me up, or get someone who will!" the angry white haired woman yelled. As she started

1

dialing the number for an ambulance, Kaily groaned. It was going to be a long summer.

-

The next day, Kaily woke up, slowly opening her eyes to the sunny light gleaming through the windows. Shadows of the wind chimes in her grandmother's small back yard danced on the thin comforter, and their tinkling was faint but calming. She got up and smoothed back the covers of her bed, then walked to the living room. Kaily had always been a morning person, in stark contrast with her mother, who would sleep past noon every day if she could.

She looked out the front window and started braiding her red-gold hair. Yesterday had been tiring. She settled into the plushy patterned couch and let her mind wander back to yesterday's events. After the woman had fallen from the roof, she had had to be taken to the hospital. From the ER they called her daughter. The whole time she waited, Kaily listened, her face frozen in a smile, to the woman complain about the meals, the doctors, the TV stations, the room she was put in, even the name of the attending nurse.

"What kind of name is Daisy? That's a name you'd give a cow or a pig, or some other type of farm animal! Oh, blast! Not the chocolate pudding again! You'd think that if this hospital is so big, they'd have more meal options. Huh? Oh, fine, I'll eat it. But I won't like it! Now look at all those commercials! You'd think…" and on she would go. It seemed that she didn't like anything or anyone, and didn't stop telling you so. That's when Kaily's grandmother finally made an appearance.

"Oh, honey! I'm so sorry I wasn't here earlier! I called your mom when you didn't show up, and she said that the bus had dropped you off an hour ago, but I had been at my shuffleboard team practice, and that's when I heard about Roberta falling off the roof again and how a young redheaded girl had gone with her in the ambulance, so I hurried here as fast as I could, but that took some time because I had to have one of the community's drivers bring me over," she said in one breath. "My goodness you're so tall now! The last time I saw you, you were so young, but now you're all grown up! A lady! Anyway, how's Roberta? This is the third time this year she's been on someone's roof, we keep telling her it's dangerous, but she's convinced she's immortal."

"Oh, Mirriam. You're finally here. What took you so long?" Roberta asked impatiently.

"Shuffleboard practice ran late," Kaily's grandmother answered cheerfully.

Kaily stared at the two women, her gray eyes open painfully wide. Her eyes flitted from one person to the other. First she looked at the cranky, stubborn face that sagged from old age sitting on the hospital bed, then to the grinning face of her grandmother. Straight faded blonde hair cut in a fashionable bob and a face full of laugh lines. They could not have been more different, and yet they seemed really close.

The smoke alarm went off and snapped Kaily back to the present. "Oh no, the scones are burning!"

Kaily walked into the kitchen and watched, fascinated, as her grandmother rushed toward the smoking oven wearing flower printed oven mitts, threw open the door, and took out a tray of light brown biscuits from the rack.

"Thank heavens! The scones will just be a little crunchy."

Kaily surveyed the scene before her. Pots and mixing bowls lay piled up in the sink covered in dough and white, powdery flour. The island in the middle of the kitchen was covered with an assortment of measuring cups, spoons, spices, cooking thermometers, open cartons of heavy cream, milk, baking powder, and small blocks of chocolate. The counters were riddled with dirty plates, knives, a blender filled with some green liquid, and rolls of aluminum foil and waxed paper. She looked at the floor; it too was scattered with napkins, dirty towels, and fallen utensils. The kitchen was a mess.

Kaily's grandmother finally noticed her standing there. "Finally up, are we? I'm just making some breakfast, and some snacks for later on," she said, a spot of cream on her cheek and several unidentifiable stains on her apron. Kaily looked up at the clock on the kitchen wall; it was only five past six in the morning. She wondered how long her grandmother had been cooking.

"Get dressed in something comfortable, because after breakfast we're leaving," her grandmother said, "and we probably won't back in time for dinner. So if you need to, bring something to go."

What on Earth was she talking about? Kaily wondered. *I thought that old people didn't do anything all day long.* Kaily, sighed. She turned around and walked back into the spare bedroom. She had a bad feeling about this.

"A little higher, yes, just on the left. Right there, perfect! Oh it looks so much better now, doesn't it?" a redheaded elderly woman wearing an old-fashioned straw hat asked.

"Really? I think we could trim it a little more, and then it would look more symmetrical. What do you think Mirriam?" an aged brunette in gardening gloves responded.

"I think that whatever you decide, that hedge looks beautiful. But maybe we should focus on the roses in the corner. They're looking a little drab, don't you think?"

And so continued the conversation, completely ignoring the girl on the ladder holding the ancient, heavy pruning shears. Kaily had somehow been roped into being her grandmother's assistant in all her clubs. It all began in the library with the book club, when all the members used her to get the books on the top shelf. Then, at the knitting club she had to roll up all the yarn that one of the member's cats had played with. In Bridge club, she had to be the dealer, and everyone seemed to cheat! In cooking class, she did the dishes. In Shuffleboard practice, she led the stretches. And in the water aerobics, she helped all the seniors get in and out of the pool.

"Kaily, honey, we're all heading back to Eunice's house now for some tea. So can you please put the ladder back in the tool shed? We'll wait for you out here," Kaily's grandmother said. Kaily slowly got off the ladder, her sore calf muscles protesting the movement. She had been on that ladder for the better part of an hour, and was ready to fall into her bed at home and go to sleep. However, she folded up the ladder and carried it into the shed reserved for the gardening club's equipment. She had never heard of a retirement community with so many clubs and classes! It reminded her more of a community center for kids, not for 60-plus residents.

She followed her grandmother back to the redhead's house and when they got there, gratefully took a seat on one of the plushy, floral embroidered couches in the living room. Though the outside of all the houses looked the same, Kaily knew that the insides could not have been more different. Her grandmother's was full of oil paintings, and glass balls; on the other hand, Eunice's was scented and smelled of lavender. All the paintings on the walls were of mountains and rivers from the north with evergreens dotting the distance. Eunice eyed her looking at the paintings.

"Beautiful, aren't they? I used to live in Washington State with my husband, before he died. It was always so beautiful," she said wistfully, "but it's much warmer here, so I won't complain," she laughed, and it sounded like the tinkling of rusty chimes, youthful and happy, and Kaily joined in.

One by one, the other residents came pouring into the lavender living room; she recognized a few. There was the tall man with salt and pepper hair from the Bridge club who knew fifteen different ways to cut the deck, and always turn up an Ace. Then the brunette named Martha from the garden who said she used to snowboard before she learned to shuffleboard. Kaily watched the lady in an African robe waltz in, who spent all of knitting club painting a replica of a Monet watercolor that looked strangely identical to the original. Then the tall white-haired woman who burned everything during cooking class sauntered in. And finally the mousy, dark haired swimmer from water aerobics that was the fastest amongst all the class, her hair still dripping from the pool. Even Roberta had been released from the hospital and was there complaining to Eunice, who was looking at her with a vacant smile.

Eunice's living room was officially full, and Kaily's grandmother decided it was time to get everyone's attention.

"Everyone, everyone! I'd like to officially introduce you all to someone. So if I could have your attention…"

"Huh?" someone said.

"If I could have your attention, I want to introduce someone special to you," her grandmother repeated.

"What did you say?" they asked again.

"Can someone please help Donald with his hearing-aid," she replied, her smile completely intact. *How does she do it?* Kaily thought. She was starting to get a feeling of deja-vu, and she remembered how frustrated she had gotten at Roberta the day before.

"Thank you. I would like you all to meet my granddaughter Kaily, who is going to spend the summer here! Most of you have met her today during one or another of our clubs, but I wanted you all to meet her officially and welcome her to the Mimosa Drive Retirement Community, because as I'm sure she has noticed, we're not like any others!" she laughed. "Anyway, Eunice has some tea and brandy ready and the sandwiches, if any of you are hungry. And we have something without tomatoes for you Estella," she said pointing to the robed woman, "and something gluten free for you Martha. That's all! Thank you!"

Everyone stopped for a minute and looked at Kaily, waved hello, then turned back to their conversations. Kaily walked over to her grandmother and gave her a hug. The first hug she had given her since she had washed up at her door.

"Thank you for that, grandmother." she said, a little awkwardly. Normally Kaily didn't like to be the focus of attention, but for some reason that had felt good. As if now she was one of the rest, excluding the fact that she wasn't a senior citizen.

"It was my pleasure, honey. And from now on call me Nana, okay?"

"Okay… Nana," Kaily responded, beaming. For the first time, she was happy her mom had sent her here; it was going to be an interesting summer. She didn't know what she was going to do, but she knew it was going to be fun. Suddenly, they heard a commotion.

"Roberta's on the roof again!"

Yep, it's going to be interesting summer.

The Hidden Man
Moya Woods

Dear D.B.,
I'm sorry that you never got to hear all of my speech. That was my fault, I'm afraid. I just wanted it all to be a big surprise that day. It was spectacular. You know when I said that we'd ended on a rough note? Well, you were the one who pulled me back from going over. You were the one who realized what I needed and you made the biggest difference in my life. I wish we could talk more but given the circumstances, I think that might be a bit difficult. I think I'll see you around.

Love,
Your favorite brother Harold

Nine months later

A man with a hidden face, you might say. But you don't know what's really there. He hides away behind a foolish grin, and you say, "Oh. He's just another crazy old guy who has the mind of a nine year old and the IQ of 65." What you don't know is that the heart of gold hidden in his chest is the purest, kindest, most loving thing you could ever encounter. Making your crazy assumptions walking down the street, you can only feel sad or sorry for him. You find yourself judging the most interesting book with the most interesting insides by the cover that just happened to be printed upside down. Everyone has a story to tell but you just have to take time to sit down and hear it.

The annoying alarm buzzed in his ear and he wearily searched for the snooze button. Seeing the rainbow with a Pastrami sandwich the size of his window appear in the corner of his room brought him great joy. He could eat a small portion of the sandwich each day and not make another one for months! Almost too soon, though, it disappeared. Then he was pulled suddenly back to reality, though to him, it made no difference what was real and what was not. His brown suit was already ironed and hanging in the doorway. There didn't seem to be a stitch out of place. His already made, pre-wrapped Pastrami sandwich, was neatly tucked into the corner of his refrigerator, soon to be taken out and devoured. His belt hung over the hanger of his suit and his socks were neatly tucked into his shoes that sat by the doormat. Harold finally got up sleepily as his alarm rang for the third time this morning. Realizing what day it was, he did his excited dance as he pranced into the bathroom to find his comb and oversized glasses. Getting ready in the morning was Harold's favorite part of the day. He got to do every little thing in perfect order and repeat it again and again as his life went on. He glanced at the clock and realized it was already a quarter past eight! He would be getting picked up in fifteen minutes to leave for the interview and he hadn't even eaten yet. Gobbling down the pastrami sandwich, it became eight twenty on the clock. The adrenaline started pumping through him as he quickly flossed and brushed his teeth and combed his hair one last time. He raced down the four flights of stairs that lead to his apartment on the fifth floor. Harold was two minutes early and out of breath as well.

"Harold Stone," a lady called.

"That's you, Harold," his brother confirmed.

Harold stood up with a little too much confidence, knocking the chair over backwards and smashing it into a nice potted flower. He grimaced in pain as if the pot had hurt him, too.

"It's okay," the lady reassured. "We'll have the cleaning staff come by shortly. As for you, you must be Harold Stone. You have to get to your interview sir. Right this way. Come along now. It's okay. The plant will be fine. Sir, are you coming or not?"

Harold caught up to her quickly.

"First, Mr. Clair will ask you some basic questions like, 'Have you had a job before and where?' Also, sir, have you got your résumé with you?" Harold nodded, afraid to talk. He was already nervous enough.

"The interview will only take about a half an hour and Mr. Clair should direct you back to the lobby when you are finished. Is that okay with you?"

Harold nodded once again.

The door was made out of deep mahogany wood and to Harold, it was so big and seemed so intimidating. The handles were huge and made of brass. He was glad to finally get there after climbing many a flight of stairs because the elevator was broken. He didn't even begin to know how that kind lady could survive walking that many flights of stairs in her spike heels. Inside the office was an older man, probably in his late fifties, sitting behind a large, also mahogany desk (probably to match the doors) doing paperwork. He sloppily had his feet on the table and looked up when they entered the room with a stern look on his face. He motioned to a chair on the other side of the desk for Harold to sit in.

"The name is Vaughn E. Clair. Call me Mr. Clair. And yours is Harold Stone?" Harold nodded yet again.

"Résumé, please." The man stuck his hand out and waited while Harold dug through his unprofessional brief case, pulling out a white document at last.

"Thank you. And here is a form for you to fill out about your health and why you want to work here. There is a job description on there as well which I'm sure you've already seen before."

Harold was trying to listen, but Mr. Clair seemed to yammer on and on in his southern accent. When he was finally done explaining what to do, Harold took out his special blue pen used only for filling out important documents and started with his name and continued scribbling away. Previous jobs...blank. Names of former employers...blank. Past education... Harold contemplated this question.

"You done?" Mr. Clair asked.

"Yes," said Harold.

"Now, what education have you had in your years Mr. Stone?"

"Well," Harold thought, "I started out in kindergarten at West Charles Public Elementary and that went until eighth grade, and then I went to West Charles Public High School. Unfortunately sir, I haven't gone to college. You see sir..."

"My name is not sir, Mr. Stone. Call me Mr. Clair! Thank you. Now please continue."

"Well, Mr. Clair, I didn't go to college because I didn't get in anywhere. I have found my adult life quite displeasing sir, I mean, Mr. Clair. I simply haven't found a purpose yet. I was hoping that if I get this job, I would have meaning. If not, I would only feel more worthless about myself."

"Well, no college eh? I find that quite odd for such a young fellow like you with a nice suit and a good pair of shoes."

"It has nothing to do with my suit and my shoes Mr. Clair. And it has nothing to do with money either," Harold scoffed. He found this man to be very judgmental of people different than himself. It was that stupid outer shell, otherwise known as his skin and outer features, Harold had been born with that hid his personality inside. Most other people only made Harold feel worse about what was on the outside of him. They just didn't know anything about how he felt and were too judgmental to even care.

"Well, Mr. Stone, this interview is most definitely over now. Thank you for coming in. Now move along. I have things to do now. Good day."

The drive back to Harold's apartment building was quite glum and noiseless. Harold was glad that it was all over.

"You want to go out somewhere?" his brother asked.

"I guess so. Can we go to Pablo's Best Hot Dogs? I love the arcade games, especially Catch and Egg, and the dogs with relish. And the pool, even though I can't hold a cue stick straight. Oh! And there isn't any smoking 'cause smoking makes me cough. And all the clowns watch me and if I do well, they don't honk at me! Boy do I hate when they honk..." Harold trailed off, now muttering to himself.

"Okay then, Harold. Hot Dogs from Pablo coming right up."

The arcade was pretty empty but there were a few high school age kids hanging around one of the shoot a duck games. They sneered at Harold and his brother as they walked in. Harold got right to it with his favorite game, Catch an Egg, while D.B. went up to the counter to order them some cokes and hot dogs. Harold could hear the snickering boys cracking jokes behind his back. There only seemed to be more and more people against Harold in his life! Why did nobody understand how he felt? He hated his looks because they drew bad attention. He was a very nice person when you got past how he looked and talked. No one seemed to know how to not judge.

"Hey boy!" said one of the guys as they strolled over to the spot where Harold was standing. "You look like you think you can do everything in the whole wide world. Can you? What can you even do? You look about as stupid as a hammer!" His friends laughed at the apparently funny joke.

Harold's temper rose. He had never had anyone treat him so rudely. Not even the bullies in the high school he used to attend. Surprisingly, it didn't bother him. On a "normal" day, this would have driven him up a wall and caused his head to go spinning and for lots of screaming to happen. Today, he guessed, was different. He didn't know why. Maybe it was the fact that he wanted to beat someone so badly at something that it didn't register that the boys had been mean. There was a lot of pressure with them standing behind him but he popped a quarter into Catch an Egg and started to play. He caught thirty-four out of fifty eggs during the first round. The group behind him laughed at his poor score. In went another quarter and he tried it again. The second time around he only caught 26 eggs. He needed to get a higher score. He needed to prove that he was good enough for them. This was his glory moment and all the clowns across the restaurant would be there to watch it happen. If he lost, they would honk their noses at him. Harold hated when clowns did that. As he started the third game, he had the right kind of mindset going. He was so close with only two more eggs to catch. Now only one, then Bam! The machine started playing music that seemed louder than life. Harold had just won Catch an Egg for the first time in his life! He started to do the happy dance when he remembered the judgmental

10

guys standing behind him watching. They probably thought he was just some stupid disabled kid who was always begging for help.

"You think you're so cool? Well I bet I can beat you at this game over here called Alley Ball. You want to prove me wrong? Come over here and show me your skills boy! Come on punk. That's right. Over here. Okay. Ready, set, go!"

Harold was not athletic at all whatsoever but he wanted to beat someone normal for a change. He never got enough praise as it was. Even though his family had always said that they loved him, sometimes that wasn't good enough. He hadn't ever really gone bowling in his life but got the gist of Alley Ball, which was sort of the same. He rolled a ball up the ramp of the game but it only hit the ten hole. He tried again. Harold kept hitting a fairly high number each time. The guy he was playing against didn't seem to be doing very well. He started cursing. As soon as the game was over, Harold watched, astonished, as the other guy started to get angry at his friends and at the game. He smashed the mini balls on the ground until they broke. But all his bad temper was for nothing. Harold tried to tell him that he'd won but the guy didn't hear Harold. Soon enough he noticed that Harold had gotten a lower score than he did and his expression completely switched from angry to on top of the world.

"Who's so cool now?" the opponent said. Who's the big one? You? Oh, no way I'll have you beating me at any game in my dad's joint! You see, that's my pap over there behind the counter. He owns this place. Now I don't want to see you messing around here anymore. You hear me? Oh well who have we here? Some back up?" His friends snickered when D.B. walked up behind Harold.

"You are the ones who need to stay away!" D.B. commanded. "I don't care who owns what but you stay away from my brother. I have no idea what three dummies like you would be doing hanging around some place like this. Harold, we're leaving now."

"But our food just…"

"We're leaving, Harold. Come on."

D.B. sat Harold down on the couch when they got back to Harold's apartment.

"Why would you challenge someone like that? Why would you give in? I trusted you to stay where you were."

"D.B., you didn't even see me win Catch an Egg! You know how much I love that game. The one happy time in my life and you aren't there to share it with me." Harold yelled. "Even the clowns didn't honk at me! I guess I don't have to share it with you though. I can keep it all to myself!"

11

"Harold, your silly clowns aren't even real! It's all in your head and you don't get it! No one can explain to you. Not even me. You need to learn to stand up for yourself and not always rely on me!" D.B. shot back.

"But he was trying to hurt me! You saw that didn't you?" Harold tried to explain how he felt but it wasn't coming out how he wanted it to.

"It's in your head Harold!" D.B. tried but Harold had already stormed out of the room.

Harold quietly sat on his bed not doing anything. He heard his brother leave and slam the door behind him. Harold knew he'd stirred up anger inside of himself and his brother but his Paranoid Schizophrenia didn't let him know how to cope with it. Harold unfortunately, really didn't know the difference between anger and simple frustration. To him, most completely opposite things looked the same. He thought everyone who didn't help him was against him, he thought that his special clowns, ponies and other such creatures really existed and to him, real and imaginary blended.

The nightly routine came once again as Harold brushed and flossed his teeth, combed his hair and climbed into bed. He did his nightly ritual of reading for exactly a half an hour and then promptly fell into a set of pleasant dreams about pastrami sandwiches.

At breakfast the doorbell rung loudly in his ear, startling him. He jumped up a bit too quickly and the chair fell over backwards and came up to hit the table. Grabbing his juice as it nearly fell off the table, he took one last swig and rushed to open the door. He almost never got mail or visitors. The mail service only brought things to the apartment doors when it didn't fit in the mailboxes down on the first floor. The postman dressed in a crisp blue uniform handed him a letter addressed to Mr. Harold Stone. He tore it open not even saying thank you to the postman. It read,

Dear Mr. Harold Stone,   February 17, 1998

I have worked with our hiring panel long and hard to finalize our hiring decision. We have come to a conclusion that you were not the one for the position but we appreciate your interviewing. If you wish to, you may interview again in six months and we will re-staff the panel and come to yet another conclusion when necessary. Thank you for your participation.

Sincerely,
Vaughn E. Clair

12

Harold nearly broke down into tears. Emotion poured out of him through his every pore. He had tried so hard and never contemplated the option of not getting the job. But maybe it was for the best. He couldn't bring himself to accept that he wasn't the best option for the job and that Mr. Clair and the hiring panel didn't chose him because they hated him. He didn't want to try again in six months fearing that it would be the same all over again. He would get judged and discriminated against by Mr. Clair another time through. How could this happen to him? Mr. Clair must hate me, he thought. Was it because of his disability? Probably, he thought. But how could Mr. Clair know about his Schizophrenia? Having Paranoid Schizophrenia had troubled him his whole life and now as a grown man, someone who he thought was superior to him had rubbed it in that he was different.

Nothing much else happened for the rest of his day except for a bit of "controlled" anger. Nothing got smashed into the wall and no pastrami sandwiches miraculously ended up on the ceiling. Instead, three ended up traveling into his mouth and then down to digest in his stomach.

He drifted off into his nighttime wonderland that was supposed to be filled with all the food and candy you could ever eat. The ponies should have been grazing in the yellow meadow but today everything was different. He landed in an auditorium filled with around fifty chairs and a podium covered in yellow, red and orange flowers. He felt like it was summer again. A shining blue sky soared overhead, lighting the room through numerous skylights. A glass of water that resided on the podium pulsed a couple of times as people started to enter the room. A woman in an ugly brown pantsuit carefully climbed the rickety stairs towards the podium. Harold took a seat in the back. He wasn't really sure where he was or why but he went with it. Maybe something good would come out of it all.

"Welcome," the woman at the podium announced, "to the Fiftieth Annual Motivational Convention housed at the Riverside Convention Center! We have a special guest who we have flown in all the way from Brisbane, Australia. Please welcome the man with no arms, no legs and no worries, Nick Vujicic.

"Hi. My name is Nick Vujicic. As you can see, I have no arms, no legs. I do have my little chicken drumstick here, but that's not why I'm here. I'm not here for you to feel sorry for me. I'm here to teach you something. Not something you'll have a test on in three hours, not arithmetic, or science. No. I'm here to tell you a bit about myself. I want to talk about like when I started to go to school and stuff, you know and a lot of people put me down. You know what I mean? A lot of people tease each other. I mean people come up and say 'Hey! You're fat...' You know? 'Lose some weight!' And you go home and you look at yourself in the mirror and you go 'Ah! I'm fat!' right? And so many people tease each other. You know? You're too short, you're too tall, you look... whatever! Different hair and all that – it doesn't matter! See the thing is when you're in school, when you're growing up in life it actually sort of matters to people how you look. And then it matters to you because it matters to others. Why? Why does it matter how you look? Because if they don't like you, who will? If they don't accept you, then who will? And the fear that we have is that we're going to be alone. That we're not good enough and that we have to change ourselves. And so many people put me down and said, you know, 'Nick, you look too weird, and no one's really your friend and you can't do this and you can't do that.' And I couldn't change anything. It's not like I was fixing my hair one day and everything was fine. It's not like, you know... just whatever, I couldn't change my circumstance. I couldn't just one day wake up and say 'Hey, give me arms and legs. I need arms and legs.' You know what I mean? Like... you could go to a body builder and go 'Can you make me some arms and legs?' No, I'm just joking! Body builder? You get it? I'm just joking! Alright? This is, hey. I go up to people 'Can you give me a hand?' I'm just joking! It was so hard because people put me down. And I started believing that I was not good enough. I started believing that I was a failure. That I would never ever be somebody who people would like, people would accept. And it was so hard, man, and I thought to myself 'You know, I can't go on the soccer field like everybody else. And I can't ride my bike and I can't skateboard and all these sorts of things.' I started getting depressed. I thought, 'What kind of purpose do I have to live?'"

Harold thought that this guy, whoever he was, real or imaginary, that he sounded a lot like Harold himself. Always putting himself down and getting teased and all those stupid things that he knew he could overcome. It just seemed so hard and that like Nick had said, that people wouldn't accept him as he was.

"You take steps in this direction and you take steps in that direction and you know, sometimes you fall down. You might fall down like this" and he fell over on the table. "So what do you do when you fall down? Get back up! Everybody knows to get back up because if I start walking, I'm not going to get anywhere." He demonstrated, wiggling what he had of his legs and his little chicken drumstick back and forth as if trying to walk but not getting anywhere. "But I'll tell you there are some times in life where you fall down and you feel like you don't have the strength to get back up. So you sort of put a mask on your face and you come to school or work and pretend that

14

everything's okay when it's not and you go home and lay in your bed when no one's looking at you, and you don't have to impress anybody and you're yourself." Harold did this quite often. "And I just want to ask you today, do you think you have hope? Because I tell you I'm down here, face down, and I have no arms and no legs. It should be impossible for me to get back up. It *should* be impossible for me to get back up, but it's not. You see, I will try one hundred times to get up and if I fail one hundred times – If I fail and I give up, do you think that I'm ever going to get up? No. And if I try and I try again and again, there's always that chance of getting up. And it's not the end until you've given up. And just the fact that you're here should persuade you that you have another chance to get back up. And I don't know how it is to feel fat or have an eating disorder and I don't know how it feels to have a broken home, but I do know how it feels to have a broken heart and to be alone."

Harold felt alone all the time being single and having hardly any friends.

"But I just want you to know that it's not the end. It matters how you're going to finish. Are you going to finish strong? And you will find that strength to get back up, like this." Harold didn't even think it was possible what happened next. Nick pushed himself onto his head, lifting his torso but still with his legs on the table, he made himself into what looked like a bridge position. And slowly but surely, he popped his head up and was in the upright position again. The room erupted in clapping and many stood up.

"How did I get from depressed to who I am today? Because I tell you I was depressed. When I was age eight, I used to concentrate on the things I didn't have. I wished I had arms and legs and I wished I could do this but what can I do? Now, I can be angry about not having arms and legs or be thankful for my chicken drumstick. I had to ask myself a couple of questions. And I want you to, too. And the first question really was, who am I? And it's funny how the friends around you kind of determine who you are. And you start losing yourself and you start putting your security in temporary things. You start putting your happiness in things that won't last. You start trying to escape reality and you make excuses like drugs and alcohol. Especially you as adults who lead busy lives, you know. Sit down at night with a loved one and have a glass of wine or a bottle of beer and it turns into two or three or four and you begin to feel so good that you feel that you need more, and you can't think straight. Do you want to be like that all of your life? If you do, keep on doing it then. We, as humans, and I mean me too, we make excuses for things that we do wrong or things that we don't want to think about or deal with and you have to put those excuses aside and try to

15

make things in your life better. And it might not always be so easy. But in order to stand up, you have to overcome things. You have to believe in yourself and if that's really what you want to do, then you have to say to yourself 'I don't care what anyone thinks of me. I'm doing what I think is right and I believe in that. I don't care how many times I fall down. I will get back up and keep trying. And if I finally do overcome that fear or hardship, I will feel better. I won't hurt from that anymore. I may hurt from other things, but not that one. If you want it badly enough and you believe that you can do it, you can.'"

Harold stood up and clapped as hard as he thought was possible. As Harold gave Nick a hug by the book signing table in the lobby, he felt as if he was falling into a black hole. He heard a soft beeping sound that got louder as he fell farther and farther. He landed softly in what he thought was a pile of white billowy clouds. He tried to open his eyes but they seemed to be squeezed shut. Finding the feeling in his hands again, he pried his eyes open realizing that he was not on a cloud but in his bed painted like a racecar, same as it usually looked when he woke up in the morning. He yawned, contemplating what he had just experienced. He hoped that if he explained meeting Nick Vujicic to his brother, D.B. wouldn't suspect that he was getting engulfed in his hallucinations again.

Many of the things that Nick had said pulled heartstrings for Harold. There had been too many times to even begin to count that Harold had put himself down or others had. His head was buzzing with idea. He had to tell himself that he *was* good enough and that he was able to do the things he wanted to do. Nick had instilled those positive thoughts into his brain. You could almost hear the gears turning and clicking around in Harold's head. If only he had a way to tell his story and make the same impact as Nick had. He wanted to be able to say something that would be effective and touch people in a way that they would always remember. Harold wanted to make a difference in the world, not just sit around and feel worthless, which he did quite often. He was finally realizing how much he as one individual could do even when he believed he could not. He knew that he must share this mysterious revelation with at least one person who would give him credit for being included in such an experience. He was almost to the phone, his brother's phone number in hand, when the doorbell surprised him as it rang. What a coincidence, he thought. D.B. is the only one who ever comes to my house. It must be him.

"Hello," he said as he answered the door. He was surprised to see that it was a policewoman. Nothing was wrong.

"Hi. What's your name sir?" she asked.

"Harold," he replied, curious to see what she needed him for.

"A man by the name of D.B. Stone has been severely injured in a car accident. We were told that you know him." Harold gasped in horror.

"Yes. He is my brother. Is he okay?" Harold questioned.

"Well, I'm not sure if you want to see him in the state that he is in now. He is badly wounded with two broken arms, two broken legs, a spinal cord injury and a slight injury to the right front lobe of his brain. He will be in the hospital for several months but it is likely that he will make it out. He was crossing the road heading over to the supermarket when he got hit from the side by a black Chevy. Luckily, we were there to witness the scene and called the paramedics as fast as we could. He is being housed at the Sherman Hospital and is allowed to have visitors as long as they are family for now."

"Well can I come and see him now?" Harold asked.

"Yes sir, you may. I will let you go and if you have any questions for the hospital, the number is…" the woman trailed on. Harold didn't really have any questions about the situation. He quickly pulled on a pair of brown corduroy pants and a checkered shirt and added a blue tie and mismatched socks to the mix. He shoveled some cheerios down his throat and topped it all off with a swig of milk. Almost forgetting to brush his teeth, he clambered out the door. He stopped though when he realized that his brother's car was not there to pick him up. D.B.'s house was not far away though and a spare car key was hidden around the left side of the garage. He tried to remember all the way back to what D.B. had taught him about driving. The car took off a little faster than expected and whirred around a stop sign as Harold got control of the wheel.

There were not many people in the hospital on a Saturday. Harold checked in at the main desk and was told room 367 was the room number of D.B. Stone. He looked terrible all bandaged up and lying in an adjustable bed. He was the only one Harold trusted with his life, and now was in danger of losing his. Even though the lady at the door said he would probably live, he looked bad enough to be dead already. Harold figured D.B. probably looked worse than he felt. He wanted to motivate others because of D.B. Harold wanted others to know his story and how he felt he should do this for his brother. The spinal injury and the brain damage meant that he would be paralyzed. D.B. had helped Harold out and now, Harold was going to help him back with hopes that he would be somewhat restored back to his old self.

-

During the nine months that it took D.B. to recover, Harold enrolled in an oratory skills class called Oratory Skills for Improvement of Speech and Self Esteem. Harold learned to be more confident in how he presented himself and the tricks of the trade on how to hook an audience and make what you're speaking about effective. As an end-of-class event, each student was to give a speech about a certain topic of his or her choice at an annual speech competition. It was only for fun when it came to the fifteen or so people in the class and Harold went into it finally open minded about losing since it was a competition.

-

There were five more people in the lineup before it was Harold's turn to speak. He waited patiently at the side of the stage, with no fear inside of him. He knew that D.B. was out there waiting for him and that he would be so proud to have such a changed brother who was more confident in himself. Everything was going right...

"Harold, there is a call for you down the hall. We thought that since you have enough time before you speak, that you might want to take the call," the speech teacher Annie told him.

This is what made Harold nervous. Why would someone bother to call him in the middle of the speech competition?

"Is this Harold Stone?" a voice questioned.

"Yes," he replied.

"I'm calling from Sherman Hospital. D.B. had an unexpected heart attack on the way to your speech competition. If you would like to come and see him quickly, it would be much appreciated. It is quite severe and is connected to his accident earlier this year. This might be the last time you can see him, Harold."

It took about one minute for Harold to comprehend the news. He was sure that his turn was right around the corner and he wouldn't miss it for the world. But for D.B.? His only living relative? He might have to make an exception.

"Harold, we'd like you back on stage now. Your turn is in ten minutes."

"Move me to last spot in the lineup," he mumbled. "D.B. had a heart attack and I need to go see him. I might not get this chance again. May I take your car please?"

"Sure, Harold but be very careful and be quick. You might have thirty minutes at the most. Be back soon," Annie said.

He got to the hospital as fast as possible and raced up to room 367, coincidentally the same one he was in last time.

"D.B.! D.B.!" Harold turned to the doctors and nurses in the room. Is he going to be alright?" Harold wanted to know.

"You came at the right time, Harold. Say your last few words. We're sorry but this is…"

Harold didn't give them time to finish.

"I love you, D.B. I'm sorry we didn't end on a better note. I think we stopped at about F#. I wish you could understand…"

That was all that needed to be said. Harold held D.B.'s hand as he died and the heart monitor came to a continuous beep until they turned it all off. It was not such a slow and painful death but more of a peaceful releasing into the life beyond death.

As Harold was driving, a ladybug flew through the open car window and landed on his arm. You're safe with me, D.B., he thought. Now it's show time!

"My name is Harold Stone," he started. "I recently encountered a very touching but heart wrenching event in my life. Probably one that I will hold in my heart for many years to come. At the beginning of this month, I was only a person cowering in the shadows. I was made fun of for being different. But I was empowered, and this may seem silly to you all, but I was empowered in my dreams." Harold surveyed the audience seeing if there was anyone he knew. For an instant, he could have sworn he saw Nick Vujicic, the motivational speaker from his dream, hiding in the shadows under the balcony. He continued, explaining certain selected events in his dream, never calling anyone by name. When he got to the part about his brother, his eyes teared up.

"Today," he said, "My brother D.B. was supposed to be here in this audience hearing me speak for the first time in front of a large group of people. Since his accident earlier this year, I have tried to help him through his trauma and the hardships of becoming himself again. He is the whole reason that I am up here today. I wanted others to hear my story and how I learned to make a difference in the world. I wanted to help people figure out that they can make a difference in the world, too. I was so ready to have D.B. hear me speak louder than I ever have and be confident that I can do it. Unfortunately, this morning, I received news that he had a sudden heart attack and couldn't make it. He died this morning, holding my hand. This empowered me further to empower other people. Not everyone needs to be empowered by death, but by another person. Each of you can make a difference in someone's life and it doesn't take a lot of doing. Be kind to someone. Tell them their hair looks nice or something kind. You can make the difference for whether they take that last step towards the edge of the cliff. Or you could pull them back and make them realize that they are worth it. They have a reason to live. And how does this connect to me? Well, my brother D.B. was the one to pull me back from the edge. I don't think he ever realized it and now he never will. But if you give that kindness to someone, then they believe that they can empower. Empowerment has the domino effect. You know? Once you start, then someone else does it and someone else does it and before you know it, the whole world is empowered. So I encourage you to be that person. Make that change. Empower!"

He wasn't so crazy after all. Harold Stone had just made the biggest speech in his life. The first eruptions of clapping came from the judge's table in the back. He was glad that they liked it and he had never even thought that he would be in the running for the prizes. Soon, the whole auditorium was standing up and applauding with all their might. Harold took a minor bow and exited the stage. The crowd didn't cease though.

"Go back out there!" the other class members kept saying. "They loved it!"

Harold went out on stage once more and bowed again. As soon as the clapping died down, the moderator took the floor again.

"That wraps up our speeches," she announced. "Now for the judges to vote and decide our winner."

It took about ten minutes for the judges to decide but finally, the results got passed up to the front in a shiny red envelope. The woman opened it up and paused for a few seconds. "Harold Stone?" she asked.

It felt like a wave of icy cold water had just rushed over Harold. "This was way better than getting a job with some dope called Vaughn E. Clair," he thought. Harold proudly let the woman pin the big blue ribbon onto his suit. That one moment of his lasted forever! With so much pride and overwhelming emotion built up inside of him, he could have never felt happier.

-

About two weeks later, Harold was finally used to getting fan mail. One letter in particular had the address and recipient printed onto the paper instead hand written. The return address was in the back and he first noticed the name of the continent. Australia, he thought. Who would be sending me something from Australia?

The letter read:

Dear Harold Stone,

I found some of your beliefs to be the same as mine on the topics you discussed during your speech. I don't know if you know, but I was one of the judges on the panel. You described meeting a man with no arms and no legs in your dream. Can you tell me a little more about him? I think we find our passion in the same thing. Empowerment, as you said, is very powerful, hence the name. I would very much like to meet you sometime. Write me back or call me at 617-885-4242. I think you might want to check your front door. I also sent a package.

Sincerely,
Nick Vujicic

Sure enough, there was something at the door. But it wasn't a box. It was a wheel chair, but with no ordinary person in it. This person had no arms, no legs, and no worries.

Run
Cedric Wong

Running was all he could ever do. At first glance, people saw an average man, only 25 years of age, but would later discover he had the ability to run at superhuman speeds. His jet black hair and natural affinity for darkness led him to be nicknamed Raven, shortened to R. Nobody could catch him. He was the wind itself, always managing to slip past the best security to be found. But he doubted he could survive this time. The klaxon sounded, relentless in its beeping. His mission was to retrieve information on these facilities and their weapons manufacturing. *I have maybe five seconds until they figure out where I am, and half a minute for them to reach this computer room...* he thought. *Do I stay? Or run for it? Definitely stay. Running now would leave evidence behind, and I would rather be shot to death than have them find out my identity.* 20 seconds to completion. Ten seconds. Five, four, three, two, one. He yanked the flash drive from the computer and dashed to the doorway in seconds, remembering the intel he received. *500 meters down the corridor, and I'll have reached the exits to the facility. This is the only way out of the building—I'll have to use it.*

This was the most dangerous part of his mission. In this small passageway, anybody could walk in, notice him, and shoot him down without the slightest chance of survival. As he sprinted down the hallway, he noticed two armed men running down a nearby staircase. He had a split second before they noticed and started firing. Then he noticed a fire alarm switch on the wall. It was a reckless plan, but it was his only hope. He jumped high in the air, climbing up the wall using the switch as a foothold, then jumped off the wall, sailed above the guard's heads, landed on the other wall, and dashed down until he was back on flat ground. The soldiers spun around rapidly, wondering what the blurry shadow that had just passed them was. But it was too late, the spy had already reached the doorway. Agent R had another successful mission under his belt.

R worked for *The Club*, a secret group that sought to bring down the most corrupt officials, companies, and empires in the world. Each member was different, with their own set of skills and abilities. Walking into the headquarters, he encountered Agent S.

"Hey, did the great and amazing R finish another successful mission?"

R walked past, ignoring unnecessary conversation.

"Maybe it didn't go so well," S reported to a nearby colleague.

Logging onto his computer, he entered his flash drive, scanning all the information on the companies into *The Club* database. Satisfied, R walked home, grinning to himself.

Upon entering his apartment, R barely had time to register the faint blur in the corner of his eye before he was assaulted with a knife. The masked assailant grazed his arm, causing blood to seep out of the wound. Just then, a second man came out of the closet, and grabbed R, attempting to hold him down. R rolled away, but was caught with a punch to his stomach, almost passing out from the pain. The last thing he saw was the culprit tying his arms and putting a sweet smelling napkin to his face. *Chloroform…* R thought as he drifted off into unconsciousness.

R awoke in a strange room. There was nothing in the room, save a pair of handcuffs that held him to a chain on the wall. His body ached, and he wondered why he was in this place. Then he remembered the assailants in his house last night, and how he'd been captured. He needed to get out of here this instant. But it was too late, as a middle-aged man walked into the room.

"Good morning, Agent R. I hope you had a nice nap."

"Where am I?"

"Why you're in the headquarters of only the most high-tech, secure, facility in the world. You, my friend, are in *The Syndicate*."

Just hearing its name sent shivers down his spine. The *Syndicate* was a group of specialist hackers, thieves, and criminals bent on controlling the entire world from the shadows. They had always been the ultimate goal of the *Club*, and recruits were always told tales of the *Syndicate* torturing their members.

"You've been very successful in your missions lately, agent R. It would be a shame for *The Club* to lose a valuable member like you. Unfortunately, I have no permission to do so. Torture, however, is right up my alley."

The man took a switch from his pocket, and flipped it, sending electric shocks down the handcuffs, zapping his entire body.

"Where is your headquarters? Your headquarters has remained a secret for many years, and we're getting impatient."

"I can't tell you," R groaned as his body went numb. Another jolt ran down his body, almost twice as long, and he was starting to smell like smoke.

"Where is it?"

"You'll never find it!" A third blast ran down his spine, and blacking out seemed like a very good idea right then.

"WHERE IS IT?"

"NOT TELLING!" R grimaced and steeled himself for another shock, but at that exact moment, a heavily guarded man burst into the room, and whispered something to his boss.

"I will be back tomorrow. It would be wise to answer me when I return."

As the man left the room, R smiled. They had taken every precaution they could have known to do. They'd frisked him, they'd handcuffed him to a wall, and they had even changed him into a set of their uniform in his size to make sure he had no tools hidden in his clothes. However, their fatal mistake was in leaving R's hearing aid intact. With the proper intel, they would have found R was not hearing impaired at all. No, the small device by his ear was anything but a hearing aid.

"Agent S?" R heard a thump, followed by a few slapping sounds, probably S searching for the com device."

"R, it's three in the morning! Can't you wake up at a normal time for once?!"

The agent grinned, being notorious in *The Club* for being almost nocturnal, always first to get his mission for the week.

"S, this is an emergency, and I probably won't have much time to talk."

"What is it?"

"I am currently in *The Syndicate* headquarters."

"WHAT!" S exclaimed so loudly it hurt R's ears.

"How did you get in there?"

"I was kidnapped in my own apartment, if you'll believe it."

"I don't know that."

"What do your surroundings look like?"

"I'm in a room completely blank except for a pair of electrified handcuffs and me."

"Have you seen any people around?"

"There was one middle aged man with graying hair, about five feet and 10 inches tall, with an expensive looking suit and a gold wristwatch. He said he didn't have permission to kill me, so he's probably one of the lower-ranked officials of *The Syndicate*."

"I'll contact the other agents and look him up. We probably have data on him, and we can find where he's stationed if he's been spotted by someone. In the meantime, stay calm, stay put, and stay alive." S finished, reciting the basic protocol for when an agent was lost or captured.

All of a sudden, the adrenaline from the electricity faded, and R fell into unconsciousness.

R woke to see a guard roughly unlocking his handcuffs.

"Get up, *agent*," he said.

"Where are we going?"

The guard didn't respond, obviously not caring. He was forced into a different set of handcuffs, and dragged down a long hallway. Eventually, they reached a door, padlocked and reinforced. After being led in, R was amazed. The room was designed so it looked exactly like a few acres of raw, untamed jungle, right down to the tiniest details.

"Welcome, agent R." The man from the day before stepped out from behind a building.

"Why does this look like a jungle?"

"Simply put, my boy, you are here to test our newest line of mechanical soldiers. Designed to function in all terrains, this is the most uneven environment we could think of. They were obviously in need of some… fine tuning, so I've decided to test you against them. They are programmed to cause immense pain. It will not be pleasant."

At that exact moment, robots burst into the room. The man boarded an elevator and left the room. R realized he couldn't be thinking about backup, or who that man was, or even if he was going to survive this ordeal. He needed to run.

R took off at a wild sprint, and not a second too late—the robots started firing off rounds of lasers from their guns. R sprinted to a nearby tree and hid behind it while considering his options. Plan A: Try to fight. Scratch that. There were at least a dozen robots, and if what the man said was true, (although there was no reason to trust anything he said) those lasers were non-lethal, but would cause immense pain and probably severe burns as well. Including the robots' armor, he wouldn't stand a chance. Plan B: Hide somewhere and wait for rescue. Also impossible, as this forest, while fairly large, had no real hiding spots. He'd be found in minutes, and would be shot down, tortured, or possibly killed if the Syndicate had lost its patience. Plan C: Run, and find some kind of exit. That seemed like the best plan for now, as he had no idea when help would come. R ran to the door, and found it locked and padlocked. The next option was the elevator. Again, the door was locked. All of a sudden, a searing pain burned his back, as if someone had laid a hot coal on his skin. R screamed in pain, and more beams seared his back. He blacked out from the sheer pain. R hadn't stood a chance.

For the third time, R awoke in the bare room, this time to yet another electric shock.

"Well, you seem awake now, so I'll just get started then. Simply put, I have been given permission to kill you, R, as it seems that you are still unwilling to cooperate, and there don't seem to be signs of you ever giving in. Frankly, you are taking up time and space that I could easily use for other prisoners, so you're going to be executed now." As soon as he had finished the sentence another guard rushed in and tore off R's handcuffs, and dragged him down the hallway in a different direction, although not after handcuffing him again. Right after the door was shut, his guard cried out in pain, and fell dead, a knife wound in his back. R let a smile creep onto his face, because despite his clumsiness and laid-back attitude, nobody was more proficient in the art of assassination than his friend.

After pulling him up into the air vent he was hiding in, S began to whisper in a very annoyed tone. "Every single time you get caught, there I am, saving the day yet again. I should get a medal, or a trophy, or even a vacation for all the times I have to save your sorry butt from all the trouble you get in. Instead, I'm just taken for granted, forgotten, and left behind!" R sighed. S was always reacting to the slightest things.

"S, I appreciate the dramatic rescue, but could you please get me out of here?" Nodding in agreement, although still obviously displeased, S began crawling through the maze of metallic tunnels.

"Hopefully he knows where he's going, or we'll never make it out of here!" R thought. Sure enough, after maybe ten minutes of shuffling and crawling through, they kicked out a metal grate and jumped down, landing on… the ice coated ground. Snow swirled all around them, chilling R's bare skin.

"Why is it snowing?" R asked as he shivered through his thin uniform.

"We, my friend, are in Alaska. If you'll look around, you'll see some of our famous sightseeing spots, such as snow, ice, and hail!" he chuckled under his breath.

"How are we going to get out of here?"

"We walk."

"Are we walking to a plane, or a ship, or what?"

"There is no mode of transport we're walking to. When we spotted the storm, the plane left as soon as possible, in order to avoid any turbulence. So, we're walking to the nearest town, which should be about 20 miles northwest of here." R sighed. It would be a long day.

In the Corners
Minhtam Tran

On a cold, bleak autumn morning, the sky gray and the leaves a bright orange, a pale-skinned girl sat under a weeping willow in the shadows of a crumbling red building. Her hair, a rusty auburn color, was done in an elaborate waterfall headband braid, framing her face. Her eyes were strikingly gray and piercing through whoever looked her way. She sang softly to herself, then lifted herself of the ground and walked toward the school building. The bell rang shrilly, piercing the ears of those who were standing in the nearby area. A new school and the frightening idea of befriending strangers sent the girl into a mute version of her normally bubbly self. As she walked into the building, she glanced at the wrinkled paper in her hands, then looked at her class schedule. In simple print, the paper said "English 10, room A8, period 1, Ms. Clarkson." Taking deep breaths to calm herself, she looked around for room A8. A few minutes later, she entered the room and looked around at her fellow classmates who she would be with for the rest of the semester. "Make friends, make friends..." The voice in her head whispered, echoing in her brain. She spotted a group of girls her age, laughing happily, smiling. One girl stood out, her crystalline blue eyes wide and innocent. Her hair, blonde and perfectly straightened, was settled across her shoulders. Before she could scare herself out of it, she walked over to the group of girls. She saw their guard go up, their backs turned against her as if to shield themselves from the stranger. Before she could cower in fear, she said," Hi, I'm Adlena. What's your name?"

The blonde haired girl, eyes narrowed and eyebrows raised, replied, "Amelia. Are you new this year or something? I haven't seen you around before."

Quietly, Adlena responded, "Yeah, I'm a freshman."

"That is *so* cool! Can I see your schedule?"

"Yeah... here." Shyly, Adlena handed over her schedule, biting her lip.

"How are we in all the same core classes? I'm a sophomore, you're a freshman," she asked quizzically.

"Oh, I took classes over the summer," Adlena replied, a forced smile coming out of her lips.

"I cannot believe it. You probably don't know your way around, right? I can show you. We can meet up during lunch. Oh, these are my friends Emmeline and Celia." Emmeline had her hair twisted into a braid, pieces of her slightly wavy brown hair sticking out, covering her bright green eyes. Celia had short wispy brown hair, with lustrous eyes the color of hazel.

Before Adlena could respond, the teacher commanded their attention. Adlena sat next to Emmeline as the rest of the class scrambled for their seats. "Okay, class, sit down now. How about we go over the rules of class? I'm Ms. Clarkson, I've had most of you before. Remember: I don't accept mediocre work. If you're going to actually do it, do it right. And even though every year you guys hear the same rules in every class, I still have to go over them. So this year is going to be harder for you guys. More work, fewer social activities, pressure for the PSAT's and SAT's. I don't accept late work, unless there is an acceptable reason. Not an 'I had too much homework so I couldn't finish it,' but a death in the family, or 'I had the stomach flu.' You get the gist, hopefully. Tomorrow I'll give everyone their first assignment for the semester. I want to see what you guys can do. I want you to *prove* to me that you can write and aren't just lazy thinkers. Got it?" With a few nods from the students, Ms. Clarkson kept talking, from general rules to her grading rubrics. With that, the class whizzed past, most of the information going through one ear and out the other. When it was over, Adlena picked up her books, hugged them to her chest, and got up, trying to remember the way to her next class.

"Adlena! Wait up!" Amelia called, her voice ringing through the hallway. Adlena stopped, turned her head around and stopping in her tracks. "Don't you need help to get to your next class? You have... oh, we're not together. Actually, we're on separate floors. But here's your schedule back. Good luck finding it! Meet us at lunch in the corner of the cafeteria near the round tables. Bye!" And with that, Amelia left, Emmeline and Celia trailing behind.

After Spanish 5/6, Adlena was tired. Doing timed essays in Spanish wasn't her idea of fun. She walked towards the cafeteria, hearing the endless chatter and the smell of food wafting past her nose. Scoping out the large room, she finally found the round tables, off in the corner. Sitting down, Adlena pulled out a chair, at the same time reaching for her sandwich in her brown lunch bag. She spotted Amelia, Emmeline, and Celia walking over to the table, and she waved them over as she took a bite of her brie, strawberry, and chocolate grilled cheese. "Hi Emmeline, Celia, Amelia. How was your class? Here, take a seat."

Emmeline, for the first time, talked to Adlena, complaining, "I hate World History. Why didn't they let me take a different class? Ugh.... That teacher is *so* boring, like, oh my god. All we do is just sit there, and take notes.

And how are we supposed to listen when the teacher doesn't even *try* to make it interesting?"

Nodding, Celia added, "Yeah, I know right? But I had him last year, and he gave us *so* much work to do. I hate essays! I mean, what's the point of writing things down when I can just talk?"

Adlena, questioningly, said "Well, writing is another way of communication. I actually love writing a lot more than speaking. You can write things down you're too afraid to say. And if you guys ever need help, I can edit and help you write your essays and papers."

Amelia, having started eating her salad, exclaimed, "Oh my god, you *can*? The girls and I are so awful at writing! You are *amazing*. And we both have the rest of the day together, too! You must be amazing at science and math too, huh? God, you are *way* too smart. The rest of us have no chance!"

Adlena blushed, and then replied, "Well, I love writing the best, but everything else is great too. I actually love school; when I was little, I would get sick a lot, but I wouldn't let my parents make me stay home. I'd go to school, and everyone would try and get me to go home because they didn't want to get sick."

"Wow, that is intense. I always tried to get *out* of school! My parents just let me bail out every time I wanted to skip. Going shopping with my girls... yeah, those were good times. But now, everything is about SAT scores, PSAT scores, GPA, homework, classes. Can't I get a *break*?"
Celia and Emmeline looked at each other, their eyes conveying their disagreement.

"Well, you know I can help you, like I've said. It's really no trouble; I only do volunteer work twice a week over the weekends. Sometimes I cook, but that's about it." Adlena replied, her voice almost down to a whisper.

Amelia opened her mouth to speak, but just then the bell rang. "Time to go to class, I guess. What's next, Adlena? Oh, right, Modern World History. Come on, I'll show you to the classroom." The two girls walked to class, in a silence amidst the boisterous conversations around them.

And from then on, the day whizzed past, flashing before Adlena's eyes in a flurry of lectures. The next day, Adlena found herself approaching the old school building timidly, looking around to find Amelia, Emmeline, and Celia. Spotting them, she walked hurriedly through the crowds, her feet dancing around in a complicated pattern. "Emmeline! Hey, wait up!" she said, her voice loud, though still drowned out in the sea of voices.

"Oh, hey Adlena. How's it going? You must be freezing cold without a jacket! Here, take mine." Emmeline shrieked, taking off her jacket.

Adlena shrugged it off, saying, "Oh, I'm fine. Besides, being out in the cold builds character, right?"

Celia nodded, saying, "Calvin and Hobbes, right? I love that series. Amelia, don't you?"

"Well, I don't know. I'm so worried about school this year. My parents told me that if I don't get B's or above, I don't get to have my party." Turning to Adlena, she said, "The party is something I throw every year. It's exclusive to only the *best* of the school. This party makes or breaks a person's reputation. If I don't hold it, who will?" Amelia whined, her eyes embedding into Adlena.

Celia gulped, saying, "Emmeline or I could have it; both of us have large enough houses. Plus, Adlena can always help us, right?"

Amelia smiled bemusedly, replying with a voice as sweet as honey, "Oh, no. We all know you three can't hold a party. You don't know the first thing about throwing a party. I'll just need to figure out how I'll get everything done. Maybe I can get someone to help me." She laughed, her voice twinkling like wind chimes.

Celia and Emmeline frowned at her last statement, though they said nothing. The bell rang, and all four of them headed to their lockers and then proceeding to English. In a few moments, they sat down at their usual arrangement in class, Celia and Emmeline in front, Amelia and Adlena in the back. They waited as Ms. Clarkson sipped her coffee, standing at the front of the class. Adlena read the board, grinning as she looked at the words "writing assignment, any form."

"Okay, class, as you can see, we are going to have a new assignment to do. What is it, you ask? I'm going to give everyone a week to write anything: a short story, an essay, a few poems, whatever you feel like. I want everyone to get comfortable writing different things outside of their comfort zone, but I need to establish a comfort zone first. You can write an essay on how horrible your life is, or whatever you feel like. I just want you to write something. Anything. Another thing: you can make this a group project. This will be due on Monday, and we'll share out. For the meantime, brainstorm with people around you. Are you guys ready? Good. Get to work." With that, Adlena saw students banging their heads on their desks, only spotting one grin in the room: her own. She turned to Amelia.

"Isn't this great? We get to write whatever we want!" Adlena shrieked, her voice echoing around the dull and silent room as students turned around and glared at her.

"No, this is horrible. I don't have time to write this assignment! We'll have so much homework to do. This is the second semester of the year, and

I'm stuck with all of this homework and evil teachers!" Amelia put her head on the desk, with either fake or genuine sobs.

Adlena swallowed, saying "Well, I mean, if you really don't have time to do it, I could help you. I'm not too busy this week." Adlena mentally scolded herself. Her Spanish teacher expected an oral presentation on the history of the Spanish language prepared by next Tuesday, and she was the only one without a group. And at home she had to cook, and look around for a job.

Emmeline frowned, saying "You don't need to do our work for us. We're perfectly capable."

"Yeah, don't worry about it. You probably have *loads* of homework anyways."

"Girls, I wasn't saying she should do the work for us. Just help m-us. I mean, this assignment can't be that bad, right?"

Still unsure, Celia replied, "Maybe. We shouldn't make anyone do our work." For the rest of the class period, the girls discussed their ideas together.

"Yeah, I think I might write a short story. It sounds fun. Maybe a mystery, like a murder. That sounds interesting, right?"

"Yeah, I guess. I don't know what to do though! My life *sucks*." Amelia whined, her voice getting higher and whinier.

"Yes, Amelia, your life totally sucks. I mean, a huge mansion-like house, being an only child, teachers giving you great grades for the little amount of effort you put in, and being the most popular kid in school. Like, oh my god, worst life *ever*." Emmeline replied, sneering.

"Whatever, Emmeline." With that, the bell rang, and the four of them packed up their things.

Once again, Adlena's day flashed by, full of new essays and homework to do. She walked home, arriving at the small cottage outside of the downtown area. Her mom was in the house, sleeping with her brown curls falling around her face. "Ada?" a little voice whispered, softly and sweetly. It was Liza, Adlena's little sister. She had red hair, brighter than Adlena's, falling in bouncy ringlets. She had bright green eyes, the color of emeralds.

"Yes, Liza?" Adlena loved her little sister, and she guessed that the feeling was mutual. Their family was a small one of three, most likely soon to be two. Their mother was sick, but she had no health insurance and had to use her sick time to stay home and rest. Unfortunately, that time was about to end, and then Adlena would have to find a job to take care of everyone.

Liza was blissfully ignorant of anything bad in the world, but her journey to reality would come soon enough.

"Mommy sleeping again. Can Ada read a story?" Liza asked, her tongue skipping parts of Adlena's name.

"Of course, Liza. Let me just start making dinner and do a little homework first, okay?" Adlena said, smiling and walking to the kitchen.

Liza frowned, whimpering "Why Ada cook now? I want to read a story! What food is Ada cooking?"

"Food that you are going to eat! It's going into *your* stomach!" Adlena poked Liza's stomach, and Liza squealed, the complaints momentarily forgotten. With that, Adlena looked through the almost-empty fridge, grabbing some food. After making a small picnic, Adlena took out her laptop, and checked her email. She had gotten Emmeline, Celia, and Amelia's email addresses already. She opened up a new document and started brainstorming ideas for the assignment. She knew she wanted to write a poem, but on what? Food would be okay, but it wouldn't be long enough. Besides, she didn't like odes. Or maybe one on life? But that would be too personal. She finally decided on nature. Nature is good, right? A tree in autumn, she decided. Autumn was the best season.

-

After writing the poem, she wrote another, this time on music. She loved jazz and classical music, the swells and melodies that cascaded from the voices of instruments. Her house was near a jazz club, with saxophones stringing notes together. There was also a small bakery, which had flaky croissants that melted in Adlena's mouth. Adlena wanted to cook when she was older, but writing sounded like a fun profession too. Adlena went up to the loft, small and airy, where the siblings shared a "bedroom." Liza was lying down, her eyes closed, sleeping silently on her side. Around the small mattress was a shelf of books with a chair next to it, which the girls used for their table. "Liza, do you want to read a story now?"

Liza sat up, her eyes crinkled in the corners. "Ada done with homework?" she asked sleepily, her voice groggy.

Adlena smiled weakly, whispering, "Yes, Ada's done with work. Does Liza want to go outside and read?" Nodding, Liza walked up and picked a book off the shelf, cradling it in her small arms. Together, the two girls go out into the back, where there is a small stream outside. Adlena brought a blanket with a picnic basket, which the girls spread out near the creek, beneath a tree. Liza eagerly looked through the basket, taking out two slim thermoses, a few plastic-wrapped sandwiches, and a few persimmons.

The two girls curled up on the blanket, unwrapping the sandwiches. There was a small peanut butter and jelly and a tomato, mozzarella, and basil. Adlena handed Liza a persimmon, washed and soft enough to bite into. Adlena started reading quietly, her voice soft and soothing. There was a soft breeze, rustling the leaves of the tree they were sitting under. They could hear the creek gurgling next to them as the sprinkle of rain came in. Still reading, Adlena draped her jacket over her sister's shoulders. As Liza fell asleep, Adlena packed up the food, closed the book, and scooped her sister into the house and tucked her into bed.

-

Adlena looked up from her computer, reading the clock that hung loosely on the wall: *11:21*. Adlena walked down the ladder quietly, meeting her mother downstairs. Her mother, still fast asleep, was snoring quietly on the armchair. Gently, Adlena picked her frail mother up and carried her into the bedroom downstairs. She walked out to the kitchen again, and then looked through the fridge. Finding nothing, she sighed. Sleep sounded good to Adlena, so she went back up the ladder to her room, and gently pushed her sister over and closed her eyes. She could see the stars in her mind's eye, far and bright.

-

The next morning in Ms. Clarkson's class, Amelia was hysterically crying, Celia and Emmeline rolling their eyes at each other. "I couldn't do my assignment because - sob - my parents banned me from using the computer." She whimpered, her mascara and eyeliner smudging from the heaving sobs.

"You can write it in class today, Amelia. It's not like you actually needed the computer to write the story. Besides, at least you don't have to work. Celia and I didn't get home until 2:00 AM because of our night shift at the Yo-Club. We're even worse off than you." Emmeline spat out, her voice annoyed.

"Yeah, okay. Maybe. We can figure it out later. All three of us can work together. Do you want to work with us, Adlena?"

"Oh, I'm okay. I already finished two poems." Adlena replied, her cheeks red from blushing.

"My god, really? You're so lucky." Amelia drawled, her voice wistful. The class was dismissed, and all four of the girls packed up their things. "Adlena, we'll meet you in the cafeteria after our next period, okay?"

-

After Spanish, Adlena saw the three girls walking towards their lockers. Adlena went the same direction as them, because her locker was in the same general area. She could hear the girls talking amongst themselves.

"I'm telling y'all, we should just take her poem and be done with it. She will be *so* easy to manipulate." Amelia gushed, her voice a loud stage whisper.

Emmeline, her voice unsteady, replied, "Why should we just take her work? She seems pretty nice, albeit shy."

Amelia, frowning, replied, "Because I need to hold this party. Besides, I need a good grade on this assignment, and y'all do as well. I mean, she already wrote two poems anyways. It's not like we're making her do extra work."

Celia and Emmeline came to a silent agreement, Celia replying, "Okay. But this is your work that she's doing. Emmeline and I are writing something else."

"Fine then, girls, be that way. But when I get an A and you two a D? It's all on you. Now, if you'll excuse me, I need to go get a poem from an idiotic freshman." Amelia scoffed, flipping her blonde hair over her shoulder and walking off, her high heels clicking across the floor.

Adlena gasped, and then hid behind a wall until she heard the three girls head to the cafeteria. She stopped quickly by her locker, and grabbed her lunch, walking fast towards the cafeteria. She couldn't believe they said that about her. She wasn't easily manipulated, right? Actually, she was. Sighing, Adlena kept walking towards the cafeteria, trying to pretend she hadn't heard their conversation.

"Adlena! Hey, sit over here!" Amelia yelled over the din of the voices.

"Yeah, I'm here." Adlena replied with a twinge of annoyance in her voice.

The lunch was awkward, only filled with the sounds of chewing. For the rest of the day, Adlena fell into her usual routine of no talking. She walked home, where her sister clung to her shoes in excitement. "Ada home! Ada home!" Liza sang joyously, dancing around in a complicated pattern.

"Yes, Ada's here. Come on, do you want to dance outside?"

Liza nodded, shrieking, "Outside, outside!" The two sisters went into the kitchen, Adlena lifting Liza up to sit on the small counter as she prepared their snack.

"Okay, Liza, let's head out. Just let me get my homework, okay?" Adlena sighed, then ran to the front of her house to get her book bag. "Liza, you're not wearing your jacket! Here, let's go get them." Adlena grabbed a scarf and a warm pea coat for her little sister.

The two of them walked a little farther than usual, up to a small stream near the walking trails. They found a little clearing and spread out their food and blanket. Adlena grabbed her laptop, turning it on to check her email. A message popped up from Amelia.

"Hey Adlena, I was wondering if you could help me write my thing for Ms. Clarkson's class. I'm just super busy; I have to plan my party. So if you could help me write a poem or something, that would be great."

Adlena typed quickly, and sent Amelia her poem on music. It was simple, but it flowed well as far as Adlena knew. Not like she had ever shared her poems she wrote in her journal with anyone.

Amelia obviously wasn't so busy with party planning, because she responded immediately with, "Oh my god, this is *amazing*. Thank you so much! Love you to pieces! My god."

Adlena was excited. She had the whole weekend to write, and Liza was going to be with her all weekend eating and talking her ear off. She let herself smile for a brief moment before closing the computer and talking to her sister.

-

Adlena's heart was racing. Here was the moment of truth. When people would finally hear her poems, for the first time. Amelia was smiling from ear to ear, her hair curled in perfect ringlets that day, her eyes still the same color as sapphires. "Amelia, would you like to read your work?" Ms. Clarkson asked, forcing the students to talk to the entire class.

"Of course I would, Ms. Clarkson." Amelia replied sweetly.

"Music, the sound of beauty, rolling off the tongues of the instruments, the voices sweet and soulful like the players themselves. The notes formed in an effortless melody, from hours of listening and deciding the perfect harmonies. The sounds, rolled together into a beautiful wave, full of power and elegance. The whisper of voices, or running footsteps down the stairs, captured perfectly in one note, one moment of time, one wisp of a note, a harmonic, a melody. A noise, waiting eagerly to come out and be heard, a moment of truth, the single note." Amelia read, her voice saying the words for the first time with confusion, the words fluttering off her mouth in an unfamiliar rhythm.

Ms. Clarkson clapped with the rest of the class, thought staring back and forth between Adlena and Amelia. Adlena gulped, as she knew she had been whispering the words to herself, memorized after the time she had spent composing the perfect piece. That was the end of class, and Ms. Clarkson asked for Adlena at the end of class. Adlena walked up, her heart racing faster and faster as she walked closer towards Ms. Clarkson's desk. "Miss Adlena, that poem was very touching. However, it doesn't seem like Miss Amelia's style, wouldn't you agree?" Ms. Clarkson's eyebrows were raised, her voice containing disapproval.

"People are full of surprises. Maybe she had an epiphany over the weekend." Adlena replied, her voice cracking with nervousness.

"Perhaps. I recommend you hurry to your next class now." Ms. Clarkson said, her voice demanding. With that, Adlena headed to Spanish. She could hear Ms. Clarkson ask for Amelia, though, and she waited outside the door quietly, not making a sound.

"Miss Amelia, your poem was very well-written; however, it sounded a bit like plagiarism. Just to be safe, I want to ask you a few questions. What's the poem about?"

"Oh, it's about nature. You know, trees and flowers and all of that stuff."

"Very good. And what style is it in?"

"Um... Amelia style?"

"Alright, I'll take those answers. But you're getting a D on the assignment. The poem was about music. Next time you plagiarize, cover your tracks a bit better."

Adlena gulped, and ran to Spanish as fast as she could.

-

Adlena walked to the cafeteria, dread filling her gut as she realized she was losing what fragments of friends she had. It wasn't her fault her friend had moved away to New York. And the fact that she was a loner anyways. And to lose friendships? She was scared. Her biggest fear was that she was going to be left alone, without anyone to comfort her or tell her everything would be okay. And this was the start of that chain.

"I cannot believe you made me get a D on that assignment! My parents will *never* let me have a party now. This is all your fault." Amelia screamed, glaring at Adlena as soon as she walked to the cafeteria table.

"I'm sorry! But you should have read the poem better." Adlena murmured quietly.

"I don't want to hear what you have to say, Little Miss Writer! Get out of my life. You shouldn't even be here. You're a loser. Leave!" Amelia sneered, pushing Adlena back so that she fell on the ground.

Feeling tears in her eyes, Adlena walked away, and went outside to the benches and grabbed her food. She heard footsteps behind her and she tried to cover up her sobs as best as she could. "What do you want?" she mumbled, her voice cracking.

"We just wanted to say we're sorry. We shouldn't have let Amelia taken your work and yell at you for it. We've seen this happen so many times... Amelia just loves to get through school without working for it." Celia whispered, handing Adlena tissues.

"Let's just start over and be friends. Amelia's an idiot, and we told her so. She's not very happy about that." Emmeline said, smiling a bit.

"Thanks, you guys. You're not that bad, after all." Adlena sniffed. And with her little sister and two new friends, she knew in her heart her worst fear wouldn't come true anytime soon.

The Descendant of Captain Kidd
Henry Thomas

The year is 1778. War is raging all around the American Colonies. My name is Henry Kidd, the descendant of the notorious privateer-turned-pirate Captain William Kidd himself. There are legends that he was invincible; neither steel nor musket ball could hit him. There are awe-inspiring stories of the treasure that Kidd left behind; something so valuable that he went mad keeping it safe. The *Adventure Prize*, his noble vessel on which he sailed the seven seas, was the exact model of my own ship, the *Aquila*. After many years of hard work in the colonies, I have managed to amass a crew of 21 men, 14 cannons, and 4 swivel guns. My ship is a thing of beauty, made out of fine Oak and Redwood lumber, topped off with iron ribbing to keep it stable. An intricately carved eagle in dark blue serves as the masthead. I think it fits perfectly, considering that *Aquila* means "eagle" in Latin.

My first mate, Robert Faulkner, or "Gibbs," we call him, was the original owner of the ship, but I helped him fix it up when it was in poor condition, and then I proved my seafaring knowledge on a naval mission in the Caribbean. Gibbs is one of the smartest men I know, and at this moment, he comes toward me bearing a large leather-bound book.

"Ahoy there, Cap'n! I've just found us a logbook for her," he says, nodding at the *Aquila*. "Now, anytime you care to make upgrades to the ship, in weaponry or in her hull, we can record yer purchases," he continues. Feeling the bulge of recently earned pounds in my pocket, I open up Gibb's book, to see what I can get. There is a swivel gun ammunition upgrade, and it costs about £7500. I open up my coin purse. I have £7800, so my purchase is perfect.

"That'll be all, Gibbs," I say. My second mate, Connor Putnam, was a former blacksmith before the Lobsterbacks destroyed his shop. We recruited him to my crew, and he's been a faithful mate ever since. He still retains all of his blacksmithing knowledge, so it's a real help to have him on board. As I walk over to him, I can see that he is sharpening a sword - but not just any sword. My beloved Cutlass that was given to me by my father when I was a young boy.

"Is my sword in good condition?" I inquire to Connor.

"Aye, Cap'n," Connor responds, "It was looking a wee bit dull, but I sharpened it right up." He pulls out the sword and waves it around a bit before holding out the handle to me. "Why don't you try it on a tree or a log?"

"I would, but we've got something better to test it out on, Connor," I say, with a gleam in my eye. "Gibbs has wind of a rogue privateer crew or something off the coast of Boston terrorizing the merchant ships in the area. Why don't you gather up the crew, and we'll soon put a stop to it."

"Aye-aye, Cap'n." He does a quick salute and then runs off to gather the crew. I return to Gibbs, and he's got my coat and tricorn waiting for me. I pull on the outfit, and sheathe my newly sharpened sword. A sudden ringing alerts the crew that it is about time to set sail. I jump up onto the bow. The crew is hustling to get the cannons and the rigging in place, and I weave through a couple men hauling a crate of flintlocks up the deck. I make my way up the deck, and grab hold of the wheel.

"PREPARE TO SET SAIL!" Gibbs bellows.

"Raise the anchor," I yell. My call is repeated until the anchor gets hauled up from the seabed. "Alright, FULL SAIL!" I yell once again. My call is greeted by cheers from the crew, and the rigging loosens and my magnificent sails unfurl. The *Aquila* shoots off from the dock, and to the open sea we go.

-

Three days later we are in the open ocean, with the stormy waves thrashing around, whipping the ship. Everyone is in high spirits, and we have the wind at our backs. We are making good time until one of the rigging monkeys suddenly yells, "MAN O-WAR DEAD AHEAD!" It is true, the clouds and the fog have disguised its approach until now. It bears the union jack, which means it is indeed a British vessel. The question now is if it is a privateer or a regiment ship. It draws closer still, and through my spyglass I can see the distinctive red coats of the soldiers onboard.

"HARD A STARBOARD!" I yell. Immediately the ship turns right so that is abreast with the larger warship. "FIRE THE HEAT SHOT!" I shout. The cannons men gently place the oil soaked cloth wrapped cannon balls in the cannons, and there is a terrific roar and all the cannons ignite at the same moment, sending a wave of flaming cannonballs at the opposing ship. On impact, they explode and kill all nearby British soldiers. I hear one yell "Its Davy Jones f'r me!" as he slumps over the deck. The fire has severely burned the hull of the other ship, and the sails of the ship are blazing with fire. However, the man o-war is far from finished. As I see the cannons on the numerous decks of the ship being slid up, I yell "BRACE!" and everyone onboard the Aquila ducks or jumps to cover. The cannonballs are not very accurate so there is little damage done to the ship. Thankfully, the Aquila is equipped with reinforced steel and a ribcage, so the *Aquila* should be able to take a lot of damage. With the Man O'War's sails rended, it'll not being anywhere soon. With expert skill, I pull the steering wheel around, and we head straight towards the larger British ship. "PREPARE TO BOARD!" I yell to my men.

"SECURE THE AFT LINES! RAISE THE SAILS! LOWER THE RIGGING!" Gibbs yells.

My second mate, Connor is eagerly handing out boarding axes, muskets and tomahawks from a crate. "BATTLE STATIONS!" He yells. The monkeys are busy throwing their hooks at the Man O'War, hoping for purchase, and tying in the ropes so we are neck and neck with the British vessel.

The redcoats know that there is no chance to flee, and they are too preparing for our invasion.

"NOW!" I yell, and with glee my crew lets loose a terrible howl and we jump onboard the Man O'war, and begin fighting.

I jump off my aft line, and do a rolling somersault as I hit the wood of the deck, before burying my sword in the neck of a British sailor. The sounds are everywhere, swearing, yelling, and the sound of steel on steel. Occasionally I hear an explosion of gunpowder, and I see a man hunched over, with a small red hole in his chest or head. We may be outnumbered ten to one, but my crew's training is quite evident against these inexperienced British men. I flick out the concealed blade hidden on my wrist, and begin to run around on deck searching for the officers and captain of the ship. Occasionally, I run up to a British sailor and bury my small blade in his back before throwing his head on the ground, all on the move, but even with the few men I dispatch, I can tell that we are losing this battle—the sheer numbers of the British are overpowering us. I need to find the officers of the ship, and fast.

As nimble as can be, I sprint up to a long plank, and run up it until I am level with the second deck. Jumping off, I can see the first officer dueling with three of my men. He parries the sword of the first, using his momentum to throw my crewman off the ship. He tumbles overboard with a cry, and then lands in the clear sea below. He is shouting for a second, and then large dark shadows of the sea grab him, and the clear blue now becomes stained with red. The officer continues his assault by stabbing the second of my men in the neck, before shooting the third with his pistol. Enraged, I charge over to him, and we start to duel. He shouts to four of his nearby men, and what was before a one-on-one duel quickly leaves me outnumbered. However, the officer does not know that I am quite used to fighting one against overpowering odds. One of the men tries to stab at me, but I parry, and kick him in the groin. He groans, but I continue my attack, and stab him in the head. He crumples to the ground, and I advance towards the second man, using my small blade to catch him off balance, and then use my sword to slash him repeatedly across the chest. The second man dies with a spurt of blood, as I continue my furious assault on to the third man, kicking him, and then somersaulting across the man, and stabbing him in the heart, in one fluid motion, effectively dodging the remaining men's reluctant attacks, and killing another of my opponents. I again use my small blade to break the fourth man's defense, and then grab his neck and slice his throat, while turning to face the officer. He is agape at my demonic display of skill. I grab the officer in a chokehold and flip out my pistol at his head.

"Where is your captain, lobsterback?" I whisper. Quivering at my pistol, he just barely manages to get out,

"Below decks. He's attending his cargo."

"What cargo?!" I ask.

"I don't know, I swear," he says. I pull the trigger, and the man dies instantly. I gently lay his limp body on the deck, and use my two fingers to close his eyelids.

"Rest in peace," I whisper, before running to the stairway. The stairs are blocked by hordes of British sailors fighting with my crew, but I cannot stop to watch. I push past the men in my way, half running and half jumping down the stairs to the hold. I jog through the numerous rooms, until I find one with a closed door. Slowly, and carefully, I open the door, but the man inside pays no notice to me. The man inside, who I presume to be captain, is busy locking a scrap of paper inside a chest.

"Captain?" I ask. The man turns around, and unsheathes his sword.

"Aye. I am Captain William Johnston of his majesty's Royal British Navy, and I will not allow petty little thieves to TAKE MY SHIP!" He bellows the last part, and it is clear that he values the ship very much. He salutes me with his sword, and makes the first attack, a powerful lunge. It is evident that he is not some ordinary man pinched from his family by the British Navy, but had actual training. I must be on my guard.

"I am a Captain also," I say to the other man. "My full name is Henry William Kidd." The British captain's eyes widen at the name Kidd.

"Aye, tis that so?" He smirks. "I know about Kidd,"

"What do you know about me?!" I ask, half yelling. The man's smirk only widens. We fight like I've never fought in my life. My every parry, lunge, stab or slash gets countered or broken. When I try to use his lunges against me, he evades and punches me in the head. The battle is going poorly for me

41

when I notice a barrel of gunpowder near the other Captain. I quickly hip fire my pistol and the barrel explodes knocking us both off our feet. We struggle to rise, and then start our duel again. The man was closer to the explosion, so he got the full brunt of the blast, and he is not quite aware of our fight as before. He lunges once again, but I grab his sword and throw the man on the ground. I plant my knee on his chest as he struggles to rise. My concealed blade hand hovers over his chest.

"What do you know about the Kidds?" I ask, calmly, once again. The man coughs, and mumbles, "Go... to hell..." and smirks.

"Rest in peace," I say, and I flick out my blade and sink it deep into the man's chest. His eyes flare with pain, and then slowly relax as he is comforted by death's cold embrace.

I get off the man, and hobble over to the chest he was desperately trying to lock. He didn't get to finish locking it, but unfortunately, the key is nowhere to be found. I reach for my pistol as I realize it needs to be reloaded. I cock the flint back ½ of the way, and pour some gunpowder into the small hole on the side of gun. I shove a cartridge, a pistol ball and some torn paper to condense the explosion, inside of the pistol's steel tube, and then pull the flint all the way back. I pull the trigger right over the chest's lock, and it gets shredded by the deadly ball. I open the lid of the chest, expecting jewels, or gold, or pounds, but there is nothing inside but a piece of paper. As I hold it up to the candlelight, I realize that it is not a piece of paper, at all but a part of a torn treasure map! As I walk up the stairs on to the deck, past the sullen British sailors being forced into lifeboats to get off the now sinking warship, I hop back over to the *Aquila*, and show Gibbs the document. We look at it for a little while before he exclaims, "Oh! 'Tis an old map of the Colonies," He looks at the map for a little longer before saying, "Aye! That's Northern Canada!" There is a small star in the northernmost part of Canada. "Aye! We must go to Canada! That must be where the treasure is..." He stops speaking for a moment and his face becomes increasingly sullen.

"What is it?" I inquire.

"That's suicide, that is," He nods to the map. "That be the graveyard of ships. Many a good vessel has gone there but never returned."

"Gibbs!" I exclaim. "We must go!" He looks at my expression for a moment before turning to my celebrating crew.

"SET A COURSE FOR THE GRAVEYARD OF SHIPS!" He yells. The crew are too happy to grumble at this request, in light of their recent victory. "Bundle up," Gibbs mutters to me. "It's gonna be cold where you're headed."

A week later, the Aquila is heading far North, farther past Boston or New Hampshire or even Maine. The weather has dropped significantly, and the cold is evident in the crew's steamy breath and rosy cheeks. Everyone has three layers of clothing on, just in case.

One of the lookouts suddenly shouts,

"ICEBERG DEAD AHEAD!" There is a note of panic in his voice, and I spin the steering wheel hard to port, just narrowly missing the huge iceberg. Once again, I hear "ICEBERG AHEAD," from yet another lookout, and I decide that this is no longer quite safe.

"LOAD THE GRAPESHOT!" I yell, and my call is repeated until all of my cannons are loaded and ready to fire. Suddenly, all the icebergs come into view. I yell "FIRE!" And thousands of tiny cannonballs are hurtling towards the ice, shattering it and clearing a path to what appears to be a huge ice foe with a ship right in the middle. I consult the torn treasure map, which has been our primary guide to the treasure.

"This must be it," I whisper to Gibbs, as I stare at the immaculate, but somehow foreboding stranded ship.

"Cap'n, I'm afraid the Aquila won't be able to go farther than this," he says. "Take a longboat to one of the big icebergs and see if you can get to that ship. And go get that treasure," He says. I nod, and walk over to where some of my men are preparing a boat for me. I slowly step in, and my crew gently lowers me down to the icy water. I pull the oars back and forth, and with a few strong strokes, I arrive at the bank of one of the large icebergs.

Surprisingly, the ice is not slippery, and my hands find purchase as I free run up the iceberg. I jump to the next, running and sliding my way up to the ship. As I stand before it, I can still see the name of it, *The Journey*, in faded yellow letters. It isn't the *Adventure Prize*, however. As I make my way to the lower deck of the ship, I can see the frosted corpses of the damned crew of *The Journey*. The captain's quarters are remarkably similar to mine, and as I explore the dimly lit room, I turn face to face with the corpse of the captain. Even in death, he still wears a demonic grin, and his eyes are half rotted, but frozen, giving the body a truly gruesome effect. He still wears the robes he once proudly wore as a captain, and on the table in front of him, he grasps a chest, the flesh of his hands rotted away, so his bones show through his blue skin. As I gently pull the chest away from the captain, his hand breaks off, from the elbow down. Disgusted, I slice the tibia off my chest, and wrench open the old and rusted lock. I open the chest finally expecting the treasure of my ancestor, but it is another piece of withered paper. I barely have time to put the paper in my pouch before the wood I am standing on breaks, and I fall into the lower deck. Disoriented, I hear a groaning sound coming from the ship. Suddenly, I realize what is happening. My weight is tilting the frozen ship, and the ship will sink if I do not get off it!

I run up the lower, tilted side of the ship, grabbing whatever holds I can, to desperately flee the sinking vessel. By the time I reach the top, the ship has tilted almost completely straight up, and I have barely enough time to dive off the ship into the icy waters below before the murky depths reclaim *The Journey*.

Freezing, I paddle over to my long boat, and drag myself up to it. I rest for a moment, dripping water into the boat, before I make my way back to the *Aquila*. Onboard, in my quarters, Gibbs and I inspect the parchment.

"Looks like another one of those map fragments. Let's see the other one, Cap'n," Gibbs asks.

"Here," I say, matching the two pieces of wrinkled paper together. "They look like they came from the same map." Gibbs inspects the newer of the two pieces.

"Another map," he says. "Except this one's of the Carolinas," He looks at me. "This time, the star's on one of these small islands."

"Gibbs," I say, "Tell the crew to set course for South Carolina."

-

A little over a day later, the Aquila is at full sail, making good time towards our destination. The sky is a clear blue, melding nicely with the light green of the Atlantic. Gibbs is more excited than I've ever seen him, eagerly anticipating finding Captain Kidd's fabled treasure. I am standing on the bow of the ship when our bell suddenly starts to ring.

"Pirates at three o'clock!" A scout yells. Two small sailing ships suddenly emerge from some of the rocks. I have to keep my calm, as Gibbs yells "BATTLE STATIONS!" The crew stands at ready behind the cannons, and the swivel guns.

"FIRE THE SWIVEL GUNS!" I shout. There is a muffled explosion, and four small cannon balls come zooming at one of the smaller ships, destroying wood and flesh, sending the smaller vessel to the bottom of the sea. "We'll use chain shot to destroy the other ship's mast," I tell Gibbs.

"CHAIN SHOT!" Gibbs tells the crew. A moment later, and hundreds to chains are sent flying into the other ship's mast, tearing the fabric, leaving it scuttled. "Jolly good," Gibbs says with a smile.

As I pull the steering wheel around, the island that is our destination comes into view. It is mostly bare except for a huge mansion atop with trees and wildlife growing around it. It looks as if it has been deserted for a long time. We anchor the *Aquila* off the shore of the island, and I swim to shore.

The front door of the mansion is locked, but a well-placed kick shatters the rotted wood. The sound echoes through the house, and gives me a sense of ominous unfriendliness. The mansion, once beautiful, has been overgrown and tree roots have forcibly grown through walls and windows. Moldy and torn portraits glare down at me, as I walk through the halls. Towards the end of the house, there is what looks like a small museum. Stuffed animals and ivory statues in disarray lead to the impression that someone has been here. Towards the end of the room lies a small chest and even stranger—a man! As I inspect the man, I realize that he is not living at all, but there is blood seeping from a small wound in his head. He has been shot recently, and all of the sudden, I hear feet running and then a door slams. I sprint back the way I have come, only to be blocked by a large door, with a lock shaped like a clock. I push the hour and minute key around for a minute with no avail. I search around the room for clues to get past the door. There are paintings, silverware, a collection of watches and a fireplace... The watches! I hasten over to inspect the collection when I realize that the watches all display the same time. The hour hand is on the seven, and the minute hand is on the thirty-five. I walk back over to the lock and slide the respective hands into place. Immediately, the door slides up, revealing a secret tunnel. I run down it, after the sound of the fleeing footsteps. Luckily, the other person is not very fast, so I catch up to him in a minute. He is desperately trying to open the next door when I confront him.

"Do you know what that is?" I ask, pointing to the final map fragment in his hand.

"Yes," he says with a snarl. "It will lead me to the legendary treasure of Captain Kidd," He puts the paper in his pocket and throws a punch at me, which I catch, and then slam his head into my elbow, he crumples, unconscious. I quickly loot the sleeping man to get the final map fragment back. I stand up, and walk back through the house. At the water, I dive in, and swim speedily back to the *Aquila*. Onboard, Gibbs already has a towel for me to dry off, and is eagerly anticipating my find. We match the two previous fragments with the one I just found.

"Cap'n, that be Boston there..." Gibbs says. "But instead of a star, there's an X on that island."

"What island?" I ask.

"That one..." He points to the island where there is an X clearly marked. "But that is..." He stops, and then looks at me. "That be Oak Island."

"Oak Island?"

"Aye. I've sailed past it many times. It can't be where he buried the treasure. People go there all the time." Visibly disappointed, he asks "Do you still want to set a course for there?"

"Aye," I tell him. Still looking quite gloomy, Gibbs goes off to tell the crew.

-

Less than a day later, the *Aquila* is sailing back to Boston, where it originally set off from. I am uncertain whether the treasure will be on Oak Island or not, but Gibbs doesn't seem to think so. This time, when we arrive at Oak Island, he comes with me.

"You're right," I tell Gibbs. "The island certainly doesn't look much special."

"Aye," Gibbs says. I look at the map again, for a closer look.

"Wait a minute... There are some strange markings here that I didn't see before around the X," I tell Gibbs excitedly.

"Is that so? Let me see, then." I show him the map, and indeed, there are a few strange circles around the X on the island. "It might be a puzzle or something," Gibbs says.

I climb into a tall tree nearby to get a better look at the landscape. Just when I am about to give up, I see a quarter of a circle made out of lines on the ground made with rocks! That's why we couldn't see them before, because you could only see them from the air! Excitedly, I hurry around the island climbing up the tallest trees until I can see the quarter of the circle in that direction. The lines seem to all converge in a circle on a large rock!

"Look, Gibbs, I think this might be where the treasure's buried," I say excitedly, as I show him the rock. He pulls out his knife and we begin to dig on and around the rock. We are digging as fast as we can when I suddenly hear a low growling behind us. I stand up just in time as a huge grey wolf jumps on me, knocking me to the ground. I struggle to hold the wolf's baying jaws away from my face when Gibbs yells, "Cap'n!" And stabs the wolf in the head with his knife. I kick the dead animal off me, and we turn to face three more growling wolves. Another wolf charges at me, but this time, I stab it in the neck with my concealed blade while Gibbs dispatches another with his flintlock. The third wolf has just enough sense to flee from the now unfavorable odds. It runs back to the forest, yelping.

46

We get back to digging around the rock when I accidentally crack it. Gibbs helps me to pull the shards of rock away from our hole, when I nearly fall in to the hole concealed underneath the rock. Gibbs leaps to grab my hand, but grinning, I tell him, "I think we may have found it." He smiles, and I let go of his hand. I fall into a pit about four feet from the hole, dimly lit by some strange glowing mineral. I make my way down a tunnel when I reach a ledge that probably once used to be a bridge, but decades of decay have eroded it into a gaping hole. I leap across, and barely miss it. I catch a sharp rock and cry out in pain, feeling my warm blood flow down my hand. Gritting my teeth, I pull myself up, and rest on the floor of the tunnel for a moment. I shakily stand up, and continue down the tunnel. The path gets spaced farther and farther apart until I find myself leaping from mineral growth to mineral growth. Finally, at the end of the tunnel there is a doorway that is clearly man made. As I go in, I must avert my eyes, because the entire room is made up of the glowing mineral I encountered earlier. At the heart of the room, between two opposite peaks of the mineral, a ring is somehow floating, suspended in midair. It has a strange feeling of power—I know that this must be the treasure that my ancestor went mad keeping. I pick it up, and only too late do I realize that it's a trap. Several flintlocks slide into place around me, and fire. This must be the end. But when I open my eyes, I am unharmed. The ring has created a mystical shield around me that deflected the bullets. This must be magic, but right now is not the time to question this object.

The cave has started to collapse, and I find myself sprinting back the way I came, jumping over the narrow cliffs and past falling rocks. I don't stop until I reach the hole where Gibbs is waiting. His smile is second only to mine. The broadest smile of all. I have found Captain Kidd's treasure.

The Battle of Quara
Siddharth Suri

Orser's farm was doing well. The soil was fertile and he had many plants to sell. One day, as he was picking this cabbages, he heard a call and looked up. As soon as he did, his heart fell. There was a man-in-arms riding through the village, yelling the call to war. The Bayan army was to be assembled at the plains of chess in one week to fight the Maztecs. He was part of the retinue of King Ingmar; he was the commander of the archers in the army, and the king's tactical adviser's apprentice. He finished picking the cabbages, with no heart left in the task, and slowly trudged home. He dropped the cabbages into his cart, and took all his other wares to the market to sell. Orser was able to sell everything in a few hours and went home to go to sleep.

The next day, he went to the supply closet and got out his bows and arrows. The arrow shafts were falling apart, and the fletching had completely fallen off. On two of his three longbows, the bowstrings were getting frayed and in need of repair. He spent most of the day making new bows and getting new bowstrings. He also got some spare bowstrings in case anything broke. Orser put his bows in the hardened leather cases and the arrows in his arrow satchel and left them by his horse. Most of the day had gone by, so he ate dinner and went to sleep.

When he woke up, he gathered his supplies and prepared to leave. He stayed a while making sure that nothing would be disturbed, and left around midday. The fields of Chess were about twelve miles northeast of his village, so he saddled up his horse, and prepared to leave. He rode north and arrived at the site where the army was camping. The fields of chess were named such because of the changes in the color of the soil made it look like a giant chessboard. He went to the command tent to be assigned a tent, and went and set up his tent. Orser went to the cookhouse and helped the cooks by getting water and food from the supply tents.

The next morning Orser went to the supply tent and got armor and a knife. He got his horse and his bow and went into the nearby forest to practice. He was a very slow shot, but he could hit the target almost every time. He kept practicing and his movements got quicker and more precise. In the following days, as the army assembled, Orser practiced. His long time farming had taken a toll on his accuracy and speed of his shots. He worked all day for the next three days, practicing and practicing. He also worked on his knife skills; he would throw the knife at the same target until he could hit the target consistently from five meters away.

The next day, the king and his retinue had arrived, so he worked with the tactical adviser Egnatius to devise a plan for the battle. They decided to set up base in the mouth of the Quara valley, with Carson forest on one side, and the steep mountains of the Carpathi range protecting the other side. The Carson forest had such dense undergrowth, that it is almost impassable. This way, the enemy would be forced to take what little shelter they had between the forest of Bighorn and the mountains. The forest of Bighorn had very little undergrowth and provided little cover. They also set all the troops that had arrived to erect defenses by digging trenches and putting up walls of logs in front of the camp.

As the rest of the army started arriving, Egnatius and Orser set the men to assemble the siege engines they had brought, but to leave one catapult disassembled. By the time the whole army had arrived, they had around 20 catapults and 30 ballistae, which were similar to giant crossbows. The catapult that had been disassembled had been sent through the forest with 200 men to attack the enemy from the rear. It also served the purpose of collapsing the path through which the enemies came and blocking their exit. The men prepared to fight the battle the next day.

The battle was to be fought in the Quara valley, the area where the two armies were camped. As night fell, Orser took his supplies and went to the command tent to be assigned a spot to fight at, and a unit to fight with. He was assigned to lead the archers, to direct their fire to wherever the support was most needed. He went to the barracks and met the men he would be fighting with the next day. The next day they sharpened their weapons and prepared to fight. They went to the middle of the field and sat down and relaxed. The rest of the army was assembled in the next hour, and the enemies were forming up to attack.

By dawn the next day, everyone was awake and ready to fight. Orser took his archers to the top of the wall and prepared for the advance. Suddenly a loud horn blast went over the field, and the catapult Orser and Egnatius had sent behind enemy lines destroyed the escape path of the enemy by collapsing large rocks across the path the Maztecs used to come into the valley. Then, as a two long whistle blasts went over the field, the catapults started moving forward, accompanied by the archers, swordsmen, and pikemen. As soon as the catapults were in range, the plan was to start firing and, force the enemy to advance. Then the archers, ballistae, and infantry would attack and destroy the enemy. What happened was slightly different. When the catapults were in range, two of them fired shots, but then return fire from other catapults in the Maztec camp cut short the plan, as those shots had wrecked two catapults.

A large battle raged, with catapults attacking each other, and the ballistae firing at men. Archers on both sides were cutting down men. The screams of the men were loud and frequent as they received injuries and wounds. There was a constant sound of metal hitting metal. Then, as Orser saw that nobody had the advantage, he called for the retreat and three whistle blasts brought the men back.

When everyone was safely behind the walls, a new plan was made. Now, since the enemy's escape path was blocked off, they would run out of supplies and would have to attack, and then the archers, catapults, and ballistae could stop anyone that came near. So they waited for the attack. And when none came after a few days, they became worried. Orser sent some scouts to see if there was another entrance where the enemy could get supplies. Three hours later, they came back and said there was a path through the mountains that they were getting supplies from. Suddenly, Orser had an idea, but the King was about to order an attack. He explained his plan to Egnatius and asked him to keep the king from attacking for four hours. Then he rode off into the forest to find the catapult and the men Orser and Egnatius had sent. When he found them, he explained the exact location of the enemy's catapults and asked them to fire on the catapults when the attack horn sounded.

Then he returned to the camp to get ready for the new attack. The Maztecs were forming up for battle when a horn blast sounded. A boulder came out of the forest behind the Maztec camp and landed on their biggest catapult. Coincidentally, the Maztec commanders were standing right next to the catapult, discussing tactics, and got crushed. At the same time, the Bayan army started moving forward. Their catapults fired boulders at the other army, and their ballistae wounded many men. Then as the archers got in range, the Maztecs soldiers had to raise their shields, and didn't see the advance of the Bayan cavalry and infantry. The Maztecs were cut down, and the hurriedly appointed new general came out waving a white flag. Orser was saddened to find that Egnatius had perished in the battle.

The Bayan soldiers held a ceremony for those who had fallen in battle. It was a simple ceremony, but all the men had lost comrades in the fight. They allowed the Maztecs to do the same, but were under guard throughout the time. In all, there were around 3,000 men that had perished.

The battle was over for most of the men, but not for Orser. He sent men to find the escaped soldiers that had fled into the woods so that they would not harm anyone. It took several months to track down all the soldiers, and even then, Orser thought that some had escaped. He also had to track down bandits and robbers that had taken advantage of the fact that the soldiers were gone. This task also took several months.

Orser worked with the king to devise a treaty that would keep the Maztecs from invading again. They finally decided on an agreement. They stripped the Maztec soldiers of their arms, and demanded a sum of twenty thousand silver reels and five thousand gold reels from the Maztec king in exchange for their eight thousand men. The Maztec king reluctantly agreed and the exchange was made.

Orser was appointed the chief tactical adviser at Castle Dore. He mainly wanted to go back to his farm, but the king and his advisers convinced him not to. He worked to keep the King safe, and repelled many invasions by the Baniards. He helped improve the lives of those who lived at the coast and were under constant threat by raiders. He taught the king's son to shoot a bow, and helped him learn how to command an army. He took on an apprentice and taught him everything Egnatius had taught him. Orser lived to a ripe old age, had four kids and thirteen grandchildren, and donated a lot of money to charity.

A Powerful Family
Annika Steele

The grass was growing. The clouds were trudging along the roof of the world. Leaves fluttered down to the ground from the branches of several nearby trees. So far, nothing very unusual was happening. This was very disappointing for Spencer, who, in desperate need of an inspiration for something to draw, had come out into the Meadow in search of fairies, talking trees, grumpy garden gnomes, or even an especially ugly toad. Spencer knew that her chances of finding any of these creatures (except maybe the toad) were extremely low, but she might as well try.

Sighing, Spencer lifted herself from the crevice in the burly roots of the oak tree that she frequently sought when she was in need of some "Vitamin D enhancement," as her mom called it. Cautiously stepping over the winding roots, Spencer put one hand on the trunk of the tree to steady herself and began to walk slowly around the looming oak. As the sharp shrills and calls of the birds in the meadow bounced around her head, Spencer mindlessly let her fingers trace the interweaving ridges and veins of the bark as she walked around the trunk.

She mentally weighed trying to draw the beautiful skin of tree. It reminded her of silk, how each individual thread intertwined in such complex patterns to create something wondrously endless. Lost in thought, Spencer forgot to look where she was going. All of a sudden, she was falling, tumbling downwards into a dark space. Her body was rigid with shock, like having the book you're reading yanked away from you when you've reached the middle of an exciting chapter, except much, much worse, because the ground had just been pulled away from her feet. The darkness wrapped itself tightly around her body as her limbs sprawled in all directions, reaching for something, grasping for any sort of stationary object that would stop her descent into darkness.

Thud! Her body came to an immediate halt as Spencer hit the cushioned ground. A yellow light seemed to permeate the uneven floor. Remaining in a crouched position, Spencer hesitantly looked around the "room" she was now in. It was more or less a perfect circle, with the walls expanding directly upward, like she had simply been dropped through a tube, or a vertical cylinder. The diameter of the room stretched approximately twelve feet, and the place was completely empty.

Before Spencer had a chance to panic, or respond the way any normal eight-year-old girl would, a small scrap of paper floated down into her lap. She looked up into the vast expanse above her, but she could only see what seemed to be an endless tunnel of darkness. Surprisingly enough, no fear came to her. Only a gleeful, anxious feeling filled her, similar to whenever she found the Christmas presents hidden throughout the house. Picking up the paper, Spencer read the words; "You have been chosen. If you would like to accept, please notify the messenger." Confused, Spencer wondered who the messenger was. She hadn't seen anyone as she fell down the crevice. Actually, Spencer hadn't really been able to see anything.

"How can I know if I accept what I've been chosen for if I don't know what it is that I've been picked to do?" she wondered out loud. Not expecting any kind of answer, Spencer figured her only choice was to comply with her new assignment. "Um, yeah, I accept...?" Spencer told the air.

Within moments, a business card floated down gently enough for Spencer to reach out and catch it. The card seemed to glint in the yellow light, and the silver lettering reflected the shine of the rocky walls around her. Etched into the card was the average information you would find on a business card; a name, address, company, and a small description. On the top line, "Mr. Director" was ominously written in place of name. The second line, the address, had simply one word: "Here."

"Well, wouldn't 'here' change?" Spencer wondered to herself. Pushing the thought aside, she realized that she had to settle for being confused, because there were far too many unanswered questions. The company sounded fake, but the letters were capitalized, so it *must* have been real. "The Department of Hidden Powers Assessment.," the next line read. That seemed somewhat self-explanatory, but included a brief description anyway: "Everyone has a super power. We have to decipher them."

Spencer was now even more befuddled than when she had picked up the card. All of a sudden, a soft whistling sound echoed through the cavern. As she was looking up, a tiny glass bottle came into view. As the jar floated down, Spencer began to make out a perfectly sized white parachute attached to the bottle. When the bottle reached Spencer, it gracefully landed at her feet, the parachute neatly collapsing around it. Bending down to pick it up, Spencer noticed that the mini vial smelled sweet, like red licorice and there was another piece of paper rolled up inside of it like a scroll.

Popping the cork, Spencer unfurled the fragment of delicate, opaque paper. Written in a smoky gray ink, sharp, handwritten letters stabbed into the page. The words were her mission: discover the powers of her family members. If she succeeded, she would be greatly rewarded. Also inside the vial was an isolated candy, draped in shriveled cellophane. As Spencer stripped off the discalced wrapper, letters engraved on the hard candy revealed themselves. "Do you like butterscotch?" it taunted.

A ravenous need to taste the familiar, swirled texture of a butterscotch candy suddenly overtook her. Unfurling her tongue, Spencer began to bring the candy slowly to her lips. Just as she began to taste the tangible emptiness that accompanied this kind of sweet treat, the floor descended, slanting downward into an unavoidable slide. With no other choice except to let herself scuttle across the smooth ground, the thrill of skidding downward began. Down, down, down she slid, with the feeling of being a leaf caught in a water-filled curb. Up ahead of her was pocket of light, closing in quickly. Before she knew it, Spencer was thrust back into her meadow, in virtually the same place she had been in when she had first been looking for something to draw.

Spencer frantically searched around for the opening in the tree. After what felt like hours of circling the tree, desperately inspecting every possible leaf or rock that could have the secret switch or lever that triggered the opening, Spencer gathered her art supplies and granola bar wrapper. As she trudged through the tall grass, the confused girl couldn't help feeling like she was being watched. The only plausible answer for how the whole falling-down-an-invisible-trench thing could have happened was that she had tripped, hit her head, and imagined the whole thing.

Slamming the back door behind her, Spencer kicked off her mud-caked sneakers and plopped down her art stuff on the table. The thing that Spencer loved most about her house was that there was always something baking. In fact, the further she progressed into the cozy two-story house, the hungrier she became. A scrumptious, delectable scent wafted into her nostrils, engulfing Spencer's senses.

As soon as she poked her head through the doorway to the kitchen, she was greeted by a familiar sight. It was her beautiful mother, trying to simultaneously stir a gurgling pot of tomato soup and talk on the phone to what sounded like a very angry insurance agent. Ever since Spencer's father had died in a car accident, it seemed like her mom was always doing twenty things at once.

"Augggh! I'm hit!" a voice bellowed. The voice belonged to none other than Patrick, Spencer's younger brother who was parading around in a pirate hat, eye patch, and was now holding a plastic sword to his chest, howling in mock agony. Spencer snickered, thinking how only this morning, Patrick had donned a full cowboy costume and was sliding around the house in socks, pretending to shoot invisible Indians.

Looking up from her concoction, Spencer's mom noticed Spencer. She reached into the cupboard for a bowl and a spoon, shoving them in her daughter's direction, all the while trying to negotiate with a very rude sounding man on the phone. As Spencer tried to quietly slurp her soup, she looked around the commodious kitchen and suddenly noticed that all of the living room furniture had been rearranged. It was as if an ogre had come in and just scooped up all the chairs and coffee tables, and then replaced the dense furniture like it was dollhouse furniture.

Click! Spencer whipped around as soon as she heard the sound of her mom's phone click off. "Mom, what happened to all the stuff in the living room?" Spencer questioned.

"Oh, I just decided we needed a little bit of change, so I moved some stuff around after I got back from the store," her mom answered.

"But you moved it around all by yourself?" Spencer gawked.

Hesitating, Spencer's mom slowly explained, "Well, I do most things by myself now..." Then, cutting herself off, she added, "Why don't you bring up a bowl of soup to your sister? She's been in her room since breakfast."

Sighing, she scooped up another bowl of soup and trudged down the hallway towards the winding staircase. Meandering down the hallway towards her sister Cassidy's room, she noticed Patrick's open door. Inside, her brother seemed to have transformed into a completely different character. His getup now consisted of a bright green cape and a screaming yellow mask. He was prancing around his room, pretending he could fly. Spencer paused, pondering how it was possible for Patrick to have just been a pirate, and now all of a sudden, he was leaping from desk to bed in an entirely new costume.

She continued down the hall, and eventually reached Cassidy's door. However, before she could even reach out to knock, a soft voice sang out. "Come in, Spence." Leaning on the doorknob, Spencer realized just how important the handles on doors were. A doorknob was the passage into whole other sections of the world. It was a bridge into different people's lives, a necessary step to creating something new. In this case, turning a doorknob was final step, the only thing keeping her from creating new experiences. Maybe one day she would turn a doorknob and it would lead her somewhere she had never been before, to a deeper chapter in her life-instead of just her sister's bedroom.

"Well what are you waiting for?" Cassidy hollered. "It's just a doorknob. It's not going to bite you." Spencer snapped to attention, thrown off by how her sister had known she was thinking about the significance of doorknobs. Barging through the doorway, she saw Cassidy sprawled on the bed, searching her laptop. Spencer put the lukewarm soup into Cassidy's outstretched hand. "How was your drawing session?" Cassidy injected, still not looking up from her computer screen.

"Uh... good," Spencer blubbered. It seemed like Cassidy always knew what Spencer was up to, even though they rarely discussed these kinds of things with each other. "So..." Spencer hummed, awkwardly trying to creep into Cassidy's spinning office chair. "Have you ever had something really weird happen to you that you couldn't explain?" she spewed. There was a pause.

"You mean like you've gone somewhere or done something that seems so impossibly unreal that the only explanation is that it must have been a dream or some sort of crazy hallucination?" Cassidy demanded, eyes ablaze. Spencer was flabbergasted. Her older sister had just described what had happened to her down to the very last grain of salt.

"B-b-wh-uh... yeah. Exactly. Yes," she sputtered, still reeling from the shock of Cassidy's perfect explanation.

"No, not really," Cassidy yawned nonchalantly, going back to her laptop screen. Spencer slowly stood up, leaving with a lame excuse about having to clean out the cat's litter box. (Which she never did.)

The world seemed to be spinning as Spencer threaded back down the hall, trying to balance her mind. The realization came crashing in on her; Cassidy, Spencer's sister, had a superpower. She could read minds. Well, maybe. No, she could read minds. Kind of. Ever since they were little kids, Cassidy always seemed to know what was troubling Spencer. She always knew what was on her mind, and even when Spencer provided the most minimal amount of detail possible, Cassidy still gave the best advice. So, in a way, Cassidy could read minds. Maybe she had the real power. It was all so much—SHPLURK!

A tiny Nerf dart hit Spencer in the small of her back. Following the bullet was a wild cackling. Whipping around, Spencer's eyes fell upon a tiny, four foot policeman: Patrick, completely decked out in a midnight blue cop outfit, pointing a Nerf gun directly at Spencer. Fortunately, the tiny bullet he had shot had been enough to push Spencer into the perfect mindset. A huge grin seeped across her face, like an egg being cracked into a bowl of batter.

Not only was Cassidy a mind reader, but Patrick was a shape-shifter. With superhuman speed. Spencer grabbed Patrick's little shoulders and planted a firm kiss right on his nose. "Aha! Yes! Thank you!" Spencer yelped. Meanwhile, Patrick was starting to turn green and was making barfing sounds as if he had just witnessed a grotesque killing instead of having just been kissed. "Sorry little bro," Spencer chuckled. "I got a wee bit carried away there."

"No kisses! Ever!" Patrick thundered, sprinting back into his room. Spencer giggled to herself, skipping down the stairs. As she got the bottom, she was immediately bombarded by the sight of what must what have been twenty cardboard boxes piled up on top of each other around the doorway.

"Oh, Spence, sweetie, please be careful! Those are the delivery packages," hollered Spencer's mom.

"Delivery packages?" Spencer echoed.

"Yes, I decided to volunteer to take on organizing the scout packages, she explained. "I just carried them up here from the Kennings house, so sorry that they're a little scattered," she justified. Spencer couldn't step around the boxes, so she tried to push some out of the way. However, when she attempted to lift one of the packages, she was shocked to find that it must have weighed at least forty pounds. How had her mom carried all these packages down the street by herself?

Trying to instead climb around the boxes, she could hear her mom consoling Spencer's Aunt June on her job loss. Although her aunt had lost her job over a job over a year ago, and Spencer's dad had died just a few months ago, Spencer's mom continued to be the strong one, comforting her sister.

When Spencer was slapped in the face by the savory aroma of a heavy, cheesy, meaty lasagna that was being toasted to a perfect crisp, the last mental puzzle piece fell into place. The lasagna, you see, was a meal that Spencer's mom was providing for the homeless shelter. It had dawned on Spencer what her mother was capable of: super strength. Even though she could have broken down after her husband died, it only fueled her need to help others. She was like the sturdy screw that never rusted or bent. She was the super glue that held everything together. Although she could be grieving over the death, showing her weakness and vulnerability, she remained strong for her family and community, continuing to be someone who could be relied on.

It was amazing how perfectly her family fit together; mind reader, shape shifter, super strength. It was incredible how all these crazy powers and capabilities had gone unnoticed for so long. Spencer thought back to the business card that said everyone had a power. Maybe that was true. Maybe some were just harder to depict than others. Categorizing someone's strengths may not always be easy or possible, Spencer realized. Maybe they would always remain a mystery.

My Broken Little Family
Katherine Renner

Between the lines of fear and blame
And you begin to wonder why you came
Where did I go wrong, I lost a friend
Somewhere along in the bitterness
And I would have stayed up with you all night
Had I known how to save a life
-The Fray, "How to Save a Life"

"Bye, thanks for the ride. See you tomorrow, Alison!" I grinned and slammed the car door shut, still bouncing from leftover energy after a fantastic volleyball practice. My friend Alison's SUV pulled down my driveway, up the street, and out of sight. I made my way to the garage door happily. The sun was setting behind my friend Piper's house across the street, bathing everything in golden light. The new green leaves rustled in the cool May breeze. The first of the crickets were beginning to sing their song, chirping "summer's coming, summer's coming." The evening was beautiful. Of course it was—they always were where I lived. My neighborhood was the typical American suburb. Each family was the same: a mom, a dad, two point five kids, and maybe a dog. There were rules about how short your grass had to be, and whether or not you could have clothes lines or chickens or an RV in your driveway. Soccer games and summer camps and piano lessons. Public school, playgrounds, Fourth of July barbecues. PTAs, SUVs, bottomless ATMs. Typical, happy American families enjoying their perfect little lives. On the outside, anyway.

-

I was starving. The rich smell of homemade spaghetti wafting from the kitchen was driving my taste buds wild. I walked in and drop my bag. I opened my mouth to greet my mom and freeze. The entire kitchen freezes, and in my mind this was a snapshot, like one of my photos that I took with my new camera. What would I caption this, I wondered vaguely. In under a second, I went from ecstatic and energetic to terrified and frozen. The emotions bouncing around the room were so strong I could taste them, hear the unspoken words in the silence, feel the tension in the air vibrating, giving me a headache. The feelings surrounded me, put me in a bubble outside the conflict in the middle of the kitchen, like I was a spectator in this battle. And

58

while it may appear that I was, I was not. I was not a spectator, I was not a referee, I was a contestant, the one dragged into the battle and trying desperately to end it and abandon it at the same time. A resounding sound of panic ringed in my ears, and it was, "Oh no, oh no, oh no, they're fighting again." This freeze frame was of my mom and my older sister Anna. My mom was at the stove, stirring the tomato sauce, her mouth open as she yelled. My sister stood by the table, arms folded, and glaring daggers. Hair hung lank around her face. Pants barely held up on her tiny hips by a belt looped several times around. The sweatshirt she'd been wearing for three days. Oatmeal stains and fly away wisps, hate rays aimed toward my mother. As if in slow motion, my mom's head turned and she noticed me for the first time. Time began to move at a normal speed, and Anna stormed away, pounded up the stairs, and slammed her bedroom door so hard the walls rattled.

My mom forced a smile. "Hi, sweetie. How was practice?" She set dinner on the table and left the room without waiting for an answer. I walked with shaky legs and racing thoughts to the table and sat. Staring at the spaghetti that was so appetizing a few minutes ago, I realized I was no longer hungry. My stomach was always tied in knots when I was upset. As I forced some dinner down, the image of my mom and Anna fighting faded. But another, worse picture quickly took its place. It was of the counter behind me, and the bottles that sit upon it. Pills of every size and powders of every kind. In bottles and jars, containers squat and white or short and transparent orange. And a caption arrived in my head, unbidden, unwelcome: *They are making her crazier.* And try as I might, I could not make it go away.

-

I didn't find out the truth about Anna until last July. I was 11. Mom and I were in the garden pulling weeds. I remember the exact conversation. "Can we take a break?" I asked. "It's really hot."

"Sure."

I wanted to ask Mom something but I wasn't sure how. My stomach had gone cold. I worked up the courage and... "Mom? Why is Anna so moody all the time? Like, why is she always angry? Is it just because she's 15 and is a teenager so it's just like normal teenage behavior? But then why does she see Dr. Samuels? He's a therapist, right? Is that normal?"

My mom looked at me like she was flabbergasted I was even asking. "Lydia...," she said slowly, "Anna has an anxiety disorder." I cocked my head uncomprehendingly. My mom sighed, and clarified, "Lydia, your sister is mentally ill."

Mentally ill.
Mentally ill.
My sister is mentally ill.

-

The day after volleyball, after spaghetti, after the fight, Anna stayed home from school—just as she had for the past week. The first day she stayed home, I had asked if she was sick. My mom had shaken her head. According to Mom, Anna wasn't sick. She was just "having a hard time." Mom never elaborated more than that.

-

I had learned by the time I was seven that eavesdropping was my best source of information. No one ever told me anything. So much was left unexplained. I would listen from the top of the stairs in my footy pajamas, trying to get some answers about my sister. I mean, they waited eleven years to tell me about Anna's anxiety disorder. And even then, they didn't explain what an anxiety disorder was. Google and silent footsteps leading me to hushed conversations became my new best friends. It still wasn't enough. It was like they thought I was blind and deaf. Like I didn't notice that she and my mom were always fighting when I was younger. Like once I found out about her disorder, I would just be satisfied with no more explanation.

Anna's illness clarified some things. The mood swings. The pitching of fits. The countless therapy trips. The medication. But mostly it just brought up more questions, more things I had to figure out on my own. I was not naïve. I could tell she was getting worse. Every week, new meds, different meds. They messed with her brain, her emotions, her eating habits. My mom removed all the razors from our shower. I knew Anna was cutting; it shocked me when I first figured it out. But it was obvious she was severely depressed. And whenever I hugged her (not often—she spent almost all of her time holed up in her room, and when she was out she was often throwing fits) she was skin and bones. She was starving herself. I quickly became stubbly from the lack of shaving tools, and far too conscious of my own eating habits. She was affecting me—I could feel myself picking up most of her bad habits. I knew about the cutting and the eating disorder. I just didn't know why.

-

For several days after that volleyball practice, I hid in my room while I was at home. Anna was on a rampage. Depressed and furious. She was giving up.

"Anna, go brush your hair," my mom had ordered her one morning while I ate breakfast. I tensed up and stopped breathing, sensing a fight. Staring at the newspaper headline intently, I tried to listen carefully and block it out at the same time. I wasn't sure if I wanted to hear this or not. I couldn't turn around. Anna sat there apathetically. "Anna, go brush your hair," my mom repeated.

"Why? Why does it matter?" My sister put as much scathingness into her tone as possible. But she just sounded weak.

My mom was exasperated. "Because it matters, Anna. *You matter.*"

My sister stood up and stomped into the bathroom, slamming drawers and kicking things. She returned with a hair brush, yanked it through her tangled, greasy hair for a few seconds, and then threw it clattering to the floor. Then she tried to storm upstairs. But on her way, she bumped into the table, knocking over her coffee mug. "F---!" she screamed, running upstairs. The coffee gushed to the floor, and across the table, seeping into my math homework. I could hear Anna upstairs throwing stuff and kicking her wall. My mom sighed and left the room. I got up, put my cereal bowl in the sink, and grabbed an entire roll of paper towels to mop up the mess. My sister had been reduced to depression and anorexia and treating everyone around her like they were dirt beneath her shoes, all from her own brain and the very drugs that were supposed to be helping her. Instead they were destroying her. And she was destroying my family. My mom obviously couldn't deal anymore. And my dad was always gone, trying to work to earn enough money to pay for all of Anna's therapy and medicine. As I soaked up the coffee and tried to figure out what I would tell my math teacher, I realized my family was falling apart, no matter how hard I tried to prevent it. And I was tired of trying so hard to hold it all together.

-

That night, my mom cornered me after dinner. "I want you to move your stuff from your and Anna's bathroom into ours," she commanded. This had happened before. Whenever Anna "got bad," I would have to take all my things out of the bathroom we shared so that we weren't in such close quarters. It was so annoying, like being handed an eviction notice because Anna was more important.

"Mooooooom," I complained. "It's not fair! Why do *I* always have to be the one to leave the bathroom? Why isn't Anna the one who ever gets kicked out?" Although I knew the answer at heart, this was about more than just a bathroom, I thought angrily. My parents always gave Anna special treatment. Grades, behavior, mouthing off, stepping out of line. Just because Anna had "issues," it was fine for her to go around slamming doors, throwing things, being a total b----, blowing off school. But if *I* did those things, my parents got way pissed. It was so tiring trying to be perfect all the time, trying to be the good kid. I continued my griping. "I hate using your bathroom! I have to rework my whole morning schedule and—"

One look from my mom silenced me. This was obviously not to be negotiated. Once again, I was being handed an eviction notice. In truth, I'd had one from the life I was supposed to have, the normal one, ever since I was born. Anna was that eviction notice. And so far: eviction notice served.

-

I tumbled off the school bus with my friends the next afternoon, laughing. I didn't even hear Mrs. Carson, Alison's mom, calling my name until she was five feet away. "Lydia, you're coming home with us."

"No," I assured her. "My mom's picking me up. She's right... right..." I looked around for her blue Subaru. "Well, she was *supposed* to be here." I shrugged.

Mrs. Carson told me, "She texted me earlier."

"Okaaaay..." I replied, slightly confused. Suddenly, something— intuition, women's wisdom, a sixth sense, whatever—made me realize what was going on. A sense of panic gripped me like an iron hand. No, no, no, no, no, no, no. This was not happening. I shoved the idea to the back of my mind and followed Alison and her mom to the car.

-

At Alison's house, everything is always so normal. Her mom fixed us and Alison's two little brothers a snack. We fumbled through our science homework and then watched TV on Hulu. All the while my mind was a tornado, each thought worse than the last. I tried to banish the horrible ideas and concentrate on the TV show. I kept waiting for the phone to ring. Mrs. Carson had assured me that my mom would call sometime this evening with an explanation. The minutes crawled by, and the call didn't come. I began to fear it never would. 4:00. 4:30. 5:30. 7:00. But finally, *finally*, the phone rang.

I bounded downstairs and listened while Mrs. Carson spoke with my mom. "Yeah, she's right here," she continued, handing the phone to me.

There was so much I wanted to say, but I choked. My throat closed. "Honey, are you there?" my mom asked. She sounded tired, concerned, and fed up.

"Yeah," I managed. Mrs. Carson was clattering around in the kitchen making stir fry, so I climbed the stairs with shaky legs.

"Lydia, you might want to sit down," my mom suggested.

"'Kay," I replied, still standing, her words not penetrating my brain.

"I'm at the hospital with Anna," my mother said cautiously. "Lydia, your sister was threatening to commit suicide."

No.

Numb.

Sinking. Down the wall, into a crumpled position.

Sinking. Ignoring Alison's worried stare.

Sinking. Into the darkness. Into an oblivion, a pit of denial and despair.

And then a thought that it took me almost a year to forgive myself for: *Maybe it would have been better for everyone if she had.*

-

You know those hospital shows where the patient is in a coma, and there's the heart monitoring machine? And the heart is having a hard time, but it's still holding on? There are regular beeps, as the heart faintly creeps along. And then suddenly the monitor flat-lines, with that long, loud beep signaling the end. That was what this was like. Just beeps. Echoing through my head. Like my mind was flat-lining. Like I couldn't think, blank, frozen. Like my heart had just... ceased to beat.

-

I cried myself to sleep that night. My dad had picked me up from Alison's after work. My mom was staying overnight at the hospital with Anna. Dinner was awful. My dad tried to make normal conversation. No, I thought. Nothing would ever be normal again.

-

The next day was awful. A Friday. I couldn't face going to school, but I would go crazy staying home. I went. I held it together. I am an excellent actress. I don't think anyone could tell that I was dying inside. I avoided Alison. She had been nice enough the day before, concerned but not prying. She didn't know. I could never tell her. She would never understand.

-

I held it together in front of my friends, but several times during the next week, I hid in a bathroom stall and sobbed. And sobbed. And sobbed. I cried for me and Anna and my mom and dad and my friends who would never understand and the normal life I wanted and the normal life I would never have. I sank to the floor in floods of tears and wished for the end. And the worst part was, when I was done, I had to pull myself together and go out there and pretend everything was okay. I had to face a world that didn't care about my sister and me, a world that only cared that I wasn't doing my homework, that I had mouthed off to my PE teacher, that I wasn't acting normal. But the world didn't care why. It just wanted me to get my life together and do what I was supposed to do. My teachers didn't bother to cut me even a tiny piece of slack, even though I knew my mom had told them. No one could spare some sympathy for the girl whose life was falling apart.

-

In the beginning, before Anna or me, there were going to be three. My mom had always wanted three. But my parents had trouble getting pregnant, and my mom was old enough by the time I was born that having another child could be risky. When I was younger, I wished that there had been a third. I wanted a sister. A real one. One who was... whole. I would be a good big sister. Better than Anna. But now that I was older, I had realized it was a good thing my parents didn't have another. I wouldn't want anyone else to go through this. I didn't think I would be able to protect my sister from Anna. I certainly wouldn't trust my parents to do it. They had never had time to protect me from Anna. They were too busy protecting Anna from herself.

-

A week later, the night before Anna was going to come home from the hospital, I cornered my parents in the living room. I hadn't been this nervous in who-knows-how-long. I'd been mulling this over in my head for days, thinking, thinking, and thinking: *What if I'm not the only one? What if one of my friends is in a situation like this too? I can't be the only one.* I was sick of having to hide everything from my best friends, who were practically my sisters. So I got up the courage to ask. "Mom, Dad… do you think I could ever tell my friends about… about Anna? Because I want to, and maybe they'd understand. Maybe one of them has gone through something like this and…"

I trailed off. My parents were shaking their heads. "No. Definitely not."

"But—"

My mom tried to silence me. "Lydia, this is not negotiable."

I protested, "You're not even listening or giving me a chance!"

"You can't expose this family," my parents told me.

"This is totally unfair! Why are you acting like Anna is something to be *ashamed* of?!" I ran upstairs to my room and slammed the door. But I did not cry. I was done crying. Instead I sat, and I thought. I knew I was not the only one. There were others going through this, too. I was tired of feeling so isolated. Tired of hiding from a world that scorned mental illness, one that hushed it up and put it in a box and called it anger management or issues or personal problems. Tired of living in a world where we hide our problems from our neighbors and friends so we could keep up this image of a perfect happy little family, when in reality, every family has chapters they would rather keep unpublished. But I was going to publish mine. Because the ignorant, judgmental, so-called perfect world needed to know what it was like from the inside. And maybe then they would understand, would consider, would think. Maybe the people at school would stop and think for a minute before putting me in the box of drama queen when I was in the bathroom crying; maybe they would accept the fact that just because I lived in a perfect neighborhood didn't mean I had a perfect life; maybe they would realize that I go deeper than that, that I am not the shallow girl they make me out to be, not the pure, unscarred one. Where I lived or who I was friends with did not mean smack about my life outside of school. I wanted people to realize that. I had battle scars, and wounds that weren't going to heal. And I would make my voice heard. Not everyone will understand. My parents do not know how powerful my words would be. They will try to shut me up. But I will not let them. Not while I have a story to tell. Just because no one ever wants to talk about mental illness doesn't mean we shouldn't.

Absence Makes the Heart Grow Fonder
Alyssa Long

Beep-beep-beep. My alarm clock goes off, signaling the start of another cookie-cutter day. It's always the same old: get up, go to school, come home, hang out with friends, and go to bed. I feel like I'm in a funk; a ginormous funk and I can't get out. My life may seem perfect on the outside, but trust me, being perfect isn't exactly a walk in the park.

I finally manage to pull myself out of bed and get ready. It's 6:45! I'm going to be late for school. Again. Sure enough, seconds later, Mable, my maid, comes to my door.

"Get up! You're going to be late for school," she says in her sweet-as-honey voice.

"I know," I groan. "I'll be down in five, get my breakfast ready."

I start to get ready, throwing on my Gucci jeans and a Prada shirt. Taking a quick look in the mirror, I see my honey-blonde curls fall perfectly across my shoulders. I swipe on baby blue eye shadow, making my hazel eyes pop as I apply my sweet cherry lip gloss. I do one final check, making sure that I look flawless, then slip on my Coach shoes and grab my purse. I smell my delicious breakfast of chocolate chip pancakes and scrambled eggs, Mable's classic breakfast, and head downstairs.

"Mmm…" I drawl, "That smells so good!"

"Yup! Chocolate chip pancakes, hot off the griddle, your favorite!" Mable shouts.

"Thanks Mable, you're the best!" I exclaim.

"No problem sweetie," Mable responds. "Now eat up!"

I scarf down my breakfast, letting the chocolate chips melt on my tongue. This meal is so delicious, but then - *ding dong.* That must be my best friend, Alice Cooper, here to pick me up.

"I'm coming," I shout as I run upstairs to grab my backpack.

I run out of the front door and barrel into Alice, who is standing right in front of my house.

"Owww!" she whines. "I spent one hour on my face this morning!"

"Nice," I tease. "No big surprise there."

We head off to her Ferrari convertible, ready for a fun drive to school. We pull out of my driveway onto Riley Road, sliding the top down. We cruise along the road and watch other cars pass by, their faces changing into shocked expressions when they see us.

As we pull up to the intersection, another car pulls next to us.

"Hey girl," one of the boys in the other car says.

"I would know that voice anywhere," I squeal. "Jake!!!"

"None other than, babe," Jake responds in his sexy voice. "Race ya to school!"

"Oh, it's on!" Alice says, just as the light turns green.

We shoot out of the intersection, tires squealing as we go. I look behind us and see the black marks left by our tires. We screech around a corner and I almost fly out the side, feeling lucky that I have a seatbelt on.

"Geez, Alice!" I complain. "I know we're racing, but can we NOT get killed?"

"Sorry..." She defends. "We're almost at school anyway."

"Good," I reply. "Let's go get us a parking spot."

"Yeah buddy," she drawls. "That's my bestie."

We slap hands and air-kiss, our secret handshake, and then pull into the parking lot.

"Shades on," Alice says as we put on our matching reflective aviators we bought this summer.

As soon as we park the car, we are surrounded by the wannabes. We open the car door and instantly the crowd parts, making way for the two most popular girls in school.

"There are perks to being popular," I whisper to Alice.

"Definitely," she replies. "Now off to 'Death Academy.'"

We roll our eyes and head up the gray cement stairs outside the school, passing by the statue of Frederick B. Evan, the founder of this "institution." Today, the statue is covered with graffiti and eggs, probably because of those immature 9th grade boys, but nobody seems to care. This school used to be one of the best private schools in the nation, but when the founder died, the school really went downhill. We walk through the blue double doors, to the giant locker we share, and put away our bags. Then, we head to our first class, English. Alice and I have the same schedule, thanks to my mom, who works as the counselor here. It's one of the advantages of having your mom at school. Well, probably the only perk.

Alice and I walk into English class just as the bell rings.

"Ok class, take a seat," sniffled Mr. Fredrickson, the most annoying teacher in school. "We have a lot to discuss today."

Alice looks over at me and we share an eye roll. The only reason we're in Mr. Fredrickson's class is because he gives out easy A's. You just have to pretend to be listening to his boring lectures. *Bzzzz.* I feel my phone vibrating in my bag. I sneakily lean over and take it out. It's a text from Alice.

Want to ditch next class? The message reads.

Yep, I reply, and look over at the clock. Only five minutes of class left. Four minutes. Three minutes. Two minutes. One minute.

"Ms. Peterson!" shouts Mr. Fredrickson. "What did I just say?"

I look over at Alice for help, but all she does is shrug her shoulders. She mustn't have been paying attention either.

"Ummm…" I respond. If only I could stall for a couple more seconds.

I stare at Alice, mouthing the words *help me,* and she seems to understand. Instantly, she falls sideways out of her seat, making a loud clatter. Mr. Fredrickson rushes over to see if she is okay. Five four, three, two, one *BRINGGG,* the bell rings, signaling the end of the period. I breathe out a side of relief and pick up my things, heading to the parking lot. I quickly find Alice's car and slide in, careful not to be seen by a teacher. Technically, we're not allowed off campus, but nobody pays attention to that rule anyway. We've only been caught once, but since my mom works at the school, they let us off easy with a warning. I'm scared to find out what would happen if we actually got caught. Then, Alice slides into the car, tearing me from my thoughts.

"Nice save, but how'd you escape Mr. Fredrickson?" I ask.

"Oh, I just told him I was fine and ran out of the classroom before he could say anything else," she giggled.

"Shades on," Alice commands, then pulls on her shades. "Now, where to?"

"Mall?" I suggest. "I'm in the mood for some fro-yo."

"Yum!" she squeals. "Let's go!"

We pull out of the parking lot and head to the mall, our stomachs grumbling the whole way there.

As we pull into the parking lot at the mall, Alice has a realization.

"Dang it!" she screams. "I left my purse at school. We'll have to go back and get it."

"No!" I complain. "I want fro-yo *now!*"

"Fine." Alice responds. "You go to the fro-yo place and I'll drive back to get my purse. I'll meet you at the store in like ten minutes."

"Good," I say as I step out of the car. "I'll see you then. Bye!"

I start to walk down the sidewalk to the mall, passing by the fake potted plants and smokers sitting on benches, being careful not to touch anything or anyone. Then, a car pulls up next to me and rolls down their window. Inside is a boy that looks around my age, with blonde hair and blue eyes.

"Hey," he says, flashing me a wide grin. "Do you need a ride?"

"Um..." I stammer. "Do I know you?"

"You probably don't remember me, being the most popular girl in school and all," he replies. "I'm in your science class. My name is Kennedy."

Hmmm, I think to myself. I usually remember people who are this attractive, but maybe I hadn't looked around my class enough. Mr. Ross is pretty boring, so I usually zone out for his classes.

"Well nice to meet you, Kennedy. I'll have to look for you in class sometime," I state with confidence. "And yes, I would like a ride."

"Cool!" he says. "Hop in!."

I walk around the car and go inside, surprised at how clean it is. I'm sure Alice will forgive me for ditching frozen yogurt when I tell her how cute this guy is. Kennedy pulls away from the curb and we start driving.

"So...." I mumble, trying to get rid of the awkwardness. "Nice car you have."

"I know," he replies with a smirk. "Lots of other people think so, too."

"Wait," I question. "Where are we going anyway?"

"I'm not quite sure myself," he responds. "Let's just see where the road takes us."

"Okay..." I mutter. "But just know that I don't like sushi."

"Really?" He jokes. "I don't think this will work out if you don't like sushi."

"Oh, funny." I retort. "I'm really hungry, though; can we get something to eat?"

"Sure!" He replies. "Are you up for some fro-yo?"

"For sure," I say. "I was actually just about to go get some when you picked me up."

We turn around and drive back to the mall, gabbing about everything we could possibly talk about. Surprisingly, it's really easy to talk to Kennedy, unlike some of my other friends. He's really easy-going and actually listens to you, instead of just pretending to listen. When we pull into the mall parking lot, I realized I wasn't even that hungry. I would rather just stay and talk to Kennedy for the rest of the day.

"What do you want?" Kennedy asks. "I'll pay."

"Um..." I reply. "How about a large double chocolate with gummy bears, jelly beans, and whipped cream."

"Wow..." Kennedy wonders. "That's the exact same thing I was going to get. Mind if we share?"

"Course not," I respond. "Just don't forget to get two spoons."

Kennedy goes to order the frozen yogurt and I start grinning like a maniac. I can't believe he asked me to share with him. That is so cute! Alice will never believe me when I say what happened today.

"I'm back," Kennedy shouts. "Did you miss me?"

"Nope," I joke. "Not at all."

Just then, Kennedy's phone rings.

"Sorry, it's my mom," he apologizes. "I'll be right back."

He walks away to answer his phone, and I can only hear snippets of the conversation. It sounds like he is fighting with his mom over something, but I'm not sure what. After about five minutes on the phone, Kennedy comes back.

"Sorry about that," he says. "Are you ready to go now?"

"Sure..." I reply curiously. Why would Kennedy want to go so soon?

"I have something to tell you," Kennedy squeaks out. "It's kind of important."

"What?" I exclaim. "I knew something seemed weird with you."

"Yeahh..." he mumbles. "Today was actually my last day at this school. I'm moving to Minnesota tomorrow."

"What?!" I shout. "Why didn't you tell me this before?"

"I guess I just really wanted to go on a date with you and I didn't want the fact that I was moving away to come between us," he gushes. "I hope you'll forgive me."

"Of course I'll forgive you," I cry. "But I'm just sad that this is the last time I'm going to see you. You're the first guy I've ever truly liked."

"Really?" he asks. "If I ever come back, you'll be the first one I call."

"Thanks," I sigh.

"Let's go," he states. "Tell me what house is yours and I'll drop you off."

"Ok," I reply. "Even though I've only known you for a short amount of time, it feels like I've known you forever."

"I know," he whispers. "I know."

—

Two months later

"Are you sure you're okay?" Alice asks, as she closes our locker. "It's been a month and you still haven't gotten over Kennedy."

"As I've said a thousand times, I'm F-I-N-E," I say. "Kennedy is actually really nice, and cute, and he has pretty eyes, and beautif—"

"AUDREY!" Alice shouts, "He moved away two months ago. You have to get over him and move on. When are you going to understand that?"

"But it's true, Alice," I argue, "I think I'm in love."

"Are you kidding me?" Alice questions. "He's probably forgotten about you already."

"Whatever…" I grumble. "I'm leaving. Come talk to me when you learn how to be a supportive friend."

As I walk away from Alice, I can hear her calling my name from behind me. I don't answer. After our last conversation, I just don't feel like talking to her. Ever since I met Kennedy, I haven't been the same. I haven't dated anybody for two months, that's a new record for me, and I've been spending a lot more time by myself. I hop into my car not yet knowing where I'm going and pull out of the parking lot. Out of instinct, I start to drive to the frozen yogurt place where Kennedy and I had our first and only date. Since Kennedy left, I've been there every day, and every day I get the same thing I got with Kennedy. A large double chocolate with gummy bears, jelly beans and whipped cream.

I walk into the frozen yogurt place and get in line to order. In front of me is a girl I recognize from my science class.

"Hey!" I say, "It's Audrey!"

"Oh, hi," she responds, turning around. "What's up?"

"Not much," I answer, remembering that her name is Susie. "Just getting my frozen yogurt. You?"

"Haha," she laughs. "Same here. Do you want to sit with me once we get our yogurt?"

"Sure," I reply. "How about we sit over there?"

"Sounds good," she agrees. "I'll wait for you."

I order my frozen yogurt and wait for it to come out, thinking about my plans for this weekend. I have mountains of homework to do and a test that I should study for. I also made plans to go shopping with Alice, just to keep her quiet. Just then, I feel a tap on my shoulder. I turn around and see a boy that looks around my age, with blonde hair and blue eyes.

"KENNEDY!!!" I scream. "OH-MI-GOSH I MISSED YOU SO MUCH."

"I missed you too," he laughs. "But before you get too excited, I just want to let you know that I'm only here until tomorrow. Then we're going back to Minnesota."

"What?" I squeak, my face falling. "I don't want you to go back."

"I don't want to leave you again, either," he whispers.

"You don't have to," I suggest. "You could move in with me. I'm sure I could convince my parents."

"I wish I could," he replies. "But I have to finish out high school in Minnesota. You understand, right?"

"Of course I understand," I cry, "But I just don't want it to be that way."

"I know," he sniffs. "I've got to go now; I'll call you to figure out when we can meet up tonight."

Kennedy gives me a big hug and kiss, and then he leaves the building. I look down at my frozen yogurt, which is all melted by now. I hear Susie calling my name from across the store.

"Audrey!" she shouts. "Over here!"

"Coming!" I reply, wiping the tears out of my eyes.

I walk over to Susie and sit down. It's clear she can sense my sadness, because she puts her hand on mine.

"Who were you talking to?" she asks, careful not to hurt my feelings.

"This guy, Kennedy, who I really like," I respond. "He moved to Minnesota two months ago, and is visiting until tomorrow. I really don't want him to go back."

"Oh, honey," Susie sympathizes. "It's okay. You know what they say?"

"What?" I answer, starting to cry.

"If you love something, let it go. If it comes back to you, it's yours to keep, but if doesn't, then it was never meant to be."

"But I already let him go, and he came back!" I complain. "He shouldn't have to leave again."

"Absence makes the heart grow fonder," she replies. "I saw in his eyes how much he loved you. I'm positive he won't forget you."

"Really?" I question, smiling a little.

"Yes," she responds, "Now go have fun while you can!"

"Thanks," I say, and I really mean it. "You really helped."

"No problem, girlie," she grins. "And remember, I'll always be here for you. Here's my number."

Susie writes her number down on a piece of paper and hands it to me. I smile and walk away, feeling a lot better about my uncertain future with Kennedy. I'll call him as soon as I get home and make plans for tonight.

When I get home, I call Kennedy right away. We make plans for a picnic at the zoo tonight. Kennedy is picking me up in five minutes, and then we will stop at the grocery store to grab some food.

Kennedy rings the doorbell and I run to answer it.

"Are you ready?" he asks.

"Of course," I giggle. "Let's go!"

We have a great time at the zoo, stopping to see every single animal. Kennedy pays for us to go on a train ride around the zoo, and we get to see everything—even the elusive pandas. We have a picnic in the meadow, pigging out on chips, salsa and popcorn.

When I get home, I plop down on my bed and start crying. I probably won't see Kennedy for a couple more years. By then, he could get a girlfriend or forget about me completely. Even though Susie reassured me he wouldn't forget about me, I can't help think that he will. I slowly drift off into a deep sleep, tired from the day's events.

The next morning, when I wake up, I am tucked under my covers. Sometime during the night my parents must have come in and put a blanket over me. I pull myself out of bed and head downstairs, hoping today won't be as awful as I think it's going to be. I'm going to have to tell Alice that I saw Kennedy and she will probably yell at me for it.

As I pass the front door, I see a paper sticking out of it. I pull it out and see the name, *Audrey*, written in big looping handwriting. Then, right below my name, I see the words, *From: Kennedy*. Taking a deep breath, I open the letter and read it.

> *Dear Audrey,*
>
> *I'm really sorry that I couldn't stay for longer. I just want to let you know that I will never forget you. You mean everything to me, and I hope I mean the same to you. Just remember, true love doesn't mean being inseparable; it means being separated and nothing changes. I will always care for you, even if we're not together and we're far, far away from each other. A wise man once told me, "Sometimes love means letting go when you want to hold on tighter." I hope you know that I wanted to stay, but I couldn't. I had to let go, but don't worry, I'll be back. And when I come back, I'm sure you'll know where to find me.*
>
> *Lots of love,*
> *Kennedy*

I clutch the letter to my chest and walk into the kitchen. Even though I'm still going to miss Kennedy, I have faith that it will all work out in the end. I reach for the phone and dial Susie's number. It looks like my plans with Alice will have to wait.

Dinosaurs, Giant Snakes, and Ball Bearings
Nikolas Kubler

Falling to the ground, Erin began to crawl towards the gun that lay two feet away from his bloody finger tips. He heard a loud hiss and the clacking of claws. Not daring to turn, Erin began to crawl faster towards the gun. One and a half feet, one foot, half a foot. Then there was a loud screech and Erin rolled to his side as a large bird-like animal slammed into the ground where he was just moments before, its long toe claw on its second toe scraping across the floor. Crawling across the cold floor, Erin was almost to his gun when a scaly clawed foot stepped in front of his face. Looking up, Erin stared into the yellow eyes of the animal as its fanged mouth opened and let out blood-curdling screech. Diving to the side, Erin snatched his gun and shot four times at the beast. The animal fell to the ground screeching, three bleeding holes in its side. Then, another screech answered from behind Erin and before he could turn another one of the animals slammed into his back, sending him face-first into the floor. With his body screaming in agony, Erin managed to push the second animal off his back and managed to fire another shot. The creature stumbled and let out another scream. Turning, Erin saw the elevator door down the hall behind him. Limping towards it, Erin heard the creature behind him and knew it would attack again soon. With a burst of speed, Erin pressed the elevator button, then pressed it again for good measure. Then a loud hiss came from behind him, and Erin turned to see the creature stalking towards him, feathers standing high on it's head. Baring its teeth, the creature leapt at Erin, who knocked aside with his gun. Fortunately, this sent the creature stumbling backwards screeching and hissing in pain and surprise. Unfortunately, it caused his gun to be knocked from Erin's hand. As the doors of the elevator began to open, another creature ran at Erin, only to have Erin dodge and send it crashing into the elevator. Then Erin was knocked to the ground by the injured creature he'd hit. Sending its sharp claws into his back, Erin felt his vision start to go fuzzy. Then the creature roared in triumph, and the elevator finally arrived.

About half an hour earlier, Darrell was sitting on a plane, trying not to throw up. This something that, up until about fifteen minutes ago, he'd been failing at. He had already thrown up right next to the woman Nima, who was sitting next to him and whom he'd since been trying to apologize to, and on the annoying reporter Celvin (something he didn't feel nearly as bad about) who'd been sent with him from the NNC, National News Center. Darrell was really hoping that this trip had been worth it. All he knew about where he was going was that it was some science lab where people were doing animal studies. For some reason they'd been sent with ten armed guards, and a paleontologist (a dinosaur scientist) who happened to be the cute girl he'd almost thrown up on. They all seemed to have no idea where we were going either, and the pilot hadn't said much.

"My job's ta get ya where you're going, not telling ya about it!" he'd shouted when Darrell asked him about it. Darrell was bored. His stories were always boring and pointless and were usually were placed next to stupid things like toy ads and the winner of the recent cupcake competition. Darrell wanted some excitement, but at this rate, that wasn't going to happen. As he sat next to Celvin, who was babbling about some story he'd recently done about Australian birds, Darrell glanced out the window to see a black line on the horizon, standing out against the blue sea. Soon Darrell wasn't the only one who saw the island, soon the others were staring out the window at the slowly growing line. Half an hour later, Darrell saw that the island was actually a massive building, with a shining metal dome and landing pads dotting the walls. As the plane began to descend, Darrell felt his stomach flip and he raced to the bathroom and stayed there until the plane stopped.

Ten minutes later, Darrell and the other passengers were being lead into the building by a skinny blonde man in a white coat who had introduced himself as Doctor Bedmirc. As Doctor Bedmirc led them into the building, Darrell and Celvin began to ask questions for the NNC.

"So, what exactly is this place?" asked Darrell, pen ready to write down his response.

"This is the TSRL," Bedmirc replied, smiling. Turning to the group, he continued, "That stands for Time Science and Research Labs. This building is our headquarters. It's six hundred feet tall at highest and about as wide as a city." Jotting this down, Darrell began to ask another question but was interrupted by the doctor.

"The TSRL was originally made to test an experimental time machine. However, we now are testing the, uh, side effects of the machine." Stopping, at a curved metal elevator door, Bedmirc pressed three buttons on a panel next to the door.

"Come along," he said as the door opened. "Unless you want to walk, which I really don't suggest." Stepping into the elevator, Derrell finished writing down Bedmirc's response when the elevator shot downwards so suddenly almost everyone, except for Bedmirc, had to steady themselves so they didn't fall. Seconds later, the elevator stopped and the group walked into a large white circular room. Large windows led to what appeared to be science labs where figures in lab coats examined computer screens while others talked in the corner of the room. As they continued

Darrell saw a large machine in the center of the room. The machine was basically two massive pillars with a large ring in between.

"What is that?" questioned Celvin, scribbling on his notepad.

"That is..." Bedmirc's response was interrupted by a large cargo truck that entered through a larger version of the elevator they'd just seen.

"You, get those ball bearings out of here!" bellowed another scientist who'd walked out of one of the labs. Marching over, the scientist began to continue to yell at the driver as the truck went through the doors again.

"And next time we order vegetable matter, don't bring me tiny metal balls!" he shouted after the truck as the double doors slammed behind it. Confused, the group followed Bedmirc over to the raging scientist.

"Oh, Bedmirc. You're here. And you brought our guests. Have you explained the machine yet?" he questioned.

"I was just about to, James," answered Bedmirc in a semi-respectful tone.

"Sorry to interrupt," said one of the armed men, Markus, not sounding the least bit sorry, "but can any of you tell us why exactly you you want us here?" His friends grumbled in agreement. Before the two scientists could reply, the massive machine behind them began to hum.

"Oh, you're all gonna like this! Especially you Doctor Nima," Bedmirc exclaimed as energy began to course through the machine. The group stepped back, covering their ears as the hum became a roar and energy began to build up in the center of the ring.

"We'll need to open it for just a few seconds!" James shouted over the crackling and roaring of the machine. "Just long enough for them to get back through with their samples!"

"Agreed!" hollered back Bedmirc as the machine grew louder, and louder, and then stopped, leaving a crackling circle of energy inside the ring.

"Now," Bedmirc explained to the speechless group, "We...," and then Bedmirc was rudely interpreted as a large camo colored jeep went flying out the shimmering ring.

The car crashed, skidded across the smooth floor, and rolled into one of the science labs. Breaking through the glass wall, the car didn't stop until it slammed into the other side of the lab, where it lay creaking and steaming against the wall. Then a loud roar echoed from the ring of power, and a man in camouflage uniform ran through the ring and into the massive room followed by a massive two legged monster. The creature was about sixty feet long and twenty feet tall, with large sail like spines on its back connected with a thin layer of skin. It had jaws like a massive crocodile, and two large clawed arms the size of a man. Easily catching the man in its

76

massive jaws, the beast swallowed him whole before turning to the group and emitting an earth shaking roar. Then chaos ensued, scientists screamed and swarmed the stairs, and the group ran, dashing as fast as they could to the elevators, James shouting into his radio for backup and the massive creature running after them at an incredible speed. Then Derrell turned to see Markus change direction and run towards the broken car.

"Where are you going?!" Derrell shouted after him as he slowed, choosing whether to go with him or head to the elevator. The creature didn't appear to care about Markus and was almost to Derrell, who decided to head towards the others at the elevator. As they reached the elevator, Bedmirc began to frantically press the buttons on the control panel, but it was too late. The creature stopped behind us, and began to look at each of them with a look that clearly said, "Hmm, who shall I eat first?" Then the sound of a gunshot echoed through the room and the monster roared in pain and anger as the gun fired once again, hitting the creature in the shoulder. Roaring the creature turned to see a Markus in front of the car, holding a large black rifle he'd pulled from the wreckage. Firing again, Markus' eyes widened as the creature began to charge, for few creatures could survive such an onslaught. Again and again he fired but the shots had little effect on the angry beast.

Derrell looked around for a weapon to help Markus as the elevator opened. Dashing in, Darrel and the armed men began to call for Markus. As the beast struck at him, Markus put his military training to use, and dived out of the way of the creatures fanged jaws which snapped the spot he had just been in. Before the creature could turn, Markus emptied three more shots before the monster, with amazing speed, threw Markus across the the room with its jaws.

"No!!!" shouted one of the armed men in anguish as he pulled a pistol from his belt and fired at the beast. The others followed his lead and the creature turned and ran towards the elevator. Quickly pressing the button, the elevator doors began to close as the creature ran towards the group. Then, one of the men shot at the beast's head, causing it to stumble, and giving the elevator just enough time to rise to safety. Derrell and the rest of the group flinched as a loud crash came from below followed by a bellowing roar from the frustrated creature.

As the others rode the elevator to safety, Markus tried to crawl toward the science lab to hide from the creature. His leg burned from where the creature had thrown him. As he approached a shattered table, he heard the whoosh of the elevator and the roar of the creature followed by its footsteps, claws clacking against the hard floor. Barely pulling himself under the table in time, Markus lay still as possible. Looking to his left, Markus saw the creatures clawed foot slam into the ground, crushing a computer that had just sat on the desk Markus now hid under. Then the creature roared and lowered its head so its large, yellow eye stared straight at Markus, who closed his eyes.

As the elevator rose with its depressed group, an automated voice echoed through the elevator.

"Remember," the voice stated happily, "In the case of an emergency, please use the stairs instead of the elevator. Thank you."

"Fat lot of use that did," Celvin said halfheartedly as the elevator sped further upwards. A few of the armed men slid to the floor, others shook their heads in disbelief. Darrell felt sorry for them. He barely knew him, but Markus seemed like a nice guy. Pushing Celvin out of the way, Nima pressed the elevator button, making the machine screech to a stop.

"That was a spinosaurus!" Nima gasped at Bedmirc and James.

"Yes, well," Bedmirc stuttered hopelessly while James pressed the button again and muttered something along the lines of "Damn lizards,.."

"Actually, they're more like birds," Bedmirc corrected sheepishly.

"Wait, wait, wait," Derrell said with a start. "Did you say dinosaurs? I'm not an expert, but aren't dinosaurs extinct?" The others in the elevator muttered in agreement.

"You'd be right," answered James, "But that machine downstairs was a portal maker. It makes portals through time and space. We've been using them to collect samples."

"As in dinosaurs," one the armed men bellowed stepping towards James. "One of your "samples" just killed Markus. Why the hell would you bring these things here? You just killed a man and you're talking about your 'samples!'"

"And why exactly do you have a time machine?" Nima added suspiciously as the elevator rose higher and higher. "In fact, last I checked, time machines don't exist"

"This building was designed to test a time machine, but it failed," Bedmirc replied cautiously as the elevator doors began to open. "The machine exploded, and created a portal. Then we built the machine downstairs, and have been using it to study the dinosaurs."

"Nima's right," Darrell said to Bedmirc. "Since when does anyone outside the movies have a time machine?"

"It was a top secret government project!" Bedmirc replied haughtily.

"So it's a conspiracy," Celvin nodded knowingly. Then, aware of the silent stares he was getting from the others he added, "What, I've seen the movies!"

The elevator doors began to open and James was the first to step out.

"Listen, we need to focus on getting out of here. We'll have to switch to another elevator, but then we'll be able to evacuate the building. Once we're out, we can discuss the purpose of this building."

The rest of the group stepped out of the elevator, muttering in agreement, and began to head down the halls to get to the other elevator. That was when they found Erin. Nima let out a gasp, and Bedmirc let out a mix between a squeal and a moan. Kneeling over, one of the armed men picked up his name tag and looked it over, wiping off blood as he looked for Erin's identity.

"His name's Erin, and he's a security guard, or at least, he was," the man said, placing the tag back on the body. Suddenly a loud screech broke the silence, and one of the feathered beasts that had killed Erin, began to stalk towards the group.

"No," James gasped as the beast hissed and stepped towards them. "They can't have gotten out. They have high security cages. How..."

"What are they?" Darrell asked, cautiously eying the creature as it continued towards him. However it was Nima who answered.

"That's a raptor, a deinonychus I think." she said quietly.

"Right," Bedmirc whispered. "It's alone, so it probably won't attack a group like us. It must have gotten out of its cage during maintenance."

"What do mean, 'probably?'" Darrell asked, "And if it won't attack us, what happen to this guy?" He said gesturing toward Erin. Suddenly another hiss came from behind them, and two more creatures ran out from behind the group.

"Oh," Darrell said stepping back. "That's how."

"I'll deal with this," James said stepping forward brandishing a small, flat devise. "This makes a high pitched sound that'll scare them off," he explained as he pointed the device at the largest of the three raptors and pressed a red button on it. The result was instant, the raptors stumbled back, screaming and hissing. For a moment it seemed to be working, then the largest raptor leapt at James, knocking him to the ground. The armed men reached for their guns, but the other raptors began to attack, and the group was forced to retreat, Bedmirc stumbling back in shock. The two other raptors began to chase after the group, who was barely keeping ahead of the pursuers. Then, they saw it, the elevator. However, as the doors opened, one of the raptors let out a screech and leapt onto one of the armed men just before the door closed. With the beast in the elevator with them, the group tried desperately to push the raptor back. Finally two of the men shot at the raptor, sending it flying into the wall. Then the elevator stopped, then began to descend.

"Damn," one of the men said as he helped up his injured friend. "The creature's damaged the elevator, now we're on a one way ticket to the lowest part of the building."

"Wait," Bedmirc stammered faintly. This was the first time he'd spoken since James' death. "The spinosaur could have damaged some of the test chambers. Who knows what's gotten out?"

"We don't have much of a choice," Darrell replied as the elevator shot downwards.

The elevator doors opened and the group found themselves faces to face with a massive armored four legged dinosaur.

"Ankylosaurus," Nima whispered. "It's a plant eater, but it's got a massive clubbed tail. So basically, don't startle it." The group carefully edged around the massive animal, staying clear of its massive tail club. The creature seemed to have little interest in the group, and continued to look around for tasty plants. As the group continued down the hall, they soon saw that ankylosaurus wasn't alone, and many other animals including beaked oviraptors, clawed therizinosaurus, ostrich-like ornithomimus, duck billed hadrosaurs, and many others had escaped into the building.

"Wait!" exclaimed Bedmirc, as a purple and turquoise feathered oviraptor squawked and dashed past the group. "We're right next to the vehicle bay. We'll be able to escape from there." A few minutes later, the group emerged into the bay, where there were trucks (including the ball bearing truck), jeeps and many other vehicles lining a giant room.

"We'll be able to escape through the main doors." Bedmirc said as he walked across the room to the control panel on the far wall.

When they noticed the snake, it was already too late. First there was movement from behind a line of trucks. Then a massive serpent slammed through the ball bearing truck, sending small metal balls flying in every direction. Bedmirc tried to run but slipped on the the small metal balls. Before he could stand, the snake opened its mouth and swallowed him.

"No!" shouted Darrell, as the snake finished Bedmirc. Grabbing a gun from a nearby jeep, Darrell began to fire upon the serpent. Following his lead, the other men also began to fire. The snake let out a hiss and struck at the men, sending two flying and scattering the others. Grabbing a large cannon-like gun, Celvin began to fire at the snake with rapid waves of bullets.

"This gun's the bomb, ain't no one gonna stop me." he yelled as the snake hissed and slithered behind some cars. Then, to Darrell's horror, it struck at Celvin, and seconds later, he was gone, nothing but his gun remaining.

Shouting in shock, sadness, and anger, Darrell fired as many shots as he could at the serpent. Turning, the snake let out a hiss and began to head towards the group.

"What is this thing?" Darrell asked as he fired at the snake.

"It's a titanoboa," Nima answered as she fired a gun she found in a damaged jeep. "But I have no idea how to stop it." Then the snake struck again, grabbing a man in its mouth and hitting another with its massive body. Darrell, Nima, and the two remaining men, backed up as the titanoboa turned towards them, rearing to strike. Then the wall exploded and spinosaurus ran into the massive room, barreling into the snake. The group stared in awe as the two beasts fought. The snake attempting to wrap itself around the spino, and the spinosaurus slamming the snake into cars and trucks. Finally regaining his senses, the Darrell quickly activated the panel and the massive door began to open. Running through the door, the group began to head towards the nearby helicopter pad while the two massive creatures fought behind them. The titanoboa struck at the spinosaur, sending it staggering out of the hanger. The snake struck again, only to be slashed by the dinosaur's massive claws. Then, the massive serpent attempted to wrap around the spinosaurus, its fatal mistake. The spinosaurus caught the snake's head in its massive jaws and then, with one foot holding the snake on the ground, crushed the serpent's neck. Roaring in triumph, the dinosaur began to feed on the serpent, allowing the group to safely escape to helicopter pad.

After calling for evacuation somewhere around twenty times, and having to hide from multiple creatures that began to leave the building, taking shelter in the forests nearby, a helicopter finally appeared on the horizon. Thirty minutes later, the helicopter landed cautiously on the landing pad and the group ran to meet it. Then the windows of the building behind them shattered, and five raptors leapt from the building. Running, the group reached the helicopter as the largest raptor grabbed the chopper. As the helicopter rose, the raptor lunged at Darrell, pinning him to the floor of the chopper. Baring its fangs, the raptor rose its head to strike at Darrell's throat. Then a loud bang, followed by a squeal echoed through the air, and then the raptor was sent flying from the helicopter straight to the ground that lay thirty feet below. Turning, Darrell saw Nima and the two men, guns still pointing to where the creature had been.

"Thanks," gasped Darrell as Nima helped him to his feet.

"Dudes," the pilot shouted to the group. "Let's go home, eh?" And so they did.

After they were about a mile away, the radio in the helicopter began to crackle.

"Hello, hello. Can you hear me? Hello," a voice crackled through the small radio. "This is Markus Makaveli and I need immediate evacuation!"

"Oh my god!" one of the armed men gasped. "We need to go back!"

"We can't," the pilot said solemnly. "We're too far away from the island. The radio crackled again and the group silenced.

"Listen," Markus called through the radio. "I can probably last about a week, but I need some help as soon as you can. But tell people what's happening here, people need to know about this." as the group agreed, Darrell thought back to about an hour ago. Maybe being put next to brownie awards wasn't so bad.

Inner Demon

Justin Huang

"Hey, little boy, don't touch those flowers!" I waved my cane at the pest, snarling as he ran away smirking. I walked up to my flower garden, patting down the soil and checking that the sunflowers hadn't been harmed. Grumbling, I trudged back up to my porch and turned around, peering down the dimly lit road. There was nothing to see except the glow of the streetlights and a Toyota Prius parked beside the curb.

"Kids these days," I muttered. Ever since those blasted Fergusons had moved into the neighborhood, their kid Frank had been nothing but trouble—setting things on fire, stealing tools off my porches, throwing toilet paper all around my house. But his parents insisted he was perfectly harmless. Of course, that twerp was a perfect angel whenever his parents were around. I walked inside and shut the door.

Ever since that fatal incident a year ago, barely anyone had dared move into this neighborhood. I had dismissed all the stories. The things people were willing to believe! It was outrageous! There were stories about some rabid "werewolf" on the loose, killing campers and other people. And then, a few weeks ago, those Fergusons had moved in. They had moved here from Arkansas, out of state, so they hadn't heard anything. I walked through the kitchen and turned to walk up the wooden stairs leading to the second floor. Lining the wall beside the staircase was a series of four clawed slashes dug into the wall. As far as I knew, those had been there ever since I bought the house, and I never got around to repairing them. I walked into the small attic room I called the bedroom, and lowered myself onto the mattress to catch a small nap before my bingo game at 1:00 this afternoon.

-

Bounding through the night, I sniffed the air for the scent. I was getting close. I bounded between the pine trees, rustling the bushes, and ran right into a clearing. There they were, two campers sitting together around a campfire, a tent set up to the side. They were busy setting a pot over the campfire. I raced quickly across the length of the clearing and opened my jaws into a feral snarl...

-

"BEEP... BEEP..."

I glanced up groggily from my bed and looked at the digital clock set on my bedstand: 12:00 P.M. *Better eat something before I go,* I thought. *And where the heck were all those dreams coming from? I should go see my therapist this week... maybe Wednesday.*

-

Frank Ferguson was out in the yard playing with his toy truck when the old man drove past in his car.

"Hey," yelled Frank, "where are you going?" The old man shot him a disgusted look and drove on. Frank was a small boy, no older than six. His parents had moved here to start new jobs. Frank was perfectly content with moving, and with the old man living just down the street, he could play as many pranks as he wanted. It was curious, though, why Frank and his parents were the only people living on this street other than the old man. The street looked perfectly safe, and the houses alongside his were all new. It was probably because everyone wanted to live somewhere as far away as they could from the cranky old man.

"Frank, it's time for lunch," his mother yelled. Frank dropped his truck and headed inside.

-

I turned onto Park Avenue and parked alongside the yellow brick building where they hosted the daily bingo games. Painted in faint red lettering were the words "Happy Time Bingo." *Happy Time, huh? In all my time coming here, I haven't seen a single winner...* I stepped inside to greet the musty smell of old people and worn carpet. The room I walked into was rectangular, about the length of a school cafeteria. There were 20 round tables set up throughout the room, and I headed for the one in the very back. As I walked to the back, no one greeted me or acknowledged me. They knew who I was and how I reacted to social interactions. I sat down in the single chair set behind the table and readied my playing card.

-

Frank finished licking up the tomato soup from his spoon and looked outside. It was fairly sunny and he wanted to do something other than play board games.

"Hey Mom, I'm gonna head outside."

84

"Okay, just don't wander off this street," she replied.

Frank stood up and ran outside, grabbing his backpack of supplies as he went. He turned to the left of his house towards the one house he loved to prank the most. "Oh, I can't wait to see the look on that old man's face," Frank smirked. Frank turned onto the old man's driveway and stood there looking at the house. Frank had never actually been inside the house. He had never dared to wander inside while the old man was there, but now that the house was empty, Frank felt confident that he could get away with this prank. Frank walked up to the doorway and wriggled the doorknob. As always, the old man forgot to lock the door and Frank walked inside without a problem.

The first thing to hit him was the stench. It smelled like a rotting corpse and other things best not to be described. The only light came from the cracks in the walls, and all the shutters were closed. Frank wandered deeper into the house. The next room after the entrance hallway was the kitchen. Just out of curiosity, Frank opened the fridge. *Bet he has a bunch of healthy organic stuff in there,* Frank laughed silently. But what was actually in the fridge shocked and disgusted Frank. Rotten cheese and meat hung dripping through the wire racks of the fridge and what appeared to be a rat and flies swarmed among the moldy breads and vegetables. *What kind of a freak have we been living next to? Better tell Mom later...* Frank pulled out a cloth from his backpack and continued on. By this time, Frank had forgotten all about his pranks and moved onwards to ascend to the second level. Moving up the stairs, he sees a long set of gashes on the wall beside the staircase. *How in the world did those get there? Either a monster is loose in the old man's house or this guy is crazy.* Frank climbed the last stair and walked ahead to what he thought was the bedroom. Opening the door to this new room, Frank beheld a horrifying sight. This room, like the kitchen was also covered in mold, and the blankets looked like they hadn't been washed in centuries. But hanging right above the head post was what looked strangely like blood...

"What are you doing in my house, boy?!"

Frank whirled around to see the old man leaning against the door, glaring venomously. "I'm so sorry, sir, I just came in to look around, and, and I was just meaning to go." Frank tried to sidle past the old man, but was blocked by a cane. Frank opened his mouth to say something, but then stopped with his mouth halfway open. The old man had stopped moving; in fact, it looked like he was frozen. Peering closer at his face, Frank saw that the man's pupils were swirling. "What the..."

The man's eyes continued to swirl and darken in color, until they were black. By this time, Frank was terrified. He tried pushing his way past him, but he couldn't squeeze past the old man's grip. All of a sudden, the old man began to growl. It started as a low guttural moan, quickly escalating into a loud snarl. Frank backed away from the man, standing up against the corner of the far wall, the entire time, never taking his eyes off the changing figure. The old man started to buck and curled up on the ground, writhing. Frank could hear the pops of his spine as the bones in the man's body started to change. Frank took this moment to run out from the corner, leap over the writhing body, and race down the stairs. He heard no sound of pursuit as he opened the door and stepped outside onto the front porch. Frank listened intently for any noises from within the house. Hearing nothing, he crept slowly away from the house, one step at a time.

CRASH! From nowhere whipped out a long hand, the ends of which were decked in three-inch long claws. The hands tore through the wooden front door and grabbed Frank around the waist. Before having any time to scream, Frank was pulled inside the house and everything was quiet.

-

I woke up with my face on the kitchen table. I must've fallen asleep again. I stood up and stretched. I looked around the room. *Where had that nuisance of a kid gone?* All I remember was driving home after bingo and heading upstairs to take a nap, to find that nasty Ferguson boy in my house. The rudeness of some people. *Ought to talk to his parents again.* After finding the boy in the house, I don't quite remember what had happened. The only thing I recall was an intense pain and anger. It must be those meds I'm taking again.

"Hello," called a voice, "can we come in?"

Who would want to visit me? I thought. I went to the door and opened it. There stood a man and a woman, whom I knew to be my neighbors, the Fergusons. "What do you want?" I asked irritably.

"We're looking for our son. He's been gone for almost four hours now, and we don't know where he went. We know he sometimes likes to come down to your house and play..."

Haha, Play, is that what they think he's doing? I thought sarcastically.

"...and we were wondering if you've seen him."

"Actually, I have, maybe just two hours ago. He was wandering around in my house, but I fell asleep sometime or another and can't seem to remember where he's gone."

"Can we come inside just to make sure he isn't somewhere inside?"

"He probably would have wandered back out already, but sure, come on in if you want." I opened the door further to allow them inside. They walked around the house a bit, sometimes coughing violently for who knows what reason, and came back to me in the kitchen. I watched as they walked in eyes watering, with mouths pressed against sleeves—an odd habit that was starting to annoy me.

"We're going to head upstairs, look around. Maybe he hasn't heard us yet." The parents were looking increasingly worried, and had I not heard a note of desperation in their voices, I would have kicked them out right then and there. So I lead them upstairs and went back downstairs to wait.

-

The parents never found their boy. I couldn't care less, that pest was too much of a bother anyways. The Fergusons ended up moving away, claiming that the neighborhood and its inhabitants "weren't safe." I laughed at the thought. I had been living here for years, yet nothing had ever bothered me. Also, something fishy was going on. Last week, I had gone to see my therapist about my dreams. I had expected her to hear me out, but the moment I started talking, she started screaming nonsense like "Get away from me, you monster!" and huddling in the corner holding a stapler and a pair of scissors. I swear, everyone's going mad these days. Also, it's starting to become very suspicious. Every time I have one of those wolf dreams, there seems to be another killing incident. Maybe I should consider going into the fortune telling business.

-

Two years later

"Bill, wake up, wake up…"

I opened my eyes to the voice and saw a young man - Darryl, my care assistant - standing over me.

"What happened? Is something wrong?" I replied.

"Yeah, the nursing home had to be evacuated. The building was falling down. We thought it was an earthquake, but I think the real cause was a wolf."

"A wolf?"

"Yeah, I swear I saw the shadow of a huge wolf, running inside the building as we evacuated everyone outside. I think we should get some people to hunt it down."

I was confused. *If the building fell down, where were we? As far as I know, I never went outside with everyone else.* I asked Darryl about it.

"That's the weird part. I was looking around the building for anyone who still might be inside, when I found you in sleeping the only undamaged part of the building," he said slowly.

"Hmm, this is very curious," I muttered, "and also interesting. You see, before I moved into the nursing home, I lived in a house by myself. While I lived there, stories about the same wolf you're talking about happened all the time. For weeks, the police looked for this wolf, but they never found anything."

Darryl smiled. "Well then, I guess the mystery of the wolf continues to live."

A Balance in Measure
Michael Ioffe

On the first day of his reign, our newly elected president issued six executive proclamations, each one of which was bound to change the country forever. In the matter of six short seconds, six illegible scribbles on a line at the bottom of an ornate piece of paper, our country went from an idyllic democracy, the poster child of our world, to a state of tyranny and corruption, ruled by a select few called the government. Our president, who had vowed so many wonderful and beneficial changes to our not-yet-perfect country, to the land of the free, had instead done the exact opposite of his promises. He had declared that he would change our school system to be the model for everyone to see. He had declared that taxes would be lowered, and government spending would be rethought for the benefit of all the people. He declared that he would give quality healthcare for all, for free, so everyone would have access to great doctors. But men can promise, and all he declared meant nothing. Yet we, the people of our country, believed in him, voted unanimously for him, and elected him. And we, the people of our country, are responsible for not looking deeper into the candidate's lightly woven story, for not questioning his many wonderful promises. For how could it be that a candidate does not lie?

It was a dreary and quite uncomfortable day in the Town Square, as I sat on a roughened wooden plank bench that had seen more that I had in my many years, and as the coldness of the raw wood jutted into my tailbone, I sat waiting for something to happen, something big and something that, as we journalists often look for, will catch attention. But the only way to find attention is through panic and fear. Through the unknown. Such is the job of a journalist, cataloging catastrophes, and many journalists I know can't find work, so they create it. So I sat, finding a catastrophe to write about, finding the imagination to create something disastrous and entirely fake. But, unlike every single journalist that I have known, I got lucky, and on that day, as I was thinking and wondering what I could dream up, what I could create to get attention, to pique the interest of the gullible public, I looked up from the roughen cobblestone floor of the empty Square, and noticed a man. He was unbelievably bent and hunchbacked, and his gait was that of a beast, stumbling and irregular, yet he walked faster than any man I had ever seen. As I carefully observed this strange yet ordinary spectacle, I noticed a small piece of paper, insignificant and invisible to this man, fall out of his worn and incredibly thin trench coat, and land comfortably into a crevice in the cobblestone. Oblivious, the man continued on his path, and in a matter of seconds, he had exited the square, and the strange sight that had played out before my eyes ceased in its existence.

As he left, I cautiously approached the piece of paper, which was lodged deep into a break in the typically uniform cobblestone. Looking guardedly around, I saw the square perfectly empty, and after proceeding to tugging at the stray for a while, the miniscule slip let go, and arrived in the roughen palm of my hand. Upon deciphering the nearly illegible handwriting, I stopped and stared at the text on the paper which was familiar in the most shocking way - the slip of paper proclaimed the very fate of our people, the very reason or nation now lay at its knees. *Abolish 1, 6, 9, 10, 12, 22* it read. While this simple passage should have been nothing of a revelation, it brought forth to my eyes the very event that had occurred just a day ago, an event that I had blatantly ignored. After all, the slip affirmed exactly what every single newly-state-owned newspaper had not reported on the front of its cover, "President Takes Full Control Of America To Aid In Reviving Country," and what most of the public knew as common knowledge, as the truth. On the first day of his reign, our president abolished Constitutional Amendments Numbers 1, 6, 10, 12, and 22. No longer was our speech, press, and religion protected. No longer were we allowed to assemble, petition, and judge. No longer would we have elections, or have one term presidents. No longer did we have our freedom, for our nation, our great nation, had been rendered Totalitarian, had been rendered, in the most modern sense, Communist.

-

My apartment, a rundown shack stuck at the top of a rickety five story building at a point of town where the countryside meets the city, had a wooden door that would only open after a series of sizable heaves upon the painted plastic door knob. Approaching the one room flat was even more of a painful hassle: one must climb up a series of eyesoring red fire escapes clinging to the side of the worn building, all ready to fall off at the wrong step or turn. The landlord of the building, a chain-smoking Marlboro man rounder than a marble on a good day, was a shadowy character by the name of Stoyles, who came around once a month to collect the feeble rent from the ten tenants, and to scream a bit at the poor housekeeper who lived on the first floor. The ten tenants consisted of a quack doctor, by all normal standards, a divorce lawyer who had not seen work since ten years ago, and six other miscellaneous workers, all of whom had no families, and kept to themselves. Stoyles seemed to be content with his occupants, and rarely evicted anyone, other than a few hopeless drunks who happened about the bland and nearly nonexistent lobby. As I heaved open the door to my room, I looked around and admired the very reason I had settled in this little place - from the fifth story, the whole sprawl of the banal town could be viewed crisply and clearly, every little abandoned alley and fissure in the gridwork of the city could be examined from above. As I entered the room and sat down to my blunt maple workdesk, I admired this view, the only beautiful sight in a country where beauty had been lost and forgotten like an old stuffed animal, like an instrument whose strings have long been still.

My workdesk, an undermined fragment of a maple tree long ago cut down, was just stable enough to allow my anxious hand to safely write without flying into the window that divided my residence from the street fifty feet below. As I carefully sat down, to avoid crushing the cardboard-of-a-chair, I swiftly clasped an aging leaf of notebook paper from the shelf beside me, and began to capture my thoughts and realizations with the blue ink flowing from my pen. Of the whole spectacle of the president's ascent came one often ignored yet remarkable fact: while it was commonly known that the president had, along with his annulment of numerous amendments, cancelled the tenure of every single governmental organization, how had the president managed to silence and suppress each and every one of the loyal members of Congress and Court, the very men and women who took pride in bringing justice to our country? Moreover, how could a man accumulate an amount of money enough to severely bribe each and every individual, as well as their families and friends, enough that these members would be too comfortable and blind to bother speaking against the president? I scribbled these budding questions in the upper right margins of the sheet, and proceeded to let my tired being rest for the night.

-

I pushed the useless threadbare blanket off of my frigid and thinning frame, and hurled myself out of my bed and into the bright grey early morning. After taking a clumsy and awkward seat at the run-down chair, I conscientiously lifted my cumbersome pen and began to draw conclusions from my thoughts of last night. I had a strong sense that I was on the brink, on the verge, of revealing something amazing and groundbreaking, but upon realizing no such subject, I began to derive what I could from the *Gazette*, our town's previously inquisitive, and now newly state-owned, newspaper. It was now delivered to your doorstep whether you liked it or not, and the outlandish day -to -day headlines remained similar, ranging from "President

Is Geared To Change Country" to the most recent one, "President Develops Plan To Cut Spending - Removes Health Services and Education," a testament to the president's removal of almost every government department, except for the Army, which will obediently protect him during his everlasting tenure, as to allow more power for himself. I picked up the very first article, a piece entitled "New President Looking Towards the Future," about the President's simple, supposedly down-to-earth, past. One part of the article, a short couple of sentences about his tenure as the head of the Bank Ultima, confounded me.

> *When our President arrived as Chief Officer of the bank, it was already in a bad state. Although he tried hard to bring the bank to working order, the bank went bankrupt nonetheless. Thanks to the hard work of our leader, the bankruptcy process was simple and efficient, and allowed all of the workers of the company to safely leave and move to other jobs.*

Five short years earlier, when I was employed by the very newspaper that had printed this passage, I had written a brief, stubborn, and, to the general public, majorly uninteresting, article summarizing the Bank Ultima event. Unlike the many banks that suffered during the strapping financial crisis, Bank Ultima endured in part to its diminutive but strong base of ceaselessly loyal customers. Nevertheless, after the financial being of the nation regained its healthiness, Bank Ultima fired its rambunctious Chief Officer due to a supposed and highly covered-up scandal, and soon acquired a new Chief Officer, the very man most everybody knows as the President. Soon after, a markedly peculiar and perplexing black swan struck the Bank: in the matter of minutes, it had lost all its valuable assets, and was forced to file for bankruptcy protection from the government. Soon enough, the story of Bank Ultima, and the very namesake of the bank itself, was lost and drowned in the whirlpool of news that is always spinning and churning in our nation. With that, all the questions around the bankruptcy dissolved like powdered sugar in a crystal glass of water, and any reservations about their billion-dollar assets were instantly washed away. Of course, the public, which was back into another uplifting boom, was oblivious and uninterested. Another part of the article received my interest, precisely due to the fact that the Army was the only untouched department in the president's tirade:

> *While growing up, the President enjoyed spending long summer afternoons playing outside with his childhood pal Frank Doyle, and he hopes, with his impending reform on education, to relay his experiences to children around the country.*

Although the minor readership of the *Gazette* was most likely blind to the contents of the article, it is key to know that Mr. Doyle is the current head of the Army, and his supposed friendship with our leader is the reason our president has been kept in safety. But the thoughts of Bank Ultima cemented in my mind: what had happened to those billion-dollar assets? What had caused an organization as strong as Bank Ultima, an organization that had endured and suffered through the very worst of crises, to fall like a deck of cards, in an instant? And was the changing of Chief Officer's at all linked to the swindling of grand sums of money, or was this all, in the words of many, a mere and subtle coincidence? With these stimulating questions in mind, I prepared my final conclusions and revelations, and began my trip to the plainclothes offices of *Occupied*, a small Underground newspaper that had been around for a while, but contained a very small readership - as a reporter, I had worked with one of theirs. Hopefully, they would contain the resources necessary for the development of my discoveries and message, enough to spread the word about the very reason our president is at power.

-

The bedridden offices of *Occupied* were conveniently situated on the lower floor of an archetypal three-story office building located half-a-mile from my apartment, in a part of town better known for its astronomical crime rate than for its great literacy. Upon knocking on the slab of oak that stood as a door, I was greeted by a kindly lady, who welcomed me into a textbook waiting room, sans any visitors or a receptionist. Within a moment of my sudden arrival, a fully-bearded man stepped out of the single door at the corner of the room and beckoned for me to follow him - obligingly, I stood up and followed him into the room, which I perceived to be his office. As I settled myself into a metal-framed chair, I was handed a glass of water, and asked to detail my entrance.

"Sir, what do you come to me for this morning?" The man talked like a stereotypical countryman, cleanly and empathetically, without any hint of foreign or regional accent.

"I would like to inquire about possible publicity, or an article, I presume."

"On what topic?"

"On the president's term, sir."

The man's face brightened up in surprise. "And what sort of news do you have for us? Please proceed to tell your story." With that statement, I began to tell my story.

"I began working at our local *Gazette* here twenty years ago, when I had just graduated with my journalism degree. I had one breakout editorial regarding the work of a local foreman, a man who had built a school for the children of a small town in the countryside. After that, I was suited to write small summaries of pointless and uninteresting events, and after seventeen years under that commonplace job, I decided, like many journalists, to work freelance. Alas, like many other journalists, I was at a loss for work, but I could not bear to move myself to use the tactics of others and *create* news - for this reason, I spent the past three years of my life wandering about the town, and enjoying the bright air and atmosphere. Because of my position, I was able to view the impending demise of our town little by little, and I was, and still am, determined to somehow fix this occurrence. On one of my travels around town, an old man ran before me, and dropped a slip of paper, which I happened to pick up. The paper, in this exact order, read, *abolish 1, 6, 9, 10, 12, 22*. Since I had not been reading the paper, and have heard scarcely about the president's plans, this came as a revelation for me, as I realized what the president had done. But then I began to wonder: how had the president managed to suppress the members of Congress and Court, and how had they allowed him to change the laws?"

I continued, "At this point, I decided to read the newspapers, and in one entry, I came upon an interesting little fragment relating to Bank Ultima, which our president was the newly elected Chief Officer of, at the time it closed. After reading the fragment, I was reminded about an article I wrote myself about the demise of Bank Ultima, which mysteriously managed to lose billions of dollars in assets in the matter of mere moments. Another interesting part I noted was that the Chief Officer at Bank Ultima before our president was ousted due to a highly undisclosed affair - why couldn't have this affair been set up by the president, who at the time, was the Operations Officer at Bank Ultima? And with the *billions he took from Bank Ultima*, why couldn't he have the money to bribe the members of Congress and Court, as well as their families and friends, to the point where they were comfortable enough that they did not care nor see the state of the country? This, I believe, is what happened to our country, and this, I believe, is the reason our country is ruled by one man. When he decided to 'cut costs' by taking out almost every single government agency, he caused the total power of our nation's government to sway towards himself. There is now no Department of Education, no National Security, and even no Cabinet to protest against him.

As well, it must be noted that, as stated in the very same *Gazette* article, the President is childhood friends with a certain Mr. Doyle, the current head of the Army, which should explain the safety of the president, and elevates his powers against the people. Above all, for the common man, the propaganda is enough to make him falsely believe in the President."

The man behind the table looked stunned beyond belief. "What do you want me to do with your discovery?"

Here came the moment I had been working, and looking for. "I would like the public to know that our President has taken the money of the people, taken the freedom of the people, and has taken all that into his own hands. The only way we can stop this man is by overthrowing him, and for that, we need the help of the people." There was another note that I did not care to make: historically, such tyrants are not kind to the public, and with the pattern of our leader's choices, rampant killing and persecution could soon follow. I knew that the townspeople must know of the president's real motives, and that the townspeople must make the change in our future.

"Sir, our country it at a point where the people must make the decisions, and they must make them in a proper and informed way. The only way that is possible is with the help of your publication." I stated.

The man looked at me grimly and knowingly. "You will see a full editorial by the beginning of next week. I will call you back, and discuss specifics. Let's hope this will change our fate. What is your number?" After parting with our contact details, I left the room, and proceeded upon my walk home. As I was exiting my meander through the town square, I noticed a large red blemish on the brick wall at the very spot where I last saw the old man that began this entire undertaking. Taking note, I paced back to my apartment, and climbed up the fire escape.

-

Tomorrow, the editorial relating to my studies will be published in the Underground paper, as well as Underground papers across the nation. The fate of our nation, as well as the whole truth about our president, is now in the hands of the citizens. On the first day of his reign, our newly elected president issued six executive orders, each one of which was bound to change the country forever. But our president forgot about the people. About the people who need the truth, and who, once sparked, will spread like a flame, and do anything to retrieve their freedom back. Our country will be restored, and replenished. Our country will survive, and be strong, and will again be the democratic poster child of the world. But for now, our country's fate is

95

in the hands of the people. So, for now, I will be on the fire escape, watching the city from above, watching the beauty of the sky, the countryside, and all the streets, buildings, and people that make life possible. And now, life itself is in the hands of the people of our country - life itself is in *your* hands. So make your choice. And most of all, make us free, and make us proud.

Exceeding Expectations
Cleo Forman

Aly was lying on her back on the thick bed of foliage that had accumulated from the falling leaves of the nearby trees. She watched as one leaf quivered fiercely, trying with all its strength to hold onto the branch it had grown up on. One final blast of cold wind overcame it and it finally let go, drifting very, very reluctantly to the ground. The trees surrounding the clearing were tall and majestic, covered in thousands of amber and crimson leaves. They seemed to protect the clearing from all outside noise. Nothing except the piercing calls of birds could be heard. The first time she had found this place, the trek to it had been slightly treacherous, with thick ivy covering the ground and a spider web at every turn, but now she had started coming here so frequently that she could follow a trail she had worn into the undergrowth. She never shared this place with anyone, because it was her way of disconnecting from everyday life.

Aly had a fairly busy schedule. She attended her neighborhood school, but after school she had ballet nearly every day. She didn't go to ballet school; instead, her mother taught her. Her mother was tall and narrow, with grey hair and blue eyes. She was a very dignified woman, but also very maternal. Not at all like many parents of the dancers Aly knew. Her mother was a retired soloist in San Francisco Ballet. She had been an incredible dancer, and was doing her best to teach Aly all she knew. She had set up a ballet studio in the basement of their house complete with ballet barres and a wall of mirrors. Aly had class with her mom in their basement six days a week for one to three hours, depending on how much homework she had.

Aly loved dancing, and loved the fact that she was finally at the level that, while she still wasn't outstanding and there were plenty of things she still needed to learn and perfect, she could finally allow herself to focus on expressing herself through the movements. When she first started out all she could do was try her best to determine all of the minute details that defined each position. It took her years and years to get to a level where her body not only understood what it needed to do during basic movements, but it had developed the necessary components to execute them (such as flexibility and strength). It took years of trial and error in steps like pirouettes (one-legged turns), so that her body finally recognized the position it needed to be in to stay upright. It wasn't as if anyone could tell her exactly how it worked, because each person was built so differently. Each dancer must individually figure out how to make it work for themselves. Finally, after nearly thirteen years, Aly had reached the point where she could focus on slightly harder steps, variations, and really expressing herself through the movement. She finally had a glimmer of hope that her dream of becoming a professional dancer in the same company that her mother had danced in, San Francisco Ballet, could come true. So she had decided to take the first step and apply to their summer program.

-

The smell of salt was thick in the air and the sky was grey and overcast. Aly leaned over the railing, where she watched the turbulent grey water rolling and crashing over itself, spraying briny water everywhere. She and her mother were taking the ferry from the San Juan Islands in Washington to Seattle, so she could drive to the San Francisco Ballet summer intensive audition. The sight of the water reminded her of what was going on in her stomach; it was churning unhappily. Tomorrow she was going to be attending her first ever audition. She knew how good some dancers were, and she wasn't used to dancing with lots of other girls. She hardly knew whether class worked the same way as when she took from her mother. Of course, she had pressed Mom for all the details on traditional classes, all the audition experiences she remembered, and anything that could give her any kind of advantage. Nonetheless, she was terrified. She had good friends at school, but no one quite understood this aspect of her life and she knew no one who could come to the audition with her. Aly was determined to do everything she could do to ensure her dancing at the audition would be her best. If she didn't get accepted... she would feel like a failure. Her mother had not only gotten accepted at age fourteen to the summer program (Aly was fifteen), but that summer she was asked to attend the San Francisco ballet school full time. Aly knew that dancers matured at different rates, but it was so nerve-wracking not to know whether she had a chance for a career. She needed something to confirm that ballet wanted her as much as she wanted it.

Because they had left a few hours after school on Friday, they reached Seattle at around nine that night. They took a cab to a hotel they had booked that was within walking distance to Pacific Northwest Ballet School. Aly and her mother entered the hotel with their one suitcase in tow. Tall plastic-looking plants stood in large ceramic vases on either side of the sliding doors. They checked in with someone at the counter, and got their room key.

Their room was strangely homey. It had a large bedroom with twin beds, a bathroom, a living room with a television, and a mini kitchen complete with a stove, coffee maker, pans, and free popcorn. Aly immediately got in her bed, and tried to get to sleep so she wouldn't be tired during the audition. Her mother got in the bed next to hers and read silently with only the reading lamp on, so Aly could sleep. However, the butterflies didn't want her to sleep quite yet. The more she tried to sleep, the more her mind raced. Forcing herself to sleep wasn't the way to go. She got out a book, and eventually she felt sleepy.

She got up the next morning at seven, allowing herself two hours to prepare and arrive at the studio before registration at 9:30 AM. She got out of bed and got out a freshly cleaned leotard and tights from her ballet bag. She put them on, and then put on a little bit of makeup, just to accentuate her eyes and mouth. She put sweatpants over her ballet clothes, and gently shook her mom awake.

"Mom! Mom, we have to leave in about an hour and fifteen minutes. Do you want to come get some breakfast with me?

After her mom had gotten her clothes on, she groggily walked with Aly to the lobby. The scent of brewing coffee and toasted bread wafted past them. There was an elaborate breakfast buffet set up. The hotel had a tiered pastry stand with bagels, croissants, danishes, and muffins. Next to those were vats of soft, scrambled eggs, breakfast sausage, tater tots, and a huge crockpot of oatmeal. On a black marble island there was a station with cereal, milk, and yogurt. She got a bowl of oatmeal, which she topped with fresh fruit, cranberries, and brown sugar and a separate plate of some scrambled eggs. She sat down with her mom, who had gotten a bagel and cream cheese, and they sat down at one of the dining room tables that overlooked the Seattle streets, which were thick with fog.

It was time to start walking to the studio. She grabbed her black ballet bag that had her pointe shoes, ballet shoes, extra ballet clothes, and extra hairpins in it. She and her mom walked up winding hills and streets to get there. It took about fifteen minutes.

A large intimidating glass structure loomed before them. She climbed up the stairs and opened the doors. Inside, hundreds of kids stood around with their hair in tight ballet buns, stretching, talking, and signing in at the registration desk. She walked up to the desk with her mother. A lady at the desk asked her to fill out her name, address, and a short summary of her dancing experience. Her mother paid the lady thirty dollars, who then handed her a large black and white number 42 and a safety pin to attach it to the front of her leotard.

"When are you done?" Her mother asked. "And where should I meet you?"

"I'm done at eleven. It might be raining, so I'll wait for you inside the building at the bottom of the stairs," Aly replied.

"I'm going to go for a walk around Seattle. Is your cell phone on?" Her mother inquired.

"No, I don't want it ringing during class, but I'll turn it on afterwards."

"Okay. Good luck, sweetie. You'll do great. Remember to look like you're having fun, even if you are really nervous. That is what a performer is all about." Aly saw her mother wave goodbye, and then Aly turned around and walked down the hall past the registration desk to the waiting room.

The sheer number of dancers who were in the waiting area was breathtaking. Most were sitting in small huddles where they were stretching in the splits and whispering anxiously. The floor was littered with dance bags. It was obvious groups of friends from different ballet schools around Oregon and Washington had come to audition together. She had no one. She shrugged off the feeling of loneliness, and started warming up. Because Aly was fifteen, she was required to do the entire audition en pointe. She took out her pointe shoes, her ouch pouches, duct tape and her second skin. She uncovered her toes by pulling back the front of her convertible-footed tights. Second skin was something that was sold to use on burns, but instead of using it for that, many dancers placed it on areas on their feet that were prone to get blisters. She peeled off the plastic that protected the gel-like surface from drying out and put it on her big toe and her pinky toe. She wrapped duct tape around the second skin to secure it. She then put on the ouch pouches, sort of like thick toe socks, and then covered her feet once again with her tights, to make sure the ouch pouches didn't slip around. She shoved her feet into the narrow boxes of her pointe shoes, pulled on the heels of the shoes, and skillfully wrapped her ribbons around her ankles. She made sure all the extra ribbon was tucked in securely, so it didn't fall out during class. Her mother told her stories about how when she was in the company she knew a soloist who had gotten fired because her ribbons had come untucked one too many times.

She found the rosin box, once again peeled off the back of her shoe and rubbed her the heel of her tights in the rosin. This ensured that she didn't have to worry about the heels of her pointe shoes slipping off in class. Then she rubbed the tip and sides of her shoe in the rosin to keep herself from slipping when she was standing en pointe. This was important so her foot didn't slip out from under her. Unlike normal ballet slippers, pointe shoes had very little friction (how much friction could one expect from an approximately one inch square platform?), so it was even harder to maintain turnout since you couldn't cheat by simply gripping the floor with your toes.

Soon, the judges called for the fourteen to sixteen year old age group to come into a large studio that was across the hall. The studio had one wall entirely made of glass. They were on the second floor so the view was across the tops of the building surrounding them. Natural light poured into the studio. The three judges sat behind a desk at the front of the room. Columns of metal barres had been set up.

"Could everyone please line up on the barres by audition number? One here, two here, etc. Please stand with four to each side of the bar." One of the judges, a middle-aged tall thin woman with red curly hair, came and tapped the barres to show the students what she meant. Soon we were all in order by number. I was at the front on one of the middle barres, almost directly in front of judges table. "Thank you, let's start."

Everyone watched very carefully as she demonstrated the first plie combination. It was a basic warm up she had done hundreds of times. Barre was just like any other barre she had taken, except she was surrounded by nearly one hundred other dancers, so she didn't get corrections nearly as often. The red-headed judge walked up and down each barre, correcting dancers occasionally and checking to see if any stood out.

Eventually, after all the usual barre steps had been done (plie, tendu, degage, fondue, frappe, rond de jambe, and grande allegro), they moved to the center. They did grand allegro and some combinations across the floor. Very soon it was over. Aly thought that she had done relatively well, but the unfamiliar atmosphere didn't help her nerves at all, so she had messed up a couple combinations. The other girls in the class had been good, but most of them were at Aly's level and most were not that much better than she was. She didn't know what to think.

-

A bird shrieked in a nearby tree, bringing Aly back to the present. It was getting late, and the sun was beginning to set. It peeked through the trees and shot rays of sunlight across her. Her usually brown hair was turned a fiery orange color, and, despite the cold, bathed her entire body in warmth. She let herself be lost in the feeling for a few minutes, but knew she needed to head home if she were going to get there before dark. She stood up slowly, brushing some of the plant pieces off of her. She lingered while the last rays of sun disappeared, and then pushed through the woods in the direction of her home.

On her way home, she checked the mailbox, as she did every day, for her audition results. She couldn't see who the letters were from in the darkness, so she ran as quickly as she could through the tall grass that covered her front yard to her house. In the fading light, the window of her house glowed with yellow warmth and the stone chimney spewed smoke from their fireplace. She knew her mother would be inside making dinner.

She clutched the white banister as she ran up the three steps to her porch. She knocked on the stained glass window of the front door. Soon her mother's familiar face greeted her.

"Come in, come in. It's cold out. You're just in time for dinner." Her mother beckoned her into the warm foyer. Her mother was wearing her old white apron, which was covered in stains from her many cooking and baking mishaps that had occurred over the years. "Why don't you go put some clean clothes on? The chicken pot pies will be ready in fifteen minutes or so." Aly was already looking through the mail as her mother talked.

"Mom! It's here!" Aly started jumping up and down in excitement. "The audition results!" Aly could hardly restrain herself from tearing the letter open immediately, but she decided she wanted to wait until dinner to find out whether she had gotten in. "I'll open it at dinner. Right now I am going to go take a shower." Her straight-legged jeans were covered in mud and her oversized red wool sweater was spattered with dirt as well. She pulled off her boots awkwardly and set them on the shoe rack.

"Okay, honey, go take your shower. As soon as you get out we'll have dinner, and find out whether you got in."

Aly strode down the wood-floored hallway to the white linoleum bathroom. She undressed and got under the scalding water in the shower. She was getting more and more nervous about opening the letter. She wasn't sure what she would do if she hadn't gotten in. She tried to push all thoughts of the audition out of her mind and just let the hot water massage her.

"Aly, it's time to get out of the shower!" Her mother's voice awoke her from her daze. She climbed out of the tub and dried herself off with a towel. She quickly put on some warm, fuzzy pajamas, and walked to the dining room table. Waiting at her place was a chicken pot pie with a sizzling, flaky pie crust covering the filling. Her mother came to sit down with her at the table. She brought Aly's letter with her, and handed it to her. "Maybe you should open the letter before we eat, it will get greasy otherwise."

"Okay," Aly replied, "I guess. I am so so so nervous. What if I didn't get in?" *I just have to do it*, she thought to herself. *It doesn't change anything if I don't open it.* She tore open the envelope and took out the letter nervously. In her hands was a paper that said:

Dear Student,

Thank you for attending the Seattle Audition for San Francisco Ballet School's 2012 Summer Course.

We are happy to inform you that we were able to place you in this year's program.

Thank you for your interest in San Francisco Ballet School.
Sincerely,

Heigi Tomasson   Patrick Armand
Director of the School   Administrative Director

"Yes!" She ran over to her mom and gave her a big hug. Her mother hugged her back.

"I knew you would get in, Aly. You have so much talent. I know you'll go even farther than I did, you could become a prima ballerina!" Tears of pride were trickling down her mother's cheeks. "I am so happy for you, sweetie."

To Survive Without Living
Rebekah Goshorn

The morning dew sparkled in the sunlight when I woke up on that spring day. I hopped out of bed and pulled on my favorite shirt, really soft and blue with "smile" written on it. Then I put my hair up into a ponytail and ran downstairs. I put a Pop-Tart into the toaster and waited for it to heat up as I grabbed a glass of milk and a plate. My kitten came around the corner, meowing for attention. I picked her up and stroked her head, pausing to scratch behind her ears. My Pop-Tart began to smoke; I had forgotten to set the timer. I hurried over to it, but just then, the power went out. I sighed and grabbed a new Pop-Tart and ate it cold. It wasn't too bad. Just not warm and gooey. Then I pulled on my sneakers and walked outside. What I saw made me stop dead in my tracks.

I live on a busy street, right across from the grocery store. Not the most beautiful place to live, but convenient. But right now it looked like hell had broken loose. The cars were horribly entangled at the stoplight like everyone had forgotten to stop except for one person. I walked forward tentatively, wondering if anyone was stuck. There were about 10 cars in the wreckage, and the motors were still running. But when I looked in through one of the windows, no one was inside. Strangely, the doors were still in place. What was going on here? I looked at the least mangled car. The seatbelts were still buckled, and there was a coffee spill on the seat. There was no blood or sign of life anywhere, but there was also no sign of death. It was like everyone had just disappeared.

I ran across the street to the store, distressed. I forced open the door—the power was still gone. The inside was a bit messy, but completely deserted. Jars of mayonnaise and cartons of eggs were broken open and bottles of milk were lying on their sides on the floor in one aisle; bags of flour and sugar were split open in another. I ran up and down the aisles, to see if there was a clean-up crew somewhere, someone to ask what was happening. But there was no one. I shouted, but all I heard was an echo. Somewhere in the distance a single dog barked.

-

I decided to go home and wait out the craziness. Inside on the chair was the book I had been reading for a school assignment, called *Surviving*. It was a pretty fun book, about how to survive on a deserted island. But now it kind of depressed me. I would rather be on a deserted island than be here, because at least then I would know there were people out there. I read it anyway, noting that some of the stuff might help if everybody actually had disappeared. I did this after freaking out in my bedroom; of course, I'm not *that* level-headed. I went into the kitchen after reading through it, and realized something. *The power is off,* I thought to myself, *which means no one is at the power station. It* also *means that all the food is going to spoil, and that water might not run, and the stove probably won't work.* I was being logical, but it still didn't make sense. Why would people disappear in the first place? *No time to think about that now. I just have to survive, like the book says, and hope for the best.* I laughed to myself. *Maybe I'll get extra credit.*

I walked out the door and back to the supermarket. This time I went straight to the candy aisle. On the ground was a little girl's hat with a daisy tucked into the side. I sank to my knees and cried. What had happened? Why had it happened? Why her? Why anyone? But most of all, why me? I had done nothing wrong. I have a 3.8 GPA, I help out at the local homeless shelter, and clean up parks. I used to be a girl scout! I quit after I got an entire box of cookies smashed in my hair by a boy scout, but still. Why me?

I screamed, and the hot, wet, tears started streaming down my face. My arms swept boxes of gum and candied nuts off the shelves and onto the ground. I got up and ran to the aisle where the spray paint was kept and got a couple cans, and then went to the front of the building. I drew a massive picture of a girl in a daisy hat, with a single tear staining her face. Beside it I wrote "In memory of the little girl I never met. I am here, and I remember you, I keep you in my heart." I went inside, grabbed a carton of ice cream, and went home.

-

After I ate my ice cream and made myself a frozen pizza (with my pizza oven), I made a list of all the things that I would have to do if this... "situation" was permanent. I came up with this:

Shelter:
1. Warmth (wood burning stove, I have that)
2. Protection (lock door, maybe find a gun?)
3. Food (I'll make another list)
Food:
1. Perishables will have to be eaten first
2. Cans will have to be cataloged for expiration dates
3. Garden will have to be grown

4. Animals caught, domesticated (break into farm? Lucy from down the street had, like, a thousand chickens)
5. Wood burning stove will have to be stocked up with wood

I decided that all of this was fairly manageable, so I set off to do it. I found a solar power section in the store. Apparently I am really lucky, because there were solar powered fridges and freezers, along with other household appliances. Maybe I wouldn't have to get sick from eating too much ice cream. But there were only two freezers, and they weren't very big. They would hold maybe 60 gallon jugs together. And then there was the problem of getting them to my house.... Maybe I could just wire them up here? This could be my little storage area. I set them up after an hour of fiddling with wires and stood back to look at what I had made. In front of me were 2 freezers, 3 refrigerators, and a dryer. Sadly, the only thing missing was a washer. And a shower. And maybe a *dish*washer. But I was content for now; I knew this find would most likely save my life sometime in the future.

I should probably get the food into these before it all spoils. I thought to myself. I ran to the freezer section. There were frozen pizzas, ice cream, vegetables, meats, and many other things. I decided I would fill one freezer halfway with delicacies – popsicles, lunchables, and the like. The rest of it I filled with meat: steak, chicken, pork; and cheeses. The other freezer got milk and more meat but mostly bread. Rye, whole wheat, whole grain, white, 20 seed, wonder bread, sourdough, banana, zucchini, and even monkey bread.

After that I got some of those locking cupboards, like the ones you see on TV, and I filled them with all kinds of stuff, mostly for baking. Lots of sugar, too, and to keep ants and other creatures out I put them in Ziploc bags. I filled a total of three cupboards (they were really really big cupboards. Really big.) It was getting late, so I grabbed a mattress and a new pair of pajamas. I looked around and found the most expensive bed set. It was worth $450. I slept on that. It wasn't any nicer than my bed at home.

-

I woke up fresh and alert. The day passed quite quickly; I had a lot to do. I put up a fence in front of the store to keep animals out and planted some seeds I had found in the garden section. I washed my hair in the display tub after heating a bottle of water in the fire pit. I had it made here! My hair smelled fresh and I ate my fill of meats and perishable items that were in the refrigerator, because I knew that they wouldn't last long here. I went to bed with a stomachache. I had eaten too much.

The next day I woke up scared. I had had a nightmare where the little girl started crying tears of blood. I reached out for her, but she fell away like sand. Then I heard a noise. It was a blood-curdling screech. I shot up in bed; I was still at the store, but there was something else with me, I could tell. Pulling myself up slowly with the bedpost, I looked around for a weapon. I cursed myself for not grabbing a gun in the hunting department. Not that I know how to use a gun. I would probably end up shooting myself in the foot. A pocketknife would probably be better for me; I use them when I'm camping. The screech rang out again, louder than the first. Closer. I began to look around frantically for anything that I could defend myself with. I would have been content with a big stick, but I saw something better.

A metal pipe, bent a bit. I don't know where it came from, but I was thankful for it. I raised it above my head, like a baseball bat. I heard the screech again and tried to find where it was coming from. I pinpointed it to be coming from aisle 3.

A bird flew in. I swung the pole and connected. I had had nothing to worry about. I was safe here, and nothing would stop me from surviving. At least not right now. I sat back down on my bed and closed my eyes. Maybe I would sleep in today.

Death by Pumpkins
Jonathan Huang

One day in a small town called Bandon, Oregon, something extraordinary happened. It all started with Ms. Stephen on her way to her farm. Ms. Stephen was a diminutive middle aged lady. But her wit was faster than a cheetah and sharper than a sword. She was the best farmer around, despite her size, and could tell when it was the best time to plant all the different types of crops. Although she was shorter than the average person, she had hard, muscled arms and calloused hands from long days working on the farm. She was also a very stubborn person and liked to do things her way.

As she was driving toward her farm, she thought about how a week ago her crops started to die, before she could harvest them. She was very frustrated at why this happened but could not find out the reason. She looked at the dirt quality, the amount of water, and even put a tall fence to keep out people or animals. But today she would be prosperous. She had recently found out that a new and improved fertilizer had been invented. The fertilizer would help crops grow faster and be more resistant to the environment. The new fertilizer would also make the crops more abundant. As she continued to drive, she saw a man walking along the road. She drove next to him and pulled over. When she got out, she proceeded to say, "Do you need a lift?"

"I do not need such a gift, but I think that you do," he said. The man was also a middle aged person of average height. He wore the dirtiest clothes and smelled rotten. His shoes were tattered and ripped like someone who had been walking on foot for days. Also, he carried no bags or luggage with him. His face was weather beaten and his hands had many callouses and scars. His hair was black and oily that seemed it hadn't been washed for numerous days. But the thing that surprised her most was his eyes. When you looked at his eyes you could see brilliant, transparent crystals dancing in his eyes. His eyes were also of the bluest shade she had ever seen. They had a mysterious look, like something was bothering him. His sing-songy voice interrupted her thoughts and he said "If you are not greedy you will go far and live in happiness too."

"I do not need a gift," she said, but only got a silent reply. He had immediately vanished like wind blowing in the air and in his place was a small pumpkin seed. She reached down and picked it up and put it in her pocket. Then she walked back to her truck and continued to drive toward her farm.

When she arrived, she opened her gate and surveyed the scene. It was disastrous and indeed a farmer's worst nightmare. All the crops had died, which created a huge mess. Because there were no more seeds available to plant, she proceeded to clean up the entire mess. The whole entire farm was littered with huge amounts of dead and rotten vegetables and it was starting to smell bad. "A year's worth of work whisked away in a couple of days," she said as she sighed. So that's what she did for the entire day, cleaning up patches of dead plants crops. As the day went by she completely forgot about her little pumpkin seed. She only remembered it as she was walking back to her truck to head home. Because the little seed fell out as she opened the gate. "What's this?" she said and remembered that strange man. She said, "Well, I am not going to waste this seed and this could be a good time to test out that fertilizer." As she was holding it, she noticed something that she had not before. The seed felt warm to the touch and was vibrating. Very intrigued, she planted the seed with some of the fertilizer and then left. But out of the corner of her eye she saw a glow. She immediately looked back at the place where it was planted but saw nothing. So she resumed walking back to her truck.

The next day, she woke up early to see the progress of her little seed. When she got there she was astounded. The little seed had grown into a large, plump-looking pumpkin overnight. The pumpkin was the healthiest and biggest pumpkin she had ever grown. She wondered what made it grow so fast and immediately thought of the new and improved fertilizer. Then without a second thought, she drove to town as fast as she could to find more seeds. She could only find couple seeds to buy. "This will have to do," she said disappointed.

When she woke up, she was very anxious to find out what would happen to those little seeds she had planted yesterday. She got dressed and very rapidly drove to her farm. The results were not what she expected. The seeds that she had planted yesterday had not even grown a bit. Then it came to her; "It must be that seed the mysterious man gave me. Not the fertilizer." Then, immediately, she got a knife and started to carve it. But then it started to glow. At first she was fearful. But then, curiosity overcame fear and she proceeded to cut the stem off. As she moved her knife closer and closer to the stem, the light increased its brightness. A sense of recklessness overcame her and she quickly cut of the stem. Then suddenly the light stopped.

She looked down; there was a cut stem and that was all. She looked around. Nothing had changed about the farm or even the landscape. Relief washed over her as she realized that nothing had changed, and she continued to cut out the inside. Once she found all the seeds from the lone pumpkin, she then planted them in her farm. After that she inspected her work and was happy. Finally she drove back home.

As the next day approached she went back to her farm to her pumpkins. To her astonishment her theory had been correct. All the seeds that she had carved out from the original pumpkin had grown in one day and were very healthy looking. So as the week went on she repeated this process for all the pumpkins she had planted. Soon she was gaining a lot of money and becoming very rich because of the "magical" pumpkins. With more money, she soon expanded her farm and bought a new house. With riches also came covetousness. She bought many new and expensive things with the money she earned. But as she got richer and richer, she started to show off her wealth arrogantly, and became greedier for luxurious and expensive things. Word soon got out that Ms. Stephen had magical farming abilities because of her excellent quality in pumpkins.

As the end of the year approached she decided she could host a party where all the residents of her town could come and witness her farm and to also to eat the pumpkin. She also wanted to show off her wealth and power to everyone else in her arrogance. But she needed extra help for some extraordinary pumpkins (she had now over 50 pumpkins in all different sizes). So the next day she sent out invitations to the entire town to help her set up her party.

So the next day, the entire town drove to her farm to look upon the huge pumpkin. Piles and piles of cars parked next to her farm; the number was countless. "I did not know that there were this many people in town," she said with a stupefied face. As the people got out, they all started pointing and murmuring with mystified and curious faces. Then she loudly announced, "Welcome to my farm! Since all of you are here, why don't we get started?" So she organized everyone to different jobs. The youngest helped with the decorations. The teens helped with hanging up the lights. The mothers helped clean up the entire farm while the men went out to the entire farm and started to get knives to carve out all the pumpkins. A man came over to her because he had noticed a faint glow coming from the pumpkin. She came over and indeed did see that the pumpkin was glowing.

"Why is this so familiar?" she said aloud. "I feel like I have seen this before." Finding no connection, she dismissed the fact with a wave of her hand and continued her work. Soon, they were done. The whole process took the entire day with the help of everyone in town.

They started the party soon after nightfall. As Ms. Stephen was surveying her work, she was filled with content with the accomplishments they had done. Everyone was happy and enjoying the pumpkin pie. The women were laughing about an old joke while the men talked about sports and football. The children were all running around with glee as they played tag and other games. As she was walking around, she noticed that there was one pumpkin left that they had not noticed. It was a small and average looking pumpkin compared to the ones she had planted before. Getting out her knife, she went on the cut it. But before she could touch a strong wind tore through the earth like never before.

The farm was in complete Armageddon. The wind soon turned into a devastating storm with branches being ripped of their trunk like ripping paper. Babies and children started to cry with terrified faces. Likewise, all the adults were pushed to the ground like ragdoll puppets. A single voice penetrated through the storm. It was loud and booming like many thunderstorms and said "Ms. Stephen, you have not followed my rules with the seed but have taken advantage over it to become greedy and ravenous in power and in objects. Therefore I punish you by taking away your gift." Then, her entire farm was torn apart. Her barn was wiped away by a wind stronger than anything recorded. Followed by her farm were her house and all the costly and valuable things. They were swallowed up by the earth; and finally her small pumpkin that she still had disintegrated right in her arms. Then, with a calamitous and loud bang the chaos ended.

After the cataclysmic event, all the people woke up to find the farm in disaster, but no one could remember what happened. No one could even find Ms. Stephen, and to this day people have never known where she could have gone. Some say that she fled the city—even the country—because of her disastrous party. Other people say that she vanished into thin air and got whisked into the sky. Maybe that is why today, Bandon, Oregon is nicknamed the Storm Capital of the World.

My Crazy Life in Los Angeles
Marissa Friedman

I rolled out of bed, remembering it was my first day at Belmont High. The morning breeze coming in through my window hit me, sending goose bumps down my spine. I pulled the string to raise the blinds above my bed, revealing the bright California sun. I immediately checked the alarm clock next to my bed to make sure I would have enough time to shower before school. My phone lit up as I pulled it off the small charging station and headed for the bathroom. I jumped in the shower and quickly washed my sandy blond hair. In ten minutes I was in and out and deciding what to wear for my first day. I pulled open the drawers of my dresser and stared blankly at the shirts and pants in front of me. I decided on dark wash skinny jeans and a light gray t-shirt. Once I was dressed, I went back into the bathroom to make sure my hair looked okay. I grabbed my phone off the white tiled counter, and ran out of my room, grabbing my backpack and sweatshirt on the way down the stairs.

"PETER!" My mom shouted from the kitchen, clearly annoyed that I wasn't downstairs yet. Since we had moved here, my mom and I haven't exactly been getting along. Our family was constantly moving because of mom's job, but this time it was different. I had finally been in one place for a year, made some really good friends, but of course, we had to move again. This was probably my tenth move since second grade.

Yesterday, mom announced that she would wait for me to leave for my first day at Belmont High, but didn't budge when I told her I would be fine to get ready on my own. She still doesn't seem to get that I was almost fifteen. I could get dressed and eat breakfast by myself.

"I'm coming, Mom!" I quickly grabbed the cereal out of the pantry and poured milk into a bright orange bowl. Of course, knowing how clumsy I was, I ended up pouring the milk all over the counter and missing the bowl altogether. Quickly, I ran across to the other side of the kitchen to grab a few paper towels to wipe up my mess. I tried again to pour the milk in the bowl, this time succeeding. The breakfast I enjoyed was in no way unique, but that's what I liked, and to some extent I liked to blend in and just go with the flow. I glanced over to the clock - 8:08 am. I realized the bus would be leaving my stop in seven minutes, I gathered my backpack, binders, and textbooks and headed for the door. I decided on leaving early so that I would have plenty of time to stop and get a coffee on my way to the bus.

Surely Mom had either the hairdryer or shower on, so I didn't even try to tell her I was leaving. The bus picked me up five blocks over from my house, but the walk to the stop was short. Our new neighborhood had a nice homey feel. We lived just outside of Los Angeles, so while walking to the bus, I passed other houses, a small pizza shop, and a coffee shop. A chilly walk and a coffee later, I arrived at the bus stop.

The ride to school was only about ten minutes, but it felt like forever. The same thoughts ran through my head each second. Over and over again. I was nervous for my first day, and I prayed every minute that it went well. After a couple more stops in other nearby neighborhoods, we arrived at the school. We had just pulled up when I realized I didn't have too much to be scared of. As it sank in more and more, I realized I would easily be able to make it through the day, and maybe even enjoy myself a little bit. The school was pretty small, so at least I would have a chance of not getting lost.

Finally, I got off the bus and began walking towards the school. Sure, I was nervous, but I was also determined to make the best of my time here, because as I had learned before, nothing lasts very long with my family. I began to walk toward the large door of the school, pulling out my planner, which had a map that would help me find my locker.

I opened my locker on the third try, and got out my materials for my first period class. I looked back to the map that I had been given on the first day and began to walk to the little "1" that had been written there by the secretary signaling my first class.

I had just turned a corner, when I saw someone who caught my eye. At first, she was just another person in the hall, but soon after my brain had processed what I saw, my head flew back around to see her again. She was absolutely beautiful. She had long dark hair that was straight and fell just above her waist. She was wearing dark wash skinny jeans, the same Chuck Taylors as mine, and a light pink Abercrombie sweatshirt. I realized I was staring, so I quickly plastered a smile on my face. Just as I did, she looked up and waved shyly at me. Her perfect complexion seemed to smile as she waved, and she quickly threw her head back laughing at some joke her friends had made seconds earlier. They stepped in front of her, blocking her from my view.

I continued on to find my first class, which was science. It only took me a minute to find it, and when I did, I slowly entered the room, taking in my surroundings carefully. The room was filled with neat lines of chairs and desks. There was a white board in the front, with markers neatly lined along the bottom. In the front corner, a larger, more official looking desk was placed with a large black chair behind it. There were a few people already in their seats, but more than half of the seats were still empty. I picked one closer to the back on the left side. Five minutes passed before the rest of the class was seated and the teacher started talking. The teacher introduced herself as Ms. Davis and quickly began discussing the syllabus for the first semester.

The day was long, but it went smoothly. I made it through all eight of my classes, talking only to a few guys who sat near me in science. After a full day of classes, I was exhausted. I rode the bus home and was greeted at the door by my mom and little sister.

"Hi mom, hi Amy," I said quietly as I walked in. It was the first day, so we didn't have any homework. I sat down at the desk in my room and began to doodle. I drew a couple of random shapes, but after only a minute of doing so, my mind began to wander to the girl I saw in the hall today. *Who was she? Was she even my age? What was her name?*

I needed to know more about my mystery girl. I don't know why, but something about her was intriguing, and it was not just that she was pretty, or that she could effortlessly light up a whole hall of people. Sighing, I pushed away the thoughts of this mystery girl, plugged my phone into my little dock on my nightstand, and tried to get some sleep. It took me awhile to fall asleep, though. She was all I could think about, and I couldn't seem to get her off my mind.

I woke up in the morning, tired from my endless thinking and doodling late into the night. Again, I washed my hair, grabbed my cereal, and left.

The second day at Belmont went well, but certainly not perfect. By then end of the day, I knew who my mystery girl was: Madison Quinlan. I rode the bus back home, and walked in to find that my parents weren't home, but my sister was. My sister was 13, just over two years younger than me. She had long, straight, blond hair that hit a few inches below her shoulder. My sister and I were really close, so she talked to me about guys she liked, and I talked to her about the girls I liked. "Hey Amy!" I yelled up the stairs. I slowly made my way over to the kitchen to grab an apple, and then ran up the stairs towards her room.

"Hi Peter! How was your day?" she asked, clearly excited about something that happened during hers.

"It was really good. How was yours?" I asked, not really interested in what she was saying. I wanted to know what to do about this girl, but I didn't want to annoy my sister. She gets annoyed really easily, so I decided to wait on asking her for advice.

"Good," she said slowly.

"I have to go get ready for basketball, but I will be back in three hours," I said as I got up off her bed. I went into my room and pulled open my drawer revealing my athletic clothes. I grabbed my basketball shorts and a t-shirt, scooped up my basketball on the way out the door, and hopped on my bike. My team met regularly at a park a five-minute bike ride away from my house. We were a summer and fall team, so we stayed together both seasons. We played for a few hours each night, but as the sun began to set, we headed home. After practice, I walked up to my room, grabbed my computer and logged on to Facebook. I had a few notifications, but nothing important. I quickly logged back off, and went downstairs to retrieve my backpack.

After reading part of a novel my mom picked up from the library, I was pretty tired, and decided to go to bed. It took me over an hour to fall asleep because again, I couldn't get Madison off my mind. She was beautiful, and her smile lit up the room. Eventually I fell asleep, but my thoughts about her continued on through my dreams until I awoke to the obnoxious beeping of my alarm clock.

I followed the same schedule I had followed yesterday and the day before. I jumped into the shower, and then slipped on some clothes. After standing in front of the mirror for at least 10 minutes, I started gathering up my homework. As I ran out of my room, I quickly poked my head into Amy's room to say goodbye. She answered with a quick hug and a simple wink, and immediately got back to doing her hair.

The next morning, as I walked into my first period English class, a diagram of our new seats was on the board in front of us. My name happened to be right next to Maddie, her friends a few seats away. I was definitely excited about my new seat, but I was nervous as well. I walked through the class to my seat, and sat down to wait for Maddison.

She set her books down on the desk beside me. "Hey. So you're Madison?" My voice sounded really shaky, but hopefully she wouldn't notice.

"Yeah, that's me. And I assume you're Peter?"

I open my mouth to speak again, but Mr. Morris had already began, "Take out your copies of 'To Kill a Mockingbird' and turn to page 83."

-

It had been a few days since I came to Belmont, and Maddie and I had talked non-stop in Mr. Morris's class. We played 20 questions, talked about our families, what we ate for breakfast, and pretty much anything in between. We both hated the book we were reading in class, *To Kill a Mockingbird,* so we just ignored the constant rambling from Mr. Morris. He didn't seem to notice, or if he did, he didn't care. Maddie and I were getting along really well. She seemed genuine and sweet, not like she was faking it or trying too hard. On top of it all, she always knew what would make me laugh at any given moment. I enjoyed our hour-long conversations, without any major interruptions.

Class had just ended, and as I was heading to my locker, I saw Maddie heading to hers as well. I decided now was the best chance I would get, so I made a move towards her locker. I walked up behind her, and gently tapped her shoulder. "Hi," my voice shook as I said it, but I wasn't quite sure why. I had talked to her for hours on end and this never happened. *Probably just nerves.* I thought to myself, trying my best to push them away.

"Hey," she answered in her perfect singsong voice.

"So, I know we just met," *oh crap, the nerves again,* "And we don't know each other very well yet," *my stomach was literally flipping upside down, but I continued on, probably rambling by now.* "But I was wondering if maybe you would want to do something sometime. With me." *Well that sounded stupid. 'Do something sometime. With me.' Really?* I smiled, hoping she didn't see how nervous I was or notice how stupid that sounded.

"Sure, I mean, yeah, I would like that," she said quickly. *Guess I'm not the only one who is nervous about this.*

"Great!" I practically screamed. *Why did I have to get so excited about something so small? It was just a small step out of many, but I managed to practically scream to the whole hall about how excited I was.* "Uh," I thought for a moment about what I was supposed to be doing after school. *Basketball. Too bad, my bros would have to wait; I have a date tonight.* "Is today okay? After school?"

"Yeah, after school is good." *YES!* Out of the corner of my eye, I saw her friends come up the stairs, but as soon as they saw us, they took a small step back.

"Alright. So I should pick you up?" *What kind of a question was that? Why did I just ask her if I should pick her up? Of course I should pick her up!* "I'll meet you here at 3:00."

"Okay, I'll meet you here."

"See you later, then," I smiled, hoping she wouldn't see exactly how excited I was, but I could feel she shared some of it.

"Bye," I turned around and heard her let out a small breath she seemed to have been holding the whole time. As I walked away, her friends let out a small laugh, surely at some little joke that I would never understand. They immediately walked past me and straight to Maddie. As soon as I rounded the corner, I ran over to the guys from my science class I was now friends with.

"Hi," They greeted me as I ran to my locker. I decided telling them about my date with Maddie was a bad idea because as soon as they found out, so would everyone else. It wasn't that I didn't want everyone to know; I just wasn't in the mood for sharing.

"Hi guys," I said, probably sounding a little too excited. Clearly, they caught on quicker than I would have liked.

"What's up with you?" Andy noticed my weird tone almost immediately.

"Nothing, why?" I said, trying my best to cover up my excitement, but failing miserably.

"I don't know, you sounded really excited about something." He sounded skeptical, but I still tried my best to cover my tracks. He quickly shrugged it off, picked his backpack up, and walked towards his next class.

The rest of the guys were just standing there staring at me. I didn't know what else to do, so I just walked past them towards my locker. I grabbed my binder and textbook for my next class, Social Studies, and began to walk there.

Class was boring, but I was still excited by the thought of Maddie and going on the date. All I had in the way of my date with her was one more class. I was counting down the minutes until we could finally leave. Nothing had really been going right until I got to school that first day and saw her. It had been hard on my sister and I when we moved because we had to leave all of our friends behind. Finally though, something was starting to go my way. I was excited to spend time alone with Maddie, and get to know her more.

Although my last class felt like five hours, it eventually ended. I ran to my locker, grabbed all my things, and walked slowly towards Maddie's locker. As she said bye to her friends, I walked up behind her. She turned around, and a flicker of shock spread across her face, but it slowly melted away into a pleasantly surprised look. "Hey, you ready to go?" I asked after giving her a minute to grab her stuff from her locker.

She quickly swung her backpack over her shoulder, kicked the locker closed with her foot and said, "Yep. Let's go." We slowly walked down the hall, side by side, heading towards my car. Who would have guessed that after my constant fighting with my mom about how I didn't want to move, I would end up with such a beautiful girl. As we approached the double doors, I took an extra step in front of Maddie to hold the door open for her. We continued walking towards the parking lot, and when we reached my car, again, I held the door open for her. Once she was in, I carefully pushed the door closed, and walked over to the driver's side thinking, *how did I manage to get such a perfect girl to go on a date with me?* I pulled out of the parking lot, and took a right, heading toward the secret location of our date.

Black Chuck Taylors
Lauren Auchterloine

You can tell a lot about a person by their shoes. It's the game I play when I walk down the school hallway every day. Four inch platform heels? Tori Anderson, the most popular girl in school, and dating the captain of the football team. Black combat boots? Alice Warman, always wears black and never talks to anyone. Flip-flops that show rainbow painted toenails? Lou Brooks, one of my best friends. I look up and smile as she skips over and loops her arm through mine.

"Were you lookin' at people's shoes again, Maddie? You know you're gonna trip eventually, right?" she asks in her sweet Southern accent. I laugh as we turn the corner and head to our shared locker. Lou spins in the combination and the metal door springs open, spilling out all of our shared memories. Picture strips from photo booths, envelopes covered with notes passed in class, and a CD of our favorite songs. We keep talking while we unload our too-heavy backpacks, and that's when I see him. Tall, blonde, very cute, and completely unfamiliar, a rare occurrence in a school as small as mine.

"Hey, who's that?" I whisper to Lou, casually flicking my eyes over to the boy.

Lou glances over her shoulder, then answers, "That's Peter Simmons. Transferred here from Lake Ridge. Today's his first day." Lou's mom is the administrator, so she always knows about new people before they're here. I look immediately to his shoes: black Chuck Taylors, identical to mine. My lips curve into a smile, and Lou squeals, jumping up and down.

"You think he's cute, don't you?" She leans in, eager to hear my verdict. I bump her with my hip, then scan the crowd for Peter. Our eyes meet, and I wave, catching a glimpse of his smile before turning away.

"Lou? You ready for some covert ops?" I say with a grin.

"Always am, sugar! What do you need from the Spy Extraordinaire?" She makes a finger gun and struck a pose.

"Okay. I need you to find out as much as you can about Peter Simmons, and tell me after school."

"Yes ma'am! I'm on it!" She skips off down the hall after Peter.

-

"So, did you dig up any dirt on Peter Simmons?" I ask Lou through a mouthful of popcorn. We are splayed out on the couch in my attic, which has been our "secret clubhouse" for years. With us is Mara, the third in our trio. Lou and I had just finished filling her in, and she was now just as eager as I was to hear Lou's news.

"Alright sugar. Here is a beginner's guide to Peter Simmons: he is sixteen years old, drives a blue Ford pickup, one of those old ones, like Toby's in Pretty Little Liars..."

"Lou! Focus, please." I love Lou, but she often tends to get sidetracked from the topic at hand.

"Sorry. Where was I? Oh yeah, blue Ford pickup, plays guitar in a band outside of school called Automaton, he uses Old Spice deodorant, he's an Aquarius, wears neither boxers or briefs..."

"Lou!" Mara and I cry. Lou laughs, "Okay, I made that one up. And I don't know his star sign. But everything else is true!" I sigh and flop back into the soft pillows of the couch and stare at the ceiling. The glow-in-the-dark stars that we stuck there when we were nine still spell out M+L+M. Lou is now dancing around the room singing, "Maddie's got a boyfriend! Maddie's got a boyfriend!" until Mara pegs her with a pillow.

"They aren't dating yet, Lou," Mara giggles. "They haven't even said a word to each other."

"Awww, why are you such a downer, Mar?" Lou flops down on the pillow with a sigh. "Why, I bet that with the combined ninja powers of us all, Peter Simmons will ask Maddie out within two weeks." She got a gleam in her eye, which Mara and I know all too well is her betting face.

"Fine, I'm in. A pedicure says it takes three weeks at least," Mara calls over her shoulder as she grabs a notebook and sharpie off the shelf. Lou is famous for her bets, a fame rivaled only by that of her cheating when she loses. The Official Book of Bets is our way of keeping track. Mara tosses it to me, and I flip to the next blank page.

"October 8th. Lou bets that Madison will be asked out by Peter Simmons within two weeks," I read aloud. "Mara bets a pedicure that it will take at least three. Everyone agree?" I ask.

"Yeah," says Mara.

"Absolutely!" cries Lou, as she tosses a piece of popcorn high into the air and catches it neatly in her mouth. I look back down at my friends' prophecies. With their laughter in my ears, I silently add my own to the list. *She hopes within the week.*

-

The next morning when I walk into first period English, I look up on the board at the new seating chart.. I scan for my name, until I see 'Peter Simmons'. I allow myself a second of fantasies, then I see the name in the next tiny square: Madison Quinlan. My eyes whip up, finding him and the empty seat next to him. After handing the chart back to Mr. Morris, I walk over to my new seat and sit down. Peter glances up, then smiles.

"Hey. So you're Madison?" It sounded like he remembered me waving to him.

"Yeah, that's me. And I assume you're Peter?" I said, using all of my self-control to remain calm.

Peter opens his mouth, but before he can speak, Mr. Morris growls to the class, "Take out your copies of 'To Kill a Mockingbird' and turn to page 83."

As the room fills with the sound of flipping pages and whispers, I glance over at Peter, and find his beautiful green eyes. He grins, and I flash a smile back. *Thank you, thank you, thank you Mr. Morris.*

-

Three days of English class smiles later, I feel a tap on my shoulder while at my locker. I turn around, expecting Lou or Mara, but it's Peter.

"Hi," he says.

"Hey," I answer, as I lean back against my locker.

"So, I know we just met, and we don't know each other very well yet, but I was wondering if maybe you would want to do something sometime. With me." Peter smiles, but I see in his eyes that he's nervous.

"Sure, I mean, yeah, I would like that," I stammer. *What a pair we are,* I think, *both more nervous than a third grader at Show-and-Tell.*

"Great!" Peter blurts, and then his tan cheeks redden just a bit. "Uh, is today okay? After school?"

I can't believe what's happening. "Yeah, after school is good." Yes, after school is definitely good. Just wait until I tell Lou and Mara.

"Alright. So I should pick you up? I'll meet you here," Peter says.

"Okay," I smile, "I'll meet you here." Yes! This is really happening.

"See you later, then," Peter says.

"Bye," I squeak. He walks away, and about 0.5 seconds later Lou and Mara are in front of me, talking excitedly over each other.

"Oh my God-"

"What just happened?"

"Then we saw him talking to you-"

"Did he ask you out?"

"GIRLS!" I shout. They stop babbling. I took a deep breath. "Peter just asked me out. We're gonna do something after school! He's gonna meet me here then we'll go somewhere an – oh my God."

There was complete silence for one second, two seconds.

"I knew it! I knew it! You, darlin', now owe me a pedicure," Lou boasts, pointing at Mara. "Haha! Who called it? I did! Oh, sugar, I'm so happy for you!" She flings her arms around me and pulls me into a crazy victory dance, which Mara soon joins us in. But she jumps back almost immediately.

"Okay, girls. It's 1:45. Maddie will be going on her date with Peter at 3:00. Next class is Spanish. Lou, that's your time. Give her confidence lessons, 'cause you're the most confident person I know."

"Aww, stop it. You're making me blush," Lou giggles.

"Alright," Mara continues, "After that is P.E. Mr. Walters never takes roll, so that's my time. I'm gonna make you even prettier than you already are. Peter will never know what hit him."

I laugh more than I usually would, then say, "Okay. Let's do this." Lou ninja kicks the locker door closed, then links her arm through mine. Mara follows suit on my other arm, and we start off down the hall.

2:56. I stick my phone back in my pocket. Lou, Mara and I are in the bathroom down the hall from my locker, waiting for the bell to ring. 2:57.

"Madison, darlin', put the phone away," Lou says, prying the phone from my fingers. I sigh loudly and sit down on top of my backpack, careful not to mess up the outfit and hair that Mara has created for me: light wash jeans that make my legs look amazing, a beautiful royal blue sweater, and, of course, my Chuck Taylors. My hair is pulled up in a high bun with a few wisps draped artfully around my face, and my makeup is perfect.

"Come on Maddie, don't freak out on me now! Zen Master Madison," Mara reminds me.

And then the bell rings.

I spring to my feet. With a deep breath, I pick up my bag and head out. Lou and Mara are right behind me. I open the locker door and start replacing the books I need with the ones I don't. Mara does a last minute touch up on my hair, and Lou gives me one last hug. Then out of the corner of my eye, I see Peter walking towards me. He looks just as good as I hope I do, in a light grey t-shirt and dark wash skinny jeans. I pretend not to see him, then turn to Lou and Mara.

"Good luck!" they say simultaneously, and walk away down the hall. I watch my best friends until they disappear in the crowd, then turn back to my locker. Peter is right in front of me.

"Hey. You ready?" he asks with a gorgeous smile.

I close my locker door, sling my bag onto my shoulder, and say, "Yep. Let's go." What a week could do. Before Peter I never thought that I would be the girl walking down the school hallway with the cutest boy there. But here we are. When we arrive at the double doors leading to the parking lot, Peter holds the door open like a proper gentleman.

We weave through the parked cars until we reach his car. It was exactly as Lou had described. Once again, Peter opens the door for me. I was beginning to forget how to open a door myself. Peter closes the door behind me, and walks around to his side of the car. I laugh out loud, doing a little dance of joy, but then the driver's side door opens and I stop dancing. Peter turns the key in the ignition and the truck rumbles to life. I felt the soothing vibrations through the soles of my Chucks, and looked over at Peter. He smiles, and presses his own Chuck Taylor-ed foot down on the gas, moving the truck and us forward into what was sure to be the best afternoon of my life.

What a Wonderful Day Indeed...
Caitlin Huang

"Lou, c'mon honey! We don't wanna be late for school again, do we? It's the first day of the week, hon, we need to be on time for once!" my mom shouted to me.

"I'm coming right down, Mama!" I cried back to her. I heard her start the engine of the car downstairs in the garage. No doubt my mom would be checking her watch every half a minute, and sighing to herself as the time slowly went by. I threw on my classic outfit: a loose flowy shirt, my silver key necklace studded with red jewels, light wash skinny jeans, and a pair of well-worn cowboy boots, brown leather, and pointed at the tips. We lived in an average house that was built ages ago. It looked like a sad, melting pile of wood when we first saw it. The stairs creaked a low tune, like a grandpa snoring softly in the middle of the night. The grass had all died away, leaving a pale, dusty miniature desert guarding and watching over the house, keeping all life forms away.

My dad, a builder, had rebuilt the house back to a clean and crisp place, perfect for housing a family of three. It took a while to make the house what it is today, but in the end, all the blood, sweat, and tears were all worth it. Now, the house is painted a creamy yellow, with white trim. A white picket wood fence lines the border of the house and the front lawn. Out in the front yard, the grass had been brought back, swaying slightly in the gentle whisper of the breeze. Tall red roses dance and decorate the front line of the house, stopping where the pathway had been set. Large, round stones curved this way and that, lead up to the main door. And the best part, the front door, is a deep royal red, and has a reflective gold handle, that is so simple, but made you smile every time you stood in front of it.

I slung my backpack over my shoulder, and rushed into the car. We got to school just two minutes before the late bell rang. My mom, being the administrator of my school, slipped inside the door to her office, and disappeared. But not before she blew me a goodbye kiss. I skipped happily over to my best friend, Madison Quinlan. She was staring at the bottom of people's feet.

"Were you looking at people's shoes again, Maddie?" I teased her. "You know you're gonna trip eventually, right?" She chuckles to herself and shakes her head. To Maddie, shoes are the ultimate statement of who you are. She links her slender arm through mine, and together, we walk over to our shared locker. I unlock the lock, and open our locker door. Inside, the many pictures and strips from photobooths decorate and cover the locker door. A light-up studded mirror sits in the middle, and glittery magnets hold love notes and secret letters in place.

As we close our locker door, we both turn our heads around in time to see a boy with a blonde clean-cut hairstyle. He looked like he just stepped out of a Sports Illustrated magazine. His well-muscled and tan arms and legs stood out, as he was wearing black Chuck Taylors, the exact same as Maddie's. Ha, that was funny. *Twinsies*, I think in my head. I side glance to Maddie and I watch as her eager eyes twinkle and sparkle as she studies him. He turns his head, sees her staring, and smiles back to her.. Her face turns a deep pink, and I feel her hand find mine, and squeeze it, nearly taking out my circulation. He smiles and his eyes too, take her in. After he turns his head away, I feel Maddie's grip on my hand loosen slightly, and the slight exhale of her body. I raise my eyebrows and stare at her; *it's always going to be the new kids, huh?* I thought to myself. If you know your friend well enough, you can usually predict what they will do even before they know it themselves. And I had a sneaking suspicion that somehow, Peter and Maddie would end up together.

"That's Peter Simmons," I informed her, studying her face closely, and narrowing my eyes. My mom was the administrator of our school, so of course, I knew every student that got enrolled.

"He is one pretty good looking guy, I gotta tell you. And you know that I don't say that just to anybody that I see. Weird. Huh. Is he in our grade? I wonder if he's going to be any of our classes?" she murmured quietly to herself. I raised my eyebrows and smiled suspiciously. Maddie had the highest standards for boys and I was shocked that she even made that comment. In the past years, Maddie has caught the eye of many boys, and each time, she turned them down sadly, shaking her head. I couldn't blame the boys for liking her though. Maddie has long luscious dark brown, perfectly sculpted wavy hair that stopped just in the middle of her back. Her perfect lips were always in a flirty pout that was always covered in a thin layer of lip gloss. Her facial features *perfect*, even without makeup. She wasn't short, but she wasn't a giant. Being five foot five, Maddie was the "average" in a regular tenth grade class. Her bright eyes shone with excitement, but also had a sense of confidence and calmness. She held herself up well, with an attitude that also didn't hurt. I was lucky to have her as my best friend. Without her, I would have no idea where I would be in life. Maddie has always helped me with my life decisions and problems. If I called her at 3 in the morning, she would be there to talk to me, until she knew that the problem was solved. Maddie was too nice like that, and also, too nice to other people too. She always put herself second before others, and that is what I love most about her.

"Can you like, um, maybe, you know...find out more about... Peter?" she asked tentatively.

"Of course sugar, anything for my best friend here!" I called back to her as I skipped down the hall towards Peter. As I stalked the long, white hallways, taking my time as I walked, I knew that this could be the beginning of something new.

-

After school, we met at Maddie's house, and sat in the attic, eating popcorn. Mara, another friend from school, was there too, sprawled out on the couch, her legs propped up on the small, wooden table that sat in front of it.

"Come on Lou, just spill it all out already!" Maddie urged. Her eager and impatient eyes watched me, and begged me to tell her what I had successfully found out so far. I leaned back into the pillow and stared up at the ceiling and smiled slightly. We were listening to Carrie Underwood, since I insisted. I love country music, and I have always grown up hearing it, so naturally, it was my favorite genre of music. Maddison played the piano, and of course, studied classical. But she listens to pop too. Mara on the other hand, just loved music in general, and liked any song that she came across.

"Okay. Beginner's guide to the ever famous Peter Simmons...He is 16 years old, drives an old blue pickup, just like the one Toby from Pretty Little Liar's..."

"Lou, come *on*, focus here!" Maddie impatiently said. One thing you should know about me is that I tend to get sidetracked easily and I have a very short attention span. Not really a good combination, when you're the daughter of the administrator of your school, and are expected to be the role model.

"Okay. Where was I? Oh yeah; blue pickup, Old Spice deodorant, he's an Aquarius..." I trailed off and smiled evilly like a villain in a superhero comic book. ."..and he wears neither boxers or briefs," I said between smirks.

"LOU!" Mara and Maddie both shout. I double over laughing.

"Okay, fine. I made that last part up," I reassure them. Suddenly feeling a surge of excitement, I get up onto my feet and dance around the room, yelling, *Madison's got a boyfriend, Madison's got a boyfriend!*

"Lou, they aren't dating *quite* yet, you know." Mara tells me.

"Aw, Mara, don't be such a pessimist. I bet that this cutie Peter will definitely have asked Maddie-bear out by the end of two weeks. If he does, you owe me a good, high-quality pedicure, hon," I dared her.

At school, I am known for my bets. I have bets with anyone, anywhere. No matter what it is about, or where we are, bets are just "my thing." The next day we arrived at school, my mom and I went about our usual routine: we rushed to school, got there about two minutes before the late bell rang, and my mom slipped back into her office, ready to make the morning announcements over the P.A system. I looked around for Mara and Maddie, and walked with them to Mr. Morris's class and sat down in between them, which was my preferred seat. But by Thursday, we would have a new seating arrangement, as said by our teacher.

I walked into Mr. Morris's class the next day, hoping that Maddie, Mara, and I would be sitting close to each other, and that just maybe, hopefully, Peter would be close too. As I glanced at the whiteboard, searching for my name, and I immediately saw Maddie to my left, and Peter to her immediate left also, with Mara, in front of us. I squealed and snapped my fingers in a Z formation, jumping slightly up and down with excitement. *This was just too much of a coincidence* I thought. I looked over to Maddie and Mara, and they both smiled back at me excitedly, their eyes bright, and I knew that they were in on it too. We all rushed to our seats just as Peter walks into the room. Maddie turns her head, and a faint smile plays on her lips as Peter looks around the room, and starts to walk towards us.

"So you're Maddie, right?" Peter asked her.

"Uh, yeah. You're... Peter?" Maddie echoed back.

"Sure am." Peter replied. He gave Mara and I a short, quick nod of acknowledgement.

I give Maddie a wink, and tip my cowboy hat at her while Mara nods her head approvingly. For the rest of the class period, I watched as Maddie and Peter chattered away like sneaky little squirrels, playing 20 Questions, leaving the rest of the world behind them. The rest of the days passed, with Madison and Peter losing themselves in their conversation, while the teacher babbled on about the book *To Kill a Mockingbird.* Mara looked at them, then chuckles and rolls her eyes. I laugh, and shrug back at her. *As long as she's happy.* I thought to myself. *I really hope that my darlin' will finally meet her man. She deserves it more than anyone.*

-

A couple days later, Mara and I were coming up the stairs from recess to find Peter and Maddie talking by her locker. I frowned at Mara, and she frowned too, equally confused as I was. He leaned one shoulder onto the locker, his thumbs jacked into his pockets, movie star style. Mara started to

127

proceed further, taking a step, but I thrust out my hand, and set the back of it against her stomach and signaled for her to wait. We both backtracked a couple steps, just so that they were barely out of our view. Maddie's eyes seemed eager and excited, her face flushing a deep pink, while Peter's nervous feet kept rocking back and forth, heel to toe. I watch as he gives her a short nod, and then waves goodbye. As soon as he leaves, both of us run up to Maddie, our shoes squeaking from the rain outside, and demanding her to tell us what happened.

"Madison Quinlan! What just happened there?" Mara demanded.

"Darlin, I have never seen you so nervous and red in my entire life, girl. What happened?" I screeched.

"Did he finally ask you out Maddie-bear?" Mara exclaimed, jumping up and down, barely holding in her excitement.

"HE DID, didn't he, sugar?" I demanded.

"*GIRLS,*" Maddie shouted at us, laughing. "Calm *down*....and maybe. Fine...yes, he did."

"*I* KNEW *IT. SEE? I WAS RIGHT. I knew that he would ask her out before two weeks was over!* I am one good psychic, huh? Someone over here owes me a pedicure!" I told them, coughing in between words, winking at Mara. Maddie just leaned back into her locker, and shook her head, putting her hand over her forehead.

"So basically," Maddie started, "he just asked me out and we're going somewhere after school, and he's meeting up with me here at 3, and he's going to take me somewhere. I don't really know where though...."she trails off.

A moment of silence passes between all three of us, and then...

"AHHH! Maddie! I'm so happy for you girl, you, out of all people deserve him, because you're too nice not to be alone. But we need to cover this first: Madison's going to her date with Peter at 3. It's 1:45 right now, so that means we only have an hour and fifteen." Mara informed us.

"She'll need a new outfit, her makeup done, and some girl advice for this. Agreed, Lou?" she asked me.

"Of course hon'. But don't worry, we'll help you get ready, and in no time, you'll look like a fairytale princess!" I assured her. As we walked to our class, arm in arm, we smiled to ourselves, and I think to myself, *what a wonderful day...*

2:56 PM

"Maddie, hon, put the phone away girl!" I told her, taking the phone from her hands. It will only be a matter of time before we send Maddie off to her first date with Peter. While Mara busily worked through Maddie's hair and makeup, I stood off to the side, giving Maddie some confidence and relaxation advice. We were in the school bathroom, standing in front of the six feet by three feet spotless mirror. On the counter, there was makeup brushes, hairspray, hair brushes, a mini on-the-go curling iron, and all of our phones. It was a whirlwind of hair and makeup mayhem. I smiled at her brightly, encouraging her, and telling her she was beautiful, trying to keep her heart rate as low as possible. She wore light wash skinny jeans and a royal navy blue sweater. She sported a bun, with curled pieces hanging down, framing her stunning face. As we packed up our things from the bathroom and walked out the door, I heard Maddie take long deep, but shaky breaths.

"Maddie, hon, it's okay. You're going to be fine. It's alright..." I reassured her. She looked at me and gave me a smile of thanks. As Peter advanced towards us, coming down the narrow and long hallway, we quickly gave her hugs, and left silently. Maddie took one last deep breath, and as Mara and I walked away out the back door, we heard Peter say, *Hey, you ready?* With a reply of *course, let's go* from Maddie. We took a sneak peek back, and saw them both smiling, heading out in the other direction.

As Mara and I walked out the opposite door, the sunlight hit our face, shining a bright beam into our eyes. We put our hands up to our face, shielding them from the powerful rays. Across the student parking lot, I saw Peter open and close the door for her, and driving away to the yet to be discovered place. Mara and I stood there in the parking lot for a little while more, soaking up the glorious rays that fit perfectly with the mood. And as we got into the car, we looked at the parking space where Peter's car had been, and smiled happily to ourselves. *What a wonderful day*, I thought to myself. *What a wonderful day, indeed...*

-

I got to school a full five minutes early. Yeah. Big improvement from my two minutes, huh? But of course I would be here early. How long did you think I wanted to wait to hear what had happened? As usual, I walked over to the lamp post, our usual waiting spot. I glanced at my rainbow tie-dyed snap on watch. I sighed, and started to tap my toe, a habit I had yet to break, whenever I got impatient. Finally, I saw the familiar shimmering light blue BMW, pull into the parking lot. In the driver's seat, sat Maddie. Right next to her in shotgun, was Mara, touching up her lip gloss. I ran up to the car, too eager to wait. I probably looked like a psycho-maniac. My hair was flying behind me like a torn apart sail on a sailboat; dysfunctional and out of control. My mouth was slightly open, and my lips were plastered to my teeth, making my expression look a little more than crazy. I finally reached the car, and I was panting like a small puppy, eyes bright and eager, ready for playtime.

"So? Are you going to tell us what happened Madison?" I asked her, even though she probably already knew I was giving her no choice.

"Are you really giving me a choice here, Lou?" she replied back, smirking. I shook my head at her, telling her no.

"Mara, has she told *you* yet?" I asked.

"Nope. Not yet. She wanted to wait, to tell us both at the same time. Ugh, it has been *killing* me this whole car ride. Just *killing me.*" Mara said to me, as she rolled her eyes and shrugged her shoulders slightly. The three of us just stood in silence after that. Mara and I staring at Maddie, and Maddie staring back. The bell rang just then, and all three of us snapped to our senses, throwing our backpacks over our shoulder, the books slamming against each other inside of it, hitting our backs with a muted thud. We ran to the building, occasionally bumping into each other with our too-heavy backpacks.

We arrived at our first period class, breathing hard, our eyes just slightly crazed. We sat down in our seats in the school auditorium. Standing on the stage was our drama teacher, Mrs. Keith. Brunette, and slightly graying, Mrs. Keith was in her mid-forties, but you couldn't tell from the way she acted. Graduating out of college with a degree in musical theater, Mrs. Keith performed on the Broadway show, and was also a dance teacher outside of school, coaching at the Belmont Dance Company. She had an elite team of girls who traveled to different places all across the country, competing in group dances, solos, trios, and duets. Her students were phenomenal, winning in the top ten every time.

"Okay, boys and girls! We're going to do an improv skit today. Brandon, Nick, Brooke, and Paige, come up here. Tell about the time you were most happy. GO!"

"Um...so, I got into varsity soccer...and yeah," Brandon managed.

"*Sigh*. Seriously? Is that all you can do? Come on, step up your game. I know you can do better. Paige, your turn," Mrs. Keith said, shaking her head.

"OMG. So like, I get to like, go to....this modeling thing. And like, yeah," Paige said. In the corner of the stage, Mrs. Keith was shaking her head in disappointment.

"Okay. Do you know what? How about this. The whole *entire* class has to write a one page minimum story about the time you were most happy or excited about something. Since obviously you guys are lazy-butts and clearly aren't thinking straight, you guys will have to come back next week with a one page minimum story. I don't care what it is, and you don't have to share it if you don't want to, but when you act, I want you to remember about what you wrote, and why you were so happy, and use that emotion in your acting. Alright?" Mrs. Keith said, looking pointedly at Brandon and Paige. We sighed, and mumbled a quiet yes. For the rest of class, we sat there listening to Mrs. Keith talk about something. Of course, I would know what that something was if I had been paying attention. But I was too busy trying to rack my brain for something for my paper. I finally had a light bulb go inside my head, and I had a feeling that the three of us, Mara, Madison, and I would have about the same story, if not the *exact* same story.

The following week

"Are you thinking of sharing, Maddie?" Mara asked.

"Maddie, girl, you *have* to share. Or at least tell *us*. I mean, I was about to scream when you told us that you were going to tell us how your date went, by writing it, and reading it to us *next week*. In fact, I did scream. And....today, is "next week." So you have to tell us. Come on. Why wait so long?" I asked her. I couldn't wait one day, let alone one week. You could imagine how my week went; spending long hours contemplating what could possibly happen. Did they just go to dinner? Did they go to the movies? A hoedown? Personally, I would've liked to go to a hoedown and the country fair, and eat cotton candy. I mean, how much more fun can things possibly get?

"Haha. Yeah, sorry about that. But I really wanted to make it super special and perfect when I told you guys. But yeah. I'm not going to share it with the class, but you guys can go ahead and read it." Maddie said, finally giving in. *Yes*, I thought. She handed the paper to us, and Mara and I both scanned our eyes over the paper hungrily, walking blindly to drama class. I felt a hand pressing softly on the small of my back, guiding me towards where I needed to go. Or maybe I just imagined it. But I was so engrossed in Maddie's paper that I couldn't really be sure.

-

He opened the door for me and smiled warmly. His eyes matched the color of the sky; bright blue and cloudless. They shone with genuine compassion and interest, and made me momentarily stunned. I smiled back at him with effort, trying to keep the butterflies away. As I got into his car, I took a deep long breath of the scent, trying to remember it. It had a rusty floral smell to it, the leather seats mixed in with the tree-shaped air freshener that was dangling from the rearview mirror. He closed the door for me and walked to the other side. I buckled my seatbelt, and he did the same, while turning the key into the ignition at the same time.

"So, where are we going?" I asked tentatively.

"Haha. You'll see... don't worry, you're going to love it. It's the most beautiful place in the entire world," Peter replied, winking. The engine roared, making the seats rumble just slightly under me. We drove out of the parking lot, and into what could be called a fairytale.

My body was rigid and tense, my hands folded neatly onto my lap. I answered with quick, short answers, which was unusual for me. Too polite and maybe too quiet, I was a nervous wreck, and only talking to answer his questions. But then I remembered back to Mr. Morris's English class. I was smiling and laughing, saying whatever was on my mind. I didn't care what other people thought, because of course, I was too caught up in our conversation. Being around him, and just enjoying his presence, I blocked out everything else that was going on around me. I was carefree and relaxed, completely opposite to what I was now. I decided that I should just let my guard down a little; not worry so much. After all, what could possibly go wrong with a perfect guy like him?

We chattered away like little squirrels again, only this time, we didn't have to be sneaky and quiet. We were alone now, with no one to interrupt us; in our perfect little world of unending happiness. I found myself talking louder and louder, my voice getting more eager and quirky sounding. I was a princess, and he was to be my Prince Charming. I was happy and content, and I knew that we just had to be together forever.

We arrived at a small parking lot, and I was brought back to reality. I had forgotten that we were actually going somewhere instead of just staying in his truck and talking. I looked out the window, and I saw a small house that was freshly painted sitting on the sidelines of the sandy beach. The waters were calm, gently waving in and out. He smiled again, and I smiled brightly back at him.

"Come on," he told me. I didn't need to be asked twice. I got out of the car, and walked over to him. I felt his hand, big and rough, but gentle, envelope my own. He led me down to the house. We stopped at the threshold, and he let go of my hand, and I couldn't help but feel a sense of disappointment. I wanted him to hold my hand, caress it and keep it warm. He stuck his hand behind a small mailbox, and lift open a small flap that was well blended into the wall, that you could barely tell it was there. He came out with a key, and inserted it into the key slot in the door. Once the door was unlocked, he pushed it open, took my hand once again, and led me inside. I squinted my eyes, trying to adjust them to the sudden darkness. He flipped on a light switch, and my eyes took in the small room in front. It was kind of cramped, but cozy and welcoming. It felt as if I had owned it and lived in it forever.

He walked over to a storage closet, and pulled out two picnic chairs.

"Here," he said to me. "Take these and prop them out on the sand. I'll bring out some food that I ordered."

Wow. So, he already thought to order some food. As I walked out of the house, I slipped off my peep-toe flats, and kicked them near the house. I let my toes wiggle in and sink into the sand, feeling the soft grainy texture in between my toes. I set the two chairs right next to each other, facing out into the deep waters. I sat down in one of them, and watched the sun slowly sink below the horizon. The sky was a color palette; the colors getting deeper and more intense as it neared the water line. Starting out from a light pale blue behind me, to a soft pink, to a bright orange, and a shimmering yellow, it finally settled in on the bright round sun, just dim enough to gaze at.

In one hand, he brought out a foldable table, with a cup full of napkins and forks. In his other hand, he held a bag of KFC.

"I hope you like barbecued chicken," he said to me sheepishly, as if he couldn't decide on what to get. He set the bag on the table and sat down into his chair, his form slowly relaxing. We watched the beautiful quiet scene in front of us, neither of us moving or talking.

"Hungry?" he asked after a while.

"Yeah, actually," I admitted.

We took out the food, the plastic bag crinkling and fluttering in the slight breeze. We told jokes as we ate, and told embarrassing stories of our past, laughing hysterically, then trying to stop, realizing it probably wasn't as funny as we thought it was to them as it was to us. This went on and on, us eating, then laughing, and eating again. We finally finished the food, and my stomach hurt slightly from laughing so hard. My cheekbones felt tired, but overall, it was worth it. A day without laughter, is a day wasted, as they say. This was definitely not a wasted day.

He got up from his chair, brushed off his shorts, and offered me a hand up. I took it, and held it. And together, we walked along the shore of the beach, the water lapping forward and back again, from our toes. We walked and walked, and it seemed as if the beach never ended. We didn't bother to say anything, and the silence didn't bother us this time. We slowed down to a stop, and stared out into the ocean. The sky was pinker now, and all the traces of blue were now long gone. He looked at me in the eyes, and I stared just as intently back at him.

He stepped closer to me with one hand pulling my waist in, so that our bodies were touching. He leaned down, and I knew at that moment, that he was going to kiss me. And I was going to let him.

I was hyper-aware of all the other little things that were happening around me. A small hermit crab peeked out from under its shell, and nestled back into it again, looking like a washed up empty beautiful sea shell. The waves were gentler now, not as abrupt and rough. It licked our ankles, and soaked up into our skin. I was cuddled against his strong body; his well-muscled arms, holding me close. A slight breeze came, and it blew in a mix of his deodorant, fabric softener, and salt water; the scent surprisingly heavenly and intoxicating. I inhaled deeply at the sweet smell, and sighed contentedly.

His lips finally hit home base, and I knew I had to be in heaven. The soft, sweet eagerness of his mouth made the butterflies come back again into my stomach. When he finally pulled away, he smiled at me, and leaned in so that our foreheads were touching. I shivered, not because of the cold, but because of our kiss. I've always read in books that first kisses can sweep you off of your feet. The dreamy heavenly sensation could cause you to be light headed, and if not for your man, holding you up as he gingerly kissed you, your legs would've turned into something like Jell-O.

Peter took my small shiver the wrong way, and wrapped his arms around me, hugging me close, acting as protector, if I needed him. We both turned our heads outwards, looking at the last remaining part of the sunset. What a wonderful day, I thought... what a wonderful day indeed.

Tracks
Calhoun Fenner

I could hear the gravel shifting under my feet as I walked, step after lonely step, down the train tracks. It was three o'clock in the morning and I was wide awake, making my way north beside the two steel rails that were my only guidance in the pitch black of night. In my pocket I had two hundred dollars and a Clif Bar, and on my back a guitar. I was leaving.

I was leaving my school. I was leaving my drunk-ass dad, and the pain of my mother's death haunting me nonstop. I was leaving the whole freaking town of Aberdeen, California, where people and their dreams go to die. Sure, I didn't have the slightest clue where I was going, or how on earth I was going to hop on a giant lumbering freight train moving sixty miles an hour. All I knew was that I had to get away.

My name is Grey. I am seventeen years old. I've lived in Aberdeen, population 250, for as long as I can remember. Four years ago, my mother was killed in a hit-and-run. The driver is still at large. After that, my dad descended into a bottomless pit of drugs and alcohol from which he has never quite dug himself out of. I live in a 550 square foot house infested with mice, rats, ants, and all sorts of fungus. My bedroom consists of a torn-up mattress and a desk, and not much else. I shower every morning in water that was lukewarm at best and my breakfast consists of one or two pieces of stale Wonder bread, washed down with a glass of sour milk. My school is a four room building, with one teacher for each year and forty kids to a class. Last year I got straight C's. Lunch is pretty much the same as breakfast, as is dinner. The only thing that I really care about is my music.

And that was why I had to go.

I stopped, as I heard the distant whistle of a train, and had a flashback to my more carefree days as a child. I remembered I used to come up to the tracks and place coin after coin on the rails. When a train would come along I would wave to the conductor and he would usually blow the horn for me. As soon as the last car would pass, I would run up to the tracks, still excited from the passing cars, and dig around in the gravel until I had found each of the flat, metal disks that had once been currency. Now they are only reminders of when I was happy. When my mom was still alive. When my dad was still capable of sobriety.

But thinking about that won't do me any good now. Back to reality. My basic plan for jumping the train was to wait until the engines were safely out of sight. Then, after finding a suitable car to jump into, preferably an empty box car with a wide open door, I would run alongside it for a few feet, throw my guitar in and then gracefully hop up into my new home for the next sixteen hours. Nothing to it.

What I seemed to have forgotten to account for was the fact that a train was a trillion pound hunk of metal that would be coming at me at a speed almost twice that of Usain Bolt in the 2008 Olympics. All of that became shockingly clear to me, however, as the train rounded the corner. Its dull yellow lights shone through the dark, giving the whole scene a surreal appearance. The train has slowed down to a speed where I just might have a very slight chance at jumping onto it because it was curving around a very tight corner. I suddenly realized that unless I moved very quickly, I would be hit and and the locomotive would hardly feel a thing as it crushed my soft body like an elephant stepping on a marshmallow.

I run to the side of the rails as the train whistles by me, first three giant yellow engines and then a line of cars that were heartbreakingly not open. I took a moment to reassess the situation: I had about five minutes before the train passed me by completely and I missed my one chance at freedom for the night. And it looked like jumping onto the train was a long shot, given the speed and weight of the cars hurtling past me. One miscalculation and I get utterly crushed.

So this brings up an interesting question. How badly do I want out of this place? Am I so determined to leave this town that I am willing to risk my life to escape?

I took a quick moment to think about that. What exactly do I have to live for here? Only the exact same modus operandi I have lived with my whole life. My dad constantly giving me a ton of crap about everything. My teachers pestering me about my grades. That really annoying Boston Terrier Zeke barking the hell out of me every time I walk by.

The answer was clear. I would rather die than go back.

The next few moments were a blur. I could feel myself running towards the train like a maniac. Adrenaline was surging through my veins. I no longer felt the weight of the guitar on my back, nor the weight of my past on my mind. I was completely free of any restraints as I flew through the air, the train coming at me like a bowling ball at a group of helpless pins.

In retrospect, I don't know how I managed to land perfectly on the small, grated metal platform attached to the end of the car. I honestly didn't even know what exactly I was aiming for when I jumped. But a few moments after I left the ground I could feel my feet connect with the steel stage, making a loud and startling clanging sound.

I cautiously leaned back against the rust colored boxcar behind me and let out a sigh of relief. Suddenly exhausted, I slowly sat down on the platform with my legs hanging out over the edge. I could see the tracks flying by beneath my feet, a sight that would normally inspire immense terror. However, having just jumped onto a speeding train that could have easily killed me, I was feeling fairly invincible at the moment. I took out my guitar, a Sunburst Fender Dreadnought Acoustic-Electric.

If you don't speak guitarist, it is okay if those words meant nothing to you. The only thing you need to know is that it is a thing of beauty. Black around the edges and fading into a dark brown towards the middle, it is the only nice thing I have ever owned. It was also my dad's from back in the days when he was the coolest guy ever. He used to play Johnny Cash for me every night before I went to sleep, and wake me up each morning with some Led Zeppelin. I can still remember rolling out of bed each morning at the crack of dawn to his rendition of Black Dog. He was good, too. Maybe even better than Jimmy Page himself.

Smiling to myself, I picked out the opening riff the song. A yellow-orange sunrise was just starting to creep over the tops of the Cascades in the distance. It was four in the morning, and I was out of Aberdeen.

-

Over the next few hours, the landscape gradually changed from the woods in which I grew up to miles of flat farmland as far as the eye can see. From what I could tell it was mostly peaches, but there were some other crops scattered among the scores of peach fields: Christmas trees, peas, apples, blueberries. I also saw a giant, half dead Pitcher Plant in a very expensive looking vase sitting on a rock near the tracks, but I wouldn't exactly consider that a crop.

Occasionally we would pass a small town scattered among the cropland. Every single one was completely rundown. The houses unkempt, the lawns and gardens completely ignored. There were giant, gaping holes in the streets filled with pools of water that had likely been there for months. As much as I hated Aberdeen, at least the people there were able to maintain a certain degree of self-respect.

And apparently, wherever this train was going, it was a nonstop trip. We passed many junctions, but never stopped at any of them. During these instances I tried to look as official as possible, which is not easy when you're sitting on the back of a boxcar, wearing a hoodie and jeans and holding a guitar. But I seemed to pull it off well enough. At least, no one stopped us as we passed through.

After about ten hours the landscape became gradually more suburban. As we passed through neighborhood after neighborhood, I noticed that the buildings were gradually growing larger and closer together. The small, pathetic towns I had seen earlier in the trip were obviously a thing of the past, and the houses we were passing now were much more upscale residences. According to my watch it was about five in the afternoon, which meant I had been awake for fourteen hours, a lot having only slept for three the previous night. I had to get some sleep.

I sighed, and realized that was never going to happen. Who can fall asleep on the back of a train? Even if I could, I would just fall off. I leaned back on the cold, hard metal of the box car and strummed a few random chords on my guitar.

And then I saw something extraordinary.

Out in the distance, just short of the horizon line, was a city. Grey and black buildings brushed the sky, gleaming in the silvery evening light. All of the lights were giving off a slight glow, making it one of the most beautiful things I had ever seen. And standing apart from the main cluster of high rises was another tower, concave in the middle with a lone tier resting on top.

This was not just any city. This was one of the most iconic cities in music history. This was the home of the Foo Fighters, the home of Nirvana, the home of Death Cab, the home of Jimi Hendrix. The home of coffee. Really, I couldn't have come to a better place.

This was Seattle.

-

I blinked. Wow. Having never seen anything higher than three stories, this was a pretty crazy moment for me. Just thinking about the fact that before long I would be walking the streets of the city was mind blowing.

I realized that, in order to maintain my freedom, I would have to ditch the train pretty soon. Considering the current speed of our train, we would be in the midst of the city in about an hour. That gave me roughly fifty minutes to jump the train before it stopped and the conductors found me and beat me up with their clubs like they do in the movies.

I had to get off at a spot within walking distance of the city, but not anywhere anyone would see me do it. There is something vaguely suspicious about a guy jumping off of a train. Believe me, I've seen it. So maybe if we went through a tunnel? I was going to have to think on that.

The minutes ticked by. The Seattle skyline was gradually getting closer, as was my window of opportunity. For the most part, my train was speeding along on a track built on a ridge just above the outlying residential districts of the city, and had been for the past thirty minutes or so. We seemed to be headed straight into downtown, which made it easier to find a jumping location close to the city, but harder to not get caught. I would have to time this perfectly.

Then, all of a sudden, there was a break in the cluster of houses. I was abruptly surrounded with trees, with not a soul in sight. My heart started beating faster than you could believe. Any moment, this incredible gift could be over and the houses would take over the natural scenery again.

So, without any more thought, I jumped.

It turns out my little gift wasn't so perfect after all. I had forgotten that I was still up on a ridge, so my fall from the tracks was a little longer than expected. After a seven foot drop that seemed to go on forever, I landed right in a cluster of blackberries. I cursed as I got up, pulling the thorny brambles out of my hair, cloths and face.

And it gets worse.

Standing right above me was a forty-something man and a kid who looked maybe seven years old. The man was wearing a red flannel jacket and Levi's, and the child, probably his son, was wearing black Wellington boots over faded blue overalls. They both had bright red hair and smelled faintly of sawdust, and were wearing the kind of shocked expression on their face, the expression you get from watching Indiana Jones and the Kingdom of the Crystal Skull and being appalled at how awful it was.

I tripped over the vines backing up, and got another face full of thorns. Lifting myself to my feet, I was able to stutter out "okay look, this isn't what it looks like," although if it looked like a crazy runaway teenager jumping off of a train he had hopped the previous night then it was, in fact, exactly what it looked like. And it was pretty clear that the guy knew that. In one flash of motion, he picked up the kid and started sprinting away, at the same time taking out his cell phone. I could just make out his words to the operator: "Hello? 911? Yes, this is an emergency..."

I was running like crazy, first out of my small grove of trees and then out into the street. I was exhausted, both mentally and physically, and a few moments ago I had definitely not been expecting to have to escape the police as soon as I got off of the train. My weary brain was wracking itself for a way out of this.

And then there it was. So clear. So simple. They'll never see it coming.

"Taxi!" I shout at a nearby yellow cab. The driver pulls over to the curb for me: an Indian man with a sleek black handlebar mustache. I promptly open the door and practically dive into the backseat.

"Take me downtown," I hastily tell the taxi driver. I expect him to at least give me a weird glance; I haven't slept, eaten or bathed in two days and I'm sure I've looked better. But no, he doesn't even give me a second look. And come to think of it, why would he? The guy's a taxi driver in the craziest city on earth. He probably sees strange things every day.

As the driver pulls out into the street, I hear sirens in the distance. A radio voice crackles on the radio:

"Attention, drivers. Do not pick up a young adult, sixteen to twenty, tall with brown hair and green eyes, located between First Street and Alaska Way Viaduct, carrying a guitar case."

The cab driver tenses. He looks at me through the rear view mirror and raises his eyebrows.

"Eighty dollars!" I blurt out.

What am I doing?! Why am I trying to bribe this guy? He's obviously a trained professional who's going to turn me into the police first chance he gets. Now I get to add bribery onto the long list of charges I have probably already accumulated.

But the cab driver just smiles, winks at me, and keeps on driving. Now I can only hope that wink meant something like "You can trust me. We are all brothers under one god, and I will help you, my fellow citizen of this earth. Peace to the world," and not "Nice try, you dirty bastard! I'm a trained professional who does not accept bribery, and I am going to turn you into the police first chance first chance I get."

Thankfully for me, it turned out to be the first kind of wink and not the second. Ignoring the distant blaring of the alarms, the man drove off towards the city.

-

Downtown Seattle. The fresh, salty air of Puget Sound fills my lungs. I am walking down near Pike Place market, soaking in the beautiful freedom I had obtained. As I stared out over the sound, I realized that this is what it was like to be truly happy.

So maybe I don't have much. Maybe I don't have very much money, maybe I don't know anyone here, and maybe I don't have any of the qualifications to get a decent job. What I do have is a strong will to go on, to put my past behind me and look ahead to the future. I will find a way to make this situation work out in my favor.

Sometimes I think back to Aberdeen, California, and wonder what happened when I left. What did everyone think? Did anyone even notice? No one seemed to notice me while I was there, so why would they now? But none of that matters anymore. I can live my new life, full of adventure and cool stuff like that, and they can stay in the black hole of hope, slowly seeing their dreams sapped away, never to return.

Not me. I see how people turn out when they give up. That's why I'm never going to do it.

An Explosion of Sadness
Liam Dubay

Ring!

The school bell rang, signaling the end of another long day. Kids of all ages rushed through the hallways and out the open doors, and I was right with them. As I ran outside, I breathed in the fresh air. Six and a half hours of confinement! Well, unless you count recess, which I don't. I think school should only be three hours long, every other day. Actually, I think I should be homeschooled, but my parents insist that I travel two miles every day in a rinky-dink old bus to this lovely prison (sorry, Springfield Middle School).

Anyway, there I was, rushing toward the school bus as our math teacher called out to us, reminding us to do our homework. Yeah, right: as if I'd labor over boring equations and confusing variables when I could be working on my science paper. I didn't care about any of my classes except science.

I chose a seat at the back of the bus, like I always do, and someone slid in next to me.

"Hi, Alder," I said without looking over. With his messy brown hair, glasses, and usually vacant expression, Alder Connaway fit the stereotype of a school nerd exactly, and the straight A's he got in school didn't help. He liked almost every subject and was pretty much my only friend at school, so he helped me with my homework a lot. In exchange, I helped him understand the ways of the school's social life (I actually had no clue what a social schoolboy was like, but Alder didn't know that).

"Hey, could you lend me your notes from English today?" I asked.

He glanced at me. "Were you not paying attention in class today?" he accused.

"What? No! I was totally paying attention! I just need to see if I missed something, that's all."

"Uh-huh. All right, I'll email them to you tonight. But, you know, you should really learn to take notes on your own. I shouldn't even be giving you the notes I took."

"Aw, c'mon, Alder," I said. "If you did that, you wouldn't have anyone to teach you the ways and mysteries of the social club."

Alder gave a mock gasp of horror, and then put his hands up in the air. "I give up," he exclaimed. "I guess I will just be your humble servant for the rest of your life, taking notes for you in class while you pass the time reading under your desk."

"Well, at least then you'd be able to raise your status from 'nerd' to the lower levels of the social status quo."

"Thanks," he grumbled, and buried his head in a book. He didn't look up until the bus pulled up, a fact which continued to amaze me. No matter how much I loved reading, I could never manage to read for more than ten seconds in a car or a bus before I got motion sickness.

We squeezed through the jostling crowd of kids clogging the narrow aisle and emerged into the afternoon sunlight. I stopped when I heard sirens wailing from somewhere, but I couldn't pinpoint the location. Alder must have heard them too, because he was staring at me with a puzzled expression, as if to say, *where are they coming from?* I shrugged, thinking it was nothing. In the suburbs of a big city like Springfield, sirens were commonplace.

A helicopter roared overhead, startling me from my train of thought. I looked up and saw a blue two on the tail: a news helicopter.

But why would a news chopper come to our out-of-the-way little community in suburban Springfield? I followed the direction of the aircraft, and felt slightly alarmed when I saw a black cloud trailing up from the ground near my house, about five blocks away. I looked over at Alder, who lived across the street from me. He looked apprehensive, if not a little excited. I felt the same way—I had never seen a fire before.

Other kids were starting to notice, too. Some were pointing at the cloud of smoke, others at the news helicopter, which was circling the area. Most were whispering excitedly.

I set off at a run toward my house, with Alder at my heels—not because we were worried (although I admit I was a little), but because we wanted to find out what was going on. After a minute, I rounded the corner and stopped in my tracks when I saw the destruction.

The smoke that I saw at the bus stop was rising from small fires that burned in the blackened shells of the houses on either side of the gaping hole that used to be Alder's house. Most of the other houses on the block had broken windows and blackened roofs. Black dust rained down, coating the police cars, fire trucks, and ambulances. Policemen swarmed the area, firefighters rushed to douse the fires, and medical and emergency responders scoured the wreckage.

Alder came around the corner at the speed of light and nearly slammed into me. I turned and gestured helplessly at the burning houses. His expression went from excitement and worry to shock, and he staggered backward like he'd been punched. Then he dropped his backpack, ignoring the fact that his laptop was inside, and raced toward what used to be his house.

"Alder!" I called, but I didn't think he heard me. I dropped my backpack next to his and ran after him.

When I ducked under the yellow tape marked POLICE LINE—DO NOT CROSS, a policeman stepped in my way, telling me to wait behind the tape, but I pushed past him. "This is *my* neighborhood," I muttered. "Don't tell me where to go."

Just as I reached the first fire truck, my mother, who was waiting with the other spectators as close as the police would let them, saw me and ran forward, ignoring the police's protests. To my embarrassment, she threw her arms around me.

"Mom, enough," I grumbled. She pulled away, looking very worried.

"I called you twice, but you didn't answer," she said accusingly.

"Oh, yeah. I forgot to charge my cellphone."

She sighed, and then looked back at our house. Compared to some of the other houses on our street, ours didn't look too bad. Most of the windows were broken, and the front door lay in pieces, but at least the house wasn't burning or collapsed.

"Where's Dad?" I asked, and Mom pointed to a spot by a couple of police cars. I looked over and saw Dad craning his neck over a stout police officer, who was shouting at him to get behind the police line. That was my dad: he never listened to authority unless he had a reason to.

"Did Alder come home with you?" Mom's voice jolted me back to reality.

"Oh, God," I said. *Alder*. How could I have forgotten about him? Here I was, chatting with my mother, while my best friend's house lay in ruins. I scanned the area until I saw Alder arguing with an emergency responder near the small crater, and ran toward him.

"...live here!" I heard Alder shouting as I came within earshot. "I have every right to be here!"

"I'm sorry, son," the responder said tiredly. "We will let you know when we have more information..."

I skidded to a halt next to Alder. "Hey," I whispered as the responder droned on.

Alder turned toward me, and I was shocked to see tears on his face. "Will," he said, not bothering to keep his voice down, "these *people* won't let me go to my own house, even though my parents are missing!" He shouted the last part, and the responder stuttered to a halt from his speech, looking surprised.

My heart sank. *His parents were missing?* But that would mean... no, there had to be another explanation.

"Maybe they're just shopping or something," I suggested halfheartedly, but I didn't think Alder bought it.

"Perhaps," he said doubtfully, "but..."

Just then a chorus of shouting from the wreckage of the house interrupted whatever he was about to say. A pair of medics rushed past with an empty stretcher, and I got a sick feeling in my mouth.

"Alder," I began, "don't—"

But he took off toward the cluster of rescue workers that had converged toward the center of the crater, so I had no choice but to follow. We arrived at the edge of the area just as several medics lifted a badly burned body out of the debris and onto a stretcher. I looked away, feeling queasy, but not before I recognized the face of Mrs. Connaway, Alder's mother.

Alder cried out in despair, and sank to his knees, sobbing. I was in shock. I wasn't sure what to do. Should I have comforted him, or should I have even been there? In the end, I just stood on the sidelines, watching Alder's grief.

After what seemed like an eternity of watching emergency workers sift through the debris (I carefully avoided looking at the body), I walked down to where Alder was, sat down, and put my arm around his shoulders. He shrugged his shoulders, like he wanted me to back off, but I kept on stubbornly (I was very good at that).

Eventually, Alder stood up, brushed the ash off of his knees, and walked over to the stretcher. He bowed his head like he was in prayer. After a while, he lifted his head, and asked one of the emergency workers a question. I strained my ears, but I couldn't hear him above the background noise. The worker shook his head, and Alder walked back to me.

"They haven't found my dad yet," he told me in a hollow voice. "So he's either working or..."

"Maybe you should call him," I suggested. He gave me a blank look, so I prompted, "You know, call you dad. You have a cell phone, right? Call him," I repeated.

A look of understanding appeared on his face, and he dug into his pocket eagerly and pulled out his flip phone. Most people would be embarrassed to be seen using such an outdated piece of technology, but Alder didn't seem to mind. He punched in the number and held the phone to his ear. After about a minute he frowned, ended the call, and tried again. Then he snapped the phone closed angrily.

"Wrong number," he explained. "It's odd; I swear I entered in the correct number."

"Maybe—" I began, but just then a car pulled up next to us.

It didn't seem like the kind of car you'd see in the suburbs, and definitely not at the scene of an emergency. It was pure black, for starters, and looked as if it belonged to the President. The windows were tinted, and when the doors opened, three men stepped out. They all wore gray suits and dark sunglasses, and went with the picture of the President's car. The only thing missing was the President.

Two of the men stayed by the car, but one of them walked up to us. He extended his hand toward Alder and ignored me (typical).

"Hello, Alder," he greeted, "nice to meet you."

"Who are you and why do you know my name?" Alder asked, in no mood to exchange pleasantries.

"These questions are best answered in a secure environment, Alder," he said cryptically. "I can answer them if you come with me."

"Excuse me?" I thought Alder was going to explode with rage. "Are you trying to kidnap me or something? My dad is missing, my house is gone, and my mother is... is..." he took a deep breath. "If you can answer those questions, then do it now; otherwise, leave!"

Mr. Mysterious nodded to his two companions, who promptly began to scan the area. "There," he said, "we can talk now. I'll answer your last question first, since it's the easiest. I know you because I knew your father."

"What?" Alder looked confused. "Oh, you must be from his work."

"Precisely, which brings us to your first question. I am..." he seemed to notice me for the first time.

"Can you be trusted?" he asked me. I don't know why, but I get that a lot from adults.

"Of course!" I replied indignantly. Then I amended, "That is, if you're not doing anything illegal or something."

"Good." He turned back to Alder. "I am Todd Dole, the director of the CIA Non-Official Cover division, where your father used to work."

Alder looked stunned. "What? You're joking, right?"

Todd Dole shook his head. "I would not joke about such a thing."

"Then what did my father do?" Alder asked. "And is that why *this* happened?" He gestured toward the ruin of his house.

"Your father was a rank-and-file CIA NOC agent," Dole replied, "NOC standing for Non-Official Cover. He was the best we'd ever had. He could have become a director, like me, but instead he chose to stay a regular agent."

"That can't be true! He was a real estate agent, not a spy!"

"That was his cover job," Dole explained. "He couldn't exactly put on his resume that he was a secret agent."

"Whoa, wait," I said. "Back up a sec. You're saying that Alder's dad is a *spy*?"

"Correct."

"What a load of baloney," I scoffed. "But if it is true, then does he have anything to do with what happened here?"

Dole sighed. "Unfortunately, he has everything to do with it. My best guess is that there was a house bomb on their first floor, designed to take him out."

Alder staggered backward. "A bomb?" he gasped. Dole nodded sadly.

"A bomb," he agreed. "It succeeded. The CIA is now without its best agent, and you are an orphan."

I couldn't believe how bluntly and gracelessly he put it. Alder looked devastated. "No," he whispered. Then he took a shaky breath like he was trying to pull himself together. I guess he didn't want to break down in front of Mr. Sympathy here.

"So, Alder," Dole said, "the real reason I'm here is because you have no other family members who can take you in. You have two choices; one, to go to an orphanage where you may or may not be adopted, or two, to come with me to the CIA—"

"What!" I exploded. "That's ridiculous! I thought there was a law against kids working!"

Alder glared at him. "You know, you're not really selling the whole 'join the CIA' thing. Are you kidding? And yeah, isn't there a law against kids working full-time jobs?"

"You would not be working, you would be protected. The people who placed the bomb here to kill your parents mean to get rid of your entire family, which includes you. At the CIA, we can protect you, in exchange for your help every once in a while."

Alder looked incredulous. "Are you crazy? Do you think I can't see through your scheme to get me a job that killed my parents?"

"I'm with you, man," I agreed. "And hey, if you want to stay at my house for now, you're more than welcome to."

Todd Dole looked very uncomfortable then, as he should have. "Consider carefully," he warned. "I can offer you protection and safety. The alternative is to go to an orphanage, which would be—"

"Like any other kid would do." Alder interjected. He squared his shoulders and faced down Dole. "I want a normal life, as normal as it can be anymore, and you can't give that to me. So thanks for the offer, but no thanks." And he turned his back on the director of the CIA and walked down to the street. I followed him, leaving an incredulous Todd Dole behind.

When we came up to a police car near my house, Alder stopped. All the energy from the encounter seemed to have left him, and his eyes seemed dead. "Why did this have to happen to me?" he asked no one in particular. He turned to me.

"Did you mean what you said about my staying at your house?" he asked.

"'Course I do," I promised, even though I had no idea if my parents were okay with it. "I wouldn't let you do anything else."

For the first time since the bus ride home, which seemed like a million years ago, Alder smiled—a small one, but a start. "Thanks," he told me. "Thanks so much."

"No problem, man," I told him. "We'll figure it out."

We stood together, watching the smoke drift up from the ruined houses, and I knew that no matter the tragedy that happened that day, everything would turn out alright.

The Cockney Seed
Will Atkinson Combs

Before I begin, there are a few things you should know: first, Cockneys speak a very strange dialect of English that shares their namesake. It consists of phrases and names of seemingly unknown or fictitious people in the place of words that rhyme with them. For example, rather than saying feet, they would say "plates of meat." Second, Cockneys stay at the age of elven to twelve infinitely, they cannot die of old age or disease, and are much harder to kill than your typical human. Third, they can regenerate limbs and certain organs, like the lungs, liver, and intestines, but not the heart or the brain. Rejuvenation, a lengthy process involving all manner of bonesaws, sutures, and various tubes and scalpels is excruciatingly painful for the Cockney donor if done cheaply (read: without anesthetic) and can have some unfortunate side effects for the donee as well, such astutely named "Tyrannosaurus arms," "baby legs," or gradual descent into Cockney-esque psychosis, but rich old codgers clinging to life make it a very lucrative business.

Theoretically, one could have a Cockney regenerate a heart, but only if you had a device to pump their blood for the time being. Fourth, Cockneys do not have parents, (they are rumored to be born from a mythical tree somewhere in Undertown), are the only people with Cockney accents, and are very protective of this. If you imitate them, they *will* kill you. Fifth, Cockneys are born psychopaths. Their organizations are made up of loan sharks, Chancehouse owners, and petty to major criminals of other sorts. While Undertown has an official organization of Peace-keepies, most of them have too little funds, or have been bribed into the Cockney payroll. While they seem to have been gaining strength in recent years, it's a slow process, and major busts remain few and far between. Cockneys also appear to have a way of passing on knowledge, so even newborns know how to handle a weapon. They also undergo a psychological decay spiral whereby they become more insane and or non-functioning until they are either put down by their equivalent of family, or someone else kills them. And now, we can begin.

It was turning out to be a bum night at the Fati Manus Chancehouse. All around me, through the opulently decorated interior, the sounds of joy, despair, and drunkenness could be heard. The noise echoing off the buttresses and dampened by the gold-with-red-trim curtains, primarily emanating from the elaborately patterned easy chairs scattered all around. *I* had already lost five grand in Scrap to the Prodder table alone.

149

And with every sparse win, the dealer, clad in his standard issue tan pants, starched white shirt, and be-sequined black vest, would look up at me from somewhere around the level of the small of my back, and force an enthusiastic, " Ev'ry cloud 'as a silva linin', sir," spitting the happy platitude in my face like it was acid. As the hand finished, I tapped the table, signaling the dealer to take the rest of my money to make chips and begin the next hand, to which he almost gleefully pronounced "Sorry, sir, I'm afraid ya're ut of bread and honey." Pounding the table, I asked for a temporary loan, to which he replied I owed too much. I then threatened him with violence, at which he threatened to call security. Slumping in defeat, I slinked away from the green covered platform and towards the door. As I dejectedly staggered back to my limply bobbing '48 model luxury Helio,(which I had bought on my last winning streak), I heard an unmistakable buzzing, clicking noise, almost like a *bzzchnk*.

As I wheeled around to face the source, I saw it was the owner of the Chancehouse, holding a modified Catacombs-made Quadviscerator shotgun.Using both hands and a foot to cock the enormous thing, the custom revolver-esque cylinder, (to allow for multiple firings without reloading), reflecting the light. Afterwards, he looked up at me and yelled "Stop wite there! Ya owe us more than wahn 'undred fousan! Na pay up 'afore I leather boot your bacon and eggs Frank Bough!" Afterwards one of his compatriots stepped forward and whispered in a proper English accent "What my boss here meant to say was, 'Stop right there! You owe us more than one hundred thousand! Now pay up before I shoot your legs off!' I apologize for the confusion. Now pay us."

As the explanation reached my brain, my fight or flight kicked in, and I chose flight. The boom of the Quadviscerator nearly deafened me, and the recoil knocked the house owner on his be-suited little arse. However, I restrained myself from stopping to laugh, as he was recocking, and this time he had fitted on recoil absorbers. As I leapt for the Helio, another boom sounded, taking the bottom half of my leg clean off. Reeling from the pain, and unable to find my opiate capsules, I crawled to the controls. As the horns of an incoming Peace-keepy vehicle blared, and the beginnings of a firefight ignited on the slowly receding airdock, I set course for the little waste heap I had haphazardly set up just after I had stumbled, drunken and numbed, into the conibear trap formally known as "life-threateningly major gambling debt."

It was an eloquent description in my mind, and to me, I was not the intended target of this famously specific snare, merely a passerby, caught by my foot, and wandering with naught the tools to remove it. I know now I was the perfect target, caught by the neck, for a guaranteed kill. It was only by some kind of divine intervention I didn't succumb in the days that followed. I was, so to speak, happened upon by a merciful trapsmith.

As darkness closed over me, I took the opportunity to have a hearty chuckle at the tiny Cockney's expense. When I awoke it was to the velvet-and-leather cabin of the Helio. Sadly, with my leg in that state, I'd have to sell it to afford a transplant from some Cockney limb dealer, and considering my offense to a major house owner, I'd have to go to one of the less reliable ones. I might even be gimpy for a few months. But, regardless of the inferno of pain in my leg, I had to soldier on.

I half-dragged, half-hopped my way through the Helio's smooth oaken door, and surveyed the tiny dump. It was a truly pitiful hut, a vibrant green fungus covering a bit more than one side, the acrid smell of leaking coolant stagnating in the air, and with barely enough room for the old Sapien-Freeze-o-Mana that I planned to lay low in for a few years. While I waited for the coded drugs to confirm with the Freezer this was indeed my decision, I reflected on the people that had gotten me into this situation in the first place.

I vividly remember the first time I saw a Cockney. I was a little boy, of about ten or so, and I was walking through the market with my mother, taking in the smell of fresh vegetables, frying meat, and the rancid yogurt that seemed to be *in* at the time. As I toddled alongside, I saw a little hand reach up and take a sausage, and then dart off between the stalls again. Being a 10 year old and feeling sorely in need of adventure, I decided to follow. As I chased the flash of fabric through a winding series of stalls, dodging both legs and the cries of my mother, I closed in on what was now revealed to be a little boy in very bedraggled clothes.

When he slowed to catch his breath I caught him by the shoulder, and asked what he was doing. He shot back, "'Re ya bacon rind or rathead?! I'm stealin', na bugger Frank Bough!" Having never seen any such misfortune, and frightened by the fearsome countenance of this mysterious boy, I simply questioned, "Why?" With a snarl he grabbed my shirt and venomously whispered, "'Cause, ya idiot, we Cockneys can't die, but we Beecham's Pill need ter eat!" Having proclaimed this, he shoved me through a gap between the stands, and ran off. As I picked myself up, my mother finally caught me, and seeing my clothes, told me I was in a lot of trouble and that we were going home for a wash. Eventually I would learn more than I ever wanted to know.

When I awoke, it took me a few tries to open the , and I eventually had to kick the door. When it fell outwards with a snap, all I could see was *green*. Not the dirty, sludgy green of the slow-flowing Mortuus Flumen, nor the phosphorescent green of the Sienimäinen Kasvannainen people who occasionally came with wares from the Valtakunta Ilman territories. Very similar to the green I once saw on a business trip to the Bazar Aledekhan, back when I was still a businessman, in the market keshek of a local merchant. A hypnotizing shade of green, as though a thousand ample ferns had been pressed into the verdurous stratum before me.

As I crawled further, the tunnel gradually grew in size, until it was large enough to stand up in. As I reached then end, I gasped in surprise. This was at two things. The first was the huge, spherical open space, filled with the same green fungi. And the second was that this fungus was the same that had been on the hut when I had arrived, which meant I had been asleep for much, *much* longer than I expected. That was my last thought before a sharp pain in my leg made me aware of the black-feathered dart sticking out of my thigh.

When I rose from that inky blackness, I felt myself being dragged along by the leg, and I gasped as I heard a torrent of the unique swearing of Cockneys. "Ya rathead father's-lover-feather-plucker! Wot were ya thinkin' givin' 'im that big gong a' half a gross!? 'E could 'ave been killed or- oh cherry pit, 'e's awake!" As the small faces crowded around me I saw I was in another place entirely. Surrounded by bright lights and surgical tables, something caught my eye, the glint of an odd, organic looking Dr. Jevalt Automatical Hyper-Implanter[PP](not surprising considering how long I had been on ice), and as the instrument descended I screamed from the incredible pain of a plum-pit sized object being forcibly inserted into my arm. And then, as quickly as it had begun, it was over. As a searing pain still throbbed in my arm, one of the Cockneys began to talk.

"Wotcha, me name is Gigantic Touch Me Knob, but ya can call me Touch Me Knob. The fin' we just stuck in your chalk farm is a seed from the Cockney Tree. Ya clock, in the past 'undred donkey's ears, the Cockneys 'ave been psychologically decayin' faster than we can be replaced. 'owever, we 'ave 'ad limited success wif implantin' seeds in non-psychopathic 'uman subjects. But current ban of them 'ave been Pin' Pong in the buff, they aw died chicken pen the seed began growin' into their frontal lobe in order ter form the basis of its psychology. So we're just garn ter 'ope that ya're. Okay? Okay."

I guess technology really had advanced, because as he finished his explanation, a diminutive red box attached to his throat by a leather strap began to translate in a crisp accent, "Hello, my name is Gigantic Bob, but you can call me Bob. The thing we just stuck in your arm is a seed from the Cockney Tree. You see, in the past 100 years, the Cockneys have been psychologically decaying faster than we can be replaced. However, we have had limited success with implanting seeds in non-psychopathic human subjects. But none of them have been strong enough, they all died when the seed began growing into their frontal lobe in order to form the basis of its psychology. So we're just going to hope that you are. Okay? Okay." As he finished, I felt, not a pain, but a profound unease, spreading from my head, all the way down to my foot. As if the most terrible deed imaginable had been given a life of its own, and decided to slither inside of my body and take the strongest of holds.

I came to a while later, and immediately retched from the overwhelming nausea that enveloped my consciousness. As I looked around, I saw my surroundings were the same, but the implanted arm was not. A vegetal, vine-like intravenous feed led into a disquietingly large bulge which came up from beneath my formerly white shirt. I almost instantaneously felt a vicious pulsing pain, akin to the unknown mass was contracting and releasing, harshly gathering the muscles that resided beneath it and then allowing them to expand into brief soreness before the next painful constriction. The pattern continued for some time and eventually faded to boring, if painful, monotony.

The constant glaring of surgical lights was broken by the suddenly overhanging head of Gigantic Bob. Rather distracted by the persistent discomfort and the gnashing of his crooked teeth, as he talked, my haze-filled Broca's area only managed to seize on "sedatives," "accelerate," and "growth process," and even then it was analogous to trying to hold on to a thoroughly lubricated penguin. Before his onerous countenance dismissed itself from my field of vision, I again witnessed the shine of a needle, this time lightly pricking the feed attached to my arm. The following days were a veritable cyclone of nausea, injections, and the omni-present and ever-growing pain in my arm, now spread all the way down to my presently distressed wrist.

Time passed, and after a period of time unbeknownst to me to this day, I began to hear gruesome cracking noises originating from that same damnable larboard appendage. Tranquilized as I was, I didn't feel the pain. The numbness, however, was almost worse in the knowledge of my incognizance and consequent helplessness to assess or control my rapidly progressing condition. The cracking, shattering, and general tearing noises continued as I steeled myself to look over at what was happening. The sight is one I will never forget, a tiny figure working its way out of what I had originally thought to be a cyst-like growth coming up off the surface of the limb, was in fact a marrow-permeating, parasitic pod, incubating around and firmly within the arm, only now struggling to burst free of its fleshy confinement.

The sound died down after about 3 minutes, my maimed arm bleeding as it twitched. The little person, who I assumed was the infant form of a Cockney, had run off into the darkness beyond the surgical lights surrounding me. The din of its laughter sounded somewhere in the distance. Not a malicious sound, more an excited laugh, as in the mirth of discovery. And it must have been discovering a awful lot, having only just come into this world, for which its inborn knowledge had effectively, if sparsely, prepared it for.

As I grasped around the tables for something I could use to sever my bonds, I had the first opportunity since I arrived in the accursed place to notice the extraneous sounds that faintly vibrated through the flourishing, fungus covered walls. And what I heard was the sounds of a warzone. Through the nausea, pain, and perpetual parade of needles, I hadn't been able to really listen, but now that they had ceased, the screams and explosions filled my perception. As I paid focused my attention, I noticed a startling, if small, divergence in language. While the war cry against whoever they happened to be fighting would normally be "Die you bloody Kingdom Come!" It was now "Die you bloodless Kingdom's Rum peacies!" As I noticed the slang "peacy," a key turned, and everything clicked into place. Now I understood why I had been dragged to a dingy offshoot of a mycological wonder, rather than a soundproofed mansion cellar, or the gilded back rooms of a Chancehouse. In the beginning I told you the Peace-keepies were slowly resurging, and I surmised that I had been frosty long enough for them to really hit their stride. That once respected assembly had been down and out for a great period, and now they were back with a vengeance.

I became greatly engrossed in puzzling out the flow and ebb of the battle. On one side I could hear the rattling, squelchingly gelatinous stomps of what I hypothesized to be some farflung descendant of the clumsy biotechnological exoskeletons that were displayed as frightening prototypes back in the day. My energies focused on the action above, my hands had been feeling around the nearby surgical stands, one of my fingers touched cold steel. Quickly slipping the knife into my palm, I maneuvered the blade under the ropes around my wrist and began to cut, the needlelike point of the knife slicing into the soft flesh as I sawed desperately at the tough fibers. As soon as I got one hand free, I went to work on the other, wincing from the pain of my bleeding wrist.

I had almost unbound my other hand when the sound of worker's boots came slamming into earshot, and beeping, accentless shouts of imminent collapse and needed transportation of biological cargo echoed from some other section of the tunnels. Apparently the Cockneys had some computerized help, a contrast mad all the more stark by the fact that when I had gone on ice, the most advanced computer had been a monstrous super-computer called Atlas, designed to figure out ciphers and calculate primes, barely capable of cranking out 10 million Babbages (Babbages being the number of operations a Babbage difference engine can perform in a second). And the technological aides were right about collapse, because no sooner had the jackbooted source of the thuds come into view, an exoskeleton put one of its flowing, sinuously viscid pseudopods through the afore darkness-shrouded cave ceiling.

As it twisted, thrashed and made a shrieking sound that assured me of its biological origins, the machine then attempted a new strategy in the form of a fluidic motion that allowed it to simultaneously stream up and out of the aperture it's weight had created, and drop several independent globules of its material down into the area, where they slapped and expanded like tender meat, and then regathered themselves and began to move via an amoebic series of oscillations toward all visible passages. It wasn't until several minutes after that the screams started. I thank the Core I only had to behold one example of the horrible process that those exoskeletal offshoots catalyzed.

It was about half a minute after the screams began that a wailing Cockney burst through an entrance screaming and clawing wildly at her head and face, which was covered by a gob of the same material the exo had been "grown" out of, and it was melting into her skull like a strong acid, pulsating as it did, drawing in flesh bone, and finally, grey matter. When the brain had finally been fully absorbed, it dropped off and proceeded to completely ignore me. As it slid under the surgical table, presumably in search of more victims, I had time to study the body of the Cockney girl, and saw a snail-like track of missing clothing and burned flesh, and came to the horrible realization that it had crawled up her body to get to her head.

As finally the last cry fell silent, I went to work on the last of my bonds, and slowly I slipped down from the table, slowly adjusting myself to the arthritic pain of muscles which, having been held still so long, had to now move once again. As I hobbled towards the closest stone corridor I noticed I had not heard the piercing of the newborn, and smiled at the fact that it had survived. While the Cockney race had put me through the worst pain of my life, it would be a shame if they were to die out, because without them, life would be dull as hell, fat cats would no longer be constrained by the threat of a Cockney neutering, *I* would no longer be able to legally gamble, and most of all, without their regenerative abilities, limb and organ loss, *my* limb and organ loss, would be a sadly permanent fact.

And when the Peace-Keepies patched me up, I learned an important piece of information, that the Snails, as I had learned was the official term, had been absorbing the Cockney's brain matter in order to assimilate their memories. They knew about the newborn, but apparently all of the people with knowledge its next hidden location had escaped or committed suicide. After a few days of recovery the brass interrogated me on what happened, I said they incinerated it in one insane last act of defiance. I walked out with a smile on my face, and a secret hope for their eventual replenishment.

The Last Dream
Tristen Wong

Wild horses rampaged across the dry and cracked dirt. Like a swarm of bees, the pitch black horses moved swiftly and silently as their eyes glowed a bright red, the color of blood. Eventually, the creatures reached a small village. A small boy saw the mares and his eyes grew wide with fear and terror. The child ran into the middle of the town, his lower lip trembling, and pointed towards the horses, standing at the edge of the town, as if waiting for a command. Suddenly, a hooded figure appeared atop the horse in the front. He had no eyes, just a small, thin mouth, which curled into a malicious smile. The moment he smiled, the darkness of the horses began to thunder into the small, helpless town.

I woke up with a start. My chest was heaving from the nightmare - the fifth one this week. Recently, I discovered that my dreams can come true in reality.

"Damn it, not again," I muttered.

I climbed out of my bed to peer out the window, hoping that those evil creatures from my dream wouldn't be waiting outside my house, like the monsters from my *other* dreams. But of course, they were all waiting there, their black glossy hooves treading the grass. Three days ago, my nightmare was of a virus that seemed like it would wipe out the population. The next morning, twenty people were found dead of an unknown cause. It's not like these kind of things happened usually. The only explanation that I could think of was my dream.

"Laurel? What are you doing out of bed at four in the morning?" inquired my mother.

I turned to see her standing in the doorway, a confused look on her face.

"Oh, I just had a dream. I'll be getting back to sleep soon," I replied.

As soon as she left, I turned my attention back to the horses, who were staring back at me with their endlessly red eyes. Just like in my dream, a dark hooded figure appeared for about five seconds, the figure grinned, and then he and all the creatures dissipated into thin air. I gasped and fell to my knees. I already knew that by morning, there would be dozens of sightings of the horses, or cases of deaths caused by the figure, which I wouldn't be surprised if it was Death. I checked to make sure my mom was asleep again, slipped on a jacket and my worn Vans sneakers, and dashed out into the chilly air. The last horse stood at the end of the street and neighed loudly at me, as if beckoning me to follow them. *It's better if I'm not seen near them. People might think I have something to do with it*, I thought as I tried to convince myself that Death had not arrived. I headed back home, hoping to get some sleep - I *am* only fifteen and I still have school. Knowing I had to go to sleep, or I'd be tired all day, I clamped my eyes shut and forced myself to drift off to sleep.

As my alarm clock blared, I clumsily hit the snooze button. I woke up drowsily and threw the covers off my bed as I climbed out.

"Hurry up! I don't want to be late!" my older brother, Alec, yelled up the stairs.

"I'm COMING!" I hastily replied.

Once downstairs, I grabbed an apple off the countertop and rushed out the door, where Alec was waiting in the car. He was a senior and I was a sophomore at Rushwood high school in Albuquerque. Alec started up the car and we drove to school. The incident last night kept running through my mind the entire time and the horses' red eyes were engraved in my mind. Everything seemed okay so far...I mean, it's not like there have been any deaths... yet.

School passed by like a blur. Alec had soccer after school so I caught a ride with my boyfriend, Finn. It was a sunny day and the light glinted off his sleek black hair. Finn saw me walking towards him and smiled a lopsided grin. I always felt terrible the day after one of my dreams and he always made me feel better, but I could never let him know about my problem. Being the down-to-earth guy he is, Finn would think I'm crazy or something. He greeted me with a "hello" and opened the car door for me before climbing into the driver's seat.

"So, are you hungry?" he asked.

"Yeah, let's go to Rosie's," I said with a smile.

Rosie's was a small diner that served the best sandwiches and fries, without a doubt. Finn and I drove to the restaurant and I ordered a tuna salad. We sat at a table, and waited for our food to come.

"I have something I need to tell you," Finn said seriously.

"You're not going to break up with me, are you?" I joked.

"Of course not! But you'll probably think I'm insane once I tell you," he mumbled.

"Okay, just tell me," I urged.

"Well, I have been having these dreams, and it's not bad or anything, but they come *true*."

I couldn't believe what I was hearing. Was Finn like me? Was that even possible? He said his dreams weren't nightmares though...so it must be *different*.

"Okay, I absolutely don't think you're crazy...because the same thing has been happening to me, since two weeks ago. Mine are nightmares though, and last night I had one about wild horses and Death. I'm really surprised nothing bad has happened...yet."

Finn's eyes grew wide as I went on. I told him I had a dream about the car accident last week. There was no way this was just a coincidence. *Are we tied somehow?*, I wondered. In the midst of us talking, a low rumbling sound started coming from outside. A feeling of dread overcame me- my nightmare was about to come true. Loud neighs were lost in the sound of the horses' hooves against the pavement outside. I peeked out the window to see giant, midnight black horses and that evil hooded figure causing destruction on the street. A woman across the road stood, frozen with fear, as Death slowly turned his head to her. He raised his scythe and sliced her head clean off her body. I stepped away from the window in horror and looked at Finn. I could tell he realized what was happening, and he grabbed my hand. We ran to the car in the parking lot and quickly got in.

"Is this your...dream?" he asked, with worry.

"Yeah. I-I think it is," I hesitated.

We didn't talk the rest of the way as he dropped me at home. Finn said he'd call me but...I doubted it. Alec came around the corner of the dining room, munching on a granola bar.

"Hey, did you hear about that giant thing with the horses in town? Like damn, that's crazy," he exclaimed.

"Uh huh," I stammered. "I have a lot of homework that I should do. See ya later."

I dropped my bag on the floor and opened my laptop. First, I looked at the news, hoping that nothing regarding the horses would pop up. Thankfully, I was right- the witnesses probably thought others would call them crazy for reporting such a thing. Next, I searched for anything on dreams coming true, and almost immediately, an article about a woman who also lived in Albuquerque and according to the story, she had dreams that came true too. Next, I typed in the woman's name- Alecia Silver. An address came up. *1872 Greensky Avenue,* I mentally made a note to myself. I reached for my phone in my bag and dialed Finn's number.

"I know you probably don't want to talk to me right now, but I found this woman in town, and she says that her dreams used to come true too. We should talk to her."

"No, we should totally talk to her. Sorry...I'm just kind of in shock..that's all," he apologizes.

Finn sounds reluctant. I can understand though, I'd be in shock too. We agreed that he'd come to pick me up tomorrow, which was a Saturday, after lunch. Later that night, I unwillingly went to bed, not wanting to be met by another dream.

From a distance, thick gray smoke was clearly visible, contrasting greatly with the pale blue sky. The clouds were shrouded by a veil of darkness as the smoke swallowed them up. Before long, the house's windows began to crack and splinter as the fire greedily consumed everything inside, sparing nothing. Waves of blazing heat radiated from the house. Flames danced along the wood. Burning chunks crashed into pieces on the ground. Nobody seemed to be inside. But there was. A teenage boy with shiny black hair and blue eyes. Finn.

The next day, it was a bright and sunny afternoon when Finn's shiny jet black car drove up the street and parked in the driveway. I grabbed my bag off the ground where I left it last night, and met Finn outside. His face was unsettled and I didn't attempt to make conversation. I told him the address and we sped off. I didn't want to make any other conversation either; I definitely did not want to mention my dream from the night before.

We arrived in front of a rickety, old washed-out green house. I looked at Finn with uncertainty, but he didn't notice. I confidently strided towards the door and rang the bell. An old withered woman answered the door.

"Hi, are you Alecia Silver?" I asked, trying to sound pleasant.

"That's me," she answered in a rough voice.

"I'm Laurel, and that's Finn. We wanted to talk to you about...some things concerning our dreams," I continued.

A strange look washed over her wrinkled face, and I could tell she knew what I was talking about.

"All right, well why don't you two come in?" she asked, her tone changing into a serious one.

I carefully walked into the house, Finn trailing behind me. Alecia shut the door and disappeared into the kitchen. I tried to ignore the cold feeling I was getting from Finn as Alecia brought us some crackers. I went on to explain about my previous dreams and how Finn and I saw it happen outside a restaurant. Finally, Finn spoke and told her about *his* dreams.

"First of all, I believe that your dreams will eventually become nightmares, as they progress," she stated to Finn.

His expression didn't change, as if he expected to hear that. I asked her if she knew a way to fix our problems.

"I do know of a way. But you will have to learn to control your dreams and your actions in them. When you have a nightmare, you need to find the source and destroy it. For example, your dream about the virus. If the 'source' was a scientist or doctor, you'd have to kill the him to prevent it from actually happening. As real as it will seem in the dream, the deaths do not occur in reality. Once you wake up, it'll only be a dream," she insisted. Finn and I had heard all we needed to know. I thanked Alecia and we left her house.

Again in the awkward silence of the car, Finn drove me to my house. This time, *he* was the one to start talking-which surprised me.

"So, are you going to try to do what she said?" he inquired.

"Of course I am!" I replied, a bit annoyed that he thought I wouldn't.

And after that, there was just more silence to welcome me. I kept looking out the window until we reached my house and immediately, I got out without a word.

That night, I had another dream. It was about a wildfire, and it spread throughout town. I tried to take hold of it, but I don't know if it worked. I ran through the burning woods, tree trunks collapsing behind me. As I reached a clearing, a camper was trying to get the flames off of himself. I steeled myself and prepared to shove him back into the hot-red fires. Heat blistered my skin and my throat felt dry.

"Help me!" he screamed, his pleading eyes growing wider each second.

I stood, frozen. I couldn't *kill* someone. What was I thinking? Even if it was a dream, it just felt so *real*. I couldn't do it. I just couldn't. So I turned and ran.

I woke up, scared of what would happen now. I'd failed. The wildfire was going to happen, and it would all be because of me. I searched around in the darkness for my phone to check the time; it was 6:00 AM. Laying in bed, I thought about how bad it could be-and when it could happen. Three hours passed by. The sun had fully rise by now, and I heard a car come to a stop outside the house. *Please, please, please let it be Finn,* I hoped. I heard the doorbell ring and shot down the stairs. It was. Finn stood in front of me, hands in his pockets and his hair mussed. His face was one of worry, and his normally enthusiastic eyes were now glazed over.

"We have to go. There's a fire starting the forest," he said softly.

Tears began to well up in my eyes. It was starting.

"This is all because of me. I couldn't do it, Finn...it just felt so real...and I couldn't do it," I whimpered.

"Hey, it's not your fault. I understand, it's hard to control. It'll take time. But we have to leave," he urged.

He grabbed my hand and half-dragged me to the car. Dark grey smoke from the burning trees billowed into the air as we got in.

"We need to get to Alecia! I need to ask her if there's another way!" I cried suddenly.

Finn swerved the car around, knowing how important it was to me. We sped into town where the fire had already started to spread to the buildings. A small cry rose from one of the houses. It was a child.

"You go find Alecia and say what you need to. I'll stay here and help. I'll meet you at the Diamond Bridge in an hour," he promised.

"But you might get hurt!" I protested.

"Go!" he ordered fiercely.

I sprinted in the direction of Alecia's house only to see it already engulfed in flames. Without thinking, I clambered through an open window. I called Alecia's name, but there was no reply. I scampered over burnt planks of wood and furniture. A limp arm hidden under one piece of wood started to reach out. A small groan was enough to tell me she was alive, and I tried to pull her out. But the plank was too heavy and all I could do was move it enough to uncover her face.

"Why are you here?" she asked, no energy left in her.

"Is there another way? I couldn't do it," I replied frantically.

She paused for a second, before telling me her answer. It was no. So that was it- there wasn't another way. I tried once more to pull her out, but I couldn't.

"You should leave. I am old and weary already," Alecia commanded.

Her face didn't have the same glow it had when I first met her; I knew she was ready to go. I whispered a goodbye and ran out of the house, tears now streaming down my face.

Finn wasn't at the Diamond Bridge. I glanced anxiously at my phone- it was already 1:15. Something must be wrong. Finn is never- and I mean, *never*- late. I dashed back to the town, most of the buildings now devoured in fire. I'd arrived just in time to see the most terrible sight I'd ever imagined. Finn had just rushed out of another house, carrying a crying toddler in his arms. Gently, he set the howling child down and immediately ran back inside.

"Finn!" I cried.

He couldn't hear me and had already sprinted in. I followed him, yelling his name as I rushed into in the house. A low rumble rose out of the ground, and I knew the house was about to collapse. I could only hope that Finn had already gotten out safely. Scrambling back out of the house, I turned back to see the house cave in upon itself, crumbling into a giant pile of broken planks and warped pipes. I looked around for Finn, but he was nowhere to be found. Feelings of sheer terror came over me as I realized he was still inside. *No no no no no he can't be dead not yet this is my fault please don't let him be hurt*, I thought. But sadly, I was right. Just like Alecia, I found him under a pile of planks. Rapidly, I lifted them off of him and threw them to the side, my strength lessening as I got closer to him. Finally, I could see Finn's entire body and the horror of it. His arms and legs were twisted at unnatural angles, and his once-silky black hair was crusted with dirt and mud. A thin stream of blood trickled from the corner of his mouth as his gaze slowly locked with mine. I sobbed once, angrily swiping my tears away. I couldn't help but think that this was all my fault. His throat bobbed as he swallowed, forcing words out.

"Why...did you...follow me...in...? You...could've gotten...hurt..." he croaked.

After almost killing him with my stupid dreams, he still worried about me. My body was racked with sobs.

"Finn, Finn, I'm so sorry...I'm so sorry, Finn," I get out, the ground swaying beneath me as my eyes start to blur from the immense amount of tears.

He laughs silently, the sound like stones grinding across metal, but it soon turned into a raspy cough. He sighs.

"Not...your fault...dreams...dreams are all...we have...left."

"Finn....please don't leave, no, Finn, stay here, stay with me," I plead, but his gaze shifts to a point over my shoulder.

"Dream for me," he whispers.

A shudder passed through his body. His electric blue eyes dull to a pale, washed out grey. I crumple into a heap next to him. Clutching his hand, I throw my head back and scream at the sky, blackened ashes floating in the air around Finn and I.

I can't cry anymore. I've run out of tears. After taking one ultimate look at Finn, I stand and wipe my tear-stained face. I can't stand it anymore. All I've done is cause pain and suffering to everyone I've ever loved. What more do I have to live for? I'll never forget Finn, and in the end, more people will just get hurt. I'm standing at the edge of the Diamond Bridge, the place I was supposed to meet Finn. Wind whooshes through my hair, whipping it around like flying ribbons. I reach into my pocket and find my wallet. Inside, I see a picture of Finn and I, his arm draped around my shoulder, both of us wearing wide grins. I take one last look at it, branding the image into my mind. Taking a deep breath, I press the photo into my chest. One final tear slides down my cheek. I close my eyes, and I let myself fall. The world turns upside down, but I still keep thinking of Finn, of everyone I've ever loved, my eyes squeezed shut so I'll never forget.

Finn's last words echo in my mind.

Dream for me.

The End
Nadia Siddiqui

July 16th, 2012

I vaguely remember having a dream about my dad last night. I've never met him and whenever I have dreams about him, he doesn't have a face. I never looked *at* my dad in my dreams; I'm always looking *into* him, into his mind. He is like me - he has the same condition. His thoughts are always so complicated, like a maze, and I have to find my way through. The psychiatrist said it's something you can only get genetically, and Mom doesn't have it, so I guess my dad did. The psychiatrist also said the government was conducting research on it at the California Brain Research Center that was just down the road.

I walked into the house and sighed to myself as I looked down at the plethora of fan mail Mom received. She never read any of it, I've never seen her open a single one. I remember looking up at the stacks of envelopes being thrown in the trash when I was younger and feeling bad for all the people who were wondering if she would reply. Mom is a singer, but I don't like her music much. It's just noisy and bothersome. I was a disappointment for her; she wanted me to take after her and become a gorgeous singer, but I can't hit a single note and I didn't exactly inherit her locks of blonde hair and big blue eyes. So I focused on making Mom proud in other ways - I remember teaching myself how to read by looking through the endless piles of mail and learning how to write by replying to some of the enthusiastic fans. None of my efforts ever made her happy, so she just left on tour for long periods of time, probably to avoid me. Welcome to my life.

Turning away from the mail, I head up the giant marble staircase to my room. I shoved the abnormally large, carved ebony door open and head over to my desk. The walls of my room were a light shade of pink with stripes of light green. In the far corner there was my bed that was way too big for just one person and in the opposite corner was my closet that was filled with clothes I never wore. My favorite part of the room was my bookshelves and my desk. The bookshelves lined an entire wall and added a sense of wisdom and depth to my room. My desk was a huge structure made of West African black wood that I adored and spent hours at, typing.

I opened up my laptop and began. I typed about everything. I put everything about my life into words so that it all made sense. Sometimes there were so many thoughts whirling around in my brain that I couldn't just focus on one, so I typed it all out to make sure it all made sense. Then I would rearrange the order of things till it looked perfect and logical. This was how I kept myself from going insane.

When I was younger, everyone thought I was stupid because I didn't talk very much and just sat with my journal all day. So one day, Mom took me to a psychiatrist to make sure I was okay. It turns out I'm better than okay; I can technically use a higher conscious percentage of my brain than most people can. Think of brains like radios - when your radio is playing, you are using 100% of it. But, the volume can be set at different levels. The average human being's volume is at one or two. My brain is at five or six. This means my mind feels like fifteen different people are talking to me at once and I'm expected to hear everyone clearly - it's *chaotic*. But it does have its perks. Everything my cerebral cortex picks up, my brain process immediately, allowing me to take in everything – it's easy to tell when people are lying or what they are feeling just by looking at them for a second and I have a photographic memory. This doesn't make my life significantly easier, though; I still have to deal with weeding out what information is relevant to my train of thought to keep me on track. So I wrote to keep myself from going crazy - to organize my mind.

Suddenly, I heard a noise come from downstairs. It wasn't a loud noise, just a soft "clink," but I figured I should check it out, just in case. You never know these days, the paparazzi are crazy. I hopped down the stairs and around to the kitchen. There was nothing. I circled back to the foyer, the piles of unread fan mail just sat there on the polished granite, untouched. Except for one envelope that was tilted off to the side. I looked around the front door; there were no signs of a break-in, so I slowly crept over to the pile of mail, my mind filling with suspicion. Shifting the top letters over, I looked for anything out of the ordinary. Again, there was nothing, but something didn't feel right. I shifted another chunk of letters off to the side. Something still wasn't right, there were more letters shifted differently than the way I had left them. I dug through the letters, pushing them off to the side until I saw something I didn't remember.

It was a leather journal that was a little smaller than the average composition book. I probably didn't notice it before, I thought to myself. But then again, when was the last time I hadn't noticed something? I opened the journal carefully, hoping for a name to be on the inside cover. The first page was ripped out, but I read on. On the upper right hand corner, there was the date, *January 8th, 1995*. It was jotted down messily, each character given little time or thought. It looked like whoever was writing this was writing urgently, but it was just an ordinary journal. It started normally:

"Today I woke up at seven o'clock and got ready for my meeting. Nothing special, just business. I have filled up about twenty other notebooks like this with journal entries. I decided to start this on when I realized everyone was taking notes in the meeting except for me; I usually just remember the contents of the discussion. So I pulled out this leather bound book I got for my birthday and I am currently pretending to take "important business notes." I started out by taking notes, of course, but it got boring quickly. So I ripped out the first page and decided to write about my life, like I always do. Anyway, in today's meeting..."

It continued on like that for a couple pages. Not particularly entertaining, but the writer was definitely relatable and sounded familiar. I closed the journal and walked up the stairs, deciding to read some more later. But I had to get back to my writing - I had a constant fear of having some sort of brain overload. I hate it when my writing is interrupted.

July 17th, 2012

I ended up falling asleep at my desk yesterday and now I have a crick in my neck. I decided to get back to reading the diary since my fingers were sore from typing, and noticed something very interesting.

"I woke up this morning to the sounds of a car alarm beeping. What a lovely way to start the day. I went downstairs for breakfast and had a bowl of Raisin Bran cereal. When I was much younger, everyone used to tease me about my love for Raisin Bran, but I liked it because the cereal tasted like oatmeal raisin cookies with milk. I head out for work early and actually enjoyed my drive over to the Research Center. Yesterday, the scientists said they would be continuing their experiment on brain development, but I could see the older scientist struggle to maintain his composure and the youngest one there was beginning to sweat. The middle aged scientist, Dr. Schneider, who was speaking, kept stumbling over his words and they seemed a little too well rehearsed. I never see them doing the research and I'm not sure what or who they are testing..."

The first thing I realized was that the writer loved Raisin Bran cereal. This would be completely irrelevant and unimportant if I didn't love Raisin Bran cereal as well – and for the same reasons – because it tastes like oatmeal raisin cookies and milk! The second thing I found interesting was that the writer worked at a research center that studied brain development. Probably at the California Brain Research Center that was down the road. And lastly, he might have the same condition as I do. What if he was related to me? What if he was my dad?

As soon as I realized this, I jumped out of my chair and knew that I would have to do something. There was no way I was going to sit around at home alone if I knew that my dad could be just around the corner. But then

166

I started thinking twice. Isn't this what all the dim-witted girls did in the movies? Act on impulse and mess everything up? But I wasn't hurting anyone, and I doubted that visiting a research center could mess anything up. I thought about it the entire day and decided to go tomorrow, after a good night's rest.

July 18th, 2012

I couldn't sleep at all last night; I couldn't stop thinking. I hate it when my brain does that- when I feel tired the entire day, but as soon as I actually get into bed, my brain decides to invite a mariachi band in and have a huge party. And when that ends, I start questioning simple things in life, like the color pink. How come it gets a name? Isn't pink just light red? What about light green, light blue, light orange, light yellow and all the other light colors in the world? Isn't that like discrimination against all the other colors? And I have a crazy discussion with myself that I have to write about and I never end up sleeping.

Anyway, I got dressed and went downstairs for breakfast and had Raisin Bran to get myself ready for the day. I can't quite explain the emotions I was feeling. I was excited, yet nervous and happy yet worried, and everything was mixing up around in my brain. Like someone threw every emotion into a blender and mixed them all together and stuffed them inside of me. So I wrote for a while to take care of that.

When I was done typing, I came downstairs and headed out the back door because I couldn't find the front door keys. I slowly walked down the street, oblivious of what was to come next. I was so clueless in that moment, so innocent. When I look back on it, I can't believe I didn't think the through further. I was just so curious at the time. I had so many questions - if I met him would he recognize me? Does he even know I exist? What if he didn't work at the California Brain Research Center anymore? Then what would I do, track him and find him or just give up. Or worse, what if he wasn't my dad?

All these questions were running through my mind and tangling up in each other, like headphones in your pocket. I had no idea how they managed to form such complicated knots, but they did. I felt like writing, but I couldn't stop for anything. I just kept walking down the road, surrendering to the mess of thoughts, letting them take over my mind. At that time, I thought all I needed to do was focus on walking, one step at a time.

I left the safety of my neighborhood and stepped past the security guard. I slowly crept away from the luxurious rows of Victorian manors and out

167

into the real world. I felt like the air was different here, not quite as scented, just natural. I strolled down the block, trying to look normal. I don't know why I felt so guilty about this, I had innocent intentions, but something just didn't feel right. I could see a large building with reflective windows and modern architecture in the distance. That was it, the Brain Research Center. I kept walking, my pace increasing as I approached the Center. I was sweating so much, it was disgusting. The air was so humid and everything just felt soggy and warm. My nervousness wasn't exactly helping that either.

I approached the commodious building, ultra-aware of my every surrounding - the expensive cars parked on one side of the lot and the beat up cars on the other side. The light orange and white roses that lined the building. The way the building reflected different colors. It was all magnified to an extreme and made my head hurt. I pulled open the front door and felt a strong blast of air conditioning hit my face, making it difficult to walk inside.

I definitely didn't think this through. What was I going to tell the receptionist, that I was looking for my dad and there was a chance of him working here? And what could she possibly say back? I would have been sweating insanely if it wasn't for the obscene amounts of cold air being blown at me from every direction.

The room was a bright white color with black and white furniture that matched the building's modern feel. It had a very sanitized feeling to it, it was all black and white and everything was in its place. I couldn't relate to it. The receptionist was sitting behind a layer of glass. She had dark brown hair and hazel eyes. She seemed really friendly and genuine, but when she noticed my presence, she tensed up and didn't flip through her papers as smoothly.

"Hi, I'm Tracy, how may I help you?" she said in a very nasal voice, looking up from her pile of papers.

"Hi, I'm Olive Valentine," I said in a shaky voice, deciding to improvise, "I came here to -"

"One moment please." she said, cutting me off as she left the room. Her voice changed tone just a tiny bit, but just enough for me to feel uncomfortable. I felt like I should leave, something really was not right here. But despite my instincts screaming at me to go now, I stayed. I guess I really am one of those dim-witted girls who messes everything up.

A very elderly scientist came out from a door at the side of the room. "Hello, I am Dr. Schneider. Are you Ms. Valentine?" he asked. He tried to sound confident, but he stumbled over a couple words. He was a little too well rehearsed. Where had I heard that name before?

"I'm sorry, I should go," I said a little too late, stepping backwards towards the door. Dr. Schneider looked right over at my shoulder and gave a curt nod. I felt a sudden, stabbing pain in my right shoulder blade. I cried out in pain as I felt my body go numb and fall to the floor.

July 20th, 2012 (I think)

When I woke up, I thought I was dead. I was in a room with nothing in it except for the glare from the bright white walls. Everything was painful and breathing was difficult. The old doctor, Schneider I think, walked in and explained everything to me. I just sat there and cried.

It turns out the government made a deal with my mom. They would pay her if they could run tests on my brain. Of course, she agreed, but only if I came to the Brain Research Center willingly. They planted a fake diary in my house, knowing I would never come by choice unless given an extraordinary circumstance. So they created one and lured me here with false hope of finding my father.

All the consent forms have been signed.
This is the end.

The Bells of Moscow
Ella Gleason

In dim light, the little girl had always loved to see her reflection looking back at her reproachfully in her mother's eyes. It was the only constant thing in her life, save the bells of the churches and cathedrals that littered the streets of St. Petersburg. No matter whether her mother came home that night, or who (or what) her mother came with, the little girl could always see her scrawny and pale self looking back at her with dark eyes so much like her mother's. She'd lie in bed at night, after her mother had or hadn't said goodnight, and think about those eyes, until the clink of change on the dresser told her it was time to sleep.

"You inherited your father's looks," the woman would say with contempt some mornings, a dark fire blazing in her eyes. The girl would always look up in awe when she saw that inferno; it seemed that whoever the woman looked at with those blazing eyes would cower and turn to ashes.

Fear. Terror. Hatred. Disgust. These were the feelings that surfaced when the girl's thoughts turned to her mother. The people that looked at her mother and balked - it was they who felt the bone-piercing fear that would visit them again in their dreams. Sometimes, there would be a glimmer of pity in their eyes, and her mother would look at them in disgust. Her hatred would chill the air. Airs of danger, mystery, and sometimes, seduction, seemed to follow the woman around. It didn't go unnoticed by the people around her. Silence followed them in streets and wide eyes stared after them. Her daughter, a small, young girl, understood none of it.

It was only when her mother danced that the girl would see happiness in the woman's expression. The woman might then see the little girl peeking from behind a wall, and she'd laugh like a tinkling bell. The woman would take her daughter's hand and lead her through the steps of something she might have done when she was the girl's age.

Prima ballerina. If the girl would ever remember anything about her mother other than those dark, dangerous eyes, it would be those two words, what her mother used to be. Mother: prima ballerina. To the girl, the words were synonymous.

Her mother stopped dancing after a while and the woman would go on screaming rages littered with words the girl didn't understand. Her mother stopped coming home after a while and the girl was left alone in a too small house where she only had the bells to accompany her. It wasn't until now, at the age of fourteen, that the girl, scrawny and pale and with her mother's dark, dark eyes, realized her mother had left her. Walked away. She wasn't

170

kidnapped or killed and she wasn't lost or scared in some dark, scary corner of Russia. The woman had simply stopped caring about the girl with eyes so much like her own.

Dreams and memories would plague her in the night, even now, when her nightmares were so far away. Her mother was not returning, not ever. Vivid dreams of her mother trying to reach her with hands and arms screaming for help, but then falling, falling, falling away, until all that was left were the dark eyes calling for help. Then there would come the ghosts of everyone the girl had ever loved and left, and they would talk to her, screaming, begging, calling for help until their final moments took them into the darkness. The ghost of starvation and abuse would come; that was her years in the orphanage when her mother wasn't there.

Then she would wake up from her nightmare crying and screaming, and she'd run to the mirror and check her eyes. But that little girl, scrawny and pale, would never be there. She'd hear a man's footsteps running to her room, and her papa would open the door, and she'd run to him, crying.

"Papa, papa!" she'd cry, the words coming to her mouth in Russian even though he went to such great lengths to teach her English. And he'd press his lips to her head and cradle her, singing softly songs she hadn't ever heard.

"Anya," he'd whisper to her when she'd ceased. He'd look into her eyes and tip her chin up with two fingers and give her a rare smile and then he'd walk away, prowling into the darkness of the grand old lonely house.

And she'd stare at him as she went, thinking all the time that she really did favor her father's looks.

So it went. But this night Anya remained quietly in bed, shaking softly and eyes wet: but still she did not cry out for her papa. He was no doubt moving restlessly about their house, missing the sleep he never got.

No, she wasn't that little girl with a whore for a mother, she told herself. She'd never be again, because her mother was gone and she would never come back. Anger coursed through her veins like ice and she settled into bed, thinking all the time of her stupidity. She had been a young and ignorant girl, and now - she'd figure that out later. All Anya did was stop the tears and go to sleep again. This time there were no dreams, no vampire-like figures waiting to kill her like they killed her mother in now distant nightmares, and certainly no dark eyes staring reproachfully from the gloom of sadness and disparity.

The morning came too soon as mornings tend to do. All Anya wanted to do was to pull the covers up again and go back to sleep. Sleep was peaceful when there wasn't the epidemic of emotion, of terror and memories that, God be good, should just be shoved back where they came from. But school was next and as much as she'd like not to, Anya had to go. She dressed quickly and slid into the kitchen. Her papa was there, reading the newspaper with a smirk and sipping coffee. He drank it black, like usual. She didn't care to see what he was reading.

In truth, Anya didn't know much about her father. She knew his name was Viktor and she also knew he was born and raised in St. Petersburg, but lived now in Moscow. He was 35 years old. They lived in a large house in the rich part of her city. It was almost like the manors she heard about, so prevalent in places like England. He was a grumpy and rich man, but still, simple and elegant. He liked fancy wines and fancier suits, but always, they had to be chic and classy. He was neat and never got more than an hour or two of sleep. He would lock himself in his room a lot, but usually, he'd spend the time playing his cigar cutter saxophone. He was very proud of his saxophone. Anya loved to listen to his saxophone, but she didn't think the neighbors shared her opinion. She'd take so much delight in learning to play it, but her papa always pushed her to spend her time learning ballet.

"You're very good," he would tell her. "You don't want that to go to waste."

Papa had once had a wife and son two years younger than Anya. The wife's name was Ellena and the son was called Peter. When Anya had first arrived at the foot of the house, scared and trembling and starved and broken from her years in the orphanage, Papa hadn't liked her.

"I did not ask for this!" he screamed, his anger blazing and cold. In some ways, he was a lot like her mother. "I will not be taking her!" Anya started to cry.

The boy from the orphanage that had brought her here, acne scarred and about 17, looked nervous. He explained with a horrible stutter that he was so very, very sorry, but laws were laws, and the father needed to take the child. He spoke so badly that it seemed he did not even speak Russian at all.

The woman stepped out from behind her father, a small boy peeking out from behind her. He was clutching his mother's leg, but he released one arm to wave at Anya. He gave her a toothy, seven year old grin, but through her tears, Anya could not return it.

"What's this?" said the woman sharply. "Who's the girl? Why the hell are they saying she's your daughter?" Silence. "Viktor! Viktor, what is this?" The questions went on.

An argument followed. Unlike Anya's mother, Peter's was uncontrolled and raging when angered. By the end of it, the teenage escort was nearly in tears. Anya still stood dumbly silent and crying. But the law was the law, and even a powerful man like Viktor Lavrov needed to listen to it sometimes.

The family went inside. Viktor yelled at her follow. She wanted to run, run and cry, but she was propelled forward, terrified. The house was huge, with lace rugs and table clothes, and chandeliers that glittered in the lights they produced. The smell of good food filled Anya's nose. There were servants running about, eying the girl nervously. Their Russian was impeccable. Even the room where she sat, tiny and alone, and was what used to be a guest room but now was her bedroom, was nicer than anything she was used to.

Viktor didn't talk to her much after that. Anya was called down for meals three times a day, and the food was plentiful and there was no end to it. But there were so many etiquettes Anya wasn't aware of, and every time Anya would make a mistake, Viktor would yell, and she'd run, crying and scared back to her room. Any other time he would talk to her, he was cold and distant.

Peter seemed eager to talk to her, but his mother, Ellena, looked at the girl with disgust and hatred and would pull her away. "The girl isn't part of this house!" Ellena would scream, distaste lacing every word. "She doesn't belong here - and who would want her? A whore's bastard!" There was so much venom laced into the woman's shrieks; Anya could never bear to hear them, and she'd run to her room again, sobs shaking her small frame.

But after a couple weeks of this, the quiet in the house turned from venom to not remorse, but hatred and a quiet and cold need for action. There had been an accident. Fire and smoke, a collision. The automobile Ellena and her son rode in crashed. The two did not survive.

Viktor completely ignored Anya after this. He simply pretended that she did not exist. But the servants of the house were kind to her, and Anya liked them. But it seemed to the little girl that Viktor saw her as no more than a mistake.

The quiet voices of the servants would echo in the hallways where Anya might wander if Viktor wasn't around. His anger was dangerous, they would say. By their fear and the murmurs of names that Anya didn't recognize it was easy to tell that blame was being thrown around like a ball in a game. Officially, as Anya half-gathered, half-guessed, proof had not yet been found and Viktor was growing the angrier for it. But one thing was for sure: Ellena and Peter Lavrov had been murdered.

When the servants would notice Anya, they'd break off quickly, abruptly. They'd smile and laugh (nervously, it seemed to Anya), and exclaim, almost in surprise.

"Ah, there's the lord's new daughter!" Anya didn't like that very much. If Viktor didn't think of her as a daughter, then she didn't think of him as a father. But she'd smile nervously, and they'd ask her if there was anything she wanted. After she said no, they'd smile like they understood. Grinning, they would take her hand, and they might lead her back to her room, or they might lead her to the kitchens, perhaps, and take her around the cooking. Sometimes they'd let her help add ingredients or stir the soups. But of course the meals in which she had helped would never be brought to the grand table.

And Anya would forget all about what she'd heard.

But while Viktor was a powerful man - it seemed the law hardly could touch him - the men he attacked with words, and sometimes, Anya thought, with violence, could not be touched.

Stories that Anya could barely read popped up in the newspaper, and all of them were about the death of the prolific Ellena Lavrov and her young, healthy son, Peter. Accusations were thrown around in the papers, and Viktor himself was heard accusing other men for sabotage, rich and fancy men like himself. "But for the moment, there is not enough evidence to convict the men on Lavrov's word alone," read one newspaper. Cold words struck by silence laced the conversations of everyone who came over, like Anya's true mother, these men were dangerous and their anger blazed cold.

But eventually the accusations were proven wrong. The other men, such as they were, were not convicted of the murder of Ellena and Peter Lavrov. But the case did not end here. The men attacked Viktor in the courts, and the words "клевета," and "иск" always appeared in the papers. Anya knew now that they meant "slander," and "lawsuit." It was the battle of three powerful, rich, and influential men that the courts either respected or otherwise, could not touch.

The case, Anya read in the papers, was won. Viktor was sued, and he lost a ridiculous amount of money. That was Anya's opinion. It seemed to her, though, that the money only seemed to be a drop in the bucket. Viktor kept the house, and he kept his cars, his furniture, the tickets to the opera or to ballets. But all of the kind servants - and the rest of the servants too - were fired.

The girl thought of these things as she prepared for school. She knew that she and papa had warmed up to each other, that there was a turning point in their relationship sometime and somewhere. They were neither friends nor confidants, and yet there was still a cold and simple camaraderie between them. He would always be there when she needed him, like on those horror-ridden nights when all she had was nightmares. Anya remained silent for the most part, and Papa followed suit. But still, they were father and daughter. There was something like love between them, but she didn't know if her papa could love anyone anymore. Anya didn't know if *she* could even love anymore. She had once loved her mother, she remembered, but love didn't mean anything.

If love meant anything, maybe her father and her mother would still be together. Maybe Papa would have never loved her mother enough to betray Ellena and Anya wouldn't even be here.

In that family, it seemed, love didn't mean anything.

Minutes passed, and the girl managed to get everything ready for school. Her ballet bag lay next to her bed, ready to be brought with her, to be used at hours of practice after school. A small sigh escaped her lips. The bag was shouldered and Anya went to the front of the house. She'd have to walk again, and in the cold, it would be a long walk. There was a long grey coat lying on the floor, where it must have fallen from a rack not far away. That went on too.

"Papa," she called out, as she did, day after day. "I'm leaving for school." He raised an arm from the kitchen, a nonchalant wave of goodbye. She left, her breath already fogging up the chilly air.

School would come and go, and ballet would do the same, and Anya would go home and eat the dinner her father had left out for her. Whatever work she had remaining, she'd do. The bells, loud and booming as she'd always remembered but different in themselves, would sing and she'd lay in bed, preparing herself for the vampires that haunted her night. But eventually, she'd sleep, and the whole process repeated.

Sometimes, when she'd go to school in the morning, she'd forget to press her skirt or comb her hair. She'd tell Papa that she was leaving for school, and he'd come out scowling and tell her that not with that hair she wasn't. He'd go on about how she was from a respectable family and that she should show it.

But Anya supposed that being from a respectable family was better than having no family at all.

"You're fourteen years old," he'd say. "Why can't you comb your own damn hair?" And he'd grimace in a way told her he was joking and she'd pretend to hate the entire thing but the two would come off better for it.

Sometimes she might ask him to cut her hair - short and classy like so many ladies were doing now. She knew she had ballet, where she knew she needed a bun, but surely there was some way to make do. But his answer was always the same, and she would always argue.

"No."

175

"Papa!" she might call.

And again and again, day after day, his answer would remain the same and he change the topic quickly and firmly. It was clear to Anya that she was fighting a lost cause, but still she did not give up.

"And what after school?" He'd ask her.

"Ballet," she said simply. "And Sasha, I'm going to spend a bit of time with Sasha before ballet starts." Sasha was her particular friend. He was a smart and clever boy about a month younger than her. Still at the age of thirteen, they would have ordinarily been separated into different grades, but smart as he was, he managed to get into the same year. He held a lot of things over her head, not only because he was so much taller than her, but because he was arrogant and cocky. Their fathers were friends, or at least Sasha's father payed Papa, and she was the first person she had met after her papa really became her papa. Not many other people liked Sasha - he was prone to temper, and it was rumored he had two fathers. Only one of them was still alive. Born in Finland, he had only moved to Moscow when Anya was ten. They had been immediate friends.

Her father frowned, still combing her hair. "If that boy so much as looks at you the wrong way, the next time you see him will be at his funeral." There was an air of seriousness to his voice.

Rising from her chair, Anya grinned. "He's likes you too, Papa." She kissed his cheek and began to leave.

"Anya! You forgot your ballet bag." The bag was discarded by the chair. A silent curse escaped her lips and she shouldered the bag.

School passed quickly for Anya, as always. Soon enough the bell had rung and students came pouring from the doors, carrying the weight of their bags. Sasha met up with her quickly, waving and shoving as he tried to make his way to her in the crowd. When he approached, he complained that they didn't have much time to spend together, not if Anya planned to reach her class in time. But they were glad to have this chance to be together - Anya had been so busy with ballet lately that they had only been able to see each other during school, where they only shared one class.

Surprise was clear on his face when she told him that she was thinking the two could visit a forest in the Green Belt, one which neither had ever been to. Anya had seen pictures, and while they were captured in an old black and white film that hid the true scene, Anya loved the look of the old gnarled trees, so closely packed.

"We wouldn't even be able to get there before your lesson starts!" he protested.

"Maybe, but I have ballet everyday. We never get to spend time together like this anymore."

Confusion soon gave way to a mullish look of nervousness. "Your father would be murderous!"

Mischief played on the girl's face. "Maybe if he found out. C'mon, Sasha, this is going to be fun!" Sasha's sigh was audible as he was pulled by the hand to streetcar. She hoped he wouldn't start throwing a fit, but as they went, apprehension faded away and Sasha seemed to be almost as excited for the trip as she was.

The two caught the trolley directly. They fit in cozily with the others on the streetcar, the constant rattling putting them into silence lest they wanted to shout to be heard. Every now and then, the trolley would stop and people would get on and off. When the two were nearing their stop, they saw one of their friends get on. He was an Indian boy whose guardian also worked with the other two's fathers. His name was Kaling, but he went by Kali for short. He was a year older than the two, and had about an inch on Anya. Sasha still towered over him. His temper could be even worse than the other boy's, but when he wasn't raging, he was kind and the other two enjoyed being around him.

"What're you two doing here?" he asked loudly. "Isn't Anya supposed to be in ballet?" Kali moved to stand near Sasha. The two were often inseparable, and it was well known that they were the very best of friends. Kaling and Anya got on well, but they weren't incredibly close. They did spend a lot of time together, when their fathers were together on some sort of business meeting.

"Supposed to be," the girl murmured. Kali grinned. "Aren't you supposed to be practicing your piano?" The boy was beautiful at the piano - he could perform the most difficult of songs as well as make his own. The man he stayed with, who wasn't actually his father but took custody of the boy when his father died, was even better. He also insisted on perfection and constant practice from the boy, who he seemed to think of as a bit of a disappointment. Kali's father was a harsh and crude man, with dirty language and dirtier jokes. Anya wasn't often allowed out of her room when he was over, but she suspected there was more than one reason for that.

"We're going to the forest, outside of town. The Khimki Forest." Sasha explained. "At least that's the general plan." He frowned. "Anya thinks it'll be fun." He grimaced at a sharp poke in his ribs from the left, where Anya stood. There was a map nearby, which Sasha gestured to. He told Kali which part of the forest they were planning to visit, but Kali spoke up.

"It's private land, you idiots! You're not allowed." There was silence save for the rattling of the streetcar for a moment. "And the owners aren't too fond of our fathers. Not at all."

That made sense. None of the kids had ever been informed what it was, exactly, that their fathers did, but it was not hard to come up with the general idea. Strange looks when their fathers went out. Unnatural silence. Mysterious murders with unknown killers. Rumors of organized crime. There was a mob in St. Petersburg, and the young kids were already more involved than they'd like to be. Already one of their old friends had suffered some bad ending. His name had been Titan, and he and his father had come from Spain. Titan and Anya had been close when they were young. They met when Anya was ten and Titan nine. By the time Anya had had her eleventh birthday, Titan was dead. The murder had upset them all.

So if the owners of the land didn't like their fathers, well, that was understandable. But obviously Kali knew something more than the others, being the oldest. And he was scared. Something more was going on. Perhaps there was more danger than the children thought, another mob here in Moscow.

But Sasha might have been the type to cut off the branch he was sitting on if it made Kali fall with him. There was that friendly rivalry between them, the sort of rivalry that long ago abandoned common sense if only for the joy of watching a friend struggle, laughing all the while. Instead of simple and practical idea of just going to a different part of the forest, he persisted. "And I'm not too fond of you," he joked. "And Anya's already skipping ballet. I think we'll survive." A smirk played on Sasha's face. "C'mon, what's the worse that could happen?"

What an unfortunate question to have asked.

It seemed to the children, after several hours, that the worse that could happen was bad indeed. The three had arrived at the forest in good time. Eventually, after laughter faded away the rest of their fear, and some backwinding after Kali convinced Sasha to go off the right track, they made it to what seemed like the end of the trail. There they stood, feeling like the conquistadores that conquered Southern America. They were explorers! Travelers! They had found new land! Those were the feelings that Anya could feel storming through her veins. The only places she had seen were two cities where violence seemed to rein, so to come to a dark corner of an unknown forest felt like an achievement to her.

The boys felt thrilled too. This was pretty fun, they decided. Soon enough Anya had convinced them to go off the trail with her. She said she could hear a stream not too far away. There they could find a place to rest, perhaps, or go further into the forest. All thoughts of ballet or piano or anger faded away.

The ground beneath their feet was slowly becoming less and less sturdy. Dust slid in packets every time they took a wrong step. They were going downhill. Steeply. Roots tangled and twisted around their feet, like tendrils or tentacles of some wild beast trying to trip them and lead them to the abyss. Even excited Anya felt a bit of nervousness singing in her bones. She voiced a thought that they perhaps ought to leave. Kali and Sasha agreed, looking uncomfortable.

They turned around, but as they faced uphill, the dust flew out some more and the rocks holding Sasha up fell away. It seemed like the forest was not fond of their leaving, and intended to do something about it.

The boy screamed and fell backward, fear shooting through him quicker than he was falling, tumbling down the side of the hill. Kali shrieked and leaped after him, but he too fell, unable to keep his balance. The surprise whipped Anya around, and the hill couldn't take her sudden movements. Almost no time had passed before she too was rolling after the boys.

The childrens' fall was not graceful. They'd hit the slope of the hill at first, and they'd bounce against it, and they'd fall again, and bounce against that. The only reprieve they found was when a limb would catch against a root or a tree or a rock and they'd feel a jerk and cry out in pain, but still, they'd continue to fall.

The hill ended abruptly. Anya was the last to reach the flat ground, being the last to fall, and she saw the other two crumpled on the ground, moaning softly. Sasha was not moving. She landed on her arm and there was a crack. For moments, she simply did not move, but lay still on the ground, whimpering softly. Tears fell from her eyes. She did not feel as if she had the strength to move.

But she heard groaning come from beside her, and gasping, too, and slowly, if she turned, she could see Kali beside her, laying on the ground with arms over his head. There was a gash on his chest and he was winded, but he did not seem to be seriously injured. Presently, he knelt beside Anya and rolled her over.

"Are you okay?" he whispered. "You're not hurt?"

It took her several times to say no, but eventually, she did. But still, tears fell from her eyes and she cradled her wrist to herself. Kali lent her his hand and she managed to sit up. Their attention focused to Sasha, and Kali's face was wet where tears fell.

"C'mon, Sasha, Wake up, Sasha. Please! Wake up!" He shook him viciously and his voice rose to a scream. "Wake up, for God's sake, wake up!"

There was silence from children and silence from the forest. Not even the birds sang. The only sound to be heard was the god awful trickling from the elusive stream. Sobs began to wrack Kali's body. Anya herself began to rock back and forth, gasping for breath. Sasha couldn't be -

He just couldn't be -

A small groan, almost imperceptible in the children's cry, issued from Sasha's lips. He moved slightly, but he gasped and clutched his ribs, crumpling into a ball. Dark, water-stained eyes lifted from behind bony hands, both pale and dark, and both Anya and Kali rose their heads to look at their injured friend. He was shivering and bruised, bloody and beaten, but Sasha, in all his injured self, was still alive.

Anya breathed a breath she hadn't known she'd been holding. "Sasha!" she cried, clutching him.

"Anya! And Kali?" Kali grasped Sasha's hands like a drowning person. The boy on the ground made to sit up, but with a sharp intake of breath and a horrid flinch, he lie back on the ground, his hands over his eyes. He seemed to be crying.

"I can't - I can't -" Sasha couldn't get it out; half a minute later, he was still moaning but seemed to be managing. "I can't see. The fall - I don't know, I can't - can't see." Terror laced the teen's words, a small tremor of fear rising in an epic crescendo that left the children trembling on the ground, tear-streaked face bleak and empty of hope. Lost in a forest belonging to hostile owners who had, in all probability, no morals. They were only three children, lost and wandering, beaten and broken. What were the chances that they would make it out?

The children, smart as they were, asked themselves the very same question but still couldn't think of more than one answer:

The chances, unfortunately, were very, very slim.

To walk instead of crawl seemed a feat impossible to achieve in their state poor that the three were in. But eventually, with the harsh use of bruised arms, battered hands, and shivering, shaking knees, the children managed to stand just enough to move one foot in front of the other. At a slow pace emphasized by stumbles and falls (particularly in Sasha's case), with moans and groans as aching limbs were pushed out of their boundaries, the children wandered through the forest, hoping to find a path or a way out.

Nothing changed in between them. The children were hurt and lost, and deep in the Green Belt as they were, it didn't seem likely they would make it out. Soft leaves in dull colors littered the ground, hiding roots and muffling the children's steps. The three clustered together, breath becoming more and more visible in the air and bitter wind nipping at exposed skin. Anya led Sasha by the hand, but there was nothing to stop him from tripping and fall almost constantly. Silent, they all wondered whether he would ever get his sight back. It didn't seem likely.

Saviour seemed to come when there was a crackle of branches near them and a harsh argument between two deep voices. Two men seemed to be fighting, but behind their cool words, there was a hint of laughter. The sound was coming nearer, just like the two. The children were overcome with relief and happiness, and yet they hesitated. Kali's prior warning still echoed ominously in their ears. Say this wasn't help, but rather, a newfound danger which could prove to be even worse than the situation the children were already in?

And so the children pulled back into the roots of a particularly large tree, a fear shooting through them that was as deeply penetrating as the chill. The descent of darkness had begun not too long ago, and the gloom and obscurity of dusk hid them well. The men, dressed surprisingly well for a walk in a forest, turned to violent words in quiet tones. Meters away, the two stopped in an argument. Voices were raised in rapid Russian, violent implications in every word. It was pure terror that the three felt now. How hard must it be for Sasha to not know where the men were!

Kali was right in the beginning. These men, they were in a mob, and they would certainly not hesitate to murder the children if they discovered them. And now, injured, lost, and hiding not far out of the sight of two killers, the children were overhearing the plan to kill the newest victim. Within her horror, Anya felt pity for whoever their next victim would be. They hadn't heard a name.

The argument between the two men followed due course, but was interrupted by a loud silence as they were joined by another. A woman's voice rang out, full of indignation and a cold anger. The men seemed abashed, but they were adamant.

"You're not going to kill him," the woman's voice admonished. There was an air of sex and mystery in her voice, and it was no wonder the two men seemed to respect her. "It's completely unnecessary! You'll get yourself caught if not killed, and you'll end up on the wrong side of Hell going down as a couple of idiots." She sounded more exasperated than angry, but a coldness as cool as the night was hidden beneath her words.

Words passed from the two mens' mouths that Anya was astonished to hear. The mobsters, whoever they were, made obscene references to a sexual relationship between the woman and their victim, and by the woman's anger, Anya could tell that at one point, some relationship must have existed. The teen couldn't believe that the men were being so rude; had Anya been in their place, she would have been terrified. The woman was powerful, especially for someone of her gender. With a swift glance to the side, the girl could see that Kali and Sasha seemed to think the same. All three were balking.

"It's not his death that I mind." The woman didn't sound flustered; rather, she sounded deadly. *She must look like a hag*, thought Anya. *I've heard stories of Baba Yaga. Could this be her?*

The woman's voice continued, like a whip cracking again and yet again. "I long for his death; it'd make all of our lives easier, believe me. One less man in that circus they call a mob. But you're going to get yourself caught when it doesn't work." There was such an air of superiority in her voice. "His wife and his son already dead in a car crash - and he knew it was you; you're lucky you're not in jail. Do you think he's so stupid as to fall for it again?"

Surprise and horror like she'd never known raced through Anya, both fighting for a place in her emotions.

A haughty laugh came from both of the two men. "Whether he falls for it or not, Viktor Lavrov will be dead by morning."

Surprise gave way to horror and Anya felt herself gasp. It was true! They were going to try to kill Papa! Her sweet and caring papa, who had accepted her when no one else would. Papa, who comforted her in the night and loved her in the day. And soon enough, he'd be dead and Anya would be back in that hellish orphanage that was always sure to haunt her in the horrid nights. A gasp understated her feelings; shrieking and screaming, sobbing, running for her papa, that was what she really felt like doing.

But the gasp, small as it was, did not go unnoticed by the three mobsters not meters away. She felt Sasha's hand tighten around her wrist and Kali go tense. There was silence in the trees and even in the elusive stream. Everything seemed to still with the tension of the children's fear.

Then there was the cracking of brackle and the children were running as fast as they possibly could, Kali in the lead and Anya dragging Sasha behind her. There was shouting from behind them and then their assailants were running too. Jumping over logs and fallen trees, leaping over that stream that only now they managed to find, quick feet on icy leaves, anything to get away. The men and the woman would get close, but then there'd be a sudden burst of energy from the kids and suddenly they'd be another five feet ahead, still running for their lives, still terrified. Sweat poured down their young faces and fatigue crept into their bodies.

But it was evident that the children could make it. They could save themselves, get out of the forest, and run, run to their papas, run to someone that would save them. All they needed to do was find the exit, to find the way out of this forest. They'd be safe, at least for time, they'd save Anya's father, and all would be well. *That's how these stories end,* Anya knew. *There's always a happy ending.*

Her hand grasped Sasha tightly. How hard must it be for him, to run unseeing in an unknown forest, to run from enemies that he couldn't even catch a glimpse of. He didn't know where to step and when to, and only his frequent stumbles stopped the other two from sprinting away, fast, fast, fast as they could.

But then there was a root, so long and outstretched that it looked like the tree itself was trying to break from the ground and run away, so spindly and twisted that it looked like the dead, so unnoticed by the blind that Sasha fell over it, falling to the ground where he wouldn't be able to stand again, where fear held him like a root held a tree. His hand fell from Anya's, and then his last lifeline fell away, because how could he run again? How could he run from the mob that he couldn't see, without Anya like a light in the night, leading him to his safety? She was his savior, and now she was falling to his side, uncertain like a philly first standing. And where was Kali, save for running with long strides, away from the danger that was sure to kill him, too?

And then the three others arrived. The men were in suits and the woman an elegant dress, her dark hair short and her dark eyes looking with disdain at the children. The two men each pulled a gun from their coats; the lady, impassive, lit a cigarette. A flicker passes through her face and she stares at Anya intently. Terror prevented the girl from noticing, where she pauses, half risen, pulling at Sasha weakly. She looked wide-eyed at the guns, and Sasha whimpered. He wanted someone to save him, for Anya to take flight again and to bring him with her. But how could she save him, when she can't quite save herself?

A trigger is pulled and Anya let out muffled scream. Still grasping her arm, Sasha hits the ground again. He's dead, blood still dripping out of the hole in his head. The girl is splattered with the stuff, but she didn't take notice. The man who shot Sasha began to smirk, cocking the gun again and pointing it to her head. Anya rose to stand, but she didn't bother to run. The birds began to sing again. *No chance,* they call. Their message is clear. Anya isn't going to make it out alive.

And so instead of running away, she stares plaintively at her soon-to-be killers, killers already, in themselves. She glances at the woman, and in that moment, in the dim light, she sees a little teenage girl, scrawny and pale, staring back at her with dark eyes so much like this woman's.

Anya's mother shrieked and in a feral movement, knocked the guns out of the two men's hands. Rapid Russian came forth in shouts, but the young girl didn't pay attention. Scrawny and pale with her mothers' eyes, she started to run again, chasing after Kali, who by then is more than 100 meters ahead of her. The screaming ensued, with Anya's mother begging for her own life. Gone was all pretence of being cool or relaxed, there was only the wild instinct of fight or flight. But since the woman couldn't do either, she threw herself at the mercy of the mobsters.

A shot fired. The young girl choked back a sob, because it was inevitable her mother's brains litter the same ground as Sasha's.

But Anya didn't look back. Her mother, once to have abandoned her, gave her life to save her. What's the point of looking back? In the past, or even directly behind her, there's only pain or misery that awaits. Ahead of her, there's the lights of Moscow not far away, just behind the edge of the forest. Anya could see it then, so close. With her final burst of energy, she exited the forest and ran into the night of chilly Moscow.

Anya managed to run for almost another kilometer before her legs gave out beneath her and she nearly fell to the ground, gasping. There hadn't been a sign of either Kali or the two mobsters. She hoped with all her heart that Kali made it out. Looking through her pockets, she found enough change to catch a street trolley, and certainly that was much quicker than running back to her house, on the opposite side of the city. But should she be wary? Would news of her escape travel so quickly that even now, there was a risk that someone would shoot her? She hoped not. She truly, truly hoped not.

The trolley came by quickly, one of the last ones before the streetcars closed down for the night. Unlike earlier in the afternoon, Anya was the only one inside, save for the driver. She felt tears press her eyes. *That was the last time I'll ever get to ride a trolley with Sasha. The last time I'll ever get to do anything with him.*

It took her hours to get back to her house. The streetcar was shut down in the middle of the downtown, far, far away from her house. She had to travel by night in an already unfamiliar area, looking for a familiar building, a landmark, or even a street name that she recognized. By the time she arrived home, light was already beginning to dawn. She was shivering from cold and fear, exhausted, thirsty, and hungry. *Is Papa even home?* she wondered. *Is he going to be angry with me?* She wouldn't put it past him. She had skipped ballet to explore the green belt with Sasha and Kali, and she hadn't returned for a whole night. Anya knew how worried he would have been, and seeing she

184

was all right, his feelings would turn from relief to anger. But he'd still be relieved. That she knew.

She was a block away from her house when she saw her papa's automobile screech out the driveway. Another automobile turned the from a couple blocks away; the sun shone on the face of the passengers, and she saw the two men from the forest. Oh, God! This was it.

Anya began to run once again. Her skirt, at the length of her knees, hindered her, but she payed no attention. Words came tumbling out of her mouth as she ran.

"Papa!" she called. The clacking and sputtering of the engine was too loud. He didn't hear her. Anya, still exhausted, began to sprint, but there was no way she could get her father's attention. He was looking out the lefthand side, while she was on the right, calling out her name. *Oh, the irony!* But Anya couldn't laugh at the situation. Her papa was about to die, all because he was paying too much attention looking for her to actually look at her!

At this rate, she wouldn't be able to stop her father's car by running or screaming. All that she might do by raising her voice would be negated as the mobsters noticed her, which they were bound to do. They would shoot her, for sure. Maybe Papa would stop and hear the gunshot, but what then? She'd be dead, and maybe Papa would be saved, but surely there was something else she could do!

Surely, surely surely. All these words flashed through her head, and she ran to her father, but the mobsters, they too had closed in behind her. She'd reach her father first, but what was the use?

She needed to make a decision!

Papa was about to see her, she could tell. But even if he stopped, and the speed he was going, he'd still crash, and there was no chance he'd survive the crash. If he did, he'd end up in the hospital, *stuck* in the hospital, where he'd be at the mercy at whoever the nurses let in. And the nurses, if threatened, why, they'd let anyone in.

The crash had to be less than ten seconds away now. But Anya was powerless. There was nothing she could do, a couple meters away from the automobile in which her father was sentenced to die. She wouldn't want to live without him! She'd be sentenced for life in that orphanage again, and she promised herself that she would never go back, never.

Within what could be the last moments of Viktor Lavrov's life, Anya, his only daughter and the most beloved thing in his life, threw herself at the car. There was a screeching halt, a thud, and the automobile of the other two men swerved into a tree. Anya could hear the obscenities leave their mouths before they were bludgeoned into unconsciousness. Lights flickered in her eyes, surrounded by rings of darkness creeping into her vision like smoke tendrils creeping into the sky. Vision left her soon enough, but she was awake enough to hear footsteps running towards her, to feel her father's hands shaking her. She could even feel his teardrops littering her face.

He brought her head to his mouth, whispering her name again and again. "Anya, Anya!" he cried. But she couldn't hear him after that, couldn't hear the soft songs she hadn't even heard in her youth. There was the tap of two fingers beneath her chin and a kiss on her forehead, all of it wasted.

But it wasn't wasted in death. Anya wasn't dead.

No, the girl was back in her youth. She was the scrawny and pale little girl with dark eyes so much like her mother's. She was dancing as a child, following the steps that her mother taught her, laughing and smiling with the woman who saved her life. She was falling asleep to the sound of the bells after a long day of playing with Sasha, or Titan, who she had once known so well.

Papa hadn't yet closed his eyes. The stars smiled down at her, and within their depths, there was always that scrawny and pale child looking back at her with dark eyes so much like her mother's.

The bells of Moscow began to ring once again.

Cretanabook
Mark Davenport

Sonton is a spot
Covered in ashes and red hot
Where dwell the miners
Breaking their backs for gold
Working in heat suits
A thousand years old.
Now remember this
As I have told
For it is your last hold.

Cretana is a place
With more than one new race
A different universe.
Cretana is a home
As it's written in the tome
A place to keep a secret.

Ertgesh is where some people go
When their minds are elsewhere
Some would see here fast or slow
Yet you are trapped forever
Trapped forever
If you go there.

Cretana is a place
With more than one new race
A different universe.
Cretana is a home
As it's written in the tome
A place to keep a secret.

Cretana – 12/2/86 NGA– Planet Ertgesh
DIARY ENTRY
From the diary of Clatt Perk

"Truly, my family is wonderful, and so was our annual harvest celebration despite our unstable debt situation. How I wish this new move of mine will not rip me from my loving Broda and my three shining children. Even basic communication will be too expensive. Many tears will be shed when they find out tomorrow. I'm sure mine will be included. I suppose I don't mind the risk to my life. It is the separation that breaks my heart. Two years without them! Why did I choose this? Never mind. It's too late now."

Cretana - 12/5/86 NGA – Sent to Planet Ertgesh
MEMO
Sonton Harvester ® Company
To: *Clatt Perk, accepted* new employee
From: Employee Recruitment Service
Re: Job Description
<Message Begins>
Dear *Mr. Perk*:

Application Accepted! Thank you for your interest in employment with the Sonton Harvester Company. The transport ship taking you from *Ertgesh*, your home planet, to Sonton will arrive outside your home in three days. Your trip will take *two hours, spanning 18 million#*. When you arrive, we will assign you quarters. You will be supplied with essential items for life, liberty, and property as long as you remain in our employ.

Here, once again, are the qualifications required for all miners:
IF: *Human*, must be Male, Mature in body, fit.

Please be advised that the atmosphere of Sonton, even though you won't be breathing it directly, will be a difficult transition from *the cool, clean, and fresh air of Ertgesh*. You may find breathing, sleeping, or exercising more difficult while your body adjusts. For these reasons, the transport ship's atmosphere will, during the course of the trip, become gradually *muggier and change chemical composition* to prepare your body for the new planet.

We eagerly await your arrival. Your preliminary contract is *two planetary revolutions*. If you wish to stay longer than that time, contact an employment official before the end of your contract period. See you in *Sector Gamma!*
Sincerely,
The Employment Team
<Message Ends>

Cretana – 12/4/86 NGA – Planet Ertgesh

DIARY ENTRY
From the diary of Clatt Perk,

"This is what I told them: After nearly one year without a job, I have decided the only way my wife and children can keep our home is to submit an employee request form to the Sonton Harvester Company #. This measure is drastic, I know #, but I can take a two year contract and hope to survive and come home to an easy life with my family. According to the form, I will be supplied essential survival resources and my wages will be sent home. I have also heard that compensation for lost employees will be sent to my family. I pray to the pillar #that my family will be safe while I am away, and that I will return in two years alive. I never thought I'd say this, but I am glad for the law recently passed by Government of Cretana#, 'no robot shall do a job that could be performed by a human, even under most extreme circumstances.' It may save my family."

Cretana – 12/6/86 NGA – Planet Ertgesh
DIARY ENTRY
From the diary of Clatt Perk

"The application to SHC was accepted! I already wish it hadn't been. This will be my last entry written in Ertgesh until they let me go. I will cross my fingers for the safety of my family during this time… although right now I would rather be homeless than leave wonderful people for this burning ball they call a gold mine#. I already knew this, but I can't believe that in this day and age, with all this technology sitting around me, we cannot communicate! Hiring a ship to take messages back and forth would cost more than my salary."

Cretana – 12/15/86 NGA – Sent to Planet Ertgesh
REGISTERED CURRENCY TRANSFER
Via: CemtoDiCretana®
From: Sonton Harvester ® Employee salary distribution account
To: The household of Clatt Perk
Amount: 10 £
<Message Begins>
"Dear *Perk Family*,
This transfer is for *Clatt's* devoted work for our cause. We once again thank you for loaning him to us.
Sincerely,

189

Sonton Harvester Company Salary Distributor Team
<Message Ends>

Cretana – 1/16/87 NGA – Planet Ertgesh
CONVERSATION
Between Broda Perk and her daughters

Broda enters the house by the back door. Chandira, her seventeen year old daughter, and her eleven year old twin sisters are waiting inside. "Hello girls!" Broda chirps on entry.

"Glad you're waiting for me to come home as always."

The twins enthusiastically chorus their carefully practiced greeting in perfect unison, thanks to Chandira's diligent drillings. Chandira is just a little slow on the routine that afternoon. Her face slips for just a moment into an expression the twins miss as they jump on their mother. She knows something is wrong. She first picks up on the slight grating tone in her mother's words. Broda's grin is just a little forced as she looks each twin in the eye and kisses the tops of their heads. They giggle. This moment is the highlight of their day ever since their father went out of their lives. Addressing the twins, Broda speaks earnestly, "and how are you two bowling balls?"#

Chandira speaks before the twins can blink. "I think electronic school at home is a nice change for them. No more homework stress. They are really good with each other for company."

Finally, Broda looks up. Chandira stands stiffly, making no move into her mother's arms. "And you Chandira; How was your stay at Rin's? Any luck with-"

"No mom. Sorry," Chandira briskly interrupts.

Broda casually breaks the hold of the locked arms around her neck. "C'mon." She beckons Chandira. "Let's talk in my room." Broda and Chandira leave the twins in the kitchen and walk into Broda's bedroom. Chandira closes the door. Her expression is dark when she turns to Broda. Broda's smile falls apart and she begins to cry softly.

"You can't hide anything from me these days, mom!" Chandira sounds more exasperated than sympathetic. "What's wrong?" She knows their voices won't carry through the house. She reaches onto the slouching bed for a worn out pillow to take her frustration out on. She feels she has had enough bad news for a lifetime.

190

Broda takes a deep breath. She knows both that her daughter is right and that she can be trusted. She has known that since Chandira handled the news of the loss of Clatt's first job. "It's your dad."

Chandira drops the hand. It is her turn to take a deep breath. "Of course it is," she sighs upon exhale.

Broda chokes out, "This month's salery is overdue."

"What?" Incomprehension is the first emotion to find Chandira as she hears the words. Why would her mother be making such a big deal about- She turns pale, and suddenly needs to sit down. The bed gives a groan as it takes the weight of Chandira's feelings. Chandira begins to shake.

"Chandira!" Broda grabs Chandira by the shoulders and looks her in the face. "He'll be fine! He's okay!" Chandira turns her face away. Her hands fumble into her pockets and check her wallet. Her fingers trace the outline of something inside; something she has kept secret from her mother.

"I need to go somewhere," she says quietly. Broda nods assent. She is sure Chandira just needs a walk to calm down and sort her out away from them. This has happened before. They both know the unspoken words on Broda's lips: *I don't want to lose you too.* Chandira kisses her mother on the cheek and darts out of the house.

As she runs, Chandira pulls out the concealed packet. Her father's last gift to her is marked with a red hex.

Cretana – 1/16/87 NGA – Planet Ertgesh
TRANSPORT PASS
One way
Passengers: 1
Name: Chandira Perk
Citizen ID: [REDACTED]
Age: 17
Fee: Paid in full
From: Planet Ertgesh – Port of Carta
To: Planet Sonton – Sector Gamma
Coach Class
Bags: 0

Cretana – 1/17/87 NGA – Planet Sonton
CONVERSATION
Between Chandira Perk and the receptionist at Sector Gamma Visitor Center
Chandira's shoes, falling apart, make resigned scuffling sounds on the orange tile floor. The receptionist is looking at his paperwork when she approaches.

He looks up. He recognizes that noise. Chandira's polite question is forming on her lips when she get a good look at the receptionist's face. It has changed from when she last saw it. For a moment, both faces register shock, then, reunited, father and daughter rush around the desk to meet each other.

Cretana – 12/1/86 NGA – Planet Ertgesh
DIARY ENTRY
From the diary of Clatt Perk

"I have decided to keep a diary and will for the next few days. I fear I will not be able to continue it for long afterword. I hope it to be read by Broda and my daughter Chandira if I do not survive this new job. Unfortunately, that is highly probable. My application is sent to Sonton Harvester early this morning. My family will be missed if it is accepted. I will write more tomorrow.

Cretana – 1/1/87 NGA
MEMO
Sonton Harvester Company
<Message Begins>
Dear *Clatt Perk,*
 It has come to our attention that your work in the mine of sector Gamma was not met the requirements of a new employee. Fortunately, a receptionist position has opened in the arrivals on Gamma Port. You will be transferred there tomorrow. There may be confusion in any employee salary sent to somewhere off planet. These problems will be resolved within one month of your switch. Sorry for the inconvenience.

Sonton Harvester Company Employee Monitor Service856

PS: Your contract still stands.
<Message Ends>

(The final two pieces of evidence were not in the original court case. They were uncovered after resolution of the crime in question. MLA procedure therefore dictated that they were put after the original court case translation and notated thus.)

Notes:

NGA refers to the era known as "Nideep Golden Age." Ertgesh is Clatt's home planet. As a point of reference to the reader, think of this as your home planet. Nideep is an underwater planet near the center of the [Cretana] universe. It has both the government and the most advanced technology in the universe underwater. A universe united government, "Government of Cretana," was developed in 1 NGA, as an end to war and a possible solution to large problems such as unemployment. This was the reason the era was called "Nideep Golden Age."

This figure (#) refers to the distance light travels in the time Ertgesh travels around its local star. Years, although universally counted in this translated documentary as having twelve months and about thirty days in each month, were varied on the different planets, which orbited their stars at various speeds and distances. This meant that time calculations were both complicated and confusing to learners.

The Sonton Harvester Company is an organization devoted to collecting ores for building or crafting from the volcanic planet "Sonton." I meant to mention this earlier. It slipped my mind. The Company is well known for dubious employee retention. Many families have lost members working for them. Those mines are dangerous because of the old equipment the company uses.

MLA procedure dictates no modification or translation of registered company names in any official document. I turned a blind eye to that for translating the Sonton Harvester Company. I retained original names (planets, people, etc.) but I feel like they might have lost something in pronunciation.
It is an Ertgesh tradition to have pet names for your children by one element of their behavior.

A red hex is the universal emergency symbol, often pasted on first aid kits. You might say the symbol is overused on something as trifling as a first aid kit.

Through the Eyes of the Undead
Sam Chappell

It's a dog-eat-dog world out there. Or in this case, a zombie-eat-human world. Yep, despite all the people who said the zombie apocalypse could never happen, it did (and the skeptical ones were often the first to be eaten). And the worst part: I'm one of the zombies. But as luck would have it, it seems the infection didn't completely corrupt my mind, so I retained my ability of human thought. Of course, the need to consume human flesh is impossible to escape, which is why I sided with the other zombies instead of the survivors. Hell, I probably would have been shot down if I went near them anyway, considering I can't speak properly. Anyway, now that I've got all the boring explanations out of the way, let me tell you a bit about my (un)life as a zombie.

-

If there's one thing that I remember perfectly, it's the series of events that led up to the defining moment of my unlife. It began one day when another zombie groaned at me to get up. That's right, those groans are actually our way of communicating. I guess the infection adjusts the brain to comprehend this "language," since I can understand it as well as I understand English. Next up is our hunting. The first thing you need to know is that zombies are far smarter than they are portrayed to be in movies and TV shows, and as a result, they were able to spread the infection quickly, bring together organized groups, and overrun the planet effectively and efficiently.

I was a member of a fairly small zombie group (i.e. thirty to forty zombies) occupying Hampton, Iowa. We had a leader for each team of five to ten zombies, and one leader that presided over the whole group. I led a team of seven zombies, and thanks to my human intelligence, we hadn't lost a single member in the time I'd been leading the team. Our assignment that day was to eliminate a few survivors who were hiding out in a supermarket.

In just a few minutes after arriving, I had a member of my team positioned at each entrance to prevent the survivors from escaping. I had them wait while I went in. Of course, the supermarket's power had been cut off, but our teeth happen to be twice as powerful as any human's, so I chewed my way through the glass. I slowly went past each aisle in the store, using the enhanced hearing of my zombie ears to listen to the survivors' movements. I managed to make it to the other side of the supermarket without being spotted, but I could tell from the various items scattered around the floor that the survivors had seen my team approaching the store.

All of a sudden, two of my team's zombies came out of a door on the other end of the aisle I was at.

"What are you doing?!" I shouted at them (in zombie-speak, of course).

Without even looking toward me, one of them simply replied, "We're too damn hungry to wait!"

It was already too late to stop them, so I hid behind the aisle as gunshots echoed throughout the supermarket. Just then, a little girl entered from a hallway near my hiding spot. Not wanting to waste the opportunity, I ran at her. Yes, I can run. I figured out early on that zombies go so slowly because their blood flow has stopped, forcing all the blood into their legs. All I had to do was puncture my ankles and I was able to run nearly as fast as I could as a human. And I don't mean to brag, but I was a pretty fast human.

I proceeded to sink my teeth into the girl's shoulder and she screamed like crazy. And believe me when I say it is REALLY hard to stop eating when you've got an entire human to yourself; especially one that's screaming like this. But I managed to control myself and left her there for the survivors to deal with. I knew it would be pretty emotionally scarring to kill a little girl (even if she was a zombie), and after I heard a shot, I had my team swarm the place and we overwhelmed the survivors.

-

When we returned to the meeting place, we saw a whole pile of human bodies in the center of the room. The other teams gave us a warm welcome and seemed happy overall.

"We've been waiting for you guys to get back!" one of the zombies hollered.

"Let's dig in!" added another.

During the feast, I got curious. "Where'd you guys find these anyway?" I asked a zombie from another team.

"Our team was chasing some survivors through a hallway," he explained. "One of them was getting out a canister of knockout gas, but he broke it open by mistake. So they're all unconscious, but fresh."

"Heh, that's one hell of a mistake to make."

"Either way, we've gotta eat."

"Of course."

After that day, the hunts continued normally until about two weeks later, when our group's leader (we call him the Chief) had me wait with him after the day's tactics meeting.

"You've been doing a great job lately, so I've got a special assignment for you," he said. "I'm sure you remember the survivor group hiding out in the field up north."

"How could I forget?" I replied. They had taken out a whole team in less than a minute thanks to all the mines they had set up.

"I want you to go to their camp and see if you can find anything out. Especially things like moving plans, attack plans, locations of other survivors, and trap details."

"But Chief, how will I get in there? Those traps will be hard to avoid."

"The traps are only set up within the field itself; the fences around it are all clear. You just need to be careful not to get caught."

"Will do."

I left the meeting place confidently, and I didn't run into any problems along the way. In what felt like mere minutes, I reached the field. As I'd been told, there were no visible traps on the outside; however, there were plenty of bushes outside the fences. I ducked down behind one of the bushes and listened carefully to the survivors. For quite a while, they rambled on about how horrible it would be for children in this time and a bunch of stuff I didn't care about. I was just about to get up and leave when two people walked in and joined the others.

"What took you so long?" someone asked.

"He lost his map," another replied. "We looked around for fifteen minutes before giving up."

"To be fair, the fights today were pretty hectic," said the one who lost the map. "Can someone make me a new map?"

"I don't think you'll need a new one," said another person. "We're leaving tomorrow afternoon, so the traps won't matter after then."

"I guess I'll just follow behind you guys, then."

I was a bit surprised: they had just openly stated that there was a map of the mine locations just lying around somewhere, and that they'd be moving. I left the bushes to look around for the map. After a few minutes of searching with my enhanced eyesight, I found it in a patch of weeds nearby. With the map and information, I returned to the meeting place.

196

After explaining to the Chief what I had learned, he thanked me and handed me a card with an address on it.

"What's this about?" I asked.

"You've been promoted," he responded, much to my surprise.

"Promoted? To where?"

"The group up in Fairmont. Their leader arrived earlier today while you were gone; I told him about you and he seemed pretty eager to have you in the group." Now, the zombie group in Fairmont, Minnesota was legendary. They literally have never failed a mission. To be promoted there from an average group like mine meant that you'd been doing something exceptionally well.

"I can't have been *that* good of a leader."

"The fact that every member of your team, from the time you became its leader, is still here, is proof enough that you have what it takes to be in the Fairmont group."

"...Alright."

I was happy to be moving to such an amazing group, but I also felt sad that I'd have to leave my friends and teammates. When I told my team about my promotion, they felt just as conflicted, but they understood that it would be better for me to join a more successful group. After we all said our goodbyes, I set off on my journey with three guards. We mostly stayed on an old road leading from Iowa to Minnesota, so the trip was pretty uneventful. Even so, we still came across a small group of survivors and lost two of my three guards. Once we were near the address on the card, the guard wished me luck and started to go the long way back to Iowa.

The headquarters was in a huge hotel. Leave it to the Fairmont group to take over a building that, in any other situation, would have already been captured by survivors. The moment I entered, I was greeted by a zombie wearing a formal-looking (but damaged) suit.

"Welcome!" he said. "You must be the new member from Hampton. I've heard a lot of great things about you."

"Um, thanks," I mumbled as he shook my hand.

"We're glad to have you here. Let me show you where you'll be staying between hunts." He led me to an elevator and pushed the button for the twelfth floor.

"You still have working electricity here?"

"Indeed. We found this place not long after the slaughter fest began, so everything is intact."

After exiting the elevator, I followed the tux-wearing zombie to a door labeled "12-9." He unlocked the door with a card key and held it open for me. Just a quick look around told me that this was a very high-class place: the first room alone had four couches, three tables, a large refrigerator with a freezer, and even a widescreen TV!

"I'm afraid I have to go back down. You'll be joining our hunts starting tomorrow, but until then, just relax and enjoy the hotel," he said before leaving.

The very first thing I did was go to the refrigerator. As I had guessed, it was stocked with human arms and other scraps of flesh. At this point, I was nearly convinced that the whole thing was just a really good dream, but I soon remembered that we don't sleep. All the same, I grabbed an arm and sat down on the couch. The trip from Hampton had been exhausting, and it's still a good idea to rest even if you don't fall asleep.

-

I was teamed up with a group of veteran-looking zombies: one had an arm missing, one had a gaping hole in his lower chest, and one only had half a face. My team's leader was one of those burly zombies with mutated arms, though he was actually pretty nice. We were assigned to take down a large survivor group hiding out in a factory. I knew it would be a bit awkward since it was my first mission in Fairmont, but I was otherwise prepared. Just a few minutes after arriving at the factory, someone busted open a pipe, covering the whole floor with water. It was then that I noticed a loose cable off in the distance and knew exactly how to use it to our advantage.

"Guys, come back to the entrance!" I yelled over the sound of the rushing water. "I have an idea!" Not long after, my team came running back to where I was. "If we can snap that cable and get it to hit the floor, we can fry all of them at once, but we need someone who can get it without touching the floor."

"Leave that to me," the leader responded. "I've got enough strength in my arms to cling to the wall and tear that cable out."

He ran over to the wall by the cable and made an incredible leap, hanging onto a protruding piece of metal on the wall. It wasn't long before we heard survivors approaching from a stairwell. We ran out the entrance and kept our backs to the walls while the leader ripped the cable out and tossed it way over to where the survivors were. After a moment of screams and loud buzzing, the leader swung out the door.

"Looks like they've all been burnt to a crisp," he said. "Your plan worked perfectly."

As the leader guided us back to the hotel, the one-armed zombie turned toward me.

"Hey, nice job," he said. "None of us would have noticed that cable." I couldn't quite tell if he was trying to make fun of me or not, but he seemed to be in a good mood.

"Thanks," I replied.

"They call me 'Righty,' 'cause of my arm." He pointed to the zombie with the hole in the chest. "That's 'Spitter.' He got a steel beam through his chest during a hunt at a construction site, and it took out his liver. Thanks to that, he can actually spit up his own unfiltered stomach acid to attack his targets." He pointed to the half-faced zombie. "And then there's 'Psycho.' He's totally nuts. Even tore off part of his own face. Lucky for us, he doesn't hold back in the least when he sees a human."

"What about the leader?"

"Oh...well, he used to be called 'Demon,' but he doesn't like the name nowadays. They say he had his skeleton replaced with robotic one just so he wouldn't have to worry about the decaying, but it seems pretty unlikely."

"Hey guys!" Spitter shouted from up ahead. "Hurry up!"

-

It wasn't until two months later that things went from great to horrible. My team had been placed on guard duty alongside another team of zombies, all of whom looked pretty pathetic. The leader and I were stationed at the main entrance while Righty, Spitter, and Psycho were down in the parking lot with the other team. We were all doubtful that there would be an attack, but that made it all the more startling when we heard gunshots coming from the parking lot. By the time we got there, survivors had flooded the place. Righty and Spitter were already on the ground in a pool of blood, as were all of the other team's zombies. Psycho was leaping around like mad to avoid the shots, but eventually fell to the floor from a headshot. Meanwhile, the leader dashed around literally punching the humans' heads off before succumbing to a combined explosion from two grenades.

Now it was just me. Fortunately, I had already hidden behind a car, but the humans were looking around for me. When one of them came particularly close to me, my instincts kicked in and I actually managed to both disarm and bite him. This gave me some time, so I hurried to a different spot. I leapt out for a surprise attack and managed to get a couple more of them, but I had failed to notice a human with a shotgun targeting me from the other side of the parking lot.

BANG!

And that was it. Everything, gone in an instant. Looking back, I accomplished quite a lot during my time as a zombie, but this attack had been too much for me to overcome. There were so many things I regretted, so many chances I missed. Who knows, maybe I could have been a big help to the survivors had I not been zombified. Maybe I wouldn't be worrying about all of this if the infection had completely taken over my mind. Maybe I could have been good.

But hey, at least there are plenty of humans in Hell.

Of Frost and Flame
Noah Gladen-Kolarsky

I slowly open my eyes, and immediately shut them as white light assaults my eyes. I hear voices, murmuring faintly. I can hear people moving around me, quickly, as if every moment meant something of great importance. I attempt to lift my hand. Even in my dazed state, I am still aware that a drug is preventing me from gaining full consciousness. I feel a soft pressure on my barely raised hand, and that is enough to push it back to the table.

At that instant, a loud boom echoes through the room. I make a second attempt at opening my eyes. I see a flicker in the haze directly in front of me. Whatever it is, it forces my eyes shut again. I make no attempt to re-open them. As exhaustion swamps my body, I briefly wonder what to make of all of this. I feel my consciousness slowly flickering away as darkness clouds over my vision.

This time, I awake feeling more normal. I hear a faint pulse in the air and the picture of a helicopter pops into my head, even though I have no recollection of ever interacting with a helicopter. Strange... Now that I think about it, I can't remember anything before I woke up. With a growing coldness in my stomach, I try to recall my name. I panic as I find that I can't.

"*It must be a side effect of the drugs,*" I think quickly. I push away the disturbing fact that I can't even remember my own name, and focus on my situation at hand.

My arms and legs are bound, and I am laying on a cold metal slab. The room I am in is so dark that I can't see any of the walls. I wonder dully where I am and why I am here. I can make out the small shapes of needles protruding from my bare chest and arms. The walls are filled with gadgets and faintly glowing contraptions.

Suddenly, a bright light pours into the room and I struggle to look at the dark silhouette rapidly closing distance between himself and the table. Suddenly, two giant lights flicker to life and fill the room with an eerie glow. I blink as my eyes adjust to the light and the scene before me.

A security camera lies in the corner of the small room, and two armed guards guard the doorway. A pasty white man with a dark brown suit strides towards me with two more guards on either side of him. When the man reaches the table, he stares down at me for what seems like a long time. Then, he rasps out in a dry, cracked voice:

"I'm surprised you're still alive, really. Any normal person would have died from that blast. Although, when one considers what you are, it isn't really all that surprising. Now. According to the reports I have, you have suffered severe memory loss. Am I right?"

He looks down at me expectantly. When I give no answer, he continues. "You are tied to that slab for a reason. You are tied there because we do not know how dangerous you are. If you refuse to cooperate, then we will have to force your cooperation. And neither of us want that."

Again, he looks down at me for a response. Again, I say nothing. I have decided that if this man wants to treat me like an enemy, then I will be his enemy. When the man realizes that I will not speak, he slowly draws out a vial and puts it on a needle. With that, he menacingly rasps out a few final words. "Fine. Just remember that this was your decision. And if you find that you are suddenly able to speak, let me know."

With that, the man jabs the needle into my left arm. Immediately, I feel a burning sensation throughout my body. I wildly look around, scanning my body for the fire that is undoubtedly cooking my flesh. But when I look at my body, it seems perfectly fine. I scream. The pale man leans over me and speaks in an agonizingly slow whisper.

"I have a solution to cure the poison. All you have to do is agree to cooperate. Just say the word, and I can make the pain go away. However, the longer you wait, the more the pain will increase. Remember, I can help if you'll just answer a few harmless questions."

In response, I glare at him. He chuckles, amused, and walks over to a chair at the far side of the room. He slowly sits down with a patronizing smirk on his face and waits.

Meanwhile, I am struggling to keep from screaming again. It feels like the poison is eating away at my bones and burning my body to ash. I glare at the man once more. I want to make this evil man feel the same pain I feel. He is my enemy. I will not tell him anything. I will not. I WILL NOT! I feel fury twist its way through my body, coiling through my muscles like a snake, eating away any composure I had. Through gritted teeth, I hiss the words, "I will destroy you."

"I highly doubt that," he says in a unconcerned tone. "But if you are serious, then by all means, go ahead and try. Getting tired yet? Remember, I have a cure."

After watching me struggle for another few minutes, he sighs, walks over to me, and starts talking again.

"Let me see if I can stir up anything for you. Tell me if anything rings any bells. Your name is Matthew. Whether that is a code name or not, neither

of us know. But as far as we know, your name is Matthew. You were some sort of commander in the Rebel Alliance
Army. Remember anything?"

As much as I want to remember, I can't. All I know at this moment is my hatred for this man. I want to destroy the chains that bind me and show him the same pain I feel now. The pain in my body increases every second. It feels like fire is burning me, consuming me, eating me, embracing me. Once more, I look down at my body. What I see astonishes me. My arm is on fire.

Strangely, I find that this fire doesn't bother or hurt me in any way. In fact, the pain of the poison has completely faded. I try again to loose myself of the chains. This time, the chains melt away as if they were bits of string. All four guard in the room have their guns pointed at me.

This reminds me of my predicament. Another wave of anger swamps me, and I see a flare cloud my vision as my torso and legs catch on fire. As if by instinct, I raise my hand and curl my hand into a ball. The guns from the guards make loud popping noises as they fire at my body. I look down, expecting my chest to explode from the impact of the bullets, but instead the bullets melt when they come near my body.

My balled hand opens and a flare of fire launches at my foes. The radius of the explosion engulfs the guards, and no more bullets come flying at my chest. Two more guards come in, and I hit them with a blast of fire. As they sink to the ground, a flash of brown catches the corner of my eye. I turn just in time to see the brown-suited man jump into an escape hatch that closes right as he passes through it.

I rush over to the hatch, and tear the melting metal off its hinges. I look down into the murky depths, and wonder if my flaming body can endure the fall that waits me inside the hatch. I decide it isn't worth it to follow the man. Instead, I spray blasts of concentrated heat from my hands to make myself spin in a clockwise direction. Again, almost by instinct, I launch my body into the air with a blast from my hands.

I shatter through layer after layer of the building, until I finally see daylight. I keep flying into the warm sunlight. When I clear the building, I look around at my surroundings. I see a vast forest, and a small town a few miles away from my location. Below me, a small outcropping in the middle of the forest has a giant hole where I came out.

Suddenly, I stop floating. Before I know it, I am falling faster and faster towards the ground. Terrified, I realize that my adrenaline from the fight must have worn off. Right before I hit, I float softly to a standing position. I am barely able to stagger a few feet into some bushes before I collapse from exhaustion.

203

When I wake up, it is morning. I have no way of knowing if it is the day after my escape or a week later. I wonder how my captors could not have found me. If I was important enough for them to chain me in a cell deep under the ground, then surely they value me enough to find me directly above their base.

For the moment, I stop puzzling over this turn of events and focus on the task at hand: finding a town and obtaining more information on the Rebel Alliance Army, which apparently I had been a part of. If I could reach the RAA, then maybe I could find some information on myself. But for now, I need to find a town. If I can find a town, then perhaps I can find food, shelter, and sanity. I set off in the direction that I had seen the town in. I set off into the dark, gloomy forest with nothing but my examination shorts on.

The forest is gloomy and dark. More than once I trip on a rock or the odd root sticking up out of the ground. I stumble through, feeling the leaves and thorns prick my face as I make my way through the forest as the day slowly fades. Once, I see a dark catlike form jump from it's hiding place right above me and land in a nearby tree. But for the most part, the forest leaves me alone. I am hungry and thirsty, and the thorns from the wild bushes in the forest have make intricate symbols on my bare chest and back.

Right as I am about to collapse from exhaustion, I see a small light making its way through the trees. I run towards it, using all the energy I have left to reach it. If I don't get help, then I might as well lie down and die. If this is an enemy, then the result will be the same. In any case, I have to take a risk to try to save myself.

When I get near the light, I see it is part of a wagon that it slowly moving along the dirt and gravel path. Two mules pull the small wooden wagon, which has barrels stored in the back. I stagger to the side of the wagon and look up to see a round elderly man holding the reins. He looks down at me with absolutely no surprise, and says in a calm, slow drawl:

"Well hello there. You be a wanderer or traveler? I gots some space still in the back, if you want a ride to town. You don' want to be stuck in here forest durin' the night, let me tell you. You look awful tired. You been travelin' awhile? Climb up here, but do it quick, now. These here mules are hard to get goin' again once they've stopped."

Baffled by the man's chatter and generosity, I slowly climb into the passenger seat right next to the man.

"You don' even got a shirt on yer back! Here, I got this last week at the market. An' you look like you could use some food and drink, too. I don' have much to spare, bein' a farmer an' all, but I still have some left over from my last meal. I don' eat much these days, gettin' older, I suppose. Anywho, heres some bread and water. It ain't much, but it'll do."

With this, the man hands me a patched shirt and half a loaf of bread with bite marks on the side. He also hands me a ragged patched shirt which looks like it used to be a greenish color.

I nod my thanks to the kind old man and nibble at the bread to make it last longer. To my disappointment, however, I find that both the bread and the water disappear into my gut too quickly. The man motions to the back of the carriage.

"You should be gettin' some rest. It's almost night, and I want to be in town as soon as possible. You don' want to be caught in this forest at night. We'll be in town by the time the sun has fully set. I'll wake you if anythin' worth tellin' you about happens. Now you get some rest."

Feeling more at ease and less suspicious with the man, I climb into the carriage and settle down between the barrels. Sleep quickly finds me; I do not dream.

When I awaken, the carriage has stopped. It is daytime, and I can hear voices all around me. I cautiously climb out of the small opening and blink as my eyes slowly adjust to the sudden light of the sun. Back in the forest, I was shielded from the light by the thick canopy. Now, it seems that we are in a clearing of some sort. I immediately realize that this must be the town the farmer was talking about.

When my eyes adjust, I look around. The cart is a stand in a sea of merchants. We are in a market of some sort, and the farmer that transported me here is selling his vegetables to a crowd of patrons. I yawn. This gets the kindly farmer's attention. He turns around with a wide grin.

"Oi! You sure did sleep soundly. I tried to wake you, but nothing would make you leave yer spot next to my goods. So I started my day as usual. And here we are. Come, you can help me unpack."

So we spent the day selling the man's produce, and chatting about current events in the world (although the conversation was mostly one sided; the man was a chatterbox). I learned that the town was stuck in the pat due to lack of money to upgrade to the latest advancements. The Rebel Alliance Army was an organization dedicated to freeing the province of Northern Europe from the World Unification Project Army. Apparently, someone known as Matthew had been a high ranking commander for the RAA, but was labeled "Missing in Action" after a huge battle between the warring sides. I asked how he knew about Matthew.

"Who doesn't?" was his simple reply. "Hes famous after all he's done."

The year was 2127, and the world had been "unified" by the WUPA after the major power countries in the world decided that the world needed absolute unity. After they decided this, they forced other countries to come under one leader through bribery, intimidation, or invasion. Eventually, all countries in the world were unified, but the utopia the power countries had imagined wasn't a reality.

Many countries had been damaged by the war, and the huge alliance known as the Earth Alliance had barely enough funds to do anything. Then the RAA formed, to recreate the earth as it once was. That is the world I lived in. The RAA is my only chance at regaining my memories and surviving in this world.

While we were talking, I had wondered how it would be possible to find the RAA and convince them that I was their lost officer. Pondering this, I continue with the repetitive work. Slowly, I realize that I will probably have to give the RAA a demonstration of some sort. I shake my head as I purge all thoughts of my murky future from my head.

The old man smiles warmly at me and points his crooked finger towards the North.

"It's obvious to even me that you have some interest in the RAA. I can give you a ride to the nearest outpost I know they control, and from there they can fly you their mysterious base. The least I can do for all yer help today is give you a ride. Let's pack up. We're gonna be wanting to travel during daylight, so hurry."

With this, we quickly put the rest of the produce in the caravan. Once this task is done, the elderly man and I climb into the front and shake the reins to make the mules start moving. After a few uneventful hours, we finally reach a surprisingly small facility that must serve as a minor outpost for the RAA. Despite its size, it still looks formidable and is a huge contrast to the poor, old-fashioned town we came from.

The old man drops me off in front of the facility.

"I can't go further than this. It's up to you to get inside. Here. I have something for you."

The old man holds out his hand, and offers me a gleaming dagger and a small pouch. The dagger has a greenish-colored hilt, green not from age, but from the ivory embedded in the stone. The hilt is leather bound and the polished blade itself looks silver in the moonlight. The man smiles at my fascination.

"This dagger has been in my family for generations. Traditionally, it was given to the firstborn son by his father, but in my case I have no children to pass it down to, and no family to entrust it to. I have a feeling you'll find more use fer it than I ever will. The pouch has some money from our sales today. You'll need it. Don' say anything; there is no need. Just walk forward and remember me kindly."

Heartened, baffled, and moved by the kindness of the old man I barely know, I step off the cart. Right before I walk towards the looming gate, I turn towards the man who doesn't even know my name. .

"Thank you for your kindness. I will remember you for the rest of my life."

I walk towards the door, and tap a button right below a microphone set into the wall. As clearly as I can, I say into the microphone, "My name is Matthew. I believe you might be looking for me."

As soon as the words have left my mouth, the gate starts opening. The speaker says in a calm, unwavering voice:

"Matthew. You have been labeled MIA. We are sending you immediately to our main base. A squad is being sent out to receive you, along with the commander of this outpost. Why didn't you report back as soon as you were able?"

I stutter, looking for words. Before I can form a comprehensible sentence, a squad of about four soldiers, a captain, and a major with many decorations on his uniform, who was strutting towards me quickly. I take a step forward. As soon as I do, an automated turret appears from out of the wall and an robotic voice asks me for my identification. Again, I grasp for words in vain.

The officer raises his hand, and the turret collapses back into the wall. He and his party come forward and look at me. The officer speaks quickly and deliberately.

"You've been gone for two years. I'm sure you can imagine how many questions those of higher authority want to ask you. As we speak, the major generals back at base will be discussing your future. Quickly. You need to get into a high speed transport ship. I can imagine how many questions you must have, but right now is not the time."

Briskly, I get led into an airfield where I am placed into the back of a small army transport plane. We don't even go inside the building, just travel around to the back. It is relatively small, with a huge hole in the side of it to allow soldiers to get in and out of it quickly in a warzone. The captain and his squad get into the plane with me, but the commander stays put. He informs me that he is needed more at his current position. Before I go, he hands me a briefcase.

"Open it once you're in the air. It will help you. Are you alright? You look different from the last time I saw you. More confused."

207

I nod, unsure what my response should be. He nods back, satisfied, and exits towards the building. With that, we quickly take off from the ground, and the outpost disappears from sight as the clouds embrace us. After we've been flying in silence for a few minutes, I decide to ask the officer a few minor questions.

"So, why did you let me immediately into your base without questioning me? How did you know I was the real Matthew?"

In a monotone, the captain answers, "we have facial recognition software. Even if we didn't, your face is recognizable to anybody who has ever served in our army."

"Where are we going?"

"You should know that well enough. You served there for a number of years."

I sigh. Should I just tell them straight out that I have no knowledge of ever being in their army, or ever being myself? I decide to wait until I get to the main base to tell them about my memory loss.

I open up the briefcase the officer gave me. Inside, there is a crisp uniform and a small black handgun with a couple clips of ammunition. I have no clue how to use the gun, so I leave it in place for now. The clothes, however, I know exactly what to do with.

I ask the captain where I could change. He points to a small door at the end of the plane and says that there is a small restroom where I can change inside. I enter and remove the smelly clothes from my body. I then change into the crisp uniform, which feels itchy on my skin. '*Better than the rags I was wearing a minute ago,*' I think to myself.

The uniform has dark blue and green colors, which I believe are the colors of the RAA. When I enter the back into the ship, there seems to be some sort of commotion. I question one of the four soldiers about the anxiety, and he replies with urgency:

"We've been spotted by one of the WUPA airships. Who knows why they're flying in these territories. All we know right now is, they're closing in fast and we need to go into action quickly. I nod quickly. The soldier runs to some other part of the ship to prepare for the incoming attack.

I rush over to my briefcase and pull out the gun. I surprised myself by the way I load it and stuff the remaining clip into my pocket. Again, almost through instinct, I draw my dagger. With my dagger in one hand and a loaded gun in the other, I feel ready for any attack possible. The feeling instantly drains away when I see two massive ships close on the left side of the ship. As soon as I have sighted the ships, a blaze of turret fire cuts through the air. One of the ships looks damaged, but is still able to fly.

Both of the ships start to tear apart our own ship with their turret fire. One of the soldiers next to me falls as the bullets whistle through the windows. I look down at him, but he has already slid out of the plane. I duck down and try to hide from the deadly bullets. One of our turrets stops firing and gets blown to pieces.

Suddenly, I hear a thump and the captain screams something about our ship being boarded. I raise my gun instinctively and unload my gun at a group of people who come crashing through the roof. It seems impossible, but they are taken care of before any more life on our side is lost. I reload my gun and empty it quickly again at the enemy ship that has come close to our ship. Something explodes on the deck in front of me, and two more lifeless bodies are sent out into the air. I stand up, suddenly feeling surprisingly calm. I blink. All flames on our ship instantly extinguish.

I raise my hand at the nearest enemy plane, and little flecks of something are shot towards it. I take a slow breath. I feel so calm. I exhale. The little flecks get bigger and turn into little icicles. Somehow, this doesn't surprise me. With each breath I take, the icicles get bigger until they start ripping holes in the metal of the ship. I lower my hand slightly, and the engines sputter and shatter. The enemy plane falls towards the ground, and a few of our soldiers cheer.

The other enemy ship, which has come close to us on the other side, has launched missiles at us. My hand clenches in a ball, and I just manage to stop it before they hit us. I fall over from the exertion. I know I can't stop anything else with my strange powers. The others on the ship realize this, and another of our turrets starts firing on the ship. Someone launches a missile at the ship. More explosions. I feel myself losing consciousness.

Three more men fall. Suddenly, our ship sends missiles of our own after the enemy plane. They don't have enough time to dodge, and their last plane explodes. Heartened by this, I faint.

The captain wakes me up, and I try to stand up.

"Try to stay put. You've been through a lot."

"What happened to our ship?"

The captain sighs. "We lost seven of our soldiers and two turrets. We are virtually defenseless at the moment. Thankfully, we are almost to our destination. You helped us win that battle. You have my gratitude for that."

I lay my head back. The dull roar of the ship's engines combined with the blast of cold air from the open side of the ship give me a headache. Groaning, I stand up. A soldier approached me and hands me my dagger.

"You lost this during the fight. I just managed to catch it before it fell off the ship," he tells me. I thank him warmly. I stuff the knife into my briefcase along with the now useless gun. A few minutes later, The copilot enters the deck, and makes an announcement to the entire ship.

"We'll be arriving in a few minutes. Due to the current state of the plane, we will have a rather bumpy landing. I advise that you find something to hold onto or buckle yourself into a seat." He smiles. "And thank you for flying warzone airlines." A few people chuckle.

When he leaves, everyone finds something to hold on to. Almost right on cue, the ship hits the ground and shakes. I hold on for dear life, praying for dear life. A few seconds later however, the bumps and shaking stops, and the plane stops on the airfield. A cheer carries through the ship.

I look around for the first time at the massive building in front of me. It is huge, with giant metal plate, turrets, soldiers, and everything else a center of war operations should have. Little doorways dot one side of the building. I assume they lead to barracks or chambers. of some sort. I am escorted to one doorway by the captain and a couple soldiers.

"This is as far as I am permitted to go. The generals have been notified of your arrival, and they will be expecting you. Good luck."

With this, the captain leaves. I turn towards the doorway and enter into the small room. As soon as I enter, the room jolts and I start to feel sick. Mere seconds go by, and then the door reopens. In the room in front of me, two massive men in equally massive uniforms stand up to greet me. I know for certain that these must be the generals I need to meet.

"Matthew. It's been a long time. We have some catching up to do," the first general says.

I take a deep breath. Now is the time to tell them about my memory loss. "I'm sorry for disappointing you," I begin, "but I'm not the Matthew you're looking for. I lost my memory, and lack any sort of military knowledge you seek from me. I have weird powers, but that's about all I know."

Both of the generals look taken aback, but reply in a surprisingly even and controlled tone. The second general speaks first. "That is quite an inconvenience. But the fact that you are here in front of us is proof enough that you still have potential. At the moment, you have three options, as I see it. You can decide to fight with us, and join our cause; you can settle down at one of our facilities, and live a comparatively normal life, or you can decide to do nothing and be thrust back into the world with no memory. Naturally, you don't have to decide now. The transporter you came on will send you back to a guest room, and you can give us your answer tomorrow."

I nod, dazzled by the options I now face. I stumble back into the transporter, and suffer through the process of entering a new part of the building. When I step out again, I am in a small room with a bed, a dresser, and a bathroom. Before I do anything else, I take a shower. It feels so good to finally be clean again. While in the shower, I ponder my decisions. *"Its obvious enough that doing nothing isn't a realistic option,"* I think. *"Settling down sounds nice enough, but is that really what I want? Is that really my purpose?"* I sigh. One decision could affect the rest of my life, right down to how long it is.

I decide to sleep. Lying in bed, I think more about my decision. *"Why not try joining the cause,"* I think. *"I mean, what's the worst that could happen?"* With that thought in mind, sleep washes over me.

When I wake up, an automated voice immediately tells me to report to the general's chamber. Confused, I change into a fresh uniform from the dresser. Once I've done this, I put my knife into a small concealed pocket inside my uniform blazer. *"Can't be too careful,"* I decide.

Finally, I step into the transporter. Again I feel nauseous as I am put through the quick transportation process. When I step out for the second time, the generals are sitting in almost the same place in the room, quietly discussing something. Their eyes brighten when they spot me.

"Matthew!" one starts. "Its nice to see you again. Have you made your decision yet?"

"Yes, I have." I reply too slowly. *"Its not too late to turn back,"* I think. I brace myself, and force the words out of my mouth before I lose the nerve to say them. "I want to rejoin your army."

Both generals beam at me. "Wonderful," the second one starts. "Unfortunately, we lack any sort of method of training you to use your powers. We can, however, give you your old notes. Hopefully you can use them wisely. But, I imagine you have some questions for us. We'll be glad to answer any you have, if we can."

"What am I?" I immediately ask.

"We don't actually know for sure," says the man. "All we know is that you were some sort of marvel invented by scientists. Even our scientists don't know how they made you. Even if they did, they died due to some reaction that happened during your birth. You did have real parents, but the scientists implemented some new technology that allowed you to control your life force or something. It wasn't clear. Unfortunately, the research on what created you was stopped once we discovered that it was too unstable and powerful to be continued with our current technology. Does that answer your question?"

"For the most part. Where are my parents?"

"Dead, regretfully. They were a couple that volunteered their child for the greater good. Sadly, they were killed by the enemy during a bombing."

"Who are the WUPA?"

"Oppressors of freedom who believe the whole world needs to be ruled by them."

"What was I?"

"You were a weapon, of sorts. A human weapon capable of destroying an entire army and completing the most difficult stealth missions. Our best soldier."

My head pounds from this sudden flow of information.

"Two more questions. Can I revive my memory?"

"No. We have no technology to allow you to recall lost memories. And even if you could, would you want to?"

I ponder this for a second. Would I really want to recover my lost memories if I could? I realize I don't have an answer to this.

"So, what am I doing next?"

"Because we have no way to train your abilities, you're on your own for that. But we can give you some basic military training. We're going to try to get you into active combat as soon as possible, in order to allow you to train yourself in your unique powers. The rest of the day will be devoted to your training and study. You should use the notes I gave you to study your abilities."

I nod. We exchange formalities, and I exit. For the next two weeks, I study my old notes on powers and manipulation. I learn at an exponential rate the basics of military training. Soon, I am receiving the most advanced training possible in the RAA. The notes from the old Matthew prove to be surprisingly informative and useful.

Apparently, I have the ability to control and manipulate heat. I can enter a state of being where I can manipulate the temperature and particles around me at will. I can enter this state of being through a trigger of an extreme emotion such as fear, anger, hate, or desperation. While in the state, I can create fire, ice, frost, or heat.

After the long two weeks of training, I am summoned to the general's chamber again.

"We have reviewed your training records, and have decided that you are ready to be put into combat, one says. Luckily, we have just discovered where the leader of the WUPA forces will be in three day's time. We have prepared a special forces team to accompany you on your mission. Your mission objective will be to assassinate the leader of the WUPA forces, Calvin Smith. I want you to reach him and terminate him through any means necessary. Once you have completed this, the war will hopefully be over. Any questions?"

I shake my head. I feel fully prepared for anything that lays before me.

"Good. Then in three days, we'll send you out on your mission."

Three days later, I report to the airfield outside of the base. There, I see a team of six special operations soldiers waiting with a black backpack for me with supplies in it. I nod briskly to them. One of the two generals is out on the airfield, and wishes me luck before my mission.

"I hope you make it home safely. If your mission is completed, there will be no need for any more lives to be lost. The war will be over. Good luck, soldier."

When I step onto the transport plane, I feel a faint feeling of loss. What if I never return? I quickly shake away the feeling. The plane takes off from the ground. I settle down, and think about the task ahead of me. I open my backpack. Inside, there is a small high powered machine gun and ammunition. I have a few smoke grenades, and a tactical helmet. Last, I have the latest bullet proof vest from the RAA. It is super flexible, and looks like it could withstand a nuclear bomb.

A few hours later, we touch down at a small airport near the city where Calvin will be. I strap in my helmet and load my gun. I have brought along my knife, and it rests in a small pouch near my heart. The marines and I creep into the city. Someone hits a button, and a convenient invisibility cloak envelops our group. When we reach the city streets, very few people are out. Our tactical helmets point out the building and floor we need to reach.

We have timed the arrival so that it is almost night. We creep through the city streets, narrowly avoiding people, and eventually reach the building. Instead of walking through the front doors, we start to scale the building. This task is made easier by the technology in our gloves, which allows us to stick onto almost any surface. About ten minutes into our climb, the invisibility cloak wears off.

"Don't pay any attention to that," says one marine. "Just keep climbing."

After about another fifteen minutes of climbing, we reach the twenty first floor of the building. One of the marines cuts open the window and we creep in. As soon as we all are inside, however, an armed guard rounds the corner. I take my gun out of my backpack and shoot with lightning speed, and he falls to the floor. Immediately, we rush forward. Realizing that Calvin had probably heard the shots, we dash to the room out helmets indicate.

Behind me, I head the fire of a gun, and a marine screams.

"Keep moving!" Someone yells. I toss a smoke grenade behind me. We finally reach the room. Right as we do, I see a man jump out of the window of the room. Without thinking, I jump out after him. Shooting with the gun as I fall, I hope one of my bullets lands.

Suddenly, a huge ship appears below us. We both land on top of the ship on some kind of cushion. The impact of the landing forces my gun and backpack from me. I instantly pop up, only to see guards streaming out of the ship. I feel the now familiar feeling of my powers starting to surface. When I look for my target, I see the same man from the facility where I lost my memory; the brown suited man. I screech in anger as I shoot a blast of fire at my target. He grins maniacally, and draws a gun, points it directly at my heart, and fires. Before my vest can be put to use, a shield of ice stops the bullet cold.

He starts backing away. Soldiers step in front of me, but I hurl them off the ship with a blast of hot air. Without warning, the ship shakes, and both me and Calvin fall down. Even before I can get up, a net is thrown at me and weights hold it down. I smirk as the ropes get burned to a crisp. Meanwhile, Calvin has taken out a weapon of some sort. Before he can use it, I lean at his with my teeth bared.

He tries to leap out of the way, but I hit him with an ice block to knock him back into me. I catch him, and hold on as I wait to die with my worst enemy. The ground raises to meet me. I twist so that Calvin is facing towards the ground, and suddenly fire envelops me.

"*Like a comet,*" I think as I crash into the ground.

-

I blink as I open my eyes. A dark shape is standing over me. I feel warm, but not a good warm.

"Matthew?" A marine is standing over me. "Calvin is dead. You killed the WUPA leader. You helped win the war."

I smile faintly. Little black dots cloud my vision. The voice of the soldier is faint, and I can barely hear half the words he's saying.

"*You.... return.... war.... hero.... later...*"

I keep smiling. It doesn't matter what happens next. I achieved my goal, and helped win the war. The black dots close in. My vision is just two holes in which a glassy picture of a soldier is standing miles away.

I feel my way to the knife at my chest. I draw it slowly. It feels so heavy. I grasp it in my hand. "*I didn't forget,*" I think. *"My only friend. I only wish I could have known your name."* With this final though, I inhale a deep breath. As

I exhale, I let the little dots fill in the last holes of my vision. Then, I float away.

Live and Die
Ari Bluffstone

A gray haze suffocates the sky, and the smell of harsh, acrid smoke fills my lungs with every breath. As the sun sets, the sky becomes dark crimson, and I notice that my blue Union frock coat is dark red not only from the glow of the hazy sunset, but from the stain of my own blood. The day slips into night, but I cannot move from the field where I lay. My arm begins to throb violently, and I let out a small cry of pain. I squeeze my rifle to my chest and shut my eyes tight. A few large tears blur my vision, and roll down my dirt-covered face. I don't wipe them away; there is nothing to prove. There is no shame in crying. The tears feel hot as they fall from my face onto the scorched earth. My body burns with fever, and it is only with great effort that my eyesight does not begin to spin into black.

With difficulty, I rub my nose with my torn sleeve, and reach in my pocket for my handkerchief. Instead I find and pull out a piece of wrinkled, light brown paper. It is poem handed down to me from my father. I smooth its creased surfaced and stare at its finely printed letters. It reads:

Sadly, but not with upbraiding,
The generous deed was done,
In the storm of the years that are fading
No braver battle was won:
Under the sod and the dew,
Waiting the judgment-day;
Under the blossoms, lay the blue,
Flowers spring from unmarked graves.

I can see the edges of my vision beginning to grow fuzzy, my stream of consciousness rushing over my head like a river. My head circles like a spinning top just on the brink of tipping to its demise. I am Jack, a patriot, lover, husband and soon-to-be father. I cannot die here. It cannot be my time just yet. As my head spins violently, black invading the edges of my vision, I feel my mind begin to leave from my body. Before I lose consciousness, I swear I see my body from above, and I notice a faint smile on those cracked, bloodied lips of the body from which I was now departing.

"Jack? You in there, big guy?"

My vision focuses slowly, colors unbending and becoming their own, lines straightening out and darkening into the outlines of shapes. The shape of a man in front of me begins to come into focus, and I can make out some details: brown hair, deep wrinkle lines, and bushy, arching eyebrows.

"Dad, yeah, sorry. Just a bit tired I guess," I say quietly.

"Well, that's to be expected when you stay up so late reading that book of yours," he says, a slight smile forming on his lips.

I smile and look away. I thought no one knew about my bad habit of reading late by candlelight. I look back at him and feel a surge of affection for the old man. Him and me, comrades in arms, us against the world! It's been that way for as long as I can remember. I feel as if I haven't seen him in forever, but actually we've been in this boat for hours now, chatting quietly and fishing.

I feel a twitch on my homemade line, and excitement creeps through my chest. I calmly try to remember everything he taught me. Wait ten seconds, then pull, hard - no sooner, no later. I wait. One, two, three, four, five... I pull. I feel the tension in the line release, and I know I've lost it. In the one moment when I needed to remember, I had forgotten.

"I'm sorry, I didn't wait long enough," I whisper, my eyes glazing with tears.

"Oh, don't worry, Jack," he said, wrapping a strong, consoling arm around my shoulders and pulling me in tight. "You'll get it next time, there's always another chance," he says reassuringly.

It seemed like we stayed like that for hours, his arm around my shoulders and my head leaning against his chest. I didn't say anything, and neither did he. We just sat there in silence, on the glass lake, the sun kissing my arms and legs. It was so peaceful, I didn't even realize that my eyes had closed.

My eyes sting as they open. I gasp as white hot pain sears through my arm.

"Aghh," I shriek, my eyes clamping shut as my muscles clench. My eyesight flutters momentarily, but I force myself to stay in reality. I don't want to chance that I might never wake again. I can tell that I'm becoming feverish; I'm sweating incessantly even though it can't be more than 40 degrees tonight. I see a gray haze in the distance, but when I blink my eyes it has disappeared.

I slowly open my travel pack, which contains my rations of bread and water. I decide to use some of my precious water to clean the wound. I clench my teeth and pour a small drop on my hand. Searing hot tears stream down my face as I scream - it is a scream of utter terror and pain which hangs in the air over the battlefield for what seems like forever.

I could now take in the severity of my wound. The bullet had splintered the bone, leaving my right arm lifeless and unmoving. The sight of it was enough to make me sick. I shut my eyes and tried to control my already rapid breathing. A pain between my eyes began to cloud my thoughts. I felt like I have amnesia, nothing sticks in my memory and I can barely remember my thoughts from minute to minute. I fight the sick feeling in my stomach and sit up. I have to stand up, I have to move and survive, but I can't. My knee had buckled while in hand to hand combat with a Confederate soldier, and I haven't been able to stand since.

While I was in a somewhat stable state of mind, I decide now was as good a time as any to attempt to stand. With much care, I try to make my damaged body stand up. Immediately my leg collapses, pain shooting up my leg. Unable to catch myself, my head connects with the ground, hard. Again, my vision goes dark and I am left unconscious.

I awake to the smell of a crisp spring breeze and sweet orange blossoms. My eyes flutter open and I am temporarily blinded by the hot sun overhead. I am laying on a blanket in a small clearing, surrounded by an orchard. In a short moment of panic, I forget where I am, and how I got here. But then I remembered. I had just come from tea with Major Conrad and was now soaking in the afternoon sun with my beautiful wife, Susan.

"Hey there," she said, her hair glowing like amber in the golden light.

"Hey," I replied.

"Did you have a good rest?" she asked.

"Blissful," I yawn.

She smiles a worried smile and puts her hand softly against my cheek. She has been through so much in her short life. She had been beaten and abused by her father until she was 15, when he died in a carriage accident. Her father was riding along the edge of the canyon when the horses spooked, taking him to his doom on the sharp rocks below. And just like that, she was all alone in the world.

When I first met her, Susan was a beautiful young girl. I spotted her at the market while buying a watermelon for a family picnic. Her hair flowed down like molten gold, and her eyes glimmered like emeralds. Despite her beauty, I could see in her face her sadness and pain. She quickly disappeared into the crowded market, but I knew I had to find her. She was something special; that much was obvious. Last summer, on the anniversary of our love, I asked her to marry me.

"Yes," she had whispered, "There's nothing I want more." I smile at the thought of this, and come out of my daydreaming to see her staring at me.

"Why are you smiling?" she asks.

"I just can't believe we're married! I... I love you."

"I love you, too," she says. I close my eyes to kiss her.

I open my eyes expecting to see Susan's beautiful face, but instead I see ranks of advancing Confederate soldiers dotting the horizon. I am done. I can't walk, let alone flee from the able-bodied men marching toward me. I reach into my pocket and remove a piece of paper. I take a pencil from my supply sack and begin to write, furiously scribbling the words down on the paper. It is to be a a will, a note that will make me more than just another unnamed, dead soldier.

"Whoever should find this note, you will notice I have been killed in battle. There is no worthier cause I would die for. My name is Jack Davies, and I'm proud to say I died protecting of my beloved country. I give everything I have to my beautiful wife, Susan. I love her more than anything in the world. Tell her that I did not die in vain, but in their protection, and I would like to die no other way. While I'll never meet my newly-born child, please go back to Kansas City and find my wife, Susan Davies. Tell her what's happened. Please, take my body to Kansas City. Take me home."

A single tear rolls down my face, and I wipe it away with a calloused hand. I am done, I know that. But I'm a Union soldier, Jack Davies, forty-seventh squadron of the great state of Kansas's militia. If there's one thing I'm doing, it's going out fighting. I am the last sentry, the last line of defense, and I will fight until my last breath. I remember the poem from my father as I pick myself up from the ground and lean heavily on my rifle. I begin to recite the familiar words.

"*Sadly, but not with upbraiding, the generous deed was done,*" I mutter quietly, the pain in my arm and leg receding. "*In the storm of the years that are fading no braver battle was won,*" I recite, my voice growing raspy with the exertion of walking. This is the fight, the fight of my life, my duty to everyone I've ever known. "*Under the sod and the dew, waiting the judgment-day,*" I say, knowing the truth this poem holds. "*Under the blossoms lay the Blue, the garlands, the Gray,*" I finish. There is a sense of finality in that last sentence. I am ready for what is about to happen. I draw my pistol, pride, anger and sadness all filling my chest.

"Union!" I shout as I unload the bullets in the pistol until it is empty and harmless in my hand. I close my eyes tight, waiting for the bullets I know will come. They say your life flashes before your eyes right before you die, but all I saw was Susan.

Unchangeable
Dahlia Jones

Letting darkness grow
As if we need its palette and we need its color
But now I've seen it through
And now I know the truth
That anything could happen
Anything could happen.
Ellie Goulding, Anything Could Happen

The gray tip of my pencil moved seamlessly in swirls as I scribbled out the numbers. Problem eleven of my math homework. And now on to the next one.

I rubbed my forehead and heaved a sigh. I didn't want to do math right then. I let my eyes wander up to the large green trees above me. Birds nestled among the leaves began to chirp back and forth to each other. I could hear people talking as they strolled on the concrete path running right behind the wooden park bench where I was stationed with my homework.

Through the canopy of tree tops, I could see thick gray clouds masking the blue sky. It wasn't an entirely dreary day, though. Hints of sun here and there, shone down over the still wet, post-rain streets. I squeezed my eyes shut and listened to the sounds of car engines, and voices, gusts of wind rustling dead leaves. I let myself relax in the center of the park I know so well, sinking deeper into the rhythm of people's footsteps.

"You always take naps while doing homework?"

I started, then smiled as my sight landed on Strider's face; his familiar messy brown hair, and deep chocolate eyes... his features so branded into my brain it would be impossible to forget.

"Just thinking," I said, and folded my notebook shut. Strider nodded.

I gathered up my books and stood up.

After a few seconds he said: "Did you get your AIT score back yet?"

I smiled. "Yeah." I pulled the unopened envelope out of my folder. Strider fished his - completely wrinkled - out of his back pocket, and held it out in front of him.

"Ready?" I asked, doing my best to ignore the nervous jitters in my stomach. The AIT, Annual Intelligence Test, determines whether or not I will move up to the next grade, and for me next year is high school. The minimum passing score for 8th grade on the AIT is a 150. And I *have* to pass.

I have so much to lose if I don't. I had agreed to open my score with Strider, but now I realized how hard it would be to fake indifference if I flunked. And all it was was a white piece of paper, folded in thirds and mailed to my house.

"On three." I glanced at Strider, but couldn't read his expression. "One..." I focused hard on ignoring the people in the park around us. "Two... three." We both ripped open the tape seals and unfolded our papers.

Strider looked up at me. "What did you get?" He leaned over to look at my grade, but I moved it out of the way.

"You first."

"I got 200," he said.

"Me too!" I exclaimed.

Strider smiled, making his eyes glow the way they do. A perfect score was all that I could have hoped for, for both of us.

Trying to keep my smile up, I walked with him to the end of the park, and across the street to a brown door on the side of a little coffee shop; my aunt's restaurant.

"Ready for Separation tomorrow?" I asked Strider, twisting open the door knob.

"Yeah," He responded, then looked away, his expression as mysterious as ever. But I knew what he was thinking. I was feeling it too. That we weren't out of the woods yet. That the course of our lives could still be drastically altered by the nonideal system of laws applied to public schools in our 22nd century society.

I pictured shooting sunshine through my veins; a last attempt at false reassurance.

And then I shut the door in my best friend's face.

-

Mirrors are weird. They give the perception that you are looking at yourself, but you are not. It is merely a reflection. My gray-blue-hazel-green eyes that I saw staring back at me didn't feel like mine. *Is this what I look like to other people?* I thought.

I pushed some of my cinnamon brown hair out of my face, turning in the mirror. My hair has never been able to decide if it's wavy or straight, something I've found annoying, but not worth troubling myself over. I ran my fingers through my hastily cut bangs to keep them from plastering to my forehead, emitting a heavy sigh. Leaning forward, I examined my face closer in the mirror. Tiny freckles dotted over my nose.

The few times in complete solitude I allow myself to feel self conscious always end in me finding every single little thing that's wrong with me. But wishing I were someone else never fixes the problem, and it certainly doesn't fix all the *other* problems in my life.

Prioritize.

Someday I will learn how to do that.

"Lyla!" My Aunt Lira's voice carried up from down the stairs.

I turned on my heel, grabbed a black cardigan sitting on my dresser, and threw open my bedroom door. I yanked it shut behind me and began shoving my hands in the armholes of my sweater as I ran down the stairs, the force of my bare feet pounding on the wooden steps vibrating through my body.

"Lyla, go sweep the cafe while I make dinner," My Aunt Lira said to me as soon as I entered the kitchen.

"Yeah, okay." I began heading toward the wooden door that connected our small house with the restaurant.

"And you forgot to put the broom away yesterday."

I nodded. Obedient. Ignoring the harshness of her tone. I placed my hand on the cool metal doorknob, and turned it. The café was dark when I shut the door behind me, but I didn't bother to turn on the lights.

Aroma's isn't really a café. We sell coffee, but it's more like a small soup house. The sun having gone down hours ago, *Aroma's* was closed. All the chairs were turned upside down on their tables, except for the vinyl bar stools. I picked up the worn-out broom leaning against the side of the trashcan, beginning my routine sweeping. I moved to behind the counter, stepping up on the raised honeycomb plastic mat in front of the kitchen, and leaned on my broom.

Just me and the still, dark, silence.

A chance to breathe.

-

My pencil strokes were more jagged now as I sat at my desk, finishing my homework. Hiding away in my room... my lonely, content sanctuary of thought. Not too different from hiding away in my mind. My clock said 10:45, but I was much too exhausted to fall asleep. I could hear faint sounds from the TV in my Uncle David's room. Aunt Lira was probably downstairs scrubbing the kitchen.

My aunt loves me, I think. She never planned on having kids, but volunteered to take me in when my mother died in a car crash when I was a baby. And I am glad for that as it was far better than handing me off to my dad. But she's stressed, and overworked, and is always complaining. She snaps at me, sometimes. Loses her temper, sometimes. And more often than sometimes I am alone. But I know she cares about me, though I am just another adult keeping up their part in the household.

I guess I'm not the best at following orders. I'm just an independent girl who's brain is wired so she can't understand anything anyone else is saying, only the things in her own mind.

Yes, that's me. Right to the core.

A streetlamp directly outside my window shone with its warm, exciting orange light. I stared at it, and everything else fell away. Only the bright, artificial light bulb filled my vision. A mimic of the sun, an imposter invading the sky.

I could feel tiredness slowly beginning to set a blur on everything. The last clear thought I remember is wishing I could fly, so I could escape into the night and never come back.

-

"You really hate peaches, don't you?"

"Mm..." I nodded as I finished emptying my fruit onto Kenzie's plate. I didn't mention that fresh peaches from the southern states were one of my favorite things. But it's been a long time since our city's been able to get anything but the slimy canned things they serve here.

"Oh, right. So leave *me* to eat them." Kenzie rolled her eyes in mock disgust, then dug in.

I nibbled on some lettuce, wishing I had an olive bread sandwich instead. I watched Kenzie try to clean some spilled ketchup off of the green sweatshirt that she wore every day, but then tuned out when she she began to babble on with the other girls at our lunch table about... something. I have never been really prone to participate in lunch conversation. Strider's lunch period is before mine, and Kenzie is a good friend, but I always feel so... *different* when I'm around her or anyone else.

Laughter, shouts and whispers all suddenly became amplified in my ears. The sounds of a cafeteria. At least in high school they let you off campus for lunch. So only a month left of this for me.

Science and World History whizzed by, and then I was walking back home with Strider once again at my side. Conversation was short with us today, as it sometimes is. Like at that moment we didn't really need to use words, just being next to each other connected us. But I doubt that Strider

223

was thinking of it that way. That was probably just my girl brain putting a deeper meaning to a simple silence.

I do that often.

A red convertible zoomed around the street corner, nearly running me over as I stepped off the sidewalk.

I know this corner well. Two blocks away from *Aroma's*, where the park starts. Two big maple trees, growing next to each other, green right now as it's the end of April. But my mind takes me back to fall, many years ago. Strider and I were carefree little kids, reckless and curious as always. His mom had taken us to the park, back before Strider's three younger siblings, when she had time for stuff like that. Somehow we had gotten ourselves up the twisty turvy trunks of those two maple trees. I remember I had a pair of plastic sunglasses that I hid in a knot of the left tree as I settled in to hide from Strider's mom. She pretended not to see us, asking herself aloud where we could possibly be. And we laughed and laughed, playing in the branches and Strider seeing how high up he could climb.

I wish I could get back to that day, live it again and again forever, never knowing my future.

Strider's hand brushed against mine, and I jumped. He smiled at me and I laughed nervously, trying to cover up how it startled me. But another memory had already been unearthed. When I was nine. The year of the nightmares. Every night.

No one knew what caused it, not even Strider himself. But it tore him to shreds. He would wake up drowning in tears, crying harder than I'd ever seen. Strider's mom got little to no sleep pretty much every night. I was over at his house constantly, confused and frankly quite terrified. *What was wrong with my best friend?*

The doctor said it could be from too much stress, or anxiety from school, but none of us believed him. Still, every week, the nightmares got worse.

I remember leaning in the door frame of his bedroom late one night watching his mother hold his hand as Strider cried and said "Make it stop, make it stop. Please..."

I wanted so much to fix the piece of him that was broken, but I didn't know how. I had bit the inside of my cheek hard to keep any tears from coming, and turned away from them. At the end of the hall Strider's little brother, who was four at the time, stood looking at me with confused wide eyes.

I lowered my head and walked the other way. I stopped when I reached the stairs leading down to the dark basement. I was standing there, lost in thought, when suddenly a bloodcurdling scream right in my ear made me stagger forward and nearly fall down the stairs. When I turned it was Strider, standing right behind me with blood dripping out of his mouth, screaming words I couldn't understand.

I think the blood part was my imagination, but he had still scared me to death.

I rarely think about that memory. And we haven't talked about the nightmares since they stopped a couple months after that. Sometimes I wonder what the nightmares were about, or why Strider never told me, but I guess it doesn't matter.

"Bye," Strider said when we finished walking through the park. Then he left me at the little brown door, just like every day before that.

I rushed inside, flung down my backpack, and put on my mocha colored apron, yanking my hair back into a loose ponytail as I emerged into a very much alive *Aroma's*.

"That's for table six," Aunt Lira called to me as I picked up a tray with two plates of food sitting on the counter.

I nodded and put on my smile, heading for a couple sitting in delighted conversation. And then back again for the next tray, and smiling, and acting personable, and picking up more food. I began to feel the rhythm of my waitress routine.

A couple hours later the café was even more populated with all our dinner customers. I wanted to take another break, but it had only been five minutes since my last one. Aunt Lira looked happy, happier than normal. She was having a nice time participating in all the laughter between customers at the bar. The wrinkles at the corners of her eyes turned up as she smiled, instead of drooping, so I knew it was genuine.

"Lyla! Is that for me?"

"Yes it is, Mr. Caverly." I handed him his bean soup, and took part in our familiar joking banter. I have made friends with the usuals at *Aroma's* over the years, though I started out as only the little girl standing in the corner, frightened and intrigued as I watched the people in my Aunt's café.

"Lyla."

I jumped and nearly dropped my empty tray, as I stepped back right into the hooded figure who had just said my name.

"What are you doing here?" I asked when I saw the person's face.

Strider hesitated, then said "I don't know." But something was off. He normally never comes to *Aroma's*, especially while I'm working.

"What's wrong?" I tried again.

"Nothing." He was lying; his shaking fingers and bloodshot eyes gave him away. I could tell something was up, but I wasn't sure how to extract the information from him.

I pulled him aside, and had just opened my mouth to say something, when Aunt Lira materialized beside me.

"What are you doing?"

"Uh..." I looked to Strider for help, but he seemed to be shrinking in his skin.

"You can talk later, you're on your shift now." Aunt Lira dried her hands on a dishtowel and I followed her back to *Aroma's* kitchen.

I glanced back at Strider one last time, only to see him leaving through the glass doors.

-

The air was sunny cold and crisp the next morning.

Strider had already left, and I was alone, running on the sidewalk towards school. City buses carrying people destined for work rode parallel to me. I ran harder, dodging young trees that lined the street.

Days like this I don't mind monotony so much. There's always a probability for a fresh start.

Once within the double doors of my school, I dragged my feet as quickly as I could into my English classroom, collapsing into my seat as soon as my backpack hit the ground.

The aftermath of insomnia.

Just as I felt myself drowning into a daydream, anticipating the long lecture to come, I was startled by an announcement from Ms. Taylor.

Today was Separation Day. Of course.

"We're going to walk quietly to the auditorium, and I want you guys to be on your most respectful behavior. We all know how important this assembly is."

And for the first time this year, the students did what she said. We filed out of the classroom in perfect nervous silence.

Once we were all sitting in plastic fold-out chairs in the auditorium, the principal of our school came out to make the introduction. But unlike the norm he didn't talk for long and soon it was time.

I found Strider's gaze from across the aisle, and held it for a second. He seemed perfectly fine, not at all like yesterday.

A man from the school district came out on stage in a navy blue suit. He walked up to the microphone and cleared his throat.

"Class A."

I held my breath. This is where we would be separated into groups. The groups that define our lives.

"Melissa Abreu, Josh Avery, Cody Benson..." The auditorium was deathly silent, save the shifting of seats and uplifting of spirits of those being named.

Getting into Class A is a one-way ticket to a good education. You get all the best teachers in high school, the most challenging classes. The government really only puts any effort into the kids they think will succeed, classes A and sometimes B.

"Kenzie Cahill..."

I glanced at Kenzie and saw her grin to herself.

"Trevor Caid, Landon Caillouette, Jaden Christley, Caroline Dupree," The list went on. And on.

I was starting to get tired of waiting intently on the edge of my seat, so I closed my eyes and focused on taking deep breaths. But that didn't stop me from hearing the announcer at about halfway through Class B say Strider's name, and then mine, and then...

I opened my eyes.

The announcer wasn't standing at the mic. He was laying flat on his back in the center of the stage. He had been shot in cold blood.

What followed was a silence much different than before.

I pressed my hands together to keep them from shaking like they were. I couldn't make myself look away from the stage, I just couldn't.

Then a loud crash - like someone bursting through the windows - rushed at me from my left. Screams were drowned out by the ringing in my ears.

I was still sitting in my plastic chair when a hand grabbed my forearm, the long fingernails biting into my vulnerable skin. I whipped my head around to see a person, their face covered by a mask. A twisted smile and glossy eyes were painted onto it with red ink; and white lines on the cheekbones and forehead created a resemblance of Asian warrior art.

Horrified, I scrambled backward, my chair falling out from underneath me, but his grip was strong. Wisps of hair and a sickly yellow color made the flesh on his hand look like it was rotting.

I cringed away from the beast, but was only saved by two kids that fell on top of my captor in their desperation to escape.

Now free, I ran as hard as I could, slipping and sliding on the tile floor of the halls as I turned corners. Bursting out of the double doors, I emerged into the fading sunlight. Heading for back alleyways behind surrounding houses and shops, I made a beeline for my home. I tripped shoving open the door to *Aroma's*, and barely bothered to regain my balance as I cried out, "*Aunt Lira!*"

But when I stopped I saw the plates shattered on the floor, the upturned tables, and the food underneath my sneakers.

Rushing out of the empty restaurant, I was now frantic and beyond terrified. There were no cars on the street. Adrenaline slowly rose up from my gut, choking me. I stood there, panicking with no idea what to do next.

And then a block in front of me, a masked man wearing all black, was running at me. No, not at me, at a group of kids tripping over each other in tears. He fired a gun at them, but missed, and the bullet stuck to the side of a building. But it wasn't a bullet, or a normal one, anyway. It looked like a metal thumbtack the size of a ping pong ball, the sharp needle embedded in the mortar between two bricks.

Who were these Mask Men? What were they doing here? I asked myself many questions, but I'm not sure I really wanted to know the answers.

After all, what is truth compared to survival?

I looked to my right, and down the center of the street was a large mass of people. I ran toward them, recognizing some faces from my school auditorium minutes ago. Everyone was screaming and falling over each other, not getting very far. Every now and then one would slump to the ground and not get up. A silent gun. The Mask Men had silent guns, aside from their thumbtack things. That's how they had shot the announcer at school.

Now shrouded in a mass of people, I was screaming too, having a hard time deciding my up from down. I fell hard on the cement, and blood leaked out of the tear in the right knee of my jeans. There were Mask Men everywhere, pointing their weapons at random skulls.

I ducked behind a woman as a grotesque yellow finger pulled a trigger. The woman keeled over, but I'm sure *I* was the one who was shot. This sudden new hollowness in my stomach... my body wanting to vomit up this foreign poison of guilt... the feeling of complete wrongness in the world...

This was wrong. *Very, very wrong.*

Another hand on my shoulder. But this time when I turned it was Strider.

"C'mon!"

"Thank God you're alive," I breathed, ready to collapse and finally wake up from this dream.

But he kept pulling me down the street. The Mask Men didn't notice us; a moving target was harder than a still one... and we *were* just another target.

My feet pounded on the pavement, creating a rhythmic beat with Strider's as we hopscotched around limbs and torsos of the fallen. But something about the faces of the dead was unsettling, making my skin prickle.

Slowly I begin to notice changes. Gray saliva dripped out of their lips. Red bumps broke out on their skin, turning into sores like the marks of meth addicts, and then disappearing again all in the matter of seconds, leaving their skin a greenish yellow. And their hair, thinning, becoming blond right before my eyes. Lighter and lighter until it was like gray fur, shedding as the tip of my sneaker touched it, the strands coated in sticky residue.

Eyes opened. They were not dead.

"Strider," I whispered, almost unable to utter the next words. "They're morphing."

He looked down, and by that time it was hard to miss.

A woman, with now very gruesome features, slowly began to rise. She stood up directly in front of us, and Strider and I were forced to a halt. She opened her mouth, revealing a pink and swollen tongue, and shrieked.

The world stood still for a second, and to me it sounded like her vocal chords were splitting and tearing apart. Then she fell, and lay face down on the concrete, still.

Slow to rise and quick to fall. These creatures should not be a problem for us.

Stepping around her, we kept running, and came across another park, almost identical to the one up the street, but with greener grass and shorter trees. In the center of the park, was a metal statue of a man riding a horse.

But the man was not metal. He was alive. Moving, turning, bringing out one of those thumbtack guns.

A prick in my shoulder made me stop running.

I was about to call out to Strider to wait, but a wave of dizziness hit me. I tried again to say something, but forming words seemed all too difficult with this headache I was getting.

I blinked, and suddenly the ground was an inch away from my face. I tried to stand up, but it felt like my legs had turned to jello. I managed to push myself into a sitting position, but my arms felt much too weak to go any farther. Especially my right arm. I craned my neck around, and there, stuck in my shoulder, was one of those thumbtack things. I reached to pull it out, but my vision was swimming, doing acrobatic tricks and spinning in circles. I could barely see a thing.

Still, somehow I managed to find the thumbtack bullet in my arm, and yank it out. The pain blinded me further, but at least I couldn't see the sticky blood gathering in the wound in my shoulder.

"Lyla!" It must be Strider. "Hurry! They're coming!"

I looked behind me and saw a vague outline of the morphed dead humans about twenty feet away, coming toward me. They were slow, but right now I could be slower.

Frantically, I tried to get my feet under me. Strider was still calling to me, but I no longer understood his words. The street was slanted in front of me as I stumbled forward. I tried to make my legs move, but they were heavy like lead, and I could barely get them an inch off the ground. I took a step, cringing from the effort, all my muscles screaming to move forward. I inched along on the concrete until I reached the sidewalk, dotted with pine cones. I screamed at my brain with all my inner might and then gravity pulled me down the hill. It felt so good to be running... But just as I began to enjoy that familiar feeling of my hair being blown back, my legs stopped again.

Uggghhhh, it was *so frustrating*! Strider again yelled for me to run, and through my loopy vision I could see he was in front of a museum, with large white pillars in front and a three story building. Yeah, it was the... something. A very famous museum, and the name was like...

FOCUS.

The poison from the thumbtack thing was starting to make me feel drowsy as well as trapped. The further I slipped away from reality, the more frightened I got of not being able to escape. I was losing control of my body, more quickly than I realized. They were coming, they must be coming, they're going to kill me.

Another painful three steps, and I stepped onto the grass that surrounded the long walkway up to the museum steps. My bare toes dragged along the dew in the grass, as I forced them in safety's general direction. I could've sworn I had been wearing shoes, but that didn't matter now. The morphed humans were at the top of the hill already. Strider was so far away, and my legs just refused to lift off the ground. I wanted to cry, or scream, or something!

"C'mon, c'mon!" Strider didn't come to help me. But he did continue to yell, and in all my life I've never wanted anything more than to reach his voice.

Noises behind me sounded like the police. Why were the police chasing me? And why weren't they dead? Glancing back, I saw the once walking corpses now laying face down in the street, their bodies contorted in odd shapes.

I wanted to close my eyes, and stop straining, but panic and adrenaline were coursing through my veins far too quickly to do that. I needed to get away, I needed to move!

Surprisingly, gravity pulled me forward once again, and I was running. A short, clipped, odd kind of run, but I was running. So close, I was almost there... But right before my fingertips touched Strider's sleeve, he turned around and ran ahead of me, away from the police that were gaining on us.

I paused, wondering why he didn't let me have my victory. That was a mistake. My run was gone again. But I tried leaning forward and using my pull to the ground as an advantage, and found a rhythm. Slowly, momentum carried me across the large expanse of grass.

"Hurry!" Strider said as he ran around to the side of the museum, and I followed him into a narrow, sunlit passageway, with the looming concrete taupe wall of the museum on the left, and large stepping stones embedded in the ground. The grass around the square stones was wilting and had a brownish tint, rather than the vibrant, almost fake green of the grass in front of the museum.

I blinked and realized that my vision had been normal for a second there. Now it was back to swirling, omitting pieces of information, and freezing and catching up like a slow video camera.

Suddenly my legs stiffened and my run stopped again. *C'mon, Lyla.* I thought. *Stop getting distracted. Willpower. RUN. RUN.*

Slowly, I resumed my jerky half-run again, keeping it up only by intense mental concentration. I just kept focusing on the pull in my chest that willed me away from my pursuers. My eyelids closed half way as I held my breath, squeezing all my muscles to keep my body together. Strider was almost to the end of the passageway that emerged into a brightly lit gravel space.

I continued to follow, trying not to trip on my own feet. I passed a stand on my left with a pretty woman in her twenties selling different types of soda. She looked at me and I almost stopped, but something didn't feel right. Her eyes were a light brown that seemed as bottomless as a water well. They were warm and cozy like a blanket, and made me feel almost *too* comfortable. I stiffened, almost losing my run from lack of concentration.

Wait... why would a woman be selling soda in the middle of a five hundred foot long, six foot wide strip on the side of a museum? I glanced behind me to further inspect the stand, but it was gone. Disappeared entirely.

Had I imagined it? That seemed close to impossible... the image was still so clear in my mind... but...

"Stop!" A museum security guard appeared at the end of the passageway, and Strider had to skid to a halt to avoid crashing into him.

I turned around and began running back down the passageway, knowing we had no other option. I felt my chest heaving in and out the cold air, which I had not noticed before, as I turned the corner and pounded up the steps of the museum, not sure where else to go. I could hear Strider following me, although it could've just been the footsteps from the numerous police officers and security guards following us. Where had all the Mask Men gone? Why were they not still hunting down people? Had they already killed everyone in the streets?

Reaching for the glass museum doors and not thinking twice about whether or not they would be locked, I flung them open and almost slipped with my bare feet on the white marble floors inside. But Strider's arm steadied me, and we headed off through a corridor on my left. We ran through halls, twisting and turning up and down flights of stairs, going in whichever direction was closest. By the time we ran out of breath, we were so lost in the bowels of the museum that no one could find us for a hundred years.

I slowly sat down on the cool stone floor. We were up high in some old Victorian or Renaissance room. There were large glass windows behind me that let in weak sunlight and provided a view, but I couldn't really tell of what because I still felt cross-eyed. And I was dizzy. So dizzy...

"Are you okay?" Strider asked me from the other end of the room.

I think I emitted a groan of some sort, then laid down. Strider said something else, but I'm not sure what. That's when something that felt like a large truck hit me in the forehead, and my vision went completely black.

-

I wasn't asleep. I just couldn't awaken myself to reality. In a way I guess I preferred that to my poison-induced inability to think straight in real life.

As time passed however, I began to think of other things. Random, unimportant details that seemed to take over my brain completely. Then at some point, I forgot all about a girl named Lyla, and my dream began.

It started out in an army camp. People dressed in camo were milling about, having loud conversations that I couldn't quite understand. I knew I was one of them, but they looked at me strangely, like I didn't belong. I realized that most of them were children, except a few volunteer counselors that were clearly in charge of us.

They herded us to a lodge in the middle of a distant, foreign place. The room, which appeared to be a cafeteria, had a high ceiling, walls constructed to look like stacked logs, and a moose head hung over an unlit fireplace. I sat at a picnic table-style bench, shivering in the cold air. Someone was barking out rules to us in a strict voice, and a chunky boy and a high school age counselor sitting next to me on the bench were playing fighting with each other, consequently shoving me into a log-shaped roof supporter.

I rolled my eyes, thinking of how immature they were, and sighed at how invisible and small I was here.

Suddenly, everyone got up and started filing out the door, so I assumed they had told us to go outside. I got up and pushed my way outside. The air was crisp against my bare arms, and I looked down at my maroon colored short sleeved top. *Where the heck was my jacket?*

But I quickly forgot about that as I saw the small lake in front of me. It was only about fifty feet in width, but wrapped in a "U" shape around a large oak tree whose roots bulged out of the ground, taking over the small bank of grass on the other side of the lake. The lake itself had dark, almost black, opaque water, and was covered in a thick layer of orange and red leaves, most likely from the oak tree, whose branches were bare. To me, the lake looked shallow, but it was probably very deep in the middle.

In front of me was a small wooden dock that extended for only about fifteen feet left to right on the lake's edge. I stepped onto it, cautious. I slowly unfurled my two small wings; their feathers were white, but mangled and spattered with dirt. I didn't know how to use them. Of course, that was the point of coming here. They wanted us to learn how to fly.

I looked at the lake's surface, and jumped.

I tried to flap, but I couldn't find the muscles in my wings. It was like they were strapped on. I glided for a few seconds, and tried to keep going to reach the tree, but instead I dropped into the lake. I lifted my wings up to keep them from getting wet, but I didn't sink like I expected. The water wasn't really liquid, it was more like goo. It was thick and sticky, and made up of chunks and oddly shaped rocks. Swimming in it was hard, because my feet kept trying to find something to step on in the disgusting mush, but they would slowly sink like quicksand instead.

I knew I needed to get to shore, though, so I kept trying, and eventually I reached the dock. Once I was on land, I started brushing the clingy leaves off of my jeans. I glanced around and saw other kids swinging on a rope from the oak tree. But instead of dropping into the lake, they would spread their own wings and fly for a few seconds before alighting on land.

I tried jumping over the lake again, and managed to glide forward, moving slower than should be possible, for a few feet. My stomach skimmed the leaves in the lake, getting my shirt smudged in black goo. I gave up and landed in the mud, but just as I was turning around to make my way to shore, my hand bumped into a rock, and it was was brought to the surface as I dragged my arm out through the mud.

It took me a few seconds of looking at the rock to realize that it was a human skull.

My throat involuntarily squeezed up and I looked down at what I was up to my chest in. Bones and bits of body parts were intermingled with the leaves and mud. The lake was made up of decomposing corpses.

I dragged myself as quickly as I could back to the dock, but I was already covered in the soup of bodies. I felt like throwing up as I looked down at my clothes, but a man just started yelling at me to keep practicing my flying. Though I wanted to shrink out of my skin, I did what I was told and continued to jump out over the lake, praying that I would reach the oak tree, until they let us back inside the lodge.

I found my jacket at one of the lunch tables and did my best to wipe off my clothes before putting it on. I sat down in the spot I was at before, and tried not to think about all the blood and bones I had just swam in.

They began passing out food on yellowed plates to everyone at my table. I avoided the scrambled eggs that seemed to very much resemble rubber, and took a bite of the cubed cantaloupe. Though it was really underripe, I was glad to see it was not from a can.

The same teenage counselor that was sitting next to me before was there again. He paused from cutting his syrup-drenched pancakes in strips and asked me what my name was. I told him Madison. I didn't actually know what my name really was, but I was pretty sure it started with an 'M'. Or something like that...

We began talking, and before long our conversation stopped making sense. That was when everything began to fade to an empty blackness, and then I found myself opening my eyes to see a white marble floor.

I sat up, a little dazed. "Strider?" I asked the air in front of me. My voice sounded weaker than I expected it to be.

"Yeah, I'm here."

"How... how long have I been-"

"Couple hours. I tried to wake you up, but..." Strider shook his head. "You were still breathing, though."

"I'm sorry. I don't really remember what happened, and I have this headache..." I closed my eyes tight to make it go away, but all that did was create black spots in my vision. "I'm really tired. I must've blacked out."

"Is the poison gone? That guy shot you."

I nodded, now remembering some of my loopy thoughts from before. "Yeah, it was weird. I kind of cost lontrol of my body." I blinked. "I mean... *lost control.*"

Strider raised his eyebrow at me.

I shrugged. Lately, my mind hadn't exactly been functioning properly, to say the least.

I stood up and walked across the room to an old four-poster bed on display from sometime in the 1800s. It had two lace pillows resting against the small headboard, and though it was on a platform, it was very low to the ground. It must've belonged to someone very important to be in a museum, but I just moved aside the red velvet ropes and sat down on the dusty bedspread.

Strider came and sat down next to me, and I untied my tennis shoes which were once again on my feet. I realized they had probably been there the whole time; the poison had just made me hallucinate.

"I had a bad dream." I said to Strider in the smallest voice possible. I was still pretty shaken up by it, and I knew he would understand.

"Oh." He looked down and studied his fingernails, his face solemn.

"It's over now, though. It's okay." I knew I was speaking for both of us when I said that.

Strider remained silent and I decided to drop the subject. But I knew my words had reached some part of him, whether he showed it or not.

We sat next to each other for a while, just *being.* I watched the last of the daylight slide away from the museum through the big windows, and looked up at the night through a skylight in the ceiling. There were no stars in the sky, and I'd like to think there were no clouds either. That with so many souls taken from the world that day, there was no light left to light up the dark.

What were we going to do next? Where would we go in the morning? So much had changed since just the beginning of that day. As far as I knew, we were the only ones left, besides the inexplicable policemen and those mask creatures. Everything was drained from inside me but despair, and I just wanted to close my eyes and never wake up.

But before I could get any deeper into that thought, Strider said "You remember that time when I stole a candy bar from the gas station?"

I smiled. "Yeah, and I snitched on you."

"And my mom yelled at me for an hour."

I laughed, remembering. "I seriously thought her head was going to explode."

"You were, I mean *are*, quite the tattle-tale."

"Am not!" I slapped his arm and pretended to be offended.

Strider laughed, and seeing him happy sparked a warm feeling in my chest.

We continued to talk late into the night, and eventually my eyelids began to feel heavy. But I felt much less pained by our situation. Because no matter what I went through, I was not alone.

-

I woke up entangled in Strider. His warmth and familiar scent made me feel safe and sound and perfectly, satisfyingly, content.

It was the weirdest thing I have ever experienced.

Fighting my irrational feelings of wanting to sink back down into him, we parted as soon as both of us fully awakened, with little more than an awkward laugh. Rising from the ancient bed, and standing up onto the platform, I suddenly went paralyzed.

Crimson, pomegranate-red blood surrounded a security guard that lay dead at my feet in a full-body halo. His torso was sliced open, from belly-button to throat, revealing the mangled insides of his body.

I sucked in a breath and covered my hand with my mouth, wondering how close to death we ourselves had been last night.

Strider stood up behind me, pulling off the thick sweatshirt he had slept in.

"What?" he asked, blissfully ignorant.

A queasy feeling took over my stomach, exhausting and disgusting me to the point that I needed to sit down. *Deep breaths*, I reminded myself, and shut my eyes. When I opened them, my vision was cloudy, and Strider was sitting next to me, his face blank but white as a sheet.

We sat there for a while, staring in silence. I've seen murders before, on the TV in *Aroma's*, and at Strider's house, but that's all just fake. It's much different when a slaughter is right under your nose.

"Okay," Strider said, trying to sound nonchalant. "We should get out of here."

I nodded and slipped on my tennis shoes, glad to be leaving.

The museum was bright in the midday sun, lit up by golden rays shining in through the large windows at the top of the walls in the area near the entrance. The ceiling here was so high my voice echoed when I asked Strider where we were headed.

He just shrugged. "I dunno. But I think we need to find food."

Only when he mentioned it did I realize how badly I needed to eat. "Yes, that's a very good idea." I responded with emphasis. Then we left the museum without looking back. I never did find out the name.

When we stepped outside, there was a girl kneeling in the grass. She had curly black hair that just reached her shoulders, and a deep tan. She looked about sixteen, and seemed very focused on something on the ground. She snapped her head up when she heard us coming down the stairs, her brown eyes piercing into us.

"Hi." I said tentatively to her when we stepped onto the grass.

She just stared back at me.

Strider stepped forward. "We were wondering if you knew a safe place to find food, or anything about the invasion yesterday. I thought we were the only survivors."

She looked us up and down, and then evidently deciding that she believed us, stood up. "Not so much an invasion as a massacre," She appeared to be a little taller than Strider, so she towered over me as she spoke. "No, I haven't met anyone else since yesterday. But I do know where to get food."

I nodded, eager.

"So what are your names?" The girl asked us.

"Strider."

"Lyla." I said.

The girl nodded. "Cool. I'm Gia." She stepped back to reveal a hole in the ground that she had been bending over. In the hole was a bundle about the size of a telephone, wrapped in what looked like candy wrappers and tied with string.

"You kids are pretty lucky," Gia said. "I was just building a bomb."

"A bomb?" Strider asked.

"Yeah, a small one."

I raised my eyebrows. I had never known anyone who knew how to build a bomb out of candy wrappers.

Gia shrugged. "I used a firecracker, but wrapped it up in some explosive stuff. I've done these before, but never one that's pressure-activated. It's pretty tricky actually."

"But why are you making it?" Strider asked again.

"The morphed humans. Not all of them die quickly. I saw a lot of them coming here last night, so I thought they might return."

I nodded, thinking maybe that was who killed the security guard.

Gia kicked some dirt over her bomb and patted it down. There was a strip of plastic left sticking out of the ground that she then yanked out, and stepped back from the bomb.

"So, food? I'm heally rungry." I said, then paused. "Uh, *really hungry.*"

"Are you sure you're okay?" Strider asked, chuckling. "Cause that's the second time today."

I blushed, and Gia gave me a weird look, but said, "Follow me." and led us down the street anyway.

Three blocks downhill from the museum, we walked past a cute-looking bakery.

"Ooh, why don't we go there?" I asked, my stomach growling at the food in the window.

"No." Gia said, startling me with the sharpness in her voice.

"Why not?" Strider asked, and I felt good that he was defending me.

"Because... we just can't go there. I have a better place."

Strider and I shared a glance, and then walked behind her in silence, until we arrived at a hotel. It was large, and appeared very upscale. Gia pushed open the doors to reveal an even fancier interior of glass chandeliers and polished marble floors.

I'd had enough of marble floors that day, but it was hard not to gape at the lobby. The wall behind the front desk was a waterfall flowing over chiseled black rock, and in the center of the room was a white marble staircase with a thin gold railing, spiraling up to the far left corner of the ceiling. I had no idea there was a hotel this fancy a mere eight blocks from my apartment.

"You guys can get food in there." Gia gestured to a sectioned off breakfast area on her left, and then headed toward the staircase and began climbing upward.

Though I was a little uneasy about this place, Strider and I did what we were told.

"It's pretty fancy here," Strider said as we wrapped various edible things from the buffet in cloth napkins.

I resisted the urge to say "Thank you Captain Obvious." and shoved a roll in my mouth instead.

A loud crash came from somewhere in the lobby, and both of us turned, tensing up. Slowly, we crept around the corner, expecting to see something terrible.

"Oh I'm terribly sorry, Madam." A bellboy had knocked a glass vase on the floor, that had shattered a few feet from a woman in a fur coat. She smiled, then walked away with one of her friends, their upturned noses leading the way.

My gaze shifted to the center of the lobby, which was filled with people, all talking in English accents, and all wearing sparkling jewels and fancy clothing like from the early 1900s.

I closed my gaping mouth to keep from catching flies, and looked to Strider, hoping he possibly had an explanation for this. But Strider just stared dumbfounded at the mass of people that had suddenly appeared out of thin air.

Just then Gia came down the stairs, and we both rushed to her.

"Where the heck did all these people come from?" I asked frantically.

"That's not important. Right now we just need to get out of here." Gia herded us toward the door, but two doormen in green uniforms and little hats stepped in our way.

"Leaving so soon?" They said in perfect unison, and I got the feeling that they weren't entirely human.

Gia quickly stepped back and took a sharp right turn, leading us into a laundry room. She dragged a maid's cart over to the wall and stood on top of it, opening up a trapdoor in the ceiling. She climbed through it and motioned for us to follow.

Strider went next, wriggling up into the ceiling like a worm. I followed close behind, but just as I hoisted myself up into the vent, a bellboy ran into the laundry room. He was holding a vacuum, which he promptly shoved up in the vent next to me.

This made the space about ten times smaller, and I tried to move forward, but it felt like the walls were closing in from all sides, getting ready to suffocate me.

Strider crawled out of the other side of the vent, which I was surprised to find was only about three feet long, and dumped out right onto the sidewalk, level with the slanted street.

Gia bent down and peered into the vent from the other side. "Lyla? Are you okay?"

I looked at the vacuum cutting into my right arm. "Um-"

"Why don't you come down here with ME?"

I glanced behind me to see the bellboy's head poking up through the trapdoor. He had the creepiest smile plastered on his face, one that made the skin on his forehead and around his eyes wrinkle up.

"It's *much* better down here."

I shivered. Gia leaned forward and grabbed the handle of the vacuum. Slowly, she started pulling it toward her, and my arm ruptured with pain as it dragged against my skin.

"Stop, Gia!" I yelled, annoyed.

"Stay with meee!" The bellboy's high pitched voice only added to my panic.

"C'mon, just crawl Lyla." Strider said.

I took a deep breath and started inching my way toward the sidewalk.

"Stay! Stay with me!" The bellboy was screaming now. "Staaay!"

I crawled a little faster, gritting my teeth as I felt the skin on my arm starting to tear against the sharp edges of the whole vacuum.

"Staaaaay!"

I tried to quell my claustrophobia by steadying my breaths, but I didn't relax until my hands were on the sidewalk, and I could pull my feet easily out of the vent.

"What was that place?" I asked once I was out, my words barely a whisper.

Gia shook her head, but didn't say anything.

We walked back to the museum, carrying our bundles of food. Gia had a rolled up olive green colored sleeping bag under one arm. I assumed she got it at the hotel, but I didn't bother asking. I was too worn out and tired and sick of all of this. I just wanted to go home and take a nap.

We avoided the grass in front of the museum, and headed instead to a small parking structure next to the chain link fence that was the right wall of the strip Strider and I had run through earlier. The structure was only two stories high, and was entirely made of concrete. We walked under the six foot clearance sign and Gia dropped the sleeping bag down about ten feet from the entrance.

A little girl stepped out from behind a black SUV. She looked maybe seven years old, and had big blue eyes, stringy light brown hair, and an innocent face. She was wearing a tan colored cardigan over a gray dress, and looked at us with a frightened expression.

"This is my half-sister, Ariana." Gia said. "She's smart, but she doesn't speak."

Ariana's eyes flickered between Strider and me, waiting for one of us to move.

"C'mere, Ari. I brought you a sleeping bag." Gia motioned for her to come over.

Ariana still showed obvious distrust of us, but reluctantly walked over and began to untie the cord around the sleeping bag. She unrolled it and found three wash cloths, some little hotel shampoos and soaps, and a hair brush. She then proceeded to lay these items out perfectly square on the sleeping bag, in order from largest to smallest.

I pretended not to notice, and turned to Strider.

"Your arm," Strider said with alarm, and I looked down to see a row of bloody scrapes and a large purple welt on my shoulder from the thumbtack gun.

"Oh, that's nothing..." I said, trying to cover it up.

"No, we need a bandage. Or, something... Gia!"

Gia turned around and inspected my arm. "We can get some salve at a convenience store across the street."

"No, no it's fine." I started to protest, but suddenly I fell over.

"Lyla! Are you okay?" Strider knelt down next to me.

I opened my eyes. "Uh, yeah. Yeah, I think so." I blinked a few times.

"What happened?" Strider asked.

"I don't know. I just...fell." I blinked again, trying to clear my vision, but the room stayed dark.

Strider helped me stand up, and I looked to the opening of the parking garage. There was sunlight outside, but it didn't reach us. It was like someone built a wall blocking off the parking structure.

"What happened to the lights?" I asked.

Strider looked at me. "What do you mean?"

"The lights. It's all dark in here."

"No it isn't." Gia said.

"Yes!" I insisted. "I can barely see any of the cars."

Strider frowned at me. "Um... Lyla?"

"No, I swear I'm telling the truth! There are no lights in here."

"I'm gonna get you that salve..." Gia started to walk outside, but I grabbed her arm.

"No! Don't go out there."

"Why?"

"Just don't. It's sot nafe." I clenched my fists. "Ugh. You know what I mean!"

"Jeez. What's wrong with you?" Gia muttered. But I was dead serious. There was something out there.

I glanced around me, and began backing up further into the depths of the parking garage. I didn't want whatever it was to see me. I could hear my heart thumping in my ears as my eyes searched for something in the dark to land on.

Gia rolled her eyes and began to head for the entrance.

"Hey. Maybe you shouldn't..." Strider said.

"Are you crazy?" Gia barked. "It's fine."

But as soon as she stepped out into the light, a long spear coming from around the corner sliced through her stomach. Gia fell to the ground.

Ariana looked up from folding her washcloths. I grabbed Strider's hand and ran to Gia's body.

"You!" I screamed at a man in a suit who was walking away from the scene. He barely glanced back at me. He had thinning hair, sharp features, and had made no effort to conceal his face. "You *demon!*" I hurled every ounce of hatred I had in my body in those words. But he just discarded his spear in the bushes and continued to walk away from us, disappearing into the strip on the side of the museum.

"How... how did you know that was going to happen?" Strider asked me.

But I just shook my head and turned away.

-

We walked with Ariana for hours. Nothing else mattered, we just had to get away from there. Strider led us for most of the way, taking us through parts of the city I'd never been before. I wondered how he knew these routes, but I didn't ask and he didn't tell me.

We finally ended up in a grimy, poorly lit subway tunnel somewhere downtown. Under normal circumstances, going down there at dusk might've been dangerous, but with most of the people dead...

"We can set up the sleeping bag here." Strider unzipped it and laid it down like a large blanket. Ariana took off her cardigan and laid it down for a pillow.

"Are you all right, Ariana?" I asked her, trying to show her support.

"Yes. I'm fine."

Strider and I looked at each other. I certainly hadn't expected her to respond.

"Oh, good." I sat down on the sleeping bag, wondering what had made her suddenly able to talk.

Before long Strider fell asleep, but I just sat with my back against the concrete wall and my knees pulled up to my chest, thinking. After a while one train of thought started melting in with the next, but then I was jarred awake when Ariana tugged on my sleeve.

"Lyla," She whispered. "I have to go to the bathroom."

"Okay." I got up quietly as not to disturb Strider and walked her to the public bathroom on the side of the subway platform. Inside, the floor and countertop were scuzzy, and the yellow light flickered every couple of seconds.

I looked at my tangled, oily hair in the dirty mirror while I waited for Ariana. When she came out, I wet my hands and tried to smooth it down, but it didn't help much.

"You're very smart, Lyla." Ariana said as she stood on tiptoe to wash her hands.

"Thanks..." I wasn't quite sure how to receive that comment, because something in her voice sounded like she didn't mean it. Her tone was too syrupy.

"But you know that Gia deserved to die."

"What?"

Ariana took a step toward me, and her eyes pierced right through my skull, so much like Gia's had when she first looked at me.

"Gia deserved to die. She needed to go, and no one could do anything about that."

I swallowed, and turned to open the door. Ariana didn't say anything more on the subject after that, but I knew I would be sleeping with one eye open that night.

-

I didn't end up keeping tabs on Ariana during the night. Instead, I had another dream.

Just like the one before, I wasn't myself in the dream, I was someone else. This time I was a runaway, or an orphan; either way I didn't have parents. I was tall, had dirty blonde hair, and was a couple years older. I lived on the streets with my little sister, who I took care of, and a friend of mine, a boy with shaggy black hair.

It was Christmastime and I was walking in the rich downtown of a foreign city. I slipped into a small jewelry store with fancy cursive writing on the windows. The inside was lit with warm orange lamps and had soft maroon carpeting.

The store owner, a short old man with glasses, was helping a couple select gifts for their families. He removed the glass on both of the two large jewelry cases in the center of the room, to show them different options.

I walked by casually, with my hands in my pockets.

"Can I help you?" A tall woman in a professional black dress came up to me.

"Yes. I'd like to see that ring there." I pointed to a small teardrop-shaped green and red jewel resting on a gold band.

"Sure." The lady removed the ring from the red velvet it was displayed on in the case.

I placed the ring in the palm of my hand, and waited. Slowly, the jewel began to move, sprouting gold legs and a tiny head. Now a gold spider with a gem on its back crawled off of the band, and walked around my hand.

"Isn't it special?" At the sound of the lady's voice, the spider crawled back onto the band and quickly hardened into a gem.

The bell on the door jingled as a crowd of customers walked into the shop. When the lady looked up, I stuck the ring in my pocket and calmly walked out the door. I tried to appear neutral as I rounded the corner and slipped in through a side door that dumped me out at the back of an underground parking garage, where my sister was waiting.

Her eyes widened when I showed her the ring. Then I told her to wait there, and I left again. I walked across the street to where there was a small grass park and a six foot wall next to it, where the street was slanted. My friend was sitting on the wall, holding two sandwiches.

He smiled when I climbed up and sat on the wall, my feet dangling over. He passed me my sandwich and I unwrapped it. We ate and talked for maybe fifteen minutes. I was laughing and my friend was trying to walk the wall like a balance beam when a policeman rounded the corner. I stopped laughing.

"Do you kids know anything about a girl who stole a ring from the jewelry store down the block?" He said it as if he already knew we did, and was just toying with us.

I didn't like that, but I had to keep my cool.

"No." I said shaking my head innocently.

"Really, well then you wouldn't mind if we-"

"I saw a girl run that way a while ago, though. She was holding something in her hand. Maybe that was her."

"Oh?" The policeman didn't look intrigued at all, but when my friend took out his skateboard and jumped off the wall, the policeman frowned and started to call after him to come back.

That was when I crumpled up my sandwich wrapper and started running in the opposite direction. I thought about going back to the parking garage, but I didn't want to lead them to my sister. So instead, I joined a crowd of Christmas shoppers in the street and put my hood up, trying to seem inconspicuous.

The policeman searched around in the crowd for a while, and was about to give up when he saw my face. I turned and ducked into the nearest building.

Once inside, I took a sharp right turn and ran up flight after flight of stairs until I chose a random door and ended up on a floor full of gray. Gray walls, gray carpet, gray desks. A bunch of people in business suits were mulling around in offices and in the hallways. Every one of them stopped and stared at me when I burst through the door.

I glanced nervously at the logo painted on the plaque of one of the offices. I was in a law firm.

Slowly, I started to reach for the doorknob back to the staircase, when the policeman yanked open the door right behind me.

I jumped and began weaving through the people in business suits, who in return started to murmur and move about, which did not make my commute any easier.

I crashed into a woman coming from the copier room, and her stack of papers went flying. The policeman behind me just pushed her aside and continued the chase. Eventually I made it back to the door of the staircase and ran out of the building as fast as I could.

When I burst out on the sidewalk I saw my friend, who yelled for me to go toward my sister, who was waiting in a small boat. I ran toward the dock, jumped in and immediately laid down in the boat, keeping low. The smell of salty sea water started to make me feel nauseous, and I began to feel a pulsing pain behind my eyeballs. I blinked, and slowly my vision began to fade to black.

The pain was gone when I washed up later on a beach, wrapped in a fuzzy red blanket in a pile of seaweed. The blanket was wet, and it was hard to untangle myself from it.

Once I did, I knew right away that something was wrong. I looked to the inside of my thigh, and there was a transparent pinkish, salmon-ish colored leech about the size of a chapstick stuck on my skin. I reached down, and tried to peel it off, but it was surprisingly strong. Using my fingernails, and nearly scraping off my skin in the process, I removed it and tossed it as far away from my body as I could.

That's when I noticed a black transparent leech of about the same size stuck to my forearm. Feeling a shiver run down my spine, I peeled this one off and checked my other arm.

Horrifyingly, I was covered in little pink, black and white transparent leeches. Realizing this almost made me scream, but instead I tried to keep my hands from shaking as I peeled them off. But the more of them I found on my body, the harder they were to remove.

Becoming more and more panicked I frantically scratched at my arms and legs, searching for that smooth, jelly-like feel of the leeches' bodies. My heartbeat raced and my skin was getting raw, but I didn't care. I just needed needed to get them OFF.

Almost not wanting to see what was there, I lifted up my shirt. But I looked down at my stomach anyway, and there, protruding from my bellybutton was a large, thick, ridged, black leech.

I screamed louder than I ever have in my life, and woke with a start to see only the greenish concrete wall of the subway tunnel.

I pushed myself up with my hands, and took a deep breath, trying to calm down.

"Nightmare?" Strider asked me.

I nodded. "It was a really drange stream."

"You mean... *strange dream*?"

"Oh, yeah. That." I said, waving my hand dismissively.

"You think they're a side-effect of the poison the Mask Man shot you with?"

I shrugged. "That's probably what my inability to talk is."

Strider smiled, nodding.

I glanced at Ariana's sleeping form. "How long have you been up?"

"While. I couldn't really sleep. With everything that's happened, it just hasn't really sunk in until now."

"I know the feeling. I keep expecting my Aunt Lira to show up and tell me it's time to go home."

Strider nodded, looking sad. I thought of his family of five that was probably all dead, and bit the inside of my cheek to keep my eyes from watering.

Just then Ariana sat up and rubbed her eyes. "We need to go to 83rd street." She said in her high-pitched voice.

"That's three blocks from here." I said.

She nodded.

"Why?" Strider asked.

"Because. We need to."

As vague as Gia. I thought, then felt bad about insulting Gia. She hadn't deserved to die, no matter what Ariana said.

Sighing, I stood up. "Okay. Let's go to 83rd street."

We hid the sleeping bag and the rest of our food and supplies in an empty newspaper box in the subway tunnel, and then Ariana marched happily down the street with her chin held high, Strider and I trailing behind.

"Here." Ariana said finally when we reached a tall gray building.

I looked at it, and not seeing anything obviously strange about it, followed her inside.

It was freezing in the building. I thought that electricity would've been down, considering the lack of people there to run the power plants.

"C'mon." Ariana jumped up and down and she waited for us to reach the elevators.

I was dead wrong about the electricity. We got in an elevator, and Ariana pushed the button that said 50, the highest floor in the building. We emerged into a room with no windows, and Ariana led us up a small flight of stairs and onto the roof.

I was about to ask her what we were doing here, when I saw him. I could tell Strider did too, because he stopped walking.

"You killed Gia." I said, feeling anger starting to take over my body.

The man turned around, startled. But when he saw me, he smiled. "Yes, I did."

"Lyla," Strider whispered, but I had realized it too. I knew that voice. It was the man from the school district who had announced which classes we were in at the assembly. That seemed like forever ago.

"You... died." I said, having a hard time processing this. "They killed you with a silent gun."

"No. It was only supposed to look like that."

All of the sudden I felt cheated, and sad, and just fed up with this whole complicated thing. I just wanted him gone, *really* dead. My arms itched to wring his neck, but I knew I wasn't strong enough.

So instead, I grabbed a metal pipe about the length of a baseball bat that was sitting by my feet and whacked him in the head.

A large, bleeding wound appeared on his temple, and he staggered backwards, closer toward the edge of the roof.

I dropped the pipe and stalked over to him, grabbing his coat.

"Wait, no! It wasn't me, talk to Mr. Amador! He said get rid of survivors. He made me do it!" The man pleaded with me, but very little of his words actually entered my brain.

I shoved him up against the three-foot concrete rim. "You are a murderer."

And then I pushed him over the edge. The wind was cold in my lungs as it whipped my breath away. I peered down to the ground, and felt dizzy at the sight of the drop. The cars parked on the street looked even smaller than ants, their tires almost blending in with the street. I looked away when the man's body hit the ground.

Now I was a murderer, too.

-

I cried the whole elevator ride down, and even after the doors opened to let us out. Once the tears started, I couldn't make them stop.

Strider put his arm around me and whispered "its okay." in my ear. But the fact of the matter was that it was not okay. Nothing had been okay since the invasion, and I thought he was smart enough to realize that.

"Someone's coming." Ariana said after I had managed to calm down and dry my eyes.

Strider stood up and peered out of the elevator doors.

I stood up as well, though my face still felt like it had expanded three times its normal size. I was always the type of girl who held her pain in instead of letting it out, but when I did cry, there was always that strange feeling afterward of being empty and full at the same time.

"Who is it?" I asked.

"I don't know, but he's holding-" Strider was cut off when a man in a black suit with close-cropped brown hair and dark eyes rounded the corner and pointed a gun at us.

"You are intruders here," he said.

We were herded by the man into the lobby on the first floor, which was now full of men in suits. However this man was clearly the leader. Two of his henchmen bowed and moved out of the way so he could set his gun down.

"So, do tell me. What are you children doing *alive*?" He asked us with mock, or maybe it was real, cheer.

"So *you're* the mastermind behind World Destruction." I said with disgust.

He chuckled and I felt my blood begin to boil.

"I am Mr. Amador, creator of the New Human Race, and most of the technology that made this first stage possible." He looked at me. "I see you are familiar with my poison shooter."

I tugged on my sleeve to try and cover the wound in my shoulder.

"America had become a pathetic country. It was a unanimous decision. I simply improved the plan a little bit."

"So you're from the government?" I asked.

"Well, with this new race there won't be a need for a government. Everyone will be perfect. Flawless in mind and body; you can't say that there's anything wrong with that." Mr. Amador smiled at the horrified expression on my face.

"It was a terrible system though, you must admit. The education, for example. Students who were in Class D had only a 15 percent chance of finding a successful job after graduating from high school. You should know about this, you've taken the AIT, right?"

"Yeah, but you're just going to kill everyone and replace them with robots to solve the problem?"

Mr. Amador took a few steps toward me. "Well... yes." He smiled, delighted with himself, and that's when Strider grabbed a knife sitting on the table behind him and shoved it in Mr. Amador's stomach.

Time stood still for a second as Mr. Amador crumpled to the ground. Then it sped up again when all of his henchmen, and also Ariana, slumped to the ground, their eyes closed as if a switch had been flicked off.

I looked around, confused and happy at what just happened.

"Strider, you did it!" I said, hugging him. "How did you know that was going to happen?"

He shrugged, looking relieved. "I didn't. But none of them blinked. Not once. I just figured if they didn't have their controller, then they probably wouldn't attack me after I killed him."

I shook my head and smiled at Strider gratefully.

"I didn't know Ariana was one of them, though." He said, glancing over at the little girl who lay on her back, still as a rock.

I looked down, remembering how she had scared me in the bathroom of the subway. "Yeah... Looks can be deceiving."

Strider slipped his hand in mine, and I felt a strangely warm shiver run through me.

Then he looked into my eyes and said, "We're free now."

-

Outside the air was cool, and a bright sun was peeking out from behind a cluster of clouds. It's true that this massacre probably changed our lives forever. I will never be able to unsee everything that has happened. But the strength that stays inside of us will be forever unchangeable.

In my hand I held three pieces of paper from Mr. Amador's desk. On them was a list of names... known survivors.

The first name on the list was Gia Carell, and the big X through it almost made me cry again. But there were seventeen names on the list that were not crossed out, and we were headed to find the first two, Hayley Vaughn and Madison Gray, right now.

Strider glanced at me out of the corner of his eye and smiled.

I smiled back. Though I had lost almost everyone I cared about, I still had one person by my side.

And frankly, I loved him more than anything in the world.

Acknowledgements

This book would not have been possible without the help of many people. First, the eighth grade class at ACCESS Academy. While not every students' work is showcased in this book, every student wrote a story, and without these stories, this book would not exist. Many thanks to our teachers, notably Ms. Heather Kelly, who reviewed and graded each story, as well as Ms. Irene Montano, Ms. Amy McBride, and Ms. Renee Morgan, all teachers who have honed our writing skills to this point. The principal of ACCESS Academy, Ms. Eryn Bagby, also deserves a great amount of gratitude for the work she does for the students at ACCESS. But most of all, we would like to thank the people reading this book, the people who are voicing our cause and work by reading these stories.